I0772300

DAUGHTER OF DARKNESS

WIELDER OF SHADOWS

ALLIE COLE

ALLIE COLE PUBLISHING

Daughter of Darkness Wielder of Shadows Copyright

© 2023 by Allie Cole

All rights reserved.

No portion of this book may be reproduced in any form without written permission from the publisher or author, except as permitted by U.S. copyright law or for the use of brief quotations in a book review.

This is a work of fiction. Any similarity to actual persons, living or dead, or actual events, is purely coincidental.

Cover Illustration by Jaqueline Kropmanns

https://jaqueline-kropmanns.de/

Character Illustrations by Alexandra Barlama

@alexandrabrlm_art

ISBN 979-8-9881241-4-6 (hardcover edition)

ISBN 979-8-9881241-1-5 (print edition)

ISBN 979-8-9881241-0-8 (ebook)

https://alliecole.godaddysites.com/

To my twelve-year-old self, who dreamed of escaping into magical worlds.

To my fifteen-year-old self, who drowned herself in books to stop thinking and feeling so much.

To my present self, who proved she could do it.

PLAYLIST

AVAION – Broken

David Kushner – Daylight

Ari Abdul – Hush

The People's Thieves – Now That We're Alone

Audiomachine - Elucidate

Lana del Rey – Yes to Heaven

Cigarettes After Sex – Apocalypse

Hozier – Work Song

Ari Abdul – Taste

Just Pretend - Bad Omens

Camila Cabello – Shameless

CALAPM – Valiant (feat. Sybrid)

Sultan + Shepard + Shallou – Raye

IMPORTANT NOTE

This book ends on a cliffhanger.

The content can entail some triggering situations for the reader, such as graphic violence, sexually explicit scenes, and sexual assault mentions.

So, please be advised and consider these warnings before reading.

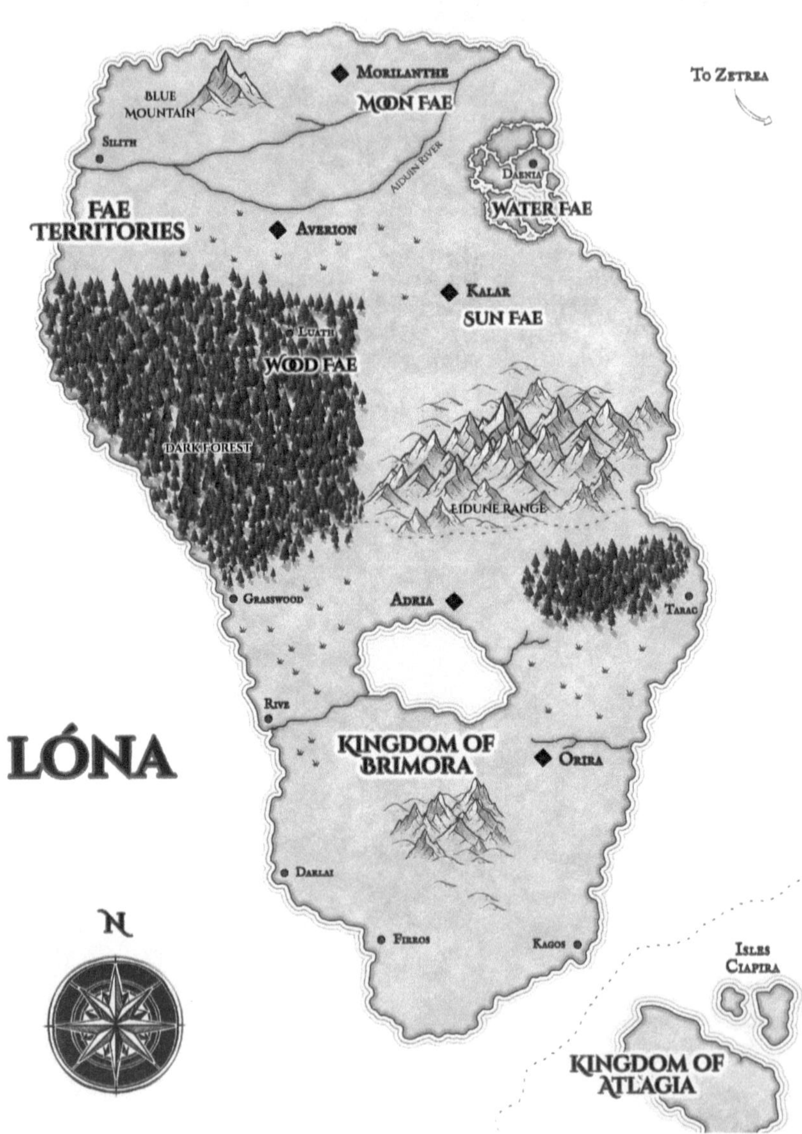

BLUE MOUNTAIN
MORILANTHE
MOON FAE
TO ZETREA
SILITH
AIDUIN RIVER
DAENIA
WATER FAE
FAE TERRITORIES
AVERION
KALAR
SUN FAE
LUATH
WOOD FAE
DARK FOREST
EIDUNE RANGE
GRASSWOOD
ADRIA
TARAC
RIVE
LÓNA
KINGDOM OF BRIMORA
ORIRA
DARLAI
N
FIRROS
KAGOS
ISLES CIAPIRA
KINGDOM OF ATLAGIA

PROLOGUE

Listen to your intuition, her voice whispers in my mind.

They know where you are. They're coming for you.

The words carry an undeniable ring of truth, erasing any trace of doubt.

Alarm bells ring in my head, growing louder as they near.

I send Ela away, with no time to explain or say goodbye. After spending the last decades doing everything in my power to ensure her safety, I must finally meet my fate.

Without me, they can't get to her. When I die, my suffering ends, and this secret dies with me. They'll never know.

As I lift my head, my gaze meets theirs. Their eyes still carry all the hate of this world, confirming I've run out of time.

CHAPTER ONE

Elanor

As I'm walking the muddy streets of the village, the smell of muck mixed with urine and trash fills the air. Lovely.

I'm not sure Grasswood can even be considered a village. It's more like a gathering of homes connected by dirt paths, with a central road along which merchants gather. The tiny houses are made of wood and stones, giving the whole place a very earthy feel.

I leave the main street after earning a few coins in exchange for wild herbs and mushrooms I've gathered from the forest. I'm hoping this will be enough to buy a piece of fresh meat. The butcher's shop is the only one not on the main road, but nothing is ever too far here, and it's only a few minutes' walk. My small pack, now emptied of its content, is almost weightless on my back as I head there.

Careful not to step in any puddles, I'm absently playing with the coins in the palm of my hand. I'm always a little on edge when I leave the safety of the forest, and the light clink grounds me. It's not like anything ever really happens around here, but I carry a knife as a precaution. My modest clothing and determined look usually dissuade anyone from approaching, but the blade is here just in case, a reassuring presence.

The smell of blood and bowels assaults me right when I walk through the door of the dimly-lit shop. I'm standing in a small room divided by a counter in the middle and a back door leading to the kitchen where they slaughter the animals and prepare the meat.

"Good day, I would like to buy some meat." I manage to say, disregarding the foul smell stuck in my throat.

The tall, brown-haired man standing behind the counter turns around at the sound of my voice. Andy is rather athletic and wide-shouldered from the hours spent carrying carcasses and expertly carving meat with knives of all sizes. His pale skin contrasts nicely with his dark eyes and the bit of stubble on his face. Overall, he's not displeasing to look at.

His family has owned this shop forever, and he will take over at some point, just like his father and grandfather before him. That's only if he manages to open his mouth and actually serve customers. I'm about to repeat my inquiry, since he's standing there completely still and silent, when he finally greets me. "Hi."

His dark gaze never meets mine for more than a second, probably because that second alone reveals more than he wishes. I think he likes me.

Everyone around here just pretends I don't exist unless I need to buy or sell something. But not Andy. He's different. He's the only one who looks at me this way. He's just shy or scared of me, which is for the best, really. The only romance I've ever experienced was that between my parents, and it was more its downfall than its peak. So, given the aftermath, I think I'm good. It would just hinder me. No thanks.

But with Andy standing in front of me, I consider it for a second. I'd probably drag him into my dark world if he ever voiced his interest in me. Or maybe he'd be the one carrying me into the light... as if that was even possible. Good one, Ela. As much as I sometimes envy those who don't have to do it all alone, those who have people around who care, I can't be one of them. The dark memories are never far behind that pipe dream.

I've gotten used to the solitude now, and I've found a strange peace and safety to it. I've created some stability, avoiding dangers as best as I can and keeping to myself in the forest. I'd need a solid reason to jeopardize that, and frankly, I don't think he's it.

As Andy's silence turns awkward, my voice sounds in the shop once again. "Andy? Is there some meat I could buy?" He blinks at the mention of his name, but before he can open his mouth to respond, his father hastens through the kitchen door and pushes him out of the way.

The older bearded man mumbles an excuse, and his stern features instantly soften when he realizes it's me. Since I started coming alone, his attitude has changed. He's not a talker, but he gives me those pitying glances and often tries to offer me lower prices, thinking I don't notice. I hate it. It makes me feel so weak and helpless.

"I'm sorry, miss, we just ran out. This is all we have left." He points to the small stand in front of us. My gaze drifts to the two pieces left on display, filled with fat and turning grey. Right. Never mind then. I guess I'm going hunting tomorrow. Again.

"I see."

"If there's anything else I can-"

"No." His mouth snaps shut with my interruption, and I realize too late I'm being rude. "Thank you, have a good day."

I give them both a quick nod and leave the shop. Once back in the street, I tuck the coins under my leather belt and head out of the village. It's getting late, and I need to be back before sundown.

With the mushy grounds squishing under my boots, a fresh gust of wind hits me as I turn the corner of the last house, clearing up the stench in my nose. Tension instantly leaves my body when the Dark Forest is in sight, welcoming me back to its comforting cover.

⚊⚊◆⚊⚊

Elanor

Careful not to leave traces and disturb the earth, I scan the grounds for signs of the game I'm hunting. Heading deeper into the woods, keeping my breathing slow and regular, I'm catching up with the animal's trail. I've been at it for hours, silently cursing myself for not making it to the butcher's shop earlier yesterday.

I come across a sunlit clearing and pause to munch on the last of my dried meat. As I chew on the hardened bits, my thoughts drift to my father.

Darkness. It's the first thing I remember about that night. It was dark, and it was cold, and I was scared. With the rocks scratching my bare hands and the roots digging into my knees, I couldn't take my eyes off his still body.

He was gone. The thought was looping in my head as my fingers dug into the wet soil, trying to catch hold of something, anything.

Gore soaked the ground. His was the only body left, but judging by the quantity of blood, at least several attackers had died at his hands or had been severely hurt before being dragged away. They left no clues for me to follow and nothing to understand why they'd come after him.

His sword was still in his hand, but my father's empty gaze was fixed on the night sky. Waves of panic and terror broke the dam I had been trying to keep in place. I had no one left now. Trembling, I stayed hours by his cooling body, unable to speak or move, waiting for the attackers to come back and take me too. But they never did.

Something shattered in me that day, and I was left with only one thing. One certainty. I would never know peace and safety again.

Insects buzzing by a cluster of wildflowers stir me from the memory of my father.

I don't remember much else about that night, but to this day, I have my guess as to the kind of monsters who could have done that to an isolated man in the forest.

Growing up, he was my everything, the strongest warrior to ever walk this earth, always there to protect me and tickle my cheeks with his scratchy kisses.

He'd been a soldier, fought in wars all across the globe before I was born, my mother by his side until she died. He never talked much about that time, except on rare occasions by the fireplace, when the burden of the memories was too much to bear. But, year after year, grief gradually overwhelmed him.

He taught me how to hunt and fight. I would watch him practice with his sword for hours, dreaming of the day I would be old enough to have my own weapon, and I remember my first lesson like it was yesterday.

Out in the clearing by our shack, he'd handed me a makeshift wooden sword and showed me how to wield it. After a few days of practice, he taught me how to parry and defend. And, of course, he kicked my ass.

I was so mad and frustrated, I think that's when I swore for the first time. And the look on my father's face was just priceless. He hated it so much when I swore. I tried keeping it under wraps with him around. But after he passed, I didn't see the point anymore. Weirdly, every time I curse now reminds me of him.

With the strong pace I'm keeping, my foot hits a root hard enough that pain reverberates in my bones. "Damn it." I wiggle my toes inside my boot until the pain dulls.

I close my eyes long enough to picture my father's face, a disapproving frown on his forehead. The memory brings a small smile to my face as I step over a fallen tree and push on. Deer tracks are leading me further north, so I speed up, not wanting to linger more than necessary.

I took up my father's sword after I buried him. At first, it was too big and heavy for me, but I kept trying, giving it my all, training for months. It was the only thing keeping me sane after his death.

I flirted with the afterlife several times myself but I can now wield his sword as well as any man would. The forest is no safe haven. Terrifying beasts and marauders hide in its dark corners, and its freezing winters are no lesser threats. I've been lucky enough to never encounter the Fae and other dark monsters who are said to roam the northern and eastern parts of the forest. I probably wouldn't be here to tell the tale if I had.

My father used to tell me stories about the Fae monsters when I was little. More like horror stories, really. They were savage barbarians ruled by strict laws, waging wars among themselves, kidnapping and killing humans at will.

He taught me how to recognize them by spotting the long and pointy ears heightening their senses. Although their eyes could appear similar to ours, the color varies based on where they are from, telling you what kind of Fae you're up against. And that's where the resemblance ends, as their speed and strength are greater than any human's.

A dried branch snaps loudly under my foot and I curse myself silently. The quiet forest as my only response, I check my surroundings.

There's no threat in sight, but I still mentally recap what my father taught me. Time doesn't kill Fae, but blades can. Some of them wield strange magic to heal their wounds, so the best way to kill a Fae is to behead it. If I encounter one, I run as fast and as far as I can.

I distinctly remember the night he made me promise to always hide from the Fae. It was the only time I ever saw fear in his eyes. I merely caught a glimpse of it, but knowing that he, too, was afraid of something robbed me of the last bit of peace I was holding onto after my mother died. He taught me about darkclaws and other beasts, but nothing ever rattled him the way the Fae did.

By the time I make another halt to drink from my waterskin, I realize the sun is much lower in the sky than I expected. It's getting late, and I should head back, even if it's empty-handed. Another mile or two, then I'll go back.

The light and shadow dance across my skin as I lift my face. With birds humming around me, I take a moment to inhale the pine and earthy smell before continuing. Although dangerous, this forest is home to me, its familiar mossy trees, fallen branches, and hollow trunks silently watching and witnessing the passing of time.

A subtle crack sounds to my right, and I quietly turn around. As if my memories had conjured him, a Fae warrior is standing maybe thirty feet ahead of me. He is heavily armored, carrying a double-bladed sword on his back, plus several knives. His weapon is unlike any other I've ever seen, so massive it rises above his shoulders.

I freeze, instinctively holding my breath. My heart is pounding in my ears as I'm trying to decide what to do. I don't think he's seen me yet, so maybe I can outrun him. Or perhaps, if I stay very still or slowly crouch against the tree, he won't notice. But, as I hesitate, his head snaps in my direction, and his gaze bores into me.

My training finally kicks in, but in the seconds it takes me to unsheathe my father's sword, he's upon me, taller and broader than any man I've ever seen. His eyes. God, his eyes. Blood red with a spark of gold. One side of his head is shaved right above his ear, which is pointy and decorated with several golden hoops. His long, almost white-blond hair is partly braided on the other side while the rest flows freely around his face.

I'm immediately struck by his appearance. I would have expected a more beastly and repulsive being, yet there's a strange appeal to him. His fair skin is softly highlighted by the rays of light piercing through the branches. *The charm of a hunter who first baits you...* As the warning sounds in my head, I am reminded of the countless men and women from the village whose bodies were found dismembered, burned, and tortured atrociously by those monsters.

Still as death, I'm holding my sword up in front of me.

"Where did you get that?" His low voice startles me. He nods towards my sword, not breaking eye contact.

It's a beautiful sword, the double-edged blade wider by the guard, with engraved symbols along its center and on the hilt. I never asked my father if they have any particular meaning. He said it was his most prized possession, so I vowed to keep and cherish it until I die.

I'm paralyzed, barely remembering to draw a breath, unsure what to say, if I can even speak. My father's warning is ringing in my ears, and it's all I can think about. I should have run and tried escaping this blood-eyed monster. He had warned me, and now I'm going to die at the hand of this savage.

"Where did you find that sword?" He enunciates each word slowly and with force, as if I didn't understand the first time.

A gust of wind hits us, whipping his hair around his cold face. His unanswered question is probably the only reason I'm still breathing, but regardless of whether I talk, I realize my odds of making it out alive are practically non-existent. Well. If I die today, I'm not dying a coward frozen in shock.

"This was my father's sword."

"Impossible." The Fae takes a step toward me and inclines his head slightly. "Let me see it."

"Over my dead body. Who are you? Why do you want to know about my sword?" I ask, emboldened by his reaction.

"Who was your father? Tell me his name," he says, flames dancing in his eyes.

"My father was Tan Vahorn." Lifting my head higher, I hold the Fae's gaze as the name leaves my lips, and for a split second, his eyes reveal a glimpse of panic. This is no random Fae. The name made him flinch, I'm sure of it!

Intrigued now, I decide to push my luck. "Did you know him?"

He pauses for a moment, carefully studying me. "I did."

My mouth drops open at the confirmation, and my grip loosens. Time stops as I blink rapidly, racking my brain for an explanation. But just as I'm about to protest, he abruptly turns and walks away.

"Wait! How did you know him? Who *are* you?"

My shaky voice does nothing to stop him. Should I go after him? Logic is telling me to run far, far away in the opposite direction. But panic suddenly takes me. My father was killed four years ago now. I have been on my own for four years, afraid of losing memories of him, of forgetting him. And now, someone who knew him, maybe better than I did if they met before my father put his fighting days behind him, is walking away! Instinctively, I step forward to follow him.

The Fae suddenly turns back. "Go back. It's not safe. If you still wish to learn about your father, come find me by the next moonsighting." A second later, he disappears behind the trees.

Elanor

I hurry back to the shack. The sun is about to set, and I really shouldn't be wandering outside this late. I'm tempted to run, but after walking all day, I'm not sure I have the energy.

Less than an hour later, the whole forest is plunged into darkness, and the usual sense of comfort I feel around here quickly turns to anxiety. Maybe I should have opted for a run. It's not the night I fear, just the creatures lurking in it, entirely imperceptible to my human eyes until it's too late. Humans who stay out after dark stop being predators and turn into prey.

Now, I can barely see in front of me, relying solely on my instinct and sense of direction to guide me. Keeping a steady but strong pace, the silence around me is astounding. That's until a branch snaps not far behind.

I immediately break into a run without looking back, my heart threatening to beat out of my chest. My legs are starting to burn, but I push on. I know I'm not far from the shack. I can make it. I'm tempted to slow to a fast walk, but I can't shake this feeling that someone or something is watching me.

When I get to the more familiar grounds of the forest near our small cottage, I come to a sudden halt and dive behind a trunk. Crouching on the ground, I wait for my breathing to slow down before scanning the area, listening carefully to the sounds around me. The wind whispers through the trees, branches crack under the weight of their leaves, and insects buzz. I didn't just survive an encounter with a Fae and my heart almost giving out to have some creature follow me back home and slaughter me in my sleep.

When I'm sure I'm completely alone, I leave my cover and run as fast as I can to the shack.

Once inside, I collapse by the small fireplace my father built all those years ago. Still shaken by the day, I don't notice the tears rolling down my face until I brush a loose strand of hair away from my eyes. I encountered a Fae warrior, lived to tell the tale, and the Fae knew of my father and his sword.

After a moment, my vision unblurs, and I manage to take several deep breaths, slowly nodding to myself. I pick myself up and start making dinner as I go over this surprising development.

I'm cutting up some vegetables when the trembling of my fingers stops me. I should forget about all this and go back to my life. Hunting. Heading to the village every now and then to sell what I can gather, or for supplies when I can afford them. Andy's silent stare when he thinks I can't see. Maybe, one day, he'll find the courage to talk to me. Then a scarier thought forms in my mind. Is that all there is to life? Surviving? With no one left who cares if I live or die?

Or, I could go back to the forest tomorrow to find the Fae and get my questions answered. Sure, it sounds extremely dangerous and frankly reckless. But also incredibly more exhilarating.

And above all else, the prospect of learning more about my father and solving some of his mysteries sparks something inside me. When he died, I chose to believe he sent me away to protect me. But maybe his ultimate act of love was not so selfless. And if I stay here, speculations will be the only thing I take to my grave.

It's decided then. I will go back into the forest.

I'm mulling the decision over, eating my broth dinner, when another predicament dawns on me. How will I find the Fae? He didn't mention a meeting point, just that I had to find him by tomorrow night. Fuck.

Exhausted, I lie down on my cot.

One last thought crosses my mind before sleep takes me. My father would probably come back from the dead to scold me if he knew what I was about to do.

⸺ ◆ ⸺

Elanor

The next morning, I check the pack containing my waterskin and other provisions one last time before heading into the forest, my sword sheathed to my back.

By the time the sun is high in the sky, I am nowhere near finding the Fae. I've been walking for hours and have seen no trace of him. It would take me most of the afternoon to return to the part of the forest we were in yesterday, which is much further east, and I have no reason to believe he'll be there.

I take a quick break to drink water and eat some dried fruits before heading north. My father always told me not to go there when talking about the Fae. Right now, that sounds like exactly where I need to go.

After several more hours wandering the forest, I pause again. I absently mutter to myself as I drop my pack to the ground. My chances of finding the Fae are decreasing by the minute, and the deeper I go in the forest, the likelihood of getting back to the shack before nightfall seems further and further away.

A touch of anger blossoms in my heart. This was stupid. Thinking there was more to this dull life, that I could find the Fae and learn more about my father. I need to head back before I put myself in more danger and it gets too dark out for me to find my way.

It's a miracle already that I haven't encountered a beast or daemon. As the thought courses through my head, I notice how silent the forest is around me. There are no birds singing and no insects chirping. Only the thick tree branches bending under the weight of their leaves are softly brushing against each other. A cold drop of sweat runs down my back and I unsheathe my sword, grasping it with both hands as the hair on my arms stands up.

Slowly, I look around, pausing on the dark brown, almost black, trunks and trying to see through the bushes near me. Reassured that nothing seems out of place, I finally let out the breath I've been holding.

A gigantic shadow looms in the corner of my vision, and I turn to face it.

A hideous bear beast with claws long enough to gut a man is standing across a small clearing. With grey-striped fur, a long muzzle, and a mouth filled with sharp teeth, the eyeless abomination releases a low growl.

Remembering my father's teaching, I know that although darkclaws can't see, their other senses are heightened. They can hear and smell from miles away. And right now, its muzzle is pointed right at me, sniffing the air loudly.

I freeze and hold my breath, trying to remain completely still in the hope that the beast will pick something else for its next meal. Or maybe it will grow tired of waiting for me to reveal my exact position. I remain in place for what feels like hours, my gaze fixed on the monstrosity.

It hasn't moved yet, so it looks like my trick is throwing it off balance. I'm seeing stars, and my lungs are starting to burn from the lack of oxygen, but I can't capitulate now. Not when a few more seconds could save or doom me.

As I'm about to burst or faint, the beast finally turns away and takes a step in the opposite direction. Feeling the most intense sense of relief, I lose my focus and release a breath before letting oxygen back inside my lungs. In response, the darkclaws immediately swirls around and closes his jaw shut. My hands start trembling, and my heart sinks as I realize my mistake. The monster begins snapping its teeth ferociously, signaling it has found its dinner.

It's too late now, and my only option is to fight it off. I'm mustering the last of my courage to face the gigantic beast when it releases the most terrifying shriek I've ever heard. This monster came through the gates of Hell, there is no convincing me otherwise. Shaking off the tremble in my fingers, I grip my blade a little harder, bracing myself for the fight to come, a fight I almost certainly cannot win.

The darkclaws growls and, without more warning, launches toward me. Mid-run, it stands on its back legs and releases another one of its horrible cries, leaving me wondering whether the last thing I'll hear will be its death song. Now looking weirdly human-like, the beast is not slowing down one bit. Its huge claws dangling at his sides, oozing a dark blue liquid, come into view. Shit. I can't let those get anywhere near me.

The beast is now upon me, swinging its arms at me. I drop to the ground at the last second and roll away, unable to strike it. I didn't expect it to be this fast!

The darkclaws turns around abruptly, listening to the sound of my steps to locate me. And then it attacks again. But this time I'm prepared. I duck and swing my sword toward one of its infected paws, slicing it off. The beast roars so loudly it's like thunder explodes in my ears. It doesn't stop, though, and its other arm comes right at me. The hit sends me rolling and crashing against a tree.

As I hit the trunk, it feels like my body breaks into a million pieces, and I lose consciousness for a moment.

Fire is burning in my chest and shoulder, and tears come to my eyes. Air has been completely knocked out of my lungs, but eventually my vision starts clearing up as I blink rapidly. I have no idea how I survived the hit.

I'm leaning against a massive tree on the other side of the clearing, trying to hold my head up and come up with a plan to make it out alive. The beast is looking straight at me, nostrils flaring at the smell of my blood. It stands there for what feels like an eternity before approaching, its sectioned arm dangling weakly by its side.

With my pulse pounding in my ears, I look frantically around for my sword, but it's nowhere to be found. I must have dropped it in the fight. Fuck. Fuck. *Fuck.* I reach for my belt knife, wondering how I'm going to be able to kill this thing with the small blade. An inferno blazes in my arm when I grip my dagger.

I've never been one to believe in divinity, but it might be time to reconsider. Maybe it'll make a difference.

With my short blade in hand, I try to stand, but my legs are not responding. Stuck against the trunk, I pointlessly try to regulate my breathing as this hideous beast is about to shred me to pieces.

I watch it stalk toward me atrociously slowly, dark blue drool dripping from its muzzle, like it knows the anticipation is sometimes worse than the act itself, and it's going to take its sweet time finishing me off. Pushing back the dread and panic, I ready my hand to strike, holding on, resisting as poison courses through my blood. The liquid is burning its way to my heart, but there's nothing I can do about it.

As I look death in the eye yet another time, I catch the glimpse of a sword, and a dark liquid sprays on my face. The last thing I see before blacking out is the severed head of the darkclaws rolling on the ground.

CHAPTER TWO

Azran

In the morning, I send scouts into the forest with instructions to report back to me if they spot her.

I still can't believe Tannyll sired a daughter and she is wielding his sword. Just like they said she would. Could it have been a trick? I almost walked away from her. I'm pulled from my thoughts by a commotion in the camp.

I leave my tent and head toward the noise to identify the cause of this ruckus. Cal is already there, listening to the report of a member of the guard. The girl has been sighted.

"Where?"

"Several miles south, not far from the caves." The guard does not dare look in my direction.

"The caves?"

Calen nods. "Az, darkclaws roam these parts."

A thunderous growl reverberates above the forest at that moment, and I break into a run.

Sprinting as fast as I can through the woods, my head is spinning. Being the fastest of the Fae, I know I will get there first and that I will be the one discovering her dead body.

Cal and I knew, in a glance, back at the camp. A human against a darkclaws? No way she can make it out alive.

As I'm racing through the forest, my mind is filled with rage. How could I have come so close and failed?

The scent of blood suddenly overwhelms my senses and I shift toward the source. There. She's lying against a giant tree in a pool of gore, deep gashes running down her chest and arms. She's holding a knife in her hand, and her eyes are widened in terror. Then the darkclaws comes into view. One of its arms is dangling weirdly, and I realize she managed to cut off one of the beast's paws.

Unleashing all my built-up fury, the beast doesn't have time to smell or register my presence as I unsheathe my double-bladed sword and slice the head off its grey-furred body.

It's all over in an instant, but when I get to the girl, she's unconscious, her chest barely moving with each ragged breath. I gather her in my arms and sprint back to camp.

The next hours are a blur. It took all of Mor's power to heal her. I stayed by her side all night, watching him clean the poison out of her wounds. The healer did his best, but she will be left with deep scars.

Mor has been with me since I was a boy and waging wars since long before then. He may be the oldest healer alive, but all magic bearers have their limits. Magic is finite energy, and each use requires life force. It regenerates with rest and time, but overexerting oneself leads to death. Healing is also the only form of magic left on this continent.

There used to be more magic bearers, but they've all become extinct over the centuries, and no one knows why.

If I had gotten there a minute later, she would be dead. I can't believe she managed to fend the beast off long enough for me to arrive. I've never heard of a human strong enough to survive even the first attack of a darkclaws. Their speed is unmatched compared to all creatures that roam this earth. All except perhaps me.

I sit down on the side of her bed. She's sleeping, her features relaxed. I release what feels like my first full breath in hours, carefully watching her and studying her face. The resemblance is uncanny, there's no doubt.

Cal pops his head into the tent, but I send him away with a glance. Not now.

⸺◆⸺

Elanor

I'm alive.

A smell of pine and wood fills the air, but I'm lying on a bed in a tent I don't recognize, the first rays of sunlight filtering through the entrance panel. The last thing I remember is the beast's head rolling on the ground and the gleam of a sword.

I catch movement from the corner of my eye. It's him, the blood-eyed Fae. His intense gaze is searching my face, questioning. He stands and approaches the bed, and as he does, a brisk wind carries his scent across the tent, a soft perfume of forest, citrus, and musk.

I try to sit up, wincing at the pain. My stomach drops when I remember how the darkclaws ravaged my body. I look down, surprised to see I'm not wearing my clothes anymore. Instead, I'm wearing a thin linen shirt that I pull aside to glance at the skin underneath and evaluate the damage.

"We managed to get the poison out of your blood and heal your wounds," he says in a low voice. "There was nothing to be done about those."

I lift the shirt and discover my chest covered in dark red scars, a reminder of the poisonous claws forever engraved in my skin. Tears start pooling in my eyes, but I swallow those down immediately, and they're quickly replaced by a mix of emotions.

Simmering rage, since his obscure instructions led me right into the darkclaws' lair. Fear, because I have no idea who is in front of me, what he's capable of, or what he plans on doing. Will he give me answers? Or was this all just an elaborate plan to trap a naïve mortal girl? I gaze into his red eyes, and fear turns into terror.

"Rest." He's almost out of the tent when the word reaches my ears.

"Wait," I croak, my throat dry. "Who are you?" There's so much I don't understand. How did he find me? Am I safe here?

Right when I think he's going to ignore me and walk out, he pauses. His head half turns towards me, his long blond hair caught in the breeze.

"I'm Azran."

The memory of his gentle voice leaves me wondering if I imagined it when I wake up several hours later.

Feeling better, I brace myself for the pain when I try standing, but it doesn't come. The Fae must have great healers. I guess it's kind of essential for people who are always waging wars.

My gaze lands on a water pitcher by the bed, and I immediately grab it. Disregarding the cup next to it, I drink directly from the pot. My throat is on fire as I swallow big gulps but I don't stop until my thirst is quenched.

A neatly folded pair of linen pants is waiting for me next to my boots, so I get dressed and explore the tent. A chest sits at the foot of the bed, a table over to one side has papers strewn across it, and a small firepit brazes with embers in the middle of the tent. Nothing extravagant, no tapestry or rugs. In the corner, I find a wash basin, indicating that Fae also try to keep clean. It's good to know they're not complete barbarians.

Determined to learn more about my mysterious and seemingly dangerous savior, I walk to the desk, hoping to take a look at the papers scattered across it.

"You're up."

Startled, I back away from the desk. Instinctively, my hands go to my back to grip my weapon and make sure it's within reach. Except my fingers are grasping nothing but air.

"Where is my sword?"

"Safely put away for now. I didn't know whether you'd be in a fighting mood upon waking up or not."

A fighting mood? Is he making fun of me? My face must betray the anger blossoming inside me because the red-eyed Fae lifts a palm in the air, calling a truce. "You managed to cut off one of the beast's paws. Impressive for a human."

"I can do much more than that. Give it back. Now."

"It's in the chest along with your knife. Unlocked."

I slowly go to it, opening it with one arm while keeping an eye on the Fae standing at the tent's entrance. He didn't lie. I pick up my sword and knife and buckle everything in place. Emboldened by the presence of the blade in my back, I decide to get the answers I've been seeking, the answers I risked my life for.

"How did I get here? And what do you know about my father? Why did you seem so shocked when you saw me wielding his sword?"

He takes a moment to look me over. Gods, what a sight I must be. A small brown-haired human, probably as pale as death after barely surviving the attack, my hair a bird's nest, hazel eyes accentuated by the dark purple shadows beneath them, carrying a sword twice my size. I must look ridiculous.

"I didn't know he had a daughter. No one did."

"How did you know him? How was he tied to the Fae? Did he fight against you?" I blurt out, unable to control myself.

"What's your name?"

"Elanor. Now answer my questions. Why am I here?" I tilt my head to the side, set on not letting him dodge all my inquiries.

"Not now. I'll tell you when you're ready to hear what I have to say. In the meantime, Calen will show you to your tent." Frozen in place, I barely register his next words. "Do not, under any circumstance, go wandering outside the limits of the camp."

"What are you talking about?! What does that mean, when I'm ready?"

"That's all I will say about this. Now go." He motions towards the tent's open panel, and that sends me over the edge.

"Who do you think you are? Summoning me to find you, then refusing to answer my questions. And now ordering me around like I'm a dog?" My rage now in full motion, I stride towards him. "If you think I'm going to quietly obey you, you've got another think coming. And I guess you *didn't* know my father, or you'd know he would have never raised a push-over."

Pointing my finger at him, I'm this close to shoving this pompous egotistical maniac. "Now, you are going to answer my questions, you entitled piece of-"

"That's enough talking for you. Leave." His gigantic hand is suddenly over my mouth. And when he growls in my face, I'm violently reminded of who's standing in front of me. I can see the rage dancing in his eyes, barely kept under lock, and it smothers my own in an instant.

I take a step back, pulling away from his deadly embrace. A vein is pumping rapidly on his forehead, and his shallow breath dances across my skin, confirming I went too far. His hateful gaze still piercing into mine, I back out and leave the tent.

***

Elanor

Just a few steps outside, I find myself in the middle of a Fae camp, surrounded by half a dozen smaller tents and several Fae warriors. Shit. It's not like anyone in Grasswood is looking for me right now, but if someone was, I realize they would never get to me.

It looks like the tents are equally spread out around the one I just left, and a huge firepit is burning in front of it, bringing warmth to the late afternoon.

Several Fae look in my direction and just as quickly look away, but a tall and imposing dark-skinned soldier comes up to me. He is wearing the same red and gold armor as everyone else. With long black locks falling on both sides of his clean-shaven face, he looks just as menacing as the others.

"I'm Calen, general of the Fae armies. But you can call me Cal." His striking blue eyes light up with his smile.

General of the what? This is no regular Fae camp. What did I walk into and who did I just talk to? It hasn't escaped me that the tent I just left is the biggest in the camp. And if this Fae is a general...

"Who are you people? Where am I?" Although this one seems nicer than the Fae I just left, I'm half-expecting another outburst of rage in response to my questions.

"We're still in the Dark Forest. The Fae you met, the one who saved you from the darkclaws, is Azran, also known as the Red Fury or the High Lord of the Fae."

A devilish smirk appears on his face and my jaw slackens for a second before I recover with a nervous smile. I'm not sure whether I'm more likely to throw up or burst into hysterical laughter. I just insulted the highest-ranked Fae of Lóna, and the most dangerous one, if I remember my father's lessons correctly. That title is earned on the battlefield, which makes my savior-captor the most revered Fae warrior alive.

I swallow a lump down my throat, which sends Calen, or Cal, laughing. Heat rises to my cheeks instantly, but no smart comment comes to mind.

Trying to keep his laughter under wraps, he leads me towards one of the smaller tents on the other side of the firepit and lifts one of its sides open to let me in.

"There's food and water inside. Get some rest."

Having had my quota of high emotions today, I capitulate and go in.

Inside, I find a small but comfortable-looking cot and, as promised, refreshments. Realizing I haven't eaten in more than a day, I grab some bread and cheese. I could eat a deer, but I try to remember to chew slowly to avoid overwhelming my body and regurgitating everything.

After swallowing another bite, my mouth drops open. It didn't even occur to me that the food could be poisoned. Well, I guess it's too late now.

I go back to devouring the food in front of me, surprised to find it so similar to ours. After eating my fill, I slouch on the cot ever so gracefully, and before I realize it, I'm dead asleep.

I wake up the next day to the sound of orders being shouted around camp. Venturing outside my tent, heart pounding in my chest and my knife in hand, I see Fae warriors packing up tents and readying horses.

A massive bay mount comes a little too close for my taste and I retreat inside to get cleaned up. I rinse my face in the small wash basin and try to tame my wild morning hair, unsuccessfully, so I tie it in a low bun with a few strands already loose on the side of my face. I buckle up my sword and head out.

"You, there! What's going on? Where are we going?" The soldier I directed my question to strides past me without even acknowledging my presence. I look around the camp, searching for a more cooperative source of information.

All the warriors are wearing red and gold armor and carrying swords the likes of which I've never seen before. Thin and curved at the end, with engravings on the hilt and blade I can't make out from where I'm standing. There are women soldiers, too, and they look just as fierce as the men.

Calen comes out of the main pavilion and gives me a nod, confirming he's coming toward me.

"We're moving out. Can you ride?" He asks once within hearing distance.

"Yes, but-"

"Good, we've readied a horse for you. Let's go."

So all the Fae are pompous asses, expecting everyone of a lower rank to obey them without question. And to them, I must really be nothing. They treat me like a child or a fancy prisoner. A child prisoner. This is great.

Although I'm usually quick to disregard safety, I'm not entirely devoid of survival instinct, and I know a lost cause when I see one. Resigned, I follow him. I still need to find answers, and they're clearly set on not giving those out for free.

The general points to a dark horse, a beautiful animal with muscular legs and a wild black mane. My father taught me how to ride, and, granted I haven't ridden in years, I should be able to not make a complete fool out of myself. Hopefully.

I mount the black horse, and then we're off. We ride throughout the day, barely stopping for food or rest. The brisk wind is my only comfort as my entire body is covered in sweat from the effort it's taking me to remain on the saddle. All I can do is hold on. Are they even aware there's a human traveling among them?

I can't feel my ass cheeks anymore, and my entire body is sore. When we finally stop before nightfall to set up camp, I'm not sure I can dismount on my own without planting myself face-first on the ground.

By some miracle, I manage to get down without falling into a heap. I stretch my sore limbs as the camp is being set up and food is being prepared. Once it's ready, I grab a bowl of stew, eat it inside my tent and crash on the cot seconds later, too exhausted to clean myself up.

I wake up at dawn, my body still aching from yesterday's ride. I slide off the bed and hobble over to the small basin by the entrance, where I splash water on my face.

Wait, it wasn't filled last night. Did a Fae walk in while I was sleeping and drooling on my cot, completely unaware? I need to be more careful around them.

Granted, if they had wanted me dead, they would have let me die at the hands of the darkclaws. But it wouldn't hurt to appear a tad more threatening. I'm not some senseless little human. I'm Tannyll's daughter, a fighter, just like them. Granted, a 5-foot-tall one, but a fighter nonetheless.

I finish washing up and put on the shirt, leather pants, and vest that were left on the foot of the cot. Disregarding how ridiculous I feel in

Fae attire, I decide to go out and face the High Lord. I need answers and the illusion that I still have some control over my fate. Being completely clueless makes me feel at everyone's mercy and on constant alert. My life has taken such a wild turn these past few days, and I'm not making sense of any of it.

Still a few steps outside the main tent, which is more like a pavilion, I'm about to go in when I hear raised voices. "[...] is no other explanation. It's Nahtar, damn it, Cal!"

I freeze, trying to discern the words as the despicable warlord and his general argue about God knows what. I'm tempted to stay here to learn more, but the voices fall silent.

Realizing they can probably sense my presence right outside, I gather my courage and walk in. I stop at the entrance, with both of them staring at me.

"All right, I'm not leaving until I get some answers or I'm escorted out by force." It appears that catches their attention. *Good*. Pushing past the awkwardness, I pick an easy question. "Where are we headed?"

"Averion, the capital city of the Fae," Calen says.

"Why should I go with you there? I want answers about my father."

The High Lord looks at Calen, who nods back and promptly leaves.

"You will get them when you're ready. Until then, you're staying with me." I step forward, ready to argue. "Unless you want to try to find your way back, face the monsters of the forest on your own, and forget all about your unanswered questions."

Prick. I pinch my lips in response. He's got me cornered, and he knows it. I have no idea where we are or how far north we've traveled. And I'm no match for the beasts roaming these parts. He drives me crazy with his superior air, and although I'm tempted to talk back, I decide against it. I haven't forgotten our previous altercation. Still unsure how far his patience extends, I storm out, defeated.

That's all I've done these past few days. Lose. My frustration is at its peak, and tears are threatening to roll down my face. No. They can't see me like this. If my only option is to stay with a horde of savages, then so be it. But right now, I need to release some of this pent-up rage.

⸻ ❖ ⸻

Azran

I didn't expect the sight of her in Fae clothing to be so disturbing. She looked fierce with her hair undone, her full lips tightly pinched together, and her hazel eyes turning darker with anger. Standing her ground, ready to pounce at the slightest sign of danger, she's their daughter, all right. If we needed any more proof of who she was, this was it. Strikingly clear.

The memories hit me any time I lay eyes on her. Unbelievable. Yet, she's here, right outside my tent.

A sliver of guilt forms in my heart. I can't tell her, not yet. I need to make sure of so many things before I do. Above all else, I have to find a way to make her stay.

After she leaves, Cal strolls back inside and I glance at him. "Erase that stupid smirk off your face."

Cal answers with his biggest smile. He's the only one I'd ever let get that comfortable with me. We've been fighting side by side for as long as I can remember, and he's like a brother to me. A very annoying brother.

"So, are you going to tell her?" He asks.

"In due time. We need answers first. How did they do it?"

"I'm not sure. I'll look into it once we're back in Averion. So, you're not going to tell her anything? At all?"

"I can't risk scaring her away or having her turn against me."

Cal chuckles. "Right, because you're only the one who-"

"That's enough." I know he wants to help, but I'm just... This is a lot. And it's all so unexpected.

With a shrug, Cal leaves me to return to his duties as my general. Although he's a real pain in the ass at times, he is also the best warrior and commander I know.

Later that day, I'm walking around the camp while she trains by her tent. I recognize Tannyll's fighting style in an instant. She's a natural with a sword. The sword that I never thought I'd see again. This could be the break we've been waiting for.

I watch her for a moment, hypnotized by her graceful motions, and the fierce determination I can read on her face. Small, with a toned body from the hours of training and hunting, I imagine. Her movements are flowing, her legs bending, and her arms stretched out, circling around. I can see she's not holding back, almost straining herself, her chest moving rapidly with each breath.

Images of her scarred chest and torn body come back to me, but I'm woken from the trance by Talín, who's now talking and smiling at her. I repress a low growl right when she notices me watching the scene. Talín catches my glance and walks away. He should know better.

I finish circling the camp and look for Calen. One of our scouts has not come back yet, which is unusual for our trained soldiers.

CHAPTER THREE

Elanor

I've taken off the vest and am now training in my undershirt in front of my tent, repetition after repetition, striking up and down. Gripping my sword and switching with my dagger from time to time, I am sweating out some of my frustration, the salty drops rolling down my forehead and back, the thin fabric of the shirt sticking to my skin.

I take a quick pause to drink water and stretch my sore limbs. Feeling like I'm being observed, I look up and catch a glance from a soldier walking toward me. I hold his gaze, showing I'm not afraid of him or anyone else here.

But he does the most unexpected thing and smiles at me, showing off his perfect teeth.

"Greetings. I'm Talín. You look like you know how to handle that sword!"

"Thanks." My brows draw closer together, but his golden eyes reveal no trace of humor or sarcasm. They're much easier to look at than those crimson eyes. And with that simple thought, I'm brought back to reality.

Glancing around, I find the High Lord looking in our direction. He's standing in front of his pavilion, unmistakably studying us.

Talín follows my gaze before smiling tightly. "It was nice to meet you. You'll see we're not all that bad!"

He walks away, and I turn back towards the main tent, only to find Azran gone. Good riddance.

I look around when a delicious aroma coats the air and my stomach growls in response. My gaze stops on an emerald-eyed, redheaded soldier walking in my direction. She's carrying a steaming bowl of food that she drops off by my tent with a quick nod. She's gone before I can thank her, her flamboyant hair flowing with the wind.

After eating my fill, I spend the rest of the afternoon training, and no one else comes to talk to me. I finally decide to take a break, and when I sheathe the sword on my back, I realize I might have pushed myself a little too hard after barely escaping death a few days ago. My whole body feels heavy and sore.

As I turn to go back into my tent, something by the border of the clearing comes into my line of sight. I pause and squint my eyes to try and identify what it is that caught my attention.

Unsuccessful, I bring my focus back to camp, where the Fae are all going about their usual activities. It's probably nothing, as none of them seems to have noticed anything out of the ordinary.

But a shape furtively circling the camp from the cover of the wide trees appears again. Suddenly it stops, and two white dots gleaming in the shadows stare back at me. Shit. There *is* something out there.

Then I decide to do the dumbest thing possible. I move closer to the outline of the trees, and the shape takes form. I'm looking at a giant black wolf flashing its canines at me. Not friendly. Before I even realize what's happening, the wolf is running toward me, attacking. And another one follows with a growl.

I have just enough time to unsheathe my sword before the first wolf jumps and impales itself on my blade, bringing me down with its fall. I crash to the ground with the black wolf on top of me, its warm blood dripping down my arm.

Straining to free myself, I finally manage to roll over and pull my blade out of its body. With no time to confirm whether the beast is dead or not, the other wolf pounces on me.

My reflexes kick in, and I make an arc with the sword. It slices through like butter, and my eyes widen when the animal's head hits the grass, coloring it red.

I'm watching the liquid paint the ground, unable to look away, when I finally remember to warn the others. But before I can call out to them, Fae warriors leave the cover of the trees and walk into the camp. Uh oh. I'm in way over my head. What's taking so long for the other Fae warriors to notice what's going on and come help me?!

The distinct sound of metal hitting metal resounds behind me, and I don't need to turn around to know they're already busy fighting off other attackers. Shit. Shit. *Shit!*

With no other choice left, I position myself toward the two attackers emerging from the forest. They came straight from the horror stories my father used to tell me. Dark marks are painted all over their faces, and they're armed to the teeth.

One of them even has a pierced tooth, with a metal ring dangling from it. How do I know? That savage is grinning at me.

"Look what we've found here. A human whore!" Says the one closest to me, only a few steps away.

"You should take your time with her," Pierced Tooth adds, still grinning.

"Come near me and die, monsters," I bark, gripping my blade tightly. They burst into laughter in response. Great job, Ela, you really showed them.

Suddenly, they stop laughing, and the first one jumps on me, his sabre getting dangerously close to my neck. I raise my blade at the last second, and the clashing of our swords almost makes me lose my grip.

His riposte comes seconds later at an unexpected speed. A gasp escapes me, and I immediately curse myself for it. Too late. His face distorts in a savage rictus, and he begins launching assault after assault.

I'm barely able to counter his blows, and with each strike, I step back, retreating before his attacks.

He's now pushed me back against a tree by the side of the camp. I block his last attempt, and our blades lock. I can't escape, and I'm straining to keep my sword up, grinding my teeth with the effort. His ugly face is almost touching mine, and his foul breath comes to me in whiffs as he's raging to gain the upper hand and finish me.

I can't hold out much longer. I need to escape this deadly trap. But I'm holding my sword with both hands, and that's barely enough to keep him from slicing my throat.

With death looming above me, I make the only decision available to me. I free one of my hands, letting his blade push against mine. As my sword starts cutting into my skin, my fingers wrap around the hilt of my knife, and I jam it into the monster's neck.

The second jab goes to his sides before I push him back. His eyes widen and his hands go to his neck, trying to contain the crimson river running down his chest as he falls to his knees.

I turn just in time to see my other assailant's expression turn from disgust to utter rage while a strange calm comes over me. They can be killed.

Pulling myself together, renewed hope in my heart, I step forward, readying my sword. I'm going to show that piece of shit what the human whore can do.

There's blood dripping down my shoulder where my blade cut in, but I don't care. All I care about is making this bastard pay for insulting me and thinking I'm a worthless little thing. I'll wipe that sick grin off his face.

I dive right at him, blade first. He is not as good a fighter as his partner, so I quickly counter his strikes and move on to offense. Hit after hit, his confidence is faltering, but mine is back. And when his guard reveals an opening, I lunge and drive my blade right through his chest.

This time I barely notice the shock on his face before he collapses to the ground. Numb and on high alert, I'm withdrawing the blade when I sense a presence at my back. With my heart pounding in my ears, I twirl around and strike without thinking.

My attack is blocked violently, and it takes me a moment to realize that Azran is standing in front of me. His blood eyes are piercing through me, clearing up the fog, and I quickly lower my blade.

While I'm heaving in great gulps of air, he looks completely unbothered. If not for the fact that he is drenched in blood, I would never have guessed he had been fighting. He looks downright murderous with his blond hair now maroon-tinted. *The Red Fury*, Calen's words echo in my mind.

"It's over. They're all dead." His eyes widen as he breathes in through his nose. "You're bleeding." Says the Fae covered in blood. I'm tempted to laugh, but his serious gaze stops me. Next thing I know, he's dragging me towards the center of the camp.

"I'm fine! It's just a scratch." I try to free myself from his grasp.

"Mor! Get in here!" He shouts at a Fae as we finally get to his tent.

"This is ridiculous, let me go! You should be the one who gets looked at by a healer. You look like death." He finally lets go of my arm and looks at me, amused. What is it about me that's so damn amusing to them all?

"Oh, but I am Death," he says in a low voice, his face once again a cold mask.

I swallow the lump in my throat while stepping away from him. I know he means that, and right now, I'm tempted to believe him.

The Fae named Mor walks in and starts examining my wound. His long dark hair is entirely braided with a strip of white silk, and he's wearing armor like the rest of the Fae. Although he has a fairly athletic build, there is no mistaking the marks of age on his face and the small wrinkles around his eyes. He must be centuries old for it to show on his Fae features. To top it all off, his pinched lips give him a serious air.

"Sit down. I need to clean the cut and close it," he says calmly as his piercing grey eyes scan my body. I'm surprised to find a hint of empathy in his stare, lying beyond the sea of wisdom.

If eyes really are the mirrors of the soul, I'm inclined to trust him, so I do as he says. But if the saying is true, then I'm not sure what that says about the crimson-eyed High Lord.

I'm still studying Mor as he looks into the leather bag he's carrying across his chest when it hits me. "You're the one who healed me that night." My pulse quickens as I remember the night I drifted in and out of consciousness, hanging by a thread, poison burning through my body.

He doesn't look up before answering, still rummaging through his bag. "If Azran had brought you to me any later, you wouldn't have made it."

"Thank you." It hadn't even occurred to me to seek out the healer who kept me alive that night and offer my gratitude. Mor quickly cleans my cut and closes it with a greyish salve that stinks terribly. He bands my shoulder and gives me a quick nod before leaving the tent. A Fae of few words.

I turn around to face Azran, who is still soaked in blood. The blood of the attackers, I'm guessing, seeing that Mor didn't linger to care for him.

The worry I saw on his face earlier seems gone, and he's back to his impassible self. I don't understand why he wastes time pretending he cares. The High Lord has made it very clear how unimportant I am, dismissing my questions and barely acknowledging my existence all day.

"Thank you," I whisper, "for getting to me in time." It was only fair I thanked him, too.

He nods and then turns his back to me to head to his wash basin. Right, another dismissal. He strips off his leather armor and soaked shirt, his movements methodical, and starts rinsing himself. As I watch him standing half-naked in front of me, a blush rises to my cheeks. I stumble back outside where the Fae are disposing of the dead and bringing order back to the camp.

I find myself walking back to the battle site, where I killed for the first time. Now that I think about it, it wasn't as hard as I thought it would be. It came to me easily, although I always imagined killing someone would take a piece of one's soul. I guess I'm more of a monster than I care to admit. The bodies are already gone, and I can only see the trail of blood left.

As I get closer to the tree line, I discover one of the wolves that attacked me, the one I stabbed. It growls when I approach. With everyone on edge, it only takes a second before a Fae rushes over. I recognize Talín as he steps between the wolf and me, readying his sword.

"No! Leave it be, there's been enough death for today." Talín looks skeptical, but he stops. "Please. I'll be careful, I promise."

He edges back, still watching me from the corner of his eye. I crouch at a safe distance to observe the animal. Its wound runs deep, but I don't appear to have hit a vital organ. Something inside me is telling me to help the wolf. Probably my conscience making a comeback, trying to prove I'm not an emotionless killer. But how? The wild animal won't let me near.

An idea forms in my mind, and I quickly head back to the camp to look for Mor. I find him sitting by the firepit, looking absently in the distance. When I stop a few feet away from him, I can tell he's properly exhausted.

"I need something strong, strong enough to knock out a man. And a needle and thread."

I straighten my back as I wait for his response, and small lines appear at the corner of his eyes.

"What on earth would you need that for?"

I pinch my lips, considering my approach. "The wolf." I nod in its direction. "Will you help or not?"

He looks me over, considering my request, and then shrugs before pulling something from his pack. It's a small leather pouch. He grabs a thick needle and some thread, and hands everything over to me. "Don't go knocking yourself out with that powder. Only a pinch is necessary."

I nod in thanks and walk back to the side of the camp. That was surprisingly easy.

The wolf is still there, blood oozing from the wound I inflicted. I approach with caution while opening the leather pouch Mor gave me.

I hope he knows what he's doing, or I'm about to lose my hand. I grab a generous pinch of the powder and, without giving myself time to rethink my decision, blow the powder in the direction of the wolf's head.

In a matter of seconds, the animal appears to have been struck by some spell. Its eyes are slowly closing, and it's out. *Damn*! That could come in handy. I carefully close the leather pouch and wait a few minutes to make sure the wolf won't wake up.

Still unmoving. I approach the animal to study the wound more closely, and in the process, I learn the wolf is male. Unsure what else to check or verify before moving forward, I run back to get some boiling water, and once the wound is clean, I get to work stitching it.

I'm holding my breath the whole time, praying he won't wake up. When I finally step back to inspect my work, it looks decent enough. I grab my supplies but leave the water by the wolf for when it wakes up.

On my way back, I'm contemplating stashing away some of that powder when I run into Mor. He doesn't say a thing, just holds out his hand in my direction with a disapproving look. Shrugging, I drop the leather pouch and the bloodied needle in his palm.

⚫

Azran

As I wash, I retrace the last hour in my head. We took all the necessary precautions, but when I first heard the wolves, I knew they were right behind. I have no idea how they found us. No one knew where we were except the members of my guard and Cal.

I spotted Elanor across the camp, way too close to the border, although I had told her not to wander far. My blood turned to ice when I saw the animals pounce on her, but attackers were coming from all sides.

I fought through the horde of enemies as fast as I could, hoping to reach her before they did. Unleashing all my wrath on them, I tore through limbs, body after body, as blood splashed everywhere.

When I finally got to her, she was still standing, attackers dead at her feet. She is a hell of a fighter. Then I smelled her blood. How could I forget that smell? It's haunted me since the night I found her with the darkclaws. Thankfully, her wounds were superficial.

She cannot die. I won't allow it, not after all this time spent searching. I take a deep breath to calm my thoughts. I need to get my head on straight, find Cal, and figure out how this could have happened.

He walks in as if reading my mind, unbothered by my nudity. We've both seen each other in worse situations.

"How did they know, Cal?"

"I'm not sure. I'm interrogating everyone after this." He looks just as angry as I am. "And you can't ever go off like that on your own again, exposing yourself, Az. You could have been harmed with no one guarding your back. You should know better!"

"Need I remind you who I am?" Fury comes back to me in an instant. "None of this matters if she gets killed." His eyebrows raise in surprise though he doesn't respond. But his silence is louder than words. I know he meant well. "I couldn't let her die..."

"I know that. Still-"

"She cannot die, you hear me?"

He nods. I know he still has doubts, but deep down, I am sure of it. She is the key to everything.

CHAPTER FOUR

Elanor

Now back in the camp, I'm set on getting some answers when I spot Calen talking to one of his soldiers. The conversation I'm about to interrupt doesn't look like a friendly one, but frankly, I don't care. "Who were they? Why did they attack?"

His head snaps towards me, and he lets out a heavy sigh. I return a pinched smile, not one bit sorry. "Rebels. Sorry you got caught up in the middle of it."

"Rebels? I thought all Fae answered to the High Lord. Why are they rebelling against him?" I turn to the soldier standing next to the general, but he avoids my gaze and leaves quietly.

"That's all I can say. You don't need to worry about them." Calen glances sideways, probably at his High Lord, if I had to guess.

I swallow a grunt of frustration and turn away. Why do I even bother with them? Clearly, neither he nor Azran will budge, and they've ensured nobody else talks to me.

Once inside my tent and away from prying eyes, I release my clenched fists, and my shoulders sag heavily. Feeling exhaustion in every muscle of my body, I grab some food, drink my fill of water, and throw my bloodied shirt on the ground.

I collapse on my cot, simply wearing my leather pants and breast band. The thin piece of fabric barely covers my chest. However inappropriate, I can't find it in me to care. I drift into somber dreams not long after.

When I wake up, it's still dark outside, but I decide to get up and check on the wolf. Looking down at myself, past the red scars, I realize I can't leave wearing only this attire. I search the tent, and I'm not sure whether I'm surprised to find another linen shirt by the entrance. Red now rosing my cheeks, I grab it and quickly put it on, wondering who keeps visiting me at night.

I quietly exit my tent and make my way through the camp. I spot a soldier on the other side, standing guard, but he's turned towards the forest, so I easily sneak past him. The tree line is now in my sight, and I can feel the tension leaving my body.

"Where do you think you're going?"

Startled, I turn around to find Azran towering over me. "What now? Am I a prisoner? I can't go for a walk?"

His dark laugh causes the hair on my arms to stand up. "Funny." His voice is devoid of any trace of humor. "Wolves are not pets," he continues with a smug look on his face. I search for a way to contradict him, but no sane argument comes to mind. "And I'm glad you decided to put a shirt on."

My brows draw together in a frown, and it takes me several seconds before his words register. "So it was you wandering around in my tent after dark like a creep. Too shy to approach me in broad daylight? Stalking is not a good look for a High Lord."

He pinches his lips slightly, and a proud smile blooms on my face as I realize the mockery has hit its mark.

"Careful what you wish for, little one." His voice barely reaches my ears, but his features transform into a suggestive grin.

Warmth rises instantly to my cheeks, and I look away before walking past him, not granting him another glance. Insufferable jerk.

When I reach the site where I last saw the wolf, the animal is gone. Feeling a tug of disappointment, I linger, searching the darkness for its shape. I'm about to turn back when it appears in front of me, limping but able to stand on its own. No canines are showing, which I take as a good sign.

"Hey," I say softly, "sorry for knocking you out yesterday, I was just trying to help." Its white eyes are staring right back at me, and I shake my head. Trying to talk to a wolf. I've really lost it.

He doesn't seem aggressive, so I slowly walk around him, watching from the corner of my eye to make sure he's not feeling vengeful. The wolf is simply studying me with his captivating eyes, following my steps.

After a few minutes of this dance, he still hasn't attacked, so I'm assuming he won't. I turn my back on the animal to head towards the lights of the camp and glimpse behind me. A smile tugs on my lips as I realize he's following me. I guess wolves can be pets, after all. Take that, High Lord.

With my new companion following me from a distance, I learn that the presence of other Fae and an encampment are no deterrents.

Maybe we killed his owner, and he thinks a new one showed up. However ridiculous that sounds, it's my best working theory. I'm not sure what the wolf wants, but he seems set on sticking by my side.

I enter my tent and turn back to find the animal lying down by the entrance, standing guard. I sit down on my cot to observe him, and I'm tempted to name him. His furry head snaps in my direction, and a name pops into my mind. *Savage.* My eyes widen in awe, but the animal resumes his guard, looking out into the night, leaving me wondering whether I just imagined that or not. I lay back down on the narrow bed, closing one eye and keeping the other on Savage.

I must drift back to sleep for a few hours because when I open my eyes again, light is streaming through the tent's flaps. Savage is still standing guard.

After eating a quick breakfast, I leave some dried meat by the wolf before heading out, unsure what the best course of action is now.

Once outside, I spot a new face among the Fae. A raven-haired soldier is hurrying through the camp, looking disheveled. I head in the same direction, set on finding out more since it's become clear I'm only going to obtain new information on my own.

As I approach the group of Fae now gathered by the central pavilion, I learn he's a scout who had gone missing or was reported killed by the rebels. He's giving his report to Calen but the timing of his reappearance seems weirdly convenient. The newcomer notices me at the same time and pauses immediately, his delicate features struck in shock. His eyes then stop on the hilt of my sword, sticking out of my back harness. The scout's intense gaze is rubbing me the wrong way.

Azran, who I hadn't seen until now, cuts in. "Inside. Now." My body stiffens at the sound of his voice. He clearly doesn't want me overhearing anything else.

⚜

Azran

I motion toward the food and refreshments at the back of the tent. I study the scout as he briefly bows in thanks and hurries to the table. I can see Cal doing the same. There is no trace of blood on his armor or weapons.

Hagmar helps himself to a cup of wine and some dried fruits before turning back towards us.

I ask him to finish his report and listen carefully to his detailed statement.

"So, you got cut off from us by the rebels, managed to escape when they came after you, too, and finally made your way back," I state, ensuring I'm not leaving anything out.

The scout nods formally before resuming martial position, still as stone, his gaze to the ground. Taking my time, I stare at him, detailing his attire, shaven jawline, and the way he carries himself, knowing damn well how unsettling the silence must be.

After an interminable pause, he finally asks the question burning his lips. "Who is the human?"

I don't bother answering and call for Talín instead as a plan forms in my head. He walks in seconds later and stops by the entrance, ready for whatever his High Lord demands of him. He's one of the youngest in the High Guard, but a good soldier.

"We need to keep moving. Talín, go ahead of us and report back if you notice anything out of the ordinary." The brown-haired soldier quickly bows and heads back out.

Once it's the three of us again, I turn back to face Hagmar and dismiss him. "That will be all. We're glad you made it back."

We watch him exit the pavilion, and Cal and I lock eyes for a second. I swear, sometimes he can read my mind. He raises an eyebrow, and I nod back in confirmation before we follow Hagmar out. I position myself by the firepit and watch as my general gives out orders to pack up the camp.

⸺◆⸺

Elanor

Back in the tent, I check on Savage before grabbing my knife to train some more and get my mind off things. I'm about to head out again when a side panel lifts up, and the mysterious dark-haired scout walks in. My blood turns to ice when my gaze meets his.

"What do you want?" By the time the words leave my mouth, Savage is up on all fours in between the stranger and me.

The dark-haired Fae returns a soft smile, which makes me even warier.

"I'm Hagmar. Just wanted to introduce myself." His voice is like honey, only honey is used to trap and kill prey. "That's a nice sword you've got there."

"Want me to show you what it can do?" My mocking tone does little to hide the unease rising in my chest. Hagmar laughs loudly at my retort, almost in confirmation of my poor performance.

Savage growls in front of me, clearly as wary as I am, and, just as suddenly, the scout's amused gaze turns feral.

I recognize the hate and murder in his eyes just in time to step back before Hagmar pulls a knife from behind his back. It's the same look I saw on the rebels' faces before they attacked me.

Savage snaps his jaw shut in a growl and pounces on the scout before he even gets the chance to try and stab me. Seconds later, soldiers storm my small tent and grab him. Too stunned to say a word, I watch as he's pulled away, still baring his teeth at me.

Screams tear through Hagmar's throat outside, and I come to my senses. Stepping outside, my gaze lands on the High Lord ordering his soldiers around, and everything falls into place. The bastard just used me as bait. I knew something was off when the scout returned to the camp, and Azran must have come to the same conclusion. Making the meaningless mortal bear the risk must have been a no-brainer. Anyone would do the trick as long as he got his proof.

More unanswered questions pop into my head with the confirmation of Hagmar's betrayal. One of the High Lord's soldiers sold him out or was with the rebels all along, lurking and waiting for an opportunity to strike.

Without a second thought, I step forward and command Savage to stay down by a hand motion. Surprisingly, the wolf obeys, and I move closer to the soldiers surrounding Hagmar on the other side of the firepit.

The green-eyed redheaded soldier is holding his head by the hair and poking her sabre in his back to keep him still. Azran is standing in front of the traitor, towering over him and taller than all the other Fae present.

I can't make out what they're saying, but I hold my breath instinctively when Hagmar spits at Azran. Time is suspended for an instant, and the atmosphere darkens. I can almost see the fury emanating from the High Lord's tense body.

I take several steps forward, hypnotized by the trial unfolding before my eyes, and get close enough to overhear a few words from Hagmar. "[...] protecting human filth. Or maybe you keep her to toy with at night. You are a disgrace to the race of the Fae!"

A frown appears on my forehead as I shake my head in disgust. I guess that confirms my father's teachings that some Fae truly do hate my kind and would rather see us all dead or enslaved.

Azran's head turns towards me and we lock eyes. Without breaking eye contact, he reaches out in front of him, tears through the Fae's chest with the brute force of his bare hand crushing flesh and bones, and pulls out his heart. Blood spatters on the High Lord's face, still twisted in a mask of rage, and a sick smile appears on his red-stained lips.

Blinking rapidly in a vain attempt to process the execution and the sheer strength it required, all I can see are the red drops decorating his skin, rolling down his chest, and coloring his hair.

I let out a shaky breath when Azran finally looks away and casts the heart into the fire. I watch him walk away, his hand dripping blood, before my gaze snaps back to Hagmar's body, still being held up by the Fae soldier. His head has gone limp and red liquid is oozing out of the giant hole in his chest.

Unclenching my fists, my nails leaving painful marks on my palms, I stumble back, and reality sets in. The High Lord didn't even flinch. After a few days, I had almost forgotten they were all monsters, especially him. I can't stay and risk being next on the execution list. I need to figure out what secrets they're keeping from me and get the fuck out of here.

The next two days are spent riding through the forest. We're barely stopping for food or rest, with everyone focused on getting to Averion. Savage is running by my side, his stitches holding decently enough, but he looks just as exhausted as I am. My entire body is aching by the end of the first day, my fingers blistering from gripping the reins so hard, and I can barely stay on my horse.

The soldiers seem unbothered, probably used to this pace, not realizing I'm not. Self-centered bastards. With each mile in the sole company of my own emotions, my anger keeps me alert and focused. Even the familiar cover of the forest doesn't help anymore. It's all turning into a blur. The only ones who seem to notice my state are Talín and the redhead riding next to me. She hasn't said a word to me, but she offered some water in between pitying glances and encouraging smiles.

By the second day though, I'm in a trance, riding all day with a headache pulsing behind my eyes and forehead. I've been in the forest for ages, and the trees are all blending in together. All I can focus on is the wind brushing my face and my body being pulled forward violently with each movement of the horse as we follow a trail I can't make out anymore.

When at last we stop for the night, I slide down my horse. Almost falling flat on my face, I reach for something to hold on to, and my hand finds purchase on a rock-hard surface. Strands of my hair are flying around my face, thankfully hiding my features as I clench my jaw and pain reverberates in my legs from the shock of the near fall.

My head snaps up when a warm hand lands on my lower back, steadying me, and I'm left staring into Azran's red eyes. I step back with a flinch, pushing back on the chest I was leaning on moments ago. The very hand that ripped out an organ in a heartbeat lets go of me, and I swear I catch a hint of worry across his brows when mine must reveal the extent of my distrust.

I step away and head straight to where Talín is signaling me, having set up my tent already.

"Here you go." He steps away. "We should arrive tomorrow." He gives me a small smile that I return before sprawling on my cot, Savage faithfully by my side. I munch on some food and quench my thirst before falling into a deep slumber.

The next day, we finally leave the Dark Forest behind us. I never thought I'd be relieved to step out of its shadows, yet here I am. We're now traveling through green hills and lush plains extending as far as the eye can see, and around mid-day, Averion comes within view.

My father told me about the Fae capital, but nothing could have prepared me for this sight. From our vantage point, I can see that the city is vast and majestic. A river runs through it, with houses and buildings on either side. All construction is white, some with turrets and bridges. And in its heart, overlooking everything, is a tall palace with a decorated dome that goes so high up it almost disappears in the clouds. Finally, my eyes land on a high wall built all around the city, protecting it. I swallow a lump in my throat as I realize that once I step foot inside the capital, getting out won't be easy.

It takes us another hour to get within the city walls, but I'm stunned by its beauty when we do. The white paved streets are flowing with life. We pass several markets, with stands each more colorful than the one before, and merchants heckling and trying to attract the attention of their next customers. I've never seen that many goods being sold in one place, ranging from spices and clothes to jewelry and weapons. The air is filled with the delicious aromas of meat pies, bread, and pastries, tempting every passerby and rider.

My eyes land on the citizens, and I quickly notice how revered the High Lord is in his capital. I was expecting more fear than reverence, but the Fae seem to be in adoration of the warlord, calling out to him, waving, and celebrating his return, though he doesn't reciprocate the greetings.

I spot several humans among the crowd now assembling and following us to the palace. My eyes widen as none look enslaved. Some are well-dressed, and most of them are smiling at the convoy. Tucking that piece of information away in my mind, I add that to the list of things I need to figure out while I'm here.

We're now approaching another high wall guarding the palace grounds. The crowd disperses as we cross under a huge white limestone arch, and we arrive in a paved courtyard. On one side, a long two-story building stands next to the stables, and on the other, a massive marble stairway leads up to the palace's decorated double doors. I watch silently as Talín disappears inside the first building after dismounting his horse. Barracks, I imagine. The redhead and the other soldiers follow suit.

Only Azran and Calen are left by my side, leading me to the imposing stairs. The palace reaches so high in the sky that I cannot discern its dome. Lifting my head up, I realize it also expands sideways around the courtyard and beyond. The High Lord and his general dismount, so I do the same, relieved to finally get off the horse for good, and Savage stops by my side. A small smile tugs on my lips when my gaze falls on him. I'm growing strangely attached to the animal. His presence makes me feel less alone and defenseless.

A large group of servants and aides come out the double doors in front of us to take away the horses, and one of them, an older lady, approaches me.

"Welcome to Averion. I'm Rina, and I will be your first maid, my Lady. If you would follow me, I will show you to your quarters."

She bows to me, and I don't move at first, too stunned to reply. My Lady? I turn back towards the two detestable Fae, but they're already strolling away inside the palace. So I follow in Rina's footsteps, with Savage right behind me.

As we step inside the palace, I'm completely awestruck. It's enormous. The entryway itself is the biggest room I've ever been in, and white marble is everywhere I look. We begin climbing a majestic stair-case and go up several floors before Rina leads me to a gigantic bed-room.

The antechamber is neatly decorated, and the room itself seems comfortable and welcoming. Nothing too ostentatious at first glance. Except maybe for the round bed covered in plush cream, brown, and rust-colored pillows in the middle of the room and the fireplace on the opposite wall. I also notice a wooden chest, a round table, a wardrobe behind the bed, and patterned rugs decorating the floors. Lastly, win-dows enhanced by sheer curtains occupy an entire wall from floor to ceiling, letting daylight in.

Rina points to an archway, and when I step into the bathing room, my jaw drops. A marble bathtub is sunken into the floor in the center of the room. Four people could probably fit in there, with room to spare.

"Should I have a bath drawn for you, my Lady? You must be ex-hausted from your travels."

Speechless, I'm staring at the Fae who is solemnly waiting for my directions. This is completely surreal.

"That would be great, thank you," I finally manage to answer. "And please, call me Ela."

Rina pinches her lips at my remark before giving me a quick nod and heading toward the bathtub. She turns several nozzles in different directions, and a few seconds later, water starts flowing into the tub. Mesmerized, I watch it being filled in a matter of minutes. I had heard about those inventions but had never seen or used one before. In Brimora, they are reserved for wealthy nobles or royalty.

Rina walks back in a few minutes later with an army of servants as I'm gazing upon the city through the room's huge windows. The view is simply breathtaking. I never thought I'd see this much beauty here, of all places.

I step back from the windows when several servants approach to undress me. With a motion of my hand, I send them away. "I appreciate you showing me around, but that won't be necessary. I'm perfectly capable of undressing myself. There's no need for all this."

Rina's eyebrows raise in surprise. She's about to object so I grab a handful of my hair. "I could use some help untangling and washing my hair, though. Please." Her features relax, and with renewed purpose in her steps, she approaches to pour salts and products into the bath. I undress completely and step into the heated water with a blissful sigh. Closing my eyes for just a second, I soak in the heavenly smells of vanilla and blackberry, wishing I could stay here for hours.

I catch my reflection in a mirror across the room. Purple circling under my crazed hazel eyes, my face so pale and dirty it's almost grey, I look like shit. My gaze drops to my chest and the red scars running through it.

"Scars only mark a warrior's value here. It's what makes you stand apart." My head snaps up with Rina's confident voice. I hadn't even realized my fingers were on my marked skin. Removing my hand, I give her a tight smile. At least these make me look stronger and less vulnerable.

Studying the other scar on my shoulder, the one I earned fighting off the rebels, I realize it's almost gone. I can barely distinguish the rosy line, and it's only been a few days. Is it possible I'm healing faster in the Fae territories? Adding that to the mental index of things I need to look into, I close my eyes and submerge my head underwater.

I come back up, and Rina's hands are now on my head, massaging a floral-scented soap into my scalp. I let her thoroughly clean my hair, savoring this luxury and allowing myself to relax for a moment.

I finish washing and rinsing myself before getting out of the bath and wrapping myself in a plush robe. I look around for my clothes and see they're nowhere to be found.

Noticing my surprise, Rina goes to the wardrobe and pulls out the most indecent gown I've ever seen. Red, with a V-neck plunge in the front and back, with two slits all the way up each side.

"What is that? I'm not wearing that. I want my regular clothes."

"They're being washed. You'll have them first thing tomorrow. And you couldn't wear those tonight, as the High Lord requests your presence at the feast."

I roll my eyes at her words. Of course there's a feast tonight. I consider not going for a second before deciding against it. Maybe I'll be able to poke around and learn more about this place. And to be honest, I'm starving. But there's no way I'm showing up dressed like that. "Is there nothing less... revealing?"

Rina pauses for a moment before heading towards the wardrobe again. She pulls out a golden gown with barely any more coverage, seeing the completely open back on it. And a strapless black one, with encrusted crystals all over it. Fuck. I'm going to look ridiculous in that. But unfortunately, it seems like the best option right now, so I point to the black dress. It also comes with detachable balloon sleeves, which should help provide more coverage, although it won't hide my scars.

To top it all off, Rina pulls out a scandalous pair of underwear made of thin black lace. I put my head in between my hands and close my eyes, defeated. "Is that what all the Fae women wear? Almost nothing?"

Rina looks at me, amused. "Hmm, it's in fashion, yes. All the ladies of the court dress this way."

Resigned, I get dressed, and Rina helps me put the gown on, as well as some black satin sandals. I leave my hair down to air dry and cover my cleavage as much as possible. Finally, Rina looks me over before giving me a nod of approval.

When I'm ready to head out, I ask for a moment alone. She leaves the room, and I find my knife and leather holster. The presence of the blade reassuring me, I fasten it to my right thigh.

I turn to Savage, lying down by the fireplace in the bedroom, his white eyes fixed on me. "I have to leave for a little bit, but I'll be back. I need you to stay here and not terrorize half the palace. And then tomorrow, we'll go explore the grounds." Explore and start finding some answers. But that, he doesn't need to know, if he understands anything I say at all. It looks like the animal that wanted to rip my throat out several days ago has now become the closest thing I have to an ally here.

Feeling as ready as I'll ever be for my first introduction to Fae society, I open the door to my quarters and find Rina patiently waiting outside, ready to lead the way.

CHAPTER FIVE

Elanor

Giant double metal doors come into view, the panels decorated with symbols and writings I can't read. With each step, the dress skirt brushes against my legs, reminding me how out of place I am here. The doors open on their own like they sensed me coming.

I freeze in the doorway when I lay eyes on the Great Hall, but Rina gives me an encouraging smile as she steps aside, and I'm drawn into a mythical realm. A series of white columns are positioned on each side of the immense room. On the far wall opposite the entrance, majestic glass panels offer a breathtaking view of the city down below and the crimson sunset painting the white buildings amethyst. Guests, both humans and Fae, are engaging in conversations and dancing while musicians play a variety of stringed instruments in a corner. The whole room is lit by chandeliers supporting hundreds of candles.

Tapestries occupy entire walls beside the columns, illustrating Fae history. Eager to learn more, I head toward the left side of the Hall to take a closer look. Circling the attendees, I stroll through the gallery and observe the rendition of the arrival of the Fae in this part of the world. There, I recognize the blond-haired and blood-eyed Fae standing on a battlefield. He appears to be gutting wild beasts and waging wars. Nothing groundbreaking there, so I move on.

The glass-paneled wall opens onto a large balcony overlooking Averion. From here, I have a clearer view of the immense city. Several avenues divide rows of residential buildings and lead to a central plaza with colorful dots in its midst. The principal market-place. Thousands of lights twinkle in the capital as its inhabitants go about their evening.

It must have taken impressive craftsmanship to build the palace this high up. Although tempted to escape the crowd, I'm too afraid to step out and stand in the cold night that high up in the sky. Instead, I turn around and face the guests attending the feast.

Rina didn't lie. The Fae are all wearing revealing outfits and gowns, showing off their bodies and sparkling jewels. I don't consider myself a prude, but I guess I didn't expect this here. Clothes are meant to be practical in my world.

Most guests are either dancing, eating, drinking, or absorbed in conversations, and only a few are glancing at me. Now what?

A familiar face stands out from the crowd. Calen switched his armor for a more relaxed evening attire, and his black locks are tied on top of his head in a bun. Back at the camp, he seemed more willing to answer my questions than his High Lord. Maybe I should try my luck with him tonight.

But before I can act on that thought, an all too unforgettable voice murmurs behind me. "Good evening."

I turn around to face Azran. His hair is pulled back, revealing his sharp features and piercing eyes. "Have you settled into your quarters?"

"I have." So now we're making small talk? He's been nothing but cold and distant since we met, and now he expects me to believe he cares about my comfort.

"I see you didn't waste time and are quickly adapting to Fae fashion," he inclines his head, and his gaze drops to the bottom half of my gown. His eyebrow twitches as he adds. "Interesting choice."

"I realize you liked playing dress-up with your toys as a child. But you've got the wrong doll." I'm growing tired of his games.

"Watch yourself. You have no idea what you're talking about," he grits out. The cold mask immediately goes back on, but there's no hiding the anger in his eyes. "If you need anything, Rina will be at your disposal." Ah. That's more like him, dismissive and to the point. He nods almost imperceptibly as if reading my mind and heads back into the crowd.

And what's so interesting about my choice of attire anyway? Considering everything, I fit in pretty well with the crowd. Brushing his comment off, I grab a small plate full of appetizers and head toward the other side of the room to check out the rest of the tapestries. As I cross the room, I catch a few glances from other guests, carefully studying me. Two Fae wearing large hats covered in feathers and sporting an ostentatious collection of necklaces don't even bother hiding their mocking laugh as I walk past them. I can feel a tingle of shame as I register they're probably making fun of me, the weird human girl attending tonight's celebration. But I don't let it show on my face and tilt my chin a little higher instead. Enjoy the show, folks. Being the topic of tonight's gossip is the least of my worries. I've dealt with far worse, though my rosied cheeks don't seem to agree.

I make quick work of the delicious hors d'oeuvres and canapes and a server pops up in front of me the minute I'm finished.

"Is there anything else I can get for you, my Lady?" The blue-haired Fae dips his chin as he takes the empty plate off my hands in a swift movement.

I mumble words of gratitude and bring my focus back to the tapestries, my hunger tamed for the moment. Azran along with Calen take center stage on a battlefield, with corpses at their feet. How long has he been High Lord of the Fae? The next panel shows him on the side of a mountain lifting a paper scroll which is enveloped in a halo of light. And then more wars. Not super insightful, but I make a note to find out what that mysterious scroll is all about. I must start somewhere.

"Good evening, Elanor."

Turning around, I find Talín smiling at me, a cup in his hand. He's wearing a stunning forest green ensemble with touches of gold that match his irises. I smile back, relieved to see a familiar face.

"You look great. I like the warrior touch," he says with a wink. The what? My face must betray my confusion as he adds, "The knife to your leg. This way people know not to mess with you. I like it!"

I look down, cheeks burning. The bottom half of my gown is sheer from mid-thigh down. Damned dress and Fae fashion! I sure gave the guests something to laugh about, this ridiculous human attempting to look dangerous, probably too slow and weak to challenge any of the Fae here.

For a second, I'm tempted to run out of here and leave this wretched place. But Talín's voice interrupts my train of thought. "Will you dance with me?"

I tilt my head to the side, unsure what to make of him. If he noticed my discomfort, he had the kindness not to show it. Instead, he's offering me an opportunity to rise above the situation. He's the nicest Fae I've met so far, going above and beyond to make me feel welcome. And at this point, I'm in dire need of an ally that's not a wolf, so I accept with a nod. He puts his drink down, takes my hand, and pulls me to the center of the room.

Azran

Calen joins me as I monitor the scene unfolding before us, my gaze fixed on Elanor, her black gown twirling around her legs. I've been watching her for a while now. Seeing her smile at Talín and now dancing with him rubs me the wrong way. I have never seen her smile before. It's... disturbing.

"Maybe that's a better technique than giving her the cold shoulder every chance you get," Cal finally says in a mocking tone.

"Don't be ridiculous."

"I'm serious, Az. She's going to find out sooner or later. And I think there's a better chance of her not gutting everyone in sight if you've managed to establish some sort of ..." He looks around to make sure no one is close enough to overhear. "Relationship."

"Hmm." It's true I have not been the most welcoming. Everyone around me obeys in the blink of an eye, and I haven't had to put forth an effort with guests in ages. She's just so... So what? Impatient. Defiant. Eager to get answers.

Elanor has made it very clear she hates my kind, and I've done nothing to dissuade her, only showing my monstrous side. If only she knew the irony of it all...

Elanor

With Talín keeping me company, the evening is not entirely dreadful. He helps take my mind off things and I'm able to dance without crushing his feet or making a complete fool out of myself.

After a few more dances, I excuse myself and retire to my room, only making one wrong turn before finding my way. Savage is in the same spot where I left him earlier, with a water bowl and an empty plate not far from him. I'll need to thank Rina for that.

I shed the treacherous black dress, disregard the lace nightgown neatly folded on the bedside table, and slip under the covers naked. A headache pounds behind my eyes and the luxuriant pillow under my head is not helping. Its warmth and softness are sick reminders of how far from home I've wandered. I yank it away and swap it with a cotton one.

The extent of my newfound circumstances is starting to hit me. I can't believe I'm this far into Fae territory. I never realized how much comfort my desolate home provided. Although I've spent the last four years barely surviving, I've also built a semblance of safety and control in my life. But now it's all gone, and I'm constantly assaulted by unfamiliar faces and strange sights.

My eyelids are starting to feel heavy, so I mentally recap what I know before I drift asleep. It's not much. I've always heard that castles have libraries. Tomorrow, maybe I can find one and do some research.

In the morning, as promised by Rina, I find my regular clothes cleaned and neatly folded in the antechamber. I put them on, buckle my sword and knife, and head out of the room with Savage, set on finding answers. We only cross paths with a few servants as we wander the wide corridors lined with windows and crystal chandeliers.

We end up outside the tower and stumble upon a palace garden. It's the most ethereal greenery I've ever laid eyes on. Several paths go through clumps of wildflowers and disappear in the distance. White flowers are blooming everywhere, some I've never seen before in my life, others I recognize, like amaryllis. Majestic trees offer shade to passersby, like ancestral beings guarding the grounds. It couldn't be more different from the Dark Forest, and it's completely breathtaking.

Savage can barely contain his excitement at the sight of grass, and looks expectantly at me. "Go," I say with a smile on my face. He's clearly been trained, and so far, I've found several commands for him to stay down, stay put, or let him be. I'll need to figure out the attack command, as it could come in handy.

Trusting that he won't maim a random servant or noble, I leave him to enjoy the outdoors and head back inside to explore the palace. Without a clue how to find the library, if there is one, I take random turns here and there. After an hour of roaming the marble halls unsuccessfully, I stop a passing servant and ask for directions. The young Fae doesn't look one bit surprised by my request and leads me right to it. Had I known it would be that easy, I would have asked hours ago. He leaves me at the top of a massive staircase, in front of giant doors that I push wide open on either side.

The main room I'm standing in is covered from floor to ceiling by bookshelves. Ladders are mounted on what looks like rails, going all around the circular room, in order to reach the volumes at the top. The center of the library is occupied by reading tables.

A door on the far wall piques my curiosity, and when I walk through it, my jaw drops open. Just like in the Great Hall, immense glass panels occupy an entire section of the room. Stepping closer, I can see the city below and, in the distance, the Dark Forest. If I had to guess, I'd say we're right above the Great Hall.

By the giant windows are oversized leather chairs and reading tables. I could picture myself spending hours here, sinking in their comfortable cushions as time passed. I'm still gazing upon the amount of knowledge amassed in this space when a new issue dawns on me. How am I going to find anything in here?

Releasing a long sigh, I begin wandering the room until a massive open book on a stand captures my attention. It contains a registry of all the texts and their corresponding location based on a system of labeled bookshelves. Thank God. I start browsing through it, unsure what I'm looking for yet. In the history category, I identify a few books that could be interesting and find their section and row next to each line.

I eye a leather armchair with envy but settle for a chair at a wooden table once I've gathered the tomes. The first one details the early days of the Fae and how they first arrived in Lóna, nothing I didn't already know. The second one doesn't reveal anything radically new, either, just more tales of war. But the third one details Azran's ascent to power. I have no clue what his intentions are, and if I'm to survive my stay in Averion, I need to learn as much as I can about him to understand who I'm dealing with.

Apparently, before there was a High Lord, the Fae weren't united, conflicts creating divides between the Wood and Water Fae, then the Sun and Moon Fae. Azran is the fruit of the union of a Sun Fae and a Moon Fae, giving him his unique features of pale skin and blond hair. I don't find an explanation for his blood eyes, but his heritage does explain his ability to rally the Fae under one banner. The Fae territory is still divided into different regions, each led by a Lord or Lady, although they all answer to Azran as their High Lord. Irann is the Lady of the Wood Fae, apparently has been so for ages, and seems to be the oldest of them all. Keryth is Lord of the Water Fae and rules over the eastern shore. Tharrion, Lord of the Sun Fae, rules over the southern plains until the Eidune Range. If the painting in this book does him any justice, he's handsome, dark-skinned, with a radiant smile. And then there's Amrynn, Lady of the Moon Fae, ruler in the north.

I find what comes next in the book particularly interesting. When Azran was fighting the last warlord resisting the Fae alliance, he sought out a soothsayer to avoid another bloodbath and went on a quest that led him deep into the Blue Mountains. There it was said he would find the key to saving his people.

Eager to learn more, I turn the page, only to find that the last ones have been torn out. I wonder what was so important on those pages that someone stole, destroyed, or hid them from prying eyes. I'm guessing Azran completed the quest, though, given that his people are united now. Except for those rebels we crossed paths with in the forest.

The thought of rebels immediately brings me chills, and I decide to call it a day. A migraine is raging behind my eyes, and I'm exhausted. Satisfied with my progress, I close the book. I'll resume my research later. But as I'm about to stand up, something catches my eye. A piece of paper is sticking out of the tome I just closed. That's weird. It's almost... hypnotizing. Now that I've seen it, I can't look away. Extending my hand, I grab it, turn it around, and almost fall out of my chair.

I'm looking at my sword, at my father's sword. The drawing is a perfect replica, with the same symbols on the blade and hilt captured on the paper. My fingers absently go to my parted lips as a pebble of truth comes to light. It must be Fae language, which means that my sword was made here or is at least known to the Fae, and it explains why I can't read it.

With some puzzle pieces falling into place, more questions arise. I close my eyes, and my fingers press on my temples to ease the storm raging underneath. This damned headache is killing me.

"You've found the library." My eyes snap open. It's him. I don't even need to turn around to know.

"I have."

"I had it built and added to the palace when I first arrived." I can feel him behind me, peeking over my shoulder. "So I take it you've learned about the sword and how I know of it." I nod, careful not to interrupt him. He seems to be in a better mood today. "It's a Fae blade, made here in Averion ages ago. It was kept at the palace, under close protection. No one dared touch it, as we believed a spell had been cast on it. And then, one day, it chose Tannyll."

My heart stops at the mention of my father's name. I tilt my head towards the High Lord, not wanting to beg for more information but hanging on to every word coming out of his mouth. He steps aside and comes fully into view.

"He lived among us for a while and fought bravely by my side. Maybe that's why the sword chose him, to reward him."

"I had no idea. When was that?" I ask.

"A long time ago," he says, looking past the glass panels into the distance. "That's enough information for the day," he adds sharply. His head snaps towards mine, and I can see the determination in his crimson eyes. There it is again, the entitled High Lord who gives and takes at will. I can't help the wave of frustration coursing through me. He must see it on my face as he adds in a low voice, "I realize this is not what you want to hear. But it will have to do for now."

"Fine. I clearly don't have a say in this, anyway. Not physically a prisoner, but not free enough to have my questions answered." His jaw clenches, probably from the effort it's taking him to remain calm. I can tell by now he's not used to people talking back to him, but I find that rather amusing. Irritating him seems to be the only way I have to maintain a semblance of control here, so I'll happily play this game. Ela, one. High Lord, zero.

He ignores my remark and instead surprises me with his next question. "Would you like me to show you around the palace? I could take you to the training grounds or the armory."

"How bold of you to willingly offer to lead me to the room with the most weapons in the palace. Or foolish." I say in a dark voice, hoping to push his buttons more.

His gaze buries into mine. "Try me. None who have tried crossing me have lived to tell the tale, so I'd choose my next move carefully if I were you." He answers in a calm voice, but his cold tone raises the hair on my arms as I realize I'm now on shaky ground. Azran has clearly never heard of sarcasm before and doesn't take threats lightly. I guess that today was really productive after all. I wanted to know more about him, and I've learned there are no traces of humor in this brute.

"Of course they're not. I wouldn't expect anything else from the High Lord of Bloodshed." I answer. There is no way in hell I'm apologizing for my comment. What would I even do if I really wanted to harm him? I'm no threat to him, and his reaction is entirely disproportionate.

With a dark smile, he goes back to his previous question. "So, is that a yes for the tour?"

"No," I say, as I stand up and push my chair back loudly on the marble floor. The look on his face is priceless. He's fuming. His eyes seem to have darkened, a palette of deep red and ambers, and I can see anger dancing in his irises. Not granting him another glance, I lift my head and walk past him to exit the library.

I head back to the garden to check on Savage, but I don't spot him immediately and wander around for a bit. It's more like a small park within the palace grounds, really. After a few minutes circling the bushes and taking in the smell of moss and flowers, a strange calm comes over me, reminding me of the safety I'd found within the Dark Forest.

Savage leaves the cover of fruit trees and comes running when he notices me. The wolf stops a few feet away, and I tentatively extend my right hand, hesitant. But Savage leans forward naturally, letting me run my fingers through his black fur.

I gaze into his white eyes, those same eyes that initially scared the shit out of me. But now I only find the confirmation of our strange bond. *Things are much simpler with you. You don't look at or talk to me like I'm an annoyance.* Of course, the wolf doesn't answer and just nuzzles against me.

I leave him be for the rest of the day and walk back to the nearest palace entrance. There are two bowls by the door, one filled with water and the other empty or licked clean. Someone has been making sure Savage is taken care of. I'll need to find out who and thank them.

With my recent encounter with Azran still in mind, I decide to find the training center he talked about. Still confused by that outburst of generosity, I'm walking through the hallways of the palace.

I could have accepted the tour, but his changing moods makes him hard to trust, on top of his condescending tone, Fae nature, and the fact that I almost died trying to find him. I still have no idea what his end game is or if it has anything to do with me, and I have no good reason to rely on him.

I head to the soldiers' barracks I first saw when we arrived at the palace. As I'm about to walk in, I run into the redhead who was riding with us. Vesta, I think her name is. She has beautiful green eyes and a striking smile.

"Oh, hi. Sorry I didn't see you there. Can I help you with something?" Her eyes sparkle as she waits for my answer.

"I'm heading to the training center to practice, if that's okay."

"Of course, let me show you around," she adds with a wide smile. Before I can argue, she's hurrying through the garrison.

I follow her through several corridors until we step into the training center. It's huge and well-equipped, with targets for sword practice, knife throwing, and archery. The walls are equipped with lanterns, the floor is covered in dark leather mats, and several Fae soldiers are training.

Vesta points to the weapons rack by the armory at the back of the room.

"You can borrow any of the weapons here, just make sure to put them back when you're done."

"Sounds good, thanks," I say, smiling. "Vesta, right?"

"Yep! I'll let you get to it. Let me know if you ever need a training partner."

She leaves me, and I realize I'm already feeling more comfortable in the space after her guidance. I position myself on an empty square on the training mat and begin with several rounds of stretching to warm up, then unsheathe my sword and go through the techniques my father taught me. One after the other, I focus on the flow of the movements. I don't know how much time passes before I finally take a break and realize the Fae are now staring at me. No, not just at me, they're staring at my sword. I repress a growl of frustration and instead give them the deadliest smile I can muster, looking each of them in the eyes. Then I go back to my training.

I must stay there for hours because, little by little, the room empties. Another Fae and I are the last ones still training in the lantern-lit room. I'm tempted to call it a day but I trade sword practice for knife throwing instead. I've never excelled with the short blades, but I know the basics and it wouldn't hurt to train some more.

The headache I've been nursing for the better part of the day is worsening. It's becoming harder and harder to focus, so I miss several throws. Frustrated, I try again and again, missing almost every single time. Another knife hits the mat with a muffled sound, and suddenly a fire ignites inside me. I let out a growl and throw the rest of the knives to the opposite side of the room without a glance. The sound of the metal hitting the stone wall is like a cold shower. Why did I just do that? I didn't even check to see if someone could be in the way. I quickly pick up the knives, put them back on the rack, and leave, my cheeks flaming.

The next day, after flipping through a couple of books in the library, I return to the garrison to train. My headache is not going away, so I can't focus on the pages for long. Now in the training center, the intense staring from Fae soldiers continues, but I brush it off. I know I've been on edge since I arrived in Averion, but being at the center of attention is not helping.

I'm in the middle of a strike when Vesta walks in, greeting everyone in the room in a bubbly voice. She notices me right away and offers to be my partner. Growing tired and a little bored with my routines, I accept. After several bouts, I'm sweating and panting. Vesta, on the other hand, is still smiling, completely undisturbed by the training.

"Are you always this cheerful and perky?" I ask, finally breaking the silence and growing frustrated by my physical condition compared to that of these seasoned soldiers.

"Yep! I've just found that an overly positive mindset suits me better. The world is dark enough as it is," she explains.

"Makes sense."

She smiles again before coming to a halt and lowering her blade. "Can I ask you something?"

"Sure."

"How did you get the wolf to follow and obey you?"

Not expecting the change in topic, I take some time to consider her question. "I don't know. I just helped heal his wound and got him some water. His name is Savage."

"Interesting. I had never heard of a human taming a wild Fae wolf before. I don't think anyone ever has. That's why they all stare so much." She looks from the corner of her eyes to the other Fae training around us. "That and your sword, of course."

"Right." I grin. "What do you know about his kind? I've been meaning to do some research."

"Dark wolves were part of a special unit of fighters during the old wars, trained specifically for close combat and to defend their warriors. Many were killed during the wars, and the race is almost extinct now. Very few Fae have actually met one, let alone cared for one. So much about them was lost. I only remember that they're said to have incredible abilities, and some even believe they can understand us." She laughs that last part off with a wave of the hand.

I nod, taking in her words. "Thanks for today. I think I'm going to head back and rinse off this sweat!"

"My pleasure. See you around, Ela."

Surprised by the use of my nickname, I quickly recover and briefly smile back at her before heading out. I like her. At least she's talking to me and not just creepily staring at me. The others, it's like they're waiting for me to say or do something wrong.

CHAPTER SIX

Elanor

I've found a routine that grounds me. Wake up, walk around with Savage, head to the training center until mid-day, eat, then do more research in the library. So far, I haven't found anything else useful. Nothing on my father, the sword, or the mysterious scroll depicted on the tapestries of the Great Hall. I'm just learning more about Fae customs and history. The similarities between our two people are actually pretty surprising. We eat the same food and trade the same goods and services to function as a society. The biggest differences lie in their propensity for barbaric wars, their use of magic, and the absence of a judiciary system.

One day, as I'm taking a pause from training by the armory, Talín joins me. The corners of my mouth lift into a smile when he walks in. I haven't seen him since the first night I got here, and right now, Vesta and he are the only Fae I'm less wary of.

"Good morning, Ela. Good to see you."

"And you. Where have you been?"

"Missing me, eh?" He cracks the biggest smile at the suggestion. "Sorry I didn't get the chance to let you know I was on a recon mission with my unit."

Although he remains pretty vague on the specifics, it's nice to feel like I'm being kept in the loop of what's going on beyond the city walls.

"Would you like to see some close-combat moves?" Talín continues with a wink. I laugh in response and position myself instinctively.

I spend the next hour carefully studying the moves he's showing me and replicating them with my knife as best I can. I'm so focused on his instructions that I don't notice the newcomer until we shift around the mat. My eyes catch a glimpse of his long blond hair, and I'm momentarily distracted. I didn't realize the High Lord trained with his soldiers.

By the time I come back to the task at hand, I realize too late that I've let my guard down. Horror strikes Talín's features when he comes to the same conclusion, and his blade scratches my forearm before he can hold his strike. Tension suddenly fills the air as he freezes, and his eyes widen in shock. I could swear the ghost of a growl reaches my ears.

I pull my arm back to examine the cut. "It's just a scratch. Don't worry about it. I should have been more careful."

"Ela. I'm so sorry. I, I-"

"It's fine, really. I lost focus for a second. My fault." I put a hand on his shoulder and gently press it. I don't know why he's making such a big deal out of it. It's really not the end of the world. Humans are not that fragile.

"Let's take a break, then. I promise that won't happen again," he adds. I try arguing, wanting to resume our training, but he insists.

"We've been at it for more than an hour. If not for you, do it for me. I need a break." His grin comes back, but I can still see the tension on his face, so I give in.

"Fine," I say.

As Talín leaves to grab some water for us, he looks toward the back of the room. I follow his gaze, and my eyes stop on the High Lord training there. High Lord of Bloodshed feels like a rather fitting nickname right about now. He's swinging a single blade, lunging, retreating, and pivoting so fast I can barely keep track of the movements. I can see his crimson eyes glaring from a distance and tension oozing from his clenched jaw. He looks terrifying. I'm still watching him when he puts the blade down to grip his double-bladed sword. And then he's dancing with death again.

His white shirt, damp with sweat, sticks to his body, and his muscular back and strong shoulders strain from the weight of the sword. My gaze drops to the front of his tunic and his outlined rock-solid muscles forming a V by the band of his low-waisted pants.

Unable to look away, heat rushes through me, and Talín chooses this exact moment to walk back in and hand me a glass of water.

"Tell me you didn't need a break, you're flushed," he says, oblivious to what I just witnessed. I smile awkwardly as I take the glass he's extending and drink my fill. "What do you say we stop here for today and go grab some food? It's almost lunchtime." He quickly looks back in the High Lord's direction.

This time I don't object, feeling pretty eager to leave myself. "Sure, let's go."

As we exit the training center, the High Lord doesn't even glance in our direction. He's been ignoring me since that day in the library.

The hateful Fae must be loving this, withholding information, dangling it in front of my face, keeping me at his mercy. The only thing I can do is try to get information on my own while I wait and make the best out of this situation.

We quickly get to the garrison's common hall and start eating after Vesta and a bunch of other soldiers join us. This almost feels normal, like I'm where I'm supposed to be. But I know better. As I'm listening to their conversation, I go over what I know. I've been here for a week, and so far, I've only confirmed that my father lived with the Fae for a time, even fought alongside them, and that my sword is a Fae blade. There are still so many missing pieces. I need to keep looking into my father's past. And I'm still curious about the attack in the forest.

Determined to find out more about what's going on with the rebels, I decide to question Talín the next day. He's a soldier, and if I manage to pull him aside, I think I can get him to tell me more about that.

❦

Elanor

"Good boy!" A smile tugs on my lips as Savage instantly executes my command and comes back to my side. These exercises are more for me than him, as he's perfectly trained.

With another gesture of my hand, I leave him to enjoy the palace gardens and head back inside, determined to get some answers. As I approach the garrison, I'm racking my brain for other ideas in case my initial guess on Talín's whereabouts proves unsuccessful, but he finds me first.

"Hey, I was looking for you." My head snaps up and he catches up with me in a few steps.

"I was actually looking for you, too."

"Really? What can I help you with?" He raises an eyebrow teasingly which sends me chuckling.

"I just wanted to talk to you and ask you some questions. I need to understand what's going on."

"Oh, I see. What do you want to know?" He doesn't let his smile falter, but his eyes betray him. I can tell he's disappointed.

I ponder my words before deciding to get straight to the point. "Who are the rebels? I know the attack was not a random coincidence. What are they after?"

He releases a slow sigh before answering. "They call themselves the Loyalists. More than twenty years ago, a powerful and high-ranked commander, Braern, mutinied the war efforts to unify the Fae. Difference of philosophy, I guess you could call it."

"Loyalists? What are they loyal to, exactly?"

"What they consider to be the true Fae purpose, to protect the Fae bloodlines, to not mix with ... humans." He glances away briefly, but I don't interrupt, eager to learn more. "During the wars, as Azran grew more powerful, uniting warlords, he started thinking about the aftermath of the war and how to rebuild. Braern thought that to fully restore the glory of the Fae, we should enslave humans and use them for labor, exploitation, and pleasure." He gives me a sorrowful look. "Ela..."

"It's fine, I can take it. I want to understand. Please."

"Our High Lord believed we should leave the humans be and instead work towards restoring the long forgotten diplomatic alliances between our peoples, reintegrating humans into our society once we were united." I nod slowly, taking in his words. "Throughout the years, the Loyalists rallied more Fae to their cause, spinning lies and tricking people with false promises. And we've been fighting them ever since, trying to put out their rebellion and protect the world we have sacrificed so much for."

"Why has the High Lord not crushed them all yet?"

"They're well organized, using many different hideouts across the territory. They move constantly and know how to remain in the shadows," he explains. "That's it, that's the whole story. But don't worry, we'll get them. I'm actually being dispatched today for a special mission. That's what I was coming to tell you."

"Oh. How long will you be gone?" I ask, looking into his golden eyes, trying to decipher his emotions.

He answers with a shrug and a tight smile. Shit. I don't think I've ever seen him worried. "Be careful out there, okay?" I add softly, looking away.

His hand on my cheek gently tilts my head, and I face him again. Each soft stroke of his thumb relegates the waves of anxiety to a distant corner of my mind.

"Don't worry, I'll be back in no time. In the meantime, keep up with your close combat training, just like we practiced, okay?"

Not sure I can speak without fumbling my words, I nod and smile back at him before he heads back to the garrison.

⸺ ◈ ⸺

Azran

After spending the better part of the day in meetings with Cal and several of our captains, I'm back in my office.

Staring out the window, the urgency of my responsibilities suddenly evades me. Ela is walking through the courtyard as Talín emerges out of the barracks to join her.

"What do you think, High Lord?" Barus clears his throat to get my attention.

Without looking away, I nod to him. "Make sure the mounts are readied for our units to ride out and that we still have enough horses to help farmers around Averion."

"It will be done, my Lord."

I can't help but clench my jaw as I watch Talín gently stroke Ela's face. She's smiling. She never smiles at me.

After another silence, my steward's voice resonates in the room. "Anything else I can help with today?"

In a gesture, I dismiss him, and my brows draw closer together as I go back to the scene unfolding before me. Talín, the little shit, cut her yesterday, and it took everything in me not to gut him right there and then. But Ela seems to like him, I think.

When she's out of sight, I go back to my desk and brood. I'm still trying to figure out how to do this, how to let the situation play out. The stakes are too high for me to make the wrong move. Everything depends on the outcome of the coming weeks and the decisions I make. Everything.

Elanor

It's well past midnight when I decide to explore the palace after the whole place has gone quiet. I've been at the library for days and haven't discovered any other promising text. That and the missing pages in the only interesting book I found tell me that the High Lord is hiding something. I just need to find where. Or maybe I'm turning paranoid, being constantly on my guard around here. I command Savage to stay behind, as he's far too recognizable with me, and head out.

I'm pretty familiar with the first levels of the palace already, so I go higher in the building. I find the massive staircase and start quietly climbing the stairs. I freeze by each landing, waiting to hear footsteps or see anything intriguing, but so far, nothing.

I stop at the entrance of another floor, feeling like my heart is going to beat out of my chest. It takes me a moment to realize I'm feeling a tug deep inside me. My gut is telling me there's something there.

Carefully, I glance at the corridor lying beyond. With no one in sight, I step in and slowly approach a series of closed doors. I go for the middle one on instinct and extend a hand to grab the knob. I need to see what lies beyond.

Someone clears their throat behind me, and I freeze, my fingers an inch from the handle. I quickly recover and turn around to find Mor staring at me with his usual serious air.

"I was just... hmm..." Nothing plausible comes to mind, and I remain silent, preparing myself to be scolded or dragged to the palace's dungeons. So much for my gut feeling.

Mor raises an eyebrow at me, and a corner of his mouth lifts briefly. "Right." He steps aside to let me walk past him. Relieved to get out of this without so much as a warning, I hurry away.

The healer is enigmatic as hell, but I'm glad he's not a talker. I could have sworn I felt a tingle of complicity between us for a second, even though it's hard to tell with his solemn demeanor.

I glance back one last time before turning the corner and see Mor turning the handle and entering the middle room before closing the door behind him.

My heart is still pounding in my chest when I return to my room. Savage lifts his head in greeting, welcoming me back after this epic failure. Well, at least I've discovered one helpful thing. I would not make a good spy.

The next day in the dining hall, I'm sitting at a table with Savage behind me as usual. I'm sipping my soup silently, absorbed in my thoughts. I need to get my hands on more information, but I have no idea how. With Talín gone, there is no one I can trust enough to ask. Or is there? Maybe I could ask Mor. After all, he let me go last night without so much as a reprimand.

As I'm considering my options, or the lack thereof, a familiar voice sounds from behind me. "Enjoying your midnight strolls through the palace, Ela?" A blush rises to my cheeks instantly, but I don't turn in my seat. I won't give Azran the satisfaction.

Damn it, Mor. I wouldn't have painted him a tattletale. My gaze snaps to the other side of the dining hall, and I make eye contact with that shameless old gossip. The healer is staring right at me, and even across the room, his eyes reveal a twinkle of amusement.

The High Lord's footsteps recede before I'm able to come up with a smart comment, and I release the breath I had been holding. I got off easy on that one, but I need to be more careful. And clearly, Mor is not an option anymore.

I don't dare wander around again after dark and the following week is a slow agony, waiting for Talín's unit to come back. I bury myself in my training, a constant headache pulsing behind my eyes. I've also lost my temper more than I care to admit, any minor inconvenience putting me on edge.

I'm trying to master a new move Vesta showed me when a ruckus sounds outside the garrison. Voices. Shouting orders. Horses. Galloping on the cobblestones of the courtyard.

I rush out to find the source of the agitation and freeze by the entrance of the garrison. It's them. They're back.

I'm looking for a familiar face in the group when the soldiers' air of gloom and the blood on their armor register. The group stops, and two of them step forward. One is clearly carrying a body covered by a tarp, and the other a bloodied bag.

Before I can process what's happening, the two Fae head into the palace, and I start running after them.

"Ela!" Vesta tries holding me back, but I'm out of her grasp in a second.

I sprint through the palace entrance and don't stop until I'm in front of the throne room's closed doors, guarded by two soldiers. I can see the drops of blood I followed here also marking the white marble floors. "Open the damn doors," I growl, baring my teeth at the guards. "Now."

⁕

Azran

Seconds after hearing my soldiers' report, Ela storms in, and the covered body at my feet stops her dead in her tracks. I estimate I have mere seconds before she explodes, so I dismiss the soldiers and my guards. There's only Cal left by my side.

"Who is it? Whose body is this?"

"Talín." I can see the terror on her face. No point in dragging this out any longer.

As the name leaves my mouth, I witness her unraveling before me, her eyes darkening, her lips trembling. I'm standing silently in front of my throne, giving her time to process, but in this deafening silence, I swear I can hear her scream of horror inside my head.

"How could you let this happen?" Her voice is barely a murmur at first, but I don't respond. It's no use. "What? You've got nothing to say now?" She's looking back and forth between Talín's body and me, with tears rolling down her beautiful face. "Forever the emotionless bastard, sending others to die for him." I sense a flicker of anger coursing through me, but I let it go. She's in shock, and her reaction is to be expected. She needs to let out her rage, and I'm the ideal candidate. "You don't even care he's dead, murdered! You're a fucking monster."

Her screams now resonate loudly in the hall. A monster. That, I am. But her words are like poison to me. I can almost feel her disgust for me. I'm not sure what's worse - seeing her like this, or feeling a distasteful sense of jealousy when faced with her distress for another.

"He told me you cared about your people and about humans, but it's all lies. You don't give a shit about anything or anyone but yourself and your power."

Baring my teeth at her, I grab the bloodied bag still at my feet and plunge my hand inside. I remove it drenched in blood, holding his pale head by the hair.

"You truly believe that? Look. Look at him! See what they do to us, to our people. I will unleash hell on them all!" My voice is shaking with uncontained rage, and her mouth opens and then closes. Her jaw is clenching hard, and tears are filling her eyes again.

Blood is dripping on the white marble floor, drop by drop, but her gaze is fixed on the severed head. Suddenly she snaps out of it. "Let him go! He's dead, and all you can think about is your war."

"I don't care enough, you said? You don't know anything about me or what I care about. I'm not him, and I'll never be. I'm the High Lord of the Fae, and I have an entire realm depending on me." I say, my whole body radiating with fury. "Unlike you, right? Not a care in the world except for your Fae lover, wishing it had been me instead of him."

"You're damn right I wish it had been you. You are the last Fae on this earth I would ever choose. I don't give a shit how powerful and important you think you are, I fucking hate you, monster! Now. Put. Him. Down."

Venom has replaced my blood, my whole body feels like it's on fire, and I snarl loudly at her.

Her eyes turn completely dark in response, and I can see her rage pulsing in black waves out of her body, barely containing itself, ready to launch. My eyes widen as I see her true nature for the first time. I'm about to put the bloodied head down when I spot movement to my left.

Cal must have seen what I saw, too, because he's abruptly moving toward Ela in an attempt to put himself between us.

The next second, he is struck by a dark wave of energy and thrown across the hall. His body hits a pillar and goes limp. I let go of the head and lunge toward him.

I'm at his side in seconds, kneeling by him, and rage replaces concern the moment I find him still breathing. I growl loudly and my head snaps towards Ela, as she takes several steps back, hesitating, her eyes widened in shock. She stumbles out before I can call out to her.

I bring my focus back to Cal as he comes back to himself with a groan, and I help him to his feet, relieved to see him standing.

"What..." He trails off as I hold him up.

"It's her, there is no doubt. And I have a feeling this is but a glimpse of what she can do."

Cal and I exchange a knowing glance. Ela and I... we're more alike than she thinks.

***

Elanor

Tears are still rolling down my face as I run out of the palace and into the city as fast as I can, taking turns randomly. I stop at last, completely out of breath, my lungs on fire, ready to vomit.

I could have killed him. This makes no sense. I don't even remember touching him. Even if I did, I'm clearly not strong enough to push him and send him rolling like that.

My chest heaving, I realize I'm standing on a busy street. It's the middle of the day, and residents are all going about their business. Only a few are glancing briefly at me, so I keep moving.

My vision is clouded by the tears filling my eyes, and there's a lump in my throat. I can hear myself babbling unintelligible words as I wonder whether grief or rage will swallow me whole.

Talín is dead. He is gone. I'll never get to talk to him again or watch him wink at me. After years of fearing the Fae, I had made a friend among them.

My eyes are burning as I try to keep them open through the tears. If I close them, I know I'll see his severed head and empty gaze staring back at me.

Sobs are now shaking my body as my heart breaks for the loss of my friend and for what maybe could have been. I can feel a familiar sense of panic slowly overwhelming me as I realize I've been abandoned yet again.

"Aerín?"

I turn around at the mention of my mother's name. A tall Fae woman is standing before me, her brown eyes widened. "My apologies, I thought you were someone else."

"What did you call me?" My voice trembles.

"You look just like her. I knew a Fae named Aerín once. The resemblance is eerie."

"Impossible. My mother's name was Aerín, but she was human, like me."

"Was your father named Tannyll?" Her brows arch in confusion.

I nod, unable to breathe or speak another word.

"How-" She pauses. "My name is Thalea. They were my dear friends. I was sorry to hear of their passing. But, my dear, they were both Fae."

I stumble back against a wall, her words like shards of ice in my heart, and my world collapses. My lips part open to let out a sound, a scream, anything to contradict what she's saying. But nothing comes out, and I'm left wide-eyed as her words carry an undeniable ring of truth.

My fingers are feeling the wall behind me as I grip the corner of the building I'm leaning on. Without a second thought, I take the turn and run like hell.

Unable to contain the shock, I stop by a large building and rush in, its darkness calling me. Standing in the shadows, my head spins as lie after lie plays in my mind. *The Fae are to be feared. Run from them, as fast as you can. You're human. You must learn how to defend yourself. Never leave home without a weapon.*

If they were Fae, what does that make me? And how could they hide this while warning me against their own people? Nothing makes sense, and my whole body feels like it's on fire. I'm trying to keep the bubbling emotions under control. But then... then I remember Talín.

Darkness takes over, and my rage explodes all around me. My sword is now in my hands, ablaze. I don't remember gripping it, but dark black and white flames are coursing along the blade in front of me.

My vision adjusts, and I can see everything clearly and in more detail. With my senses heightened, a voice, its voice, is calling for death, blood, and the end of this treacherous world.

A faint crack echoes behind me and sends me over the edge. I wield my sword in the direction it came from and set the whole warehouse aflame.

Hypnotized by the chaos, I watch it devour the walls, burning everything in its wake. I can feel its reassuring heat, almost coddling me, comforting me, telling me it's going to be all right. We're going to set the world on fire together. Fury feels like it's the only thing I've ever known, the only thing I'll ever know.

I turn around, feeling strangely calm as I watch the flames lick the ceiling. A devouring force is raging inside me and I'm pouring all my repressed emotions into it, unrestrained, until I catch my reflection in a glass panel.

A stranger stares back at me, her eyes dark and stormy, ears pointy, hair a mess of snarls and tangles. I'm a monster. One of them. I've become what I feared and hated most.

The fire is still raging around me and the wood cracks loudly. Smoke is starting to fill the warehouse while parts of the ceiling detach and fall to the ground. Crates are going up in flames all around me. Although I know deep down the fire won't hurt me, I realize the building is about to collapse. Survival instinct finally kicks in, and I make for the exit. But as I'm about to step into the street, the whole structure comes crashing down.

⸻ ◆ ⸻

Elanor

I blink weakly, feeling long strands of hair gently brushing my face. The regular rhythm of steps rocks me until I realize who I'm looking at and who is carrying me.

Then the memory of the last few hours comes crashing down, and I stir and try to jump out of his grasp. Azran freezes, his brows drawing closer together, and he carefully puts me down.

I immediately put some distance between us, crushing myself against a wall. My fingers are still tightly clenched around my sword, and I recognize the corridors leading to my chambers.

He lifts both of his hands up in the air and waits silently. He hasn't killed me yet, so I imagine I didn't hurt Calen too severely. I stare at his palms and then look down at my own, wrapped around the weapon that unleashed hell on earth.

A pit opens in my stomach as I remember the annihilating fury I harbor. I can't be around people. I can't trust myself around anyone right now, especially not him. Without a glance back, I run to my room.

Rina is waiting for me. "Out," I say. "I won't be needing your services anymore." Trying to contain the panic in my voice, I don't leave her a chance to protest. She hasn't done anything wrong, but, as painful as it is, I can't be near her or anybody else. "Out." I point to the door again. Thankfully, she complies, and I slam the door behind her.

I'm alone, at last, like I always have been, like I will remain. Never enough before, not enough for my father to keep fighting, not enough for him not to leave me. And now, too much for anyone to be around me, too dangerous and unstable.

Savage appears from under the bed, and I can't help the tears rolling down my cheeks as I spot him. He's by me instantly, resting his furry body against my legs, comforting me.

"I don't deserve you." I drop to the floor, clinging to him as my heart shatters into a million pieces. Sobs are shaking my whole body, and I'm bawling, trying to catch my breath. I'll never be able to move again. All I can think of are the lies. My entire life is nothing but an intricate web of lies, spun by my parents. Nothing makes sense anymore. And then there is the fire and the shadows. And this crushing pain in my chest.

I go over all the memories I have of my parents, trying to discern what I missed and if there could have been warning signs or hints of explanation. My father always insisted on me taking my training seriously and being able to defend myself. He knew something I didn't. That's the only thought looping in my head.

But why hide the truth? And how? How could I have gone my whole life completely unaware of my true nature? Our true nature? And even more troubling, he taught me to fear the Fae.

Question after question keeps popping up in my mind, each cutting a little deeper. No explanations, just this devastating grief, and I'm left feeling too much.

As the sun disappears on the horizon, Savage's muzzle touches my wet cheeks, pushing me to wake up, do something, anything. After what must be hours, I lift my head and stare into his white eyes. *What would you do if you were in my shoes?* What would you do if you had just learned your whole existence had been full of deceit, that you could wield a sword that could set the world ablaze, and that your only friend had died?

With no more tears left to cry, I hug Savage tightly. I know I can't stay like this forever. One hour at a time, then.

I stand up and head to the bathing room on shaky legs. Although my face is darkened by ash, no trace of power or rage is left in my eyes, just agony and exhaustion. I slowly lift a hand to my ear and notice my sharper features.

I start undressing, removing my vest and shirt, and glance at my scars. Not wanting to linger too long, I run a bath and finish undressing. Once the bath is ready, I sink into it and close my eyes.

CHAPTER SEVEN

Elanor

I remain locked in my room for two days, barely opening the door to let Savage in or out and grab the water someone has been leaving by the entrance. Rina, I'm guessing. She tried coming in a few times, but I sent her away.

The headaches are gone. I haven't had one since before the incident. They must have been connected to my repressed Fae heritage or monstrous nature, whichever.

I still can't wrap my head around what happened, what my parents did, or what I am. And then there's Talín. Although I didn't know him for long, his friendship meant more to me than I realized.

So far, I haven't had any other episodes of rage or outbursts of power, but I know it's there. I can sense it looming, waiting for the opportunity to explode again.

As long as I stay away from everyone, I won't hurt anyone else. The whole city must have heard about the incident by now, so I doubt anyone would want to be around me, anyway. I realize that's not a long-term plan, but it's the best I've got for now.

On the third day, I'm cradled in the armchair, staring endlessly through one of the windows, when the door to my room is kicked in and crashes on the other side of the wall. Vesta is standing on the doorstep, her arms crossed against her chest and a disapproving look on her face. "I tried giving you a few days to figure things out, but it looks like it's not helping. Time's up, we're getting you out of here!"

"Stay away! Don't come close." I jump out of the armchair and circle it to put the piece of furniture between us.

Dismissing my words, she comes up to me, pushes the chair aside, and grabs my hands. "I know this is overwhelming, but you can't stay locked up in here, not eating, isolating yourself from everyone."

My breath catches in my throat as I wait for the dark waves of energy to send her crashing against a wall. Nothing happens. She's just silently watching me while still holding my hands.

"I'm not alone." I finally manage to whisper as I glance at Savage, lounging by the bed.

"Hilarious, Ela. This won't solve anything, but do you know what will? Learning to control your emotions and power."

I wince as she utters the word.

"I don't want to ever touch my sword or unleash this power again." I squeeze her hands. "It can only bring death."

"That's ridiculous. The sword or the power itself is not evil, it's what you make of it that matters."

"I don't understand why you're not more upset about all this." I drop Vesta's hands and take a step back. "I almost killed Calen. I burned an entire building to the ground. Innocent people could have been in it. Wait. *Was* anyone injured?"

She shakes her head, easing the sudden panic I felt. "And Cal is fine, you barely scratched him. Come on. Let's get you out of this room."

"I can't. Not when I know I have this monstrous thing inside me." I cross my arms over my chest. "You don't understand. Everything I ever believed turned out to be a lie."

"Oh, I understand, trust me." Her change in tone catches my attention. "I did terrible things, you know. Before the wars, I, I-I slaughtered an entire village after they protected my little sister's murderer." She takes a deep breath as she begins pacing. "And then during the wars, I killed so many I lost count. I just wanted blood, not a care in the world for who ended up at the end of my sword, as long as there was someone. Anyone."

Tilting my head to the right, considering her words, I nod. "I'm sorry, I didn't know about your sister."

She shrugs. "I'm hiding a monster, too. Everyone is. That's why I hold on to the light as much as possible. Everyone has darkness inside them, Ela. It's what the world does to us. Just don't let it take over, because that's not who you are."

A single tear rolls down my cheeks before she wipes it with her thumb. "You're a stubborn and fearless warrior who needs to confront her demons, manage her emotions and learn how to control her powers." She puts a hand on my shoulder, gently pressing.

"So now you're going to eat some food, and we'll come up with a plan, yes?"

I take a deep breath and nod in agreement as she heads toward the entrance of the room. I can hear whispers outside, and a few seconds later, Rina walks in and drops off a steaming bowl of stew on the bedside table before heading right back out of the room.

I give Vesta a knowing glance. I'm not loving the ambush, but I've got to admit she's better company than the brooding thoughts I spent the last few days with. She stays several hours with me, monitoring each spoonful of stew I eat and making sure the contents of the bowl are emptied out.

"I'll come back tomorrow, Ela, I promise. Everything is going to be fine."

"Thank you," I murmur as she leaves the room, maybe too low for her to hear.

Later that day, I'm once again cradled in the armchair when Savage stands on all fours, his head toward the door. I hold my breath as the High Lord walks into my quarters. I haven't seen him since that night after I injured Calen and set his city aflame. He looks just as menacing as always, with his hair tied in a braid and his double-bladed sword on his back. Maybe he is here to render his judgment and punish me.

However, the first object of his attention is not me, but Savage. He bends down and extends a hand to pet the wolf. I'm about to warn him, but before the words can leave my mouth, Savage happily meets his gesture, leaning into Azran's touch. My mouth drops open as it's the first time my wolf tolerates someone else. Tolerate is not even accurate. The bastard is loving it.

"How are you feeling? Vesta told me you've eaten something." His focus still on Savage, I can't see his face or decipher his intentions, but I make a mental note to scold Vesta for selling me out. "Starving yourself is not a pretty way for a Fae to die. It can take years to go like that." His gaze finally snaps to mine as he stands up.

"Are you making fun of me?" I ask, already irritated by his comment and attitude. Or maybe I just don't like the fact that Savage trusts him enough to let him close.

"Not at all." But the most imperceptible tug appears on the corner of his lips. He's trying to get a rise out of me. Prick.

"Why are you here?" Although I want to appear unaffected, I can hear the tension in my voice.

"To check on you. Is that so surprising?" His shoulders sag a bit. "And I wanted to tell you about your parents, if you're ready to hear what I have to say."

I straighten up and nod vigorously, eager for an explanation to help sort out the mess my life has become. Azran looks around the room for a second before settling on my round bed and taking off his harness to put it down next to him. He doesn't look as threatening, sitting on the edge of my mattress surrounded by plush pillows.

"As you know, your father was in my army, but more than that, we were friends. He introduced me to your mother when he met her in Averion after a campaign. Aerín was a Sun Fae, hypnotizing everyone in her wake with the most joyful laugh I had ever heard, and she made Tan happy. I wedded them on Winter Solstice that same year."

He pauses, letting the words sink in and offering me a chance to ask questions. But I'm holding my breath, waiting to hear the rest. "When I first saw you in the Dark Forest, I immediately suspected your Fae heritage although I couldn't make sense of the absence of Fae features on your face. You look so much like them." He says softly. "And then your sword confirmed it all. We thought it had been lost with your father."

"How? How could I have gone my whole life completely oblivious to my Fae heritage? And theirs..." My voice fills the room, shockingly louder than his.

"Did you experience any dizziness or headaches once you arrived here?"

Surprised by the question, I nod. "I've been on edge since I stepped out of the forest, with a constant pain pulsing being my eyes. I thought I was pushing myself a little too hard. But the migraines stopped a few days ago..."

"After our encounter, I had Cal and Mor look into it. We still don't know for sure, but we think your parents had a spell placed on your family, transforming their appearance and yours at birth. Tan and Aerín had left the army by then, and we had no idea she was with child, so we can't be certain. Although rare, it's not unheard of, and the enchantment most likely started eroding as you stepped into Fae territory." I had guessed the two things were connected, but I had no clue how.

"A spell?"

"Spells are remnants of old Fae magic that left these shores long ago. They are really hard to come by, as this power is only found in healers now. And only a handful of the oldest Fae alive would have known someone powerful enough to pull it off. "

"What happened to the magic here?"

"No one knows. We used to hear about the occasional Fae able to conjure some of nature's powers, like growing plants or sparking a small flame, but no one born with that kind of ability has been sighted for centuries."

I nod. "But why? Why would they do that? It makes no sense..."

"I'm sure they thought it was in your best interest." I can't decipher Azran's expression. His troubling crimson eyes are so damn hard to read.

He leans back a bit against the pillows and crosses his hands together on top of his legs. As I'm staring at this giant sitting on my bed, I realize something else has been bothering me. "Why didn't you tell me sooner? Why keep me in the dark?"

"I didn't know for sure. My suspicions were only confirmed the other day in the throne room."

Shame suddenly overtakes me. "Is Calen okay? I didn't mean to-"

"I know. He's fine. He hadn't taken a beating in decades, so it actually did him some good." He bursts out laughing, and I freeze in shock. I never expected his laugh to make him seem so... alive. The ice-hearted Fae has humor and a personality, after all. Granted, seeing a friend get thrown across a room wouldn't qualify as amusing to most people, but it seems to do the trick for him. Catching my surprised gaze, he resumes his serious air. "I'm not just an emotionless monster, Elanor."

Hurt flickers in his eyes, but before I get a chance to respond or take back my words, he changes the topic again. "Tell me about your childhood. What do you remember about your mother?"

Taken aback, I blurt out the only thing that comes to mind. "Peaches. I remember the smell of peaches slowly cooking over the fire in our tiny cabin. She would make the most delicious peach pie. It was my favorite."

He tilts his head and smiles. "That sounds lovely."

His smile is so... disturbing.

"It was." Unable to hold his stare any longer, I glance out the window.

When I look back, he's by the door with his scabbard in hand. His head turns toward my sword lying on the floor by the entrance and, without another word, he leaves.

I find myself alone again in my room, pondering his words, his laugh and smile, and the fact that this huge Fae can move with more stealth than any other creature I've ever laid eyes on.

<hr>

Elanor

The next day, Vesta walks into my chambers as promised, flashing her brightest smile, and this time she's not alone. Rina walks in right behind her, wearing her long hair in a braid, her features strict as usual.

"Rina, I would like to apologize for my behavior..." The old Fae dismisses my apology with a wave of her hand and gives me a small smile instead. I turn to Vesta, who doesn't seem one bit surprised. I take it I shouldn't argue, then.

When I bring my focus back to Rina, she's already tidying up the room and laying out a fresh set of clothes for me, confirming she has already moved on.

Once I'm ready, Vesta, Savage, and I go down to the gardens. As much as it pains me to admit that she was right, getting some fresh air is helping, and there is no hiding it.

Vesta is beaming with pride, looking pretty satisfied with herself. She winks at me, and the childish gesture even manages to steal a smile from me.

I already feel more like myself. Shifting the looming darkness to the back of my mind for a change, I could almost pretend to be a Fae noble, casually strolling the palace grounds, wearing a pretty dress, my hair up.

I'd buy it were it not for the absence of the harness on my back. For the first time in years, I'm without my sword. I left it in the room, as I haven't been able to touch it or even look at it for more than a few seconds.

"Come on, let's go to the training center." Vesta's voice pulls me away from the futile daydream.

"What? No. I told you I'm not ready."

"Bullshit. You won't know if you're ready until you try. We're going." She gives me a sharp look and places her hands on her hips. Knowing damn well she's going to drag me there herself if I don't cooperate, I give up and start following her to the garrison after motioning for Savage to stay outside.

Thankfully, when we get there, it's just us on the mats. Less chance of hurting someone else. Vesta walks to the weapons rack, picks up a sword, and hands it to me. "Let's go. Show me what you've got."

This is a regular sword. Nothing bad can happen. I repeat to myself as I grip the hilt of the blade. Widening my stance, I position myself, and she launches the first attack.

Assault after assault, Vesta is not giving me a moment's rest or the chance to overthink my actions. I parry and block each of her blows, starting to feel more comfortable, and I move on to offense. Getting back into my routines feels good and comforting. After a while, I realize nothing is happening, everything is fine, and I'm just panting like an old donkey.

After a while, Vesta decides to change tactics. "So your parents lied to you all this time. Not very nice of them." She lunges towards me and I almost miss a step as a tingle of anger wakes up inside of me.

"Shut up before I hurt you."

"Hmm, I don't think so. On top of hiding that you're a Fae, do you think they knew about your powers?"

A low growl tears through my throat as I hammer down another blow, but she easily escapes my reach.

"And what about Talín? Did you even grieve him, or were you too self-absorbed to notice his absence?"

My vision darkens in a second, rage threatening to take over, blood pumping loudly in my ears. With a roar, I launch a deadly series of attacks, wanting her to stop talking, to leave me alone. She counters my strikes, but I'm slowly pushing her back against a wall.

I freeze when the fear in her widened eyes registers, and lower my blade. Realizing what she did, I let go of the sword in my hand and immediately make for the door.

"Wait, Ela! Wait! I'm sorry! I went too far, you know I didn't mean any of that." She catches up with me in a few steps. "I'm just trying to show you how your powers are connected to your emotions. I just wanted to help you keep them under control."

"You call that control? You would probably have been incinerated if it had been *my* sword in my hands!" I turn around violently as my screams resonate in the room.

"You're right. I'm sorry. I wanted to show you there was a way to manage this..."

"I don't need this!" Shrugging off her excuses, I leave the training center. Still shaken from Vesta's words, I head back into the palace.

On the way back to my chambers, I'm trying to calm my heart and keep my emotions in check. I'm climbing up the stairs two steps at a time when the smell hits me. Peaches.

My memories are haunting me, toying with me, but as I get closer to my room, the smell gets stronger. I walk in and identify its origin right away.

A pie is waiting for me on the table by the armchair, and its delicious aroma is filling the air. A folded note is propped against it.

"I thought it could make you smile. And if it's not to your taste, you are allowed to harass the chef until he gets it right.

Az."

The sides of my mouth lift into a smile, erasing any trace of my fight with Vesta. I grab the spoon next to the pie and dive in. When the first bite melts on my tongue, it's sheer heaven. The warm and gooey filling brings tears to my eyes, I haven't eaten anything this delicious since I was a child.

Though I might regret it later, I devour half the pie in one sitting as my lunch. Feeling better than I have in days, weeks even, I put the spoon down and lay on my bed. My stomach stretched at its maximum, I'm dead asleep before I know it.

I wake up from the nap several hours later and decide to go find Azran to thank him. Not giving myself time to change my mind, I start roaming the halls, searching for him.

I check the throne room, library, what looks like meeting rooms, and even the kitchens. No luck. Remembering the corridor Mor caught me in several days ago, I make for the upper levels of the palace. Facing the middle door this time in broad daylight, I'm about to knock when it pops open, and I run straight into the High Lord. He steps aside at the last minute, avoiding the collision.

"There you are," I say. I take a step back and tuck the front pieces of my hair behind my ear.

He arches an eyebrow in surprise. "You were looking for me?"

"I wanted to talk to you, but it looks like you're busy." I glance at the pile of papers he's holding under one arm and the thin coat over his shoulders.

"Not at all." He says, before motioning me into the room. He walks to the back of the study and drops everything he's holding onto an imposing desk.

Behind the desk, dying embers smolder in a fireplace. Heavy-laden bookshelves cover the walls, and two leather couches face each other in the center with a low table separating them. With its warm brown and ochre tones, this room contrasts nicely with the eerie and immaculate feel of the palace. It's not dissimilar to my room, actually, and it's surprisingly welcoming.

Azran is standing in front of his desk, giving me time to look around and patiently waiting for me to break the silence.

I clear my throat. "I, um, I wanted to thank you. For the pie, I mean. It was delicious."

"I'll be sure to tell the chef he still has a job in the morning." A corner of his mouth lifts slightly.

Today his eyes are more golden than red. It's the first time it strikes me, and I wonder if it depends on his mood. He catches me staring but doesn't say a thing. Embarrassed, I look away. "That's all. I'll leave you to your work."

"Wait, Ela. Stay. Please." I don't think I've ever heard him say those words to me before, so when he motions for me to take a seat, I settle for one of the soft leather couches.

He comes to sit next to me and angles his body toward mine. "I need to talk to you, too. There's something else you should know, and it's most likely the reason your parents chose to hide your identity. I didn't tell you yesterday because I was afraid it would be too much at once."

"What is it?" I gaze into his eyes, seeking the reassurance that what he's about to say won't be as bad as I think it will. I really don't know if I can take any more revelations.

"During the wars, after one of my captains, Braern, betrayed us, I came across a parchment detailing a prophecy. It spoke of a united world where Fae and humans would live in harmony. But before this came to happen, wars would divide the Fae. Only the Unifier would be able to restore peace and unite the Fae. And until then, humans and Fae would remain enemies."

"Unifier?"

"Ela... the prophecy said the Unifier would wield Nahtar."

My blood freezes at the mention of the name. I know what his next words are going to be. I can feel it in my bones.

"You must realize that your sword is far from ordinary. It's an artifact crafted eons ago, its name engraved on the blade. It didn't grant Tannyll any special powers when he wielded it, and then it was lost. Ela, I think it was meant to come to you. No matter what, Nahtar had to get to you."

A prophecy my parents knew about. Just like they knew about the sword. My heart is pounding so loudly, it's about to beat out of my chest. Maybe he hears it, too, given the worried look on his face.

"I want to see it. The scroll." I can't hide the tremors in my voice and his hand comes over mine, gently pressing it.

He scans my features before answering. "It's gone, turned to dust after I touched it. But I can tell you. I'll never forget the words."

Stone-still, I wait for him to tell me more, to reveal the exact wording, so I can tell him it's not about me. It can't be.

"Once lost, the Slayer of Darkness shall be brought back to light. Death will separate the worlds. The Unifier, born between the realms, will be the end and the new beginning." His strong grip is strangely comforting, giving me something to focus on other than his words.

"At first, I thought, hoped, it could be me. But after decades of fighting, I was nowhere near the unification of the Fae, even further from restoring any diplomatic relations with Brimora, and Nahtar still hadn't been found. Ela, you are the Unifier, born between the realms of Human and Fae." He pauses a moment before adding. "Take as much time as you need, and if you have any questions, please send for me."

I'm barely able to nod. Between the realms…

"The girl who thought she was human for twenty-two years and has been a Fae for two minutes will unite the Fae? And then bring two races who hate each other together? This can't be right. I can barely walk around without lashing out at everyone around me, and you want me to do what?" A nervous laugh escapes me as I'm babbling on, unable to bring myself to stomach this.

"Deep breath, little one. No one is asking you to do anything right now. You need time to accept this."

His collected tone calms me down for about four seconds, and then I'm frantic again. "Okay, but restore relations with the humans, how am I supposed to do that? I was just an orphan living in the Dark Forest with no one left to care if I lived or died. I'm a nobody!"

His hand is now gently brushing over mine. "You are far from a nobody to me, Ela. You don't need to worry about that now. Once we're ready, it will take years, decades even, to achieve peace with humans. Deep breaths…"

The regular movement of his hand is grounding me and helping me settle a bit. As he continues, I stare at him, overwhelmed, ready to run away, and unable to move at the same time. I just toppled over a cliff, and I'm waiting to hit the ground, but it never happens.

"Come, I'll walk you back to your room." He pulls my hand to him, helps me stand up, and doesn't let go of it. Instead, he leads me through the palace, his warm palm in mine. I don't have it in me to resist, so I let him guide me and focus on his thumb gently brushing against my skin. I don't remember the last time someone held my hand this way.

I only realize we're in front of my door when he finally lets go. The second the door closes, I lean all my weight against it, slowly exhaling the breath I've been holding. The truth is crushing me. Everything seems to be falling into place. Except nothing makes sense. Azran truly believes I'm the Unifier, which explains why he's been so secretive, calculating, and now understanding with me. He needs me to wage his war.

My emotions are spiraling out of control as I consider the paths that lay before me. My rage is simmering as I realize I've been used my whole life. A puppet manipulated by my parents, who knew about this all along and hid everything from me.

Trained to survive and kill, hidden from the world. And now the High Lord wants to use me to his advantage, to unify his people and Lóna. Unifier. If that is even truly who I am and something I can do. As I'm thinking about the implications, my laughter fills the room, surprising Savage, who looks confused as hell.

Loneliness looms over me, squeezing my heart tightly. I don't understand. Why didn't my parents tell me anything? Why keep me in the dark? And who were they really trying to protect me from? The High Lord, the war, or the traitor Braern?

Too numb to even cry, I collapse on the bed fully dressed. Savage jumps on the mattress and comes to nestle his muzzle on my lap.

Then another idea comes to mind... I can still get out of here, leave all this craziness behind. They wouldn't kill the champion of their damned prophecy, right? But first, I need to figure this out for myself. I can't just rely on his treacherous words.

A scarier thought suddenly dawns on me. Where would I go? I stop myself from dwelling on this too long and bring my focus back to the present.

I'm still trying to wrap my head around what I've just learned when I finally drift asleep.

The next day, after hours of browsing through different texts at the library, I can't find anything to discredit what the High Lord told me. There's no denying my sword is the one mentioned in the prophecy. And then there's the darkness and fury that I unleashed. Although I can't confirm this makes me who he says I am, Fae are not supposed to wield such power. It's unheard of, and I haven't found one tale recounting a similar curse.

I discover that some artifacts feed on emotions and there lies the key to my dilemma. How can I control Nahtar when I can't control my emotions? I'm wandering the world with my feelings pouring out of me and my heart bleeding endlessly.

Then another thought forms in the back of my head, fueling me with hope. Maybe this was a one-time thing that happened when the spell broke. That would explain everything and help prove I'm not their damned Unifier.

I slam that last book shut and break into a run. My steps resonate loudly in the marble corridors, but the only thing going through my mind is a prayer to anyone who will listen. The prayer that I'm right and this was an isolated incident, nothing more.

Once inside my room, my hope is instantly crushed when I glance at Nahtar, still on the floor.

Its call echoes in my core. It's talking to me, whispering to me.

I focus on it with every sense I have. At first, I can't make anything out, it's just a presence. Then a wave hits me, almost like a pulse, followed by another. The more I focus on it, the closer the waves get. I stalk towards it, lifting my hand near the hilt of the sword, trembling. And before I realize it, I'm gripping the handle, its energy flowing through me.

It has a life of its own, neither good nor bad. It just is. Strangely enough, it feels like home. Closing my eyes, I dive into the energy, retreating into my essence. I'm following an endless stream of darkness and light through a labyrinth within me.

My eyes fly open when I realize that the sword is simply the instrument, and *I* am the source of power, my pain the origin of the darkness. A part of me had hoped it was all the sword, influencing me, when all along it was just responding to my calls. Tears start rolling down my cheeks, but I wipe them off. I'm so damn tired of crying and hurting. Fuck their prophecy.

A knock on the door startles me.

CHAPTER EIGHT

Elanor

I put Nahtar down and open the door to find Vesta standing in front of me. "Hey. Can I come in?"

I step aside to let her in, and she gives me a shy smile as she takes a few steps into the room before turning around to face me.

"Did you know?" I don't give her the chance to say another word, solely focusing on unveiling the last of the secrets. But she just raises an eyebrow in question. "Did you know about the prophecy?"

She nods slowly. "I did, Ela. Look, I'm so sorry, but we were all under orders not to say a word about it."

"Everyone knew? Talín knew?"

"We all did. Azran told us we couldn't say anything, but keeping this from you has been eating at me. I'm so sorry, Ela."

Her eyes are glistening with unshed tears, so I take a deep breath while I close the door.

"So many lies and so much deceit, and here I was thinking some of you actually cared," I say in a huff. I'm doing my best to contain my emotions and not push her away, but it's taking everything I've got.

"No, Ela, we do care. I care. You have to understand I couldn't disobey my High Lord. Please, I truly consider you my friend, and in time, I hope you learn to see that, too." She pauses, waiting for an answer, but I don't respond. "And I'm sorry about yesterday, I was trying to help but I went about it the wrong way. Please, forgive me."

As I ponder her words, I realize she is genuinely sorry. I'm tempted to hold on to my anger, but I'm not sure there's any room left for that in me. And if I don't want to become the weapon Azran wants me to be, I need to find it in me to forgive.

Finally, the sad look on her face does me in, so I walk to her and grab her in a tight hug. She lets out the biggest sigh of relief as she squeezes me back.

After a moment, I pull away from the embrace. "I know you meant well. I thought about it, too, and I think you're right. I need a way to face this and control my power, but you can't keep any more secrets from me. Please. I don't think I can handle another lie."

"I promise, no more lies, Ela. And I'll help you as best I can!" She shines her biggest smile at me and tilts her head slightly to the side. Oh no, I know that look. "Also... since we're talking about facing things together, what do you say we go face an assembly of Fae nobles dressed in fancy gowns who think they're better than us?"

"What? What are you talking about?" I pull away.

"Tonight is the Summer Solstice celebration. I think it's a great occasion for you to step back into the light and regain control over your life! What do you say?"

"Have you lost your mind?" I narrow my eyes at her, pretending to assess her sanity.

"Come on, you said it yourself, you're not going to live the rest of your life locked up here, afraid of everything."

"I never said that..." But she does have a point, and I'm so sick of worrying and overthinking everything.

"Come on, it's going to be fun! I'll be here if you need anything, and you can leave anytime." She gives me a pleading look and presses her palms together in front of her chest.

"Fine. I'll go to the stupid celebration. I can't live like this any longer, surrounded by people, yet afraid of my own shadow."

"Yes! That's the Ela I know!" A smile appears on her face, and she jumps back in my arms to hug me.

Grabbing one of my hands, she pulls me in for a dance as she hums a tune. Rina walks in moments later, and her shocked air sends us both laughing.

"All right, I have to get ready if I want to stand a chance before the judgy nobles. I'll see you there," Vesta says before heading out, still giggling.

I turn to look at Rina, who is studying me intensely, and give her an apologetic smile. "Can you help me get ready?"

"Of course. I'll get the bath running and pull out a few outfits for you."

Once I'm all cleaned up and my hair is brushed, Rina shows me the different ensembles she's put together. She's lifting around several dresses, today more modest than the ones on my first night here, and an idea springs in my mind.

By now, everyone must have heard about my little adventure in Averion and what I can do. I'll no doubt be the topic of at least a few conversations. The Fae who thought she was human all her life, who can wield fire and shadows, the Unifier...

"Do we have anything a little less... traditional?" I ask, raising one eyebrow up. Rina smiles cheekily, making her look ten years younger. If they want a scandal, I'll give them one.

Elanor

Now that I'm approaching the throne room with my high heels rhythmically beating the marble floor, I'm second-guessing my decision. But several Fae have already spotted me, and it's too late to turn back.

A glass panel reflects my deadly reflection, confirming the outfit gives the intended effect. The red gown hugs my waist perfectly, and the V-neck plunge does little to hide my breasts, scars, and toned back. Double thigh-high slits reveal the black leather garters I'm wearing on each leg and the matching knives secured in their sheaths.

Rina insisted I wear a black diamond choker and put my dark hair half-up in an intricate knot, with the rest falling in loose waves. She also applied a bold red lip stain to tie it all together.

I enter the already crowded Hall and am instantly assaulted by the loud music, the explosion of colors around the room, and the buzz of hundreds of guests celebrating. The space has been completely transformed since the last time I saw it. Golden disks are suspended in the air, reflecting the lights and sparkling like a thousand suns. Vines circle the white columns, and wildflowers are displayed in all corners of the room.

Almost dizzy from the display, I search the crowd for Vesta as Fae wine and other treats are being served among the colorfully dressed guests.

"Well, that will shut them up!" Her familiar voice comes from my right.

I pivot to face her. She's wearing the most hypnotizing makeup I've ever seen, green and purple tones mixing together on her eyelids, glittering under the light of the globes suspended from the ceiling.

"Damn. You weren't joking, either!"

"I'm never joking when it comes to a good scandal!" She gives me a twirl and flaunts her stunning backless forest gown.

She grabs me by the arm and tells me the latest gossip as we go around the room. She's pointing to guests discreetly, explaining how one was dumped by his partner for being too dull in bed, and another had to call for help when they were left in a compromising position. I have no idea who all these people are or what half of this means, but I don't care. And for once, I don't think about tomorrow. I'm just enjoying this moment of complicity.

A Fae walks by us with a tray in each hand, one presenting an assortment of bites, and the other offering cups filled with a turquoise drink. I grab one of each. Vesta gives me a surprised glance, but I shrug off her concern and take a sip after swallowing the appetizer. My entire body relaxes instantly. Damn, I needed this.

Vesta keeps glancing to one of the corners of the Hall, so I turn to look and spot Calen. I've got to hand it to her, he looks handsome as ever, with his gold tunic contrasting beautifully with his dark skin and the rings in his locks reflecting the light anytime he moves. She catches me studying her and gives me a severe stare.

"Interesting..." The next look she gives me is crystal clear. Not another word on the topic. I chuckle as I think about teasing her. But when Calen comes toward us, we both freeze, although not for the same reasons, I'm sure. I haven't seen him since that day. But he's with us before I can find an escape route.

"Good evening, ladies. You both look stunning." His gaze lingers a second more on Vesta, who beams with joy.

"Calen, I'm glad to see you're doing well. I-"

"Cal, please. No one calls me Calen anymore." He cuts me off before I can address the elephant in the room.

"Fine, Cal. I haven't gotten the chance to apologize to you yet. I'm sorry for hurting you the other day. I didn't mean to."

"I appreciate it, but there's no need for apologies. It was reckless on my part to step in your way." The corners of his mouth lift in a kind smile, and I nod back at him, feeling more at ease. That wasn't so bad.

"Will you dance with me, V?" Cal is now turned slightly towards Vesta, his smile not faltering one bit as he patiently waits for the shock to leave her face.

I stifle a chuckle and push Vesta forward before she can say no.

I find an empty corner to watch them from afar, eager not to miss a second of it. Cal looks comfortable, being his charming self, but I can't say the same about Vesta. She looks like a trapped animal ready to run the first chance she gets.

I watch them twirl around the room for a moment before realizing I should have heeded Vesta's warning about this drink. Right as I drop it off on a high table nearby, two Fae accost me.

Both blond with piercing blue eyes, they look like twins. The only noticeable difference is the vine tattoo one has under his left ear.

"Lady Elanor, we've heard so much about you," says the tattooed one.

"Looks like the rumors were false. You are even more captivating in person," the other adds with a devilish smile.

"Hmm, I'm not sure I can say the same about either of you." They laugh, and I raise an eyebrow in question.

"Our apologies. It seems our compliments are not conveying the desired effect. I'm Wyn, and this is my brother, Varan." He points to the tattooed one. "It's a pleasure to meet you."

Before I get a chance to respond, their faces drain of color as they stare at something behind me.

"Clearly, the pleasure is not mutual," Azran says. "Go bother someone else, boys."

I turn around and catch his glance on my body. His red eyes stop on my lips for a moment before meeting my gaze. "They're harmless. They just sometimes forget their manners when in the company of beautiful women. Though that doesn't do you justice tonight. The knives are a nice touch." His eyes are sparkling like embers.

"Thank you," I manage to say. He's wearing a black and red collared shirt, showing off his impressive build, and a thin crown of black diamonds. His two-bladed sword has been replaced by a shorter Fae sabre at his side. Growing tense near him, I say the first thing that comes to mind. "Looks like we're matching."

A smile appears on his flawless face. "Dance with me." Before I can refuse, he grabs my hand and leads me to the center of the room, making me fall into step with him.

My gaze is fixed on the floor, and panic starts rising in my chest as I try not to stab his feet with my heels. Suddenly, his thumb is on my chin, lifting my head up to face him.

"You're doing great. Just relax."

I do as he says and soon realize I am indeed fine. Balance seems to come as a perk of my Fae nature.

"I didn't expect to see you here tonight." He's leading me effortlessly, probably having danced with half the Fae of the kingdom.

"I figured since everyone knew about me and my... exploit, I might as well get this over with and give them something else to talk about."

"Well, you are certainly giving everyone something to look at, and dancing with me should help fuel new rumors."

"I'm sure you dance at these things all the time."

"On the contrary, as High Lord, my every move is constantly observed, and I cannot dance with just anyone."

"Who can you dance with, then?"

He doesn't answer, simply observing me with his strange eyes as we twirl in another corner of the room.

We get closer to a group of Fae whose gaze is fixed on us, and I can't help thinking I'm missing something. More guests are staring now, whispering to each other as we spin before them.

My head snaps back when the depth of his implication finally registers, and a smirk appears on his face.

I roll my eyes at the ridicule of the suggestion. He's simply trying to make me feel special, so I'll play into his hand.

I contemplate ditching his stupid dance, but I don't think I can escape his strong grip without making a scene and earning ugly bruises in the process.

His next words pull me from my deliberation. "I'm truly sorry about Talín. I wish there was something I could have done to bring him back to you."

A wave of nostalgia instantly washes over me, with guilt not far behind. His name hasn't crossed my mind since Azran walked in. How could I forget... "I know it wasn't your doing. He was just a friend, but he was the first I ever made."

He nods silently and gently sends me swirling while still guiding me with his other hand. My gaze drifts to his veiny forearm and his strong hand decorated with a gold ring I hadn't noticed before. He catches me easily and pulls me back against him.

Dancing seems to come so naturally to him. He's in his element when all I can think of is the weight of his hand on my waist and his intense stare.

"Tell me what you are thinking about. This cold façade makes you terribly hard to read." Before I can comment on the irony of his observation, his hand brushes the skin between my shoulder blades and down my back.

Goosebumps flare on my skin, and his eyes turn ravenous. I open my mouth, then close it, and my breath catches in my throat as I try to formulate a response. He doesn't wait for my answer, though.

"I want to understand you, see the other side of you, the side only others get to see. Why?"

That's when I know the wine got to my head because I find myself wishing I could tell him, wishing I could take down the protective walls I've erected around my heart and let someone in. "There's no other side. It's pointless. Everyone always leaves, anyway," I finally say in a tone as sharp as I can muster.

"Not me. Never me." His voice is barely a murmur, and I'm surprised to find no trace of deceit in his eyes.

For some reason, that is even scarier than the idea of being alone forever. At least when you have no one, you have nothing to lose.

Just as the thought crosses my mind, memories of all the losses come back all at once, overwhelming me. Talín. My father. My mother. The dead Fae in the forest. The blood everywhere on the ground. A grey fog is starting to cloud my vision.

I can feel myself slipping, and I have no idea how to hold back. I try pulling away from Azran's grip, but he only tightens his hold. My eyes snap up to his, revealing my instability and the wave of darkness bubbling inside me. "Let me go."

But instead of releasing me, he pulls me even closer to him, and his head dips towards mine until his mouth brushes over my ear. "I don't think that's the show you want to give them, little one."

Suddenly, he is pulling me away from the crowd, away from the curious eyes, and behind a pillar. Both his hands are against the marble column on either side of my face. I clench my fists, and my nails start digging into my skin as my power simmers and panic rises.

"Close your eyes, take deep breaths, and just focus on my voice," he commands as he leans in, his forehead almost touching mine.

"But, everyone will..."

"No one can see you." I realize he's shielding me with his arms. "Close your eyes, it's just you and me. Look for that calm space inside and ground yourself with a peaceful memory."

But I have no such memory. My life has been marked by death and loss for as long as I can remember. Bloodied images are still running wild in my mind, pulling me further and further away.

Right when I think I'm going to lose the last bit of control I have left, with him so close to me, I catch his scent instead. Citrus and herbal musk... Without a second thought, I inhale deeply before holding my breath and counting the seconds.

I slowly exhale and take another deep breath. And again. I'm solely focusing on this, on him, and it's helping, I can feel the power receding. "Just like that. Keep breathing in and out."

When I finally open my eyes, Azran is staring at me with his hands still on either side of my head. He moves to touch my face, but the hint of worry in his eyes registers, and I can't take it.

I can't tell what's true and what's deceit. His words and actions are getting more confusing by the day. I push his arm away, step aside and make my way to the exit.

Focused on keeping a straight face, I leave the Great Hall. As I'm stomping through the corridors, I keep wondering why I started losing control and how I ended up in that position. An even more troubling thought loops in my mind. I could have exploded in the middle of the crowd had he not stepped in.

I get to my room and decide to take a bath to try and calm myself, but it's useless. Still flirting with rage, I sprawl on my bed.

I hate this, all of it. I hate what's inside of me and what I represent.

The past few days are crashing down on me, and the solstice celebration was nothing but an illusion of normalcy. I'm still retracing the last hours when I realize I didn't even thank Azran for shielding me and helping me tonight. I know I'm showing the worst of myself, but it's for the best. I'm not letting anyone in my heart ever again. Not when I've lost everyone I've ever cared about and could set the world on fire.

Pushing everyone away is my only option. For some reason, it seems easier for me to push Azran away, though. Maybe it's because he's always been so resistant to telling me the truth. He hid the prophecy from me, and lured me into his world under false pretenses when he knew all along who and what I was. He has the most to gain from securing my alliance and keeping me here, so trusting him is not an option. And I don't know, he just... irks me with his superior air and confusing words.

Also, I think it's been way too long since someone challenged him, so when you look at it this way, I'm really doing him a favor. A small smile tugs on my lips at the thought, although I don't think he would agree with me on this.

After hours of tossing and turning in bed, I give up on trying to find sleep. The night sky beyond the windows should dissuade me, but I get up and get dressed. Fuck it. I need to get out of here. I can't think clearly all cooped up in the palace.

Savage in my wake, I sneak out of my room and discreetly make my way out of the palace. A pair of guards are watching me from their posts, but no one stops me. Good.

Not long after, I'm walking out of the city gate into the plain leading to the Dark Forest, emotions still bubbling inside me. Seeking its familiar comfort, I head in that direction with Savage scouting the way ahead. God, it feels good to be out of Averion, breathing the fresh air.

When we get to the Dark Forest several hours later, I'm slightly out of breath, not having realized I was following Savage's fast pace. I slow down as we head further into the forest.

Calen

At dawn the morning following the celebration, the dance with V lingers in my mind. The look on her face when I asked her to dance was priceless. The memory brings a smile to my lips. Contemplating that for a minute, I'm pulled away from the daydream by a quick knock on the door. I sit up in bed, my knife tucked under my pillow as always, and invite whoever is on the other side to enter.

Wyn walks in carrying a missive, and I can tell by the look on his face that it's urgent. I grab it and begin reading while he waits. The first words register and panic twists my gut. My network of spies is reporting on a possible assassination attempt. It doesn't say on whom.

I dismiss Wyn, get dressed in an instant, and rush out of my chamber to find Az. Minutes later, I burst into his room, not bothering to knock. He's already up, looking over some paperwork. But given the look of exhaustion on his face, maybe he just hasn't gone to bed yet. His head snaps in my direction, and I hand him the note.

I can see the wheels turning as he processes the new information and assesses the threat. "Ela. Where is she?" His eyes are fixed on me.

"Her rooms," I say.

The same realization dawns on me as we're rushing over there. We've been trying to keep her identity a secret but what happened in the city was hard to miss or contain.

When we get to her door, Az knocks repeatedly. "Open up, Ela. It's me, we need to talk." With silence as the only response, I can tell his patience is running out.

"Fuck this," he grumbles and then proceeds to kick the door in.

We rush in, but Ela's nowhere to be found. We head to the kitchens to find Rina, but she doesn't know where Ela is, either. A growl of rage tears from Az's throat, which sends Rina crying. I manage to give her a reassuring smile before following Az out.

"Where the fuck is she?"

"The garrison, someone will have seen her leave the palace grounds if she headed out," I say.

As I enter the barracks, I quickly round up everyone. Minutes later, two soldiers come up to us to report they saw her leave the palace grounds.

"Why didn't you stop her?" Az asks darkly.

They're both looking down at their boots, but one of them offers an answer. "She was accompanied by her wolf. She was on foot."

I refrain from mentioning that Az is the one who gave the order to let her wander the grounds freely. Instead, I pull him to the side, and we head to the stables. We quickly saddle our horses, and then we're out, riding through Averion and onto the plains with the morning sun.

<hr>

Elanor

We get to a small clearing and stop for a moment, now truly out of breath from the walk. After taking in my surroundings, I close my eyes to appreciate the sun hitting my face. I breathe in the forest scent I missed so much. Moss, rotten leaves, and wet soil. God, this feels like heaven.

I'm suddenly brought back to our tiny shack and to easier times. It was a harsh life but a simpler one. Granted, it was entirely based on lies, but at least there were no schemes, and I knew who I could rely on. Myself.

My eyes snap open when Savage growls aggressively. I freeze in shock as a dozen Fae warriors step into the clearing. Some of them have dark markings on their faces. Rebels.

"Looks like we've found the bitch," one of them says. I'm scanning the clearing when I realize I've overexerted myself and won't be able to outrun all of them. I bring my focus back to the fighters to assess my chances with them. They're all armed to the teeth, and one of them is gripping a bow, almost taunting me to run and give him a chance to show off his skills. Shit.

It's not looking good, even with Savage by my side. We've never been in a fight together, at least not with both of us on the same side. Now is as good a time as ever to find out if his allegiance has truly changed.

As I move to grip my weapons, Savage doesn't wait for a signal and jumps on the closest assailant, who goes down with a scream. Before he gets a chance to stab the wolf, Savage rips his throat out. I guess I have my answer.

I use the momentary distraction to unsheathe my knife and throw it at the rebel carrying the bow. A rush of pride courses through me as the blade meets its target. But it is short-lived when I spot Savage turning to the next attacker and getting shoved by a massive shield. He rolls across the clearing until his body hits a thick trunk with a thud and lies motionless.

"Bad move, motherfucker," I snap at the ugly Fae wearing a disgusting scar across his throat and a sick smile on his face.

"Shut your mouth, bitch. Don't you know when you're surrounded?" He taunts while his posse starts laughing as they spread out to encircle me.

Rage waking up inside me, I don't give them a chance to finish the loop and lunge on a Fae wielding a short sword. In a few strikes, I overpower him and run him through with Nahtar. A second attacker takes his place. I deflect his first blow, pivot, and slice through his back.

Without looking back, I move on to the next rebel, but a gasp escapes my lips as pain flares in my leg. A sharp object is lodged in my thigh. The scarred bastard can throw knives. Great.

As I try to keep an attacker between the ugly captain and me at all times to protect myself from other flying knives, my fighting style suffers from limited mobility. And I take several other cuts, this time from the two Fae I'm facing.

Downright pissed, I realize the asshole's right, there are too many of them. I'm tempted to use my power and set Nahtar ablaze, but I stop myself. I don't want to set the forest on fire and kill both Savage and myself in the process.

Instead, I manage to unleash a dark wave of energy and send my two assailants rolling. I don't notice the knife until it's too late and already deep in my side.

The captain is now smiling at me, showing his uneven teeth. I only managed to take down five of them, and I'm hurt. They know their chances just increased.

Shoving my pain aside, I consider my options. From the corner of my eye, I can see Savage is still lying on the ground. My heart tightens, and reality dawns on me. No matter how I look at it, I don't think I can make it out alive. Fuck.

This is not how I thought I would die. Cornered by a bunch of hateful rebels I didn't know existed until a few weeks ago. But, if the time has come, I'll take as many of those pieces of shit with me as I can.

As I consider my last moments on this earth, I can't find it in me to regret it. No more prophecy or crazy responsibilities. Somehow, I even feel relieved. I'm a walking time bomb just waiting to go off, so it's probably best I don't stick around. There's no one left anyway.

I ready Nahtar, calming my breath, as much at peace with what's coming as I'll ever be. I unleash a vicious scream and lunge at my next assailant.

Azran

My mind is racing, and all my thoughts turn to her. Rationality tells me she just went out of the city to clear her mind. But deep down, a part of me is telling me she's in danger. How could I let this happen? What if they're coming for her? Today?

I suddenly feel a tug pulling me toward the Dark Forest. Of course. It's what she's always known. I nod in that direction, and Cal immediately changes course to follow me.

As we get closer to the edge, I spot tracks that could be hers, and urgency takes me. My gut is telling me that I need to get to her right now. We cannot waste a second. I've never been more sure of anything in my life. I can feel it. She needs me.

Heading deeper into the forest, we're dodging the lower branches as the horses gallop as fast as they can. My gaze is focused in the distance, trying to discern her path and not miss a turn.

I almost fall off my horse when her voice resonates in my mind. It's her. I can hear her. It's more like thought fragments and flashes. Swords clashing, pain, and rage. With no time to dwell on how that is even possible, I press the sides of my mount harder with renewed hope in my heart. She's alive somewhere in that forest.

Her next thoughts make my blood freeze. No, no, no. Over my fucking dead body she's giving up! As we're flying through the forest, she's welcoming death, making peace with it.

The most unnerving panic takes my heart in that instant. I can't lose her. I just can't. Everything depends on her. We need her too much. *I need her too much.* So I do the only thing available to me, I focus my thoughts on one image, one thing only. Life. Life by my side. *Hold on, I'm coming for you.*

Before I even spot the clearing, I can hear the echoes of the battle. Foregoing any notion of safety, I jump off my galloping horse and sprint towards the fight with Cal not far behind. I find her seconds later, bloodied but fighting like hell and still standing. A rush of pride courses through me before I turn toward the spineless cowards cornering her. They're about to learn the true meaning of fear and regret the day they were put on this earth.

Without a second thought, I unleash everything I have on them. A red veil clouds my vision, and I let out a vicious snarl as I jump on the first attacker. He doesn't even register my strike when my blade cuts through his neck, and I'm already moving on to the next rebel.

Slicing left and right, blood splashes everywhere. I growl as I feel bliss coursing through me. I'm swinging my two-bladed sword as fast as I can to get to her, barely noticing the horror in their eyes before I end them. Insignificant fools who dared to come after her, trying to take what's mine.

There's no stopping me now. Their fate was sealed the moment they crawled out of the holes they were hiding in. They're standing between me and her, and the last thing they'll ever see will be my red-crazed eyes.

CHAPTER NINE

Elanor

Right when I think this next blow will be my last, a familiar snarl fills the clearing. My breath catches in my throat as Azran jumps on the attackers.

The tip of a blade rips against my shoulder and I avoid my assailant's strike at the last second. My brows draw closer together. I need to cut this combat short. My energy is declining rapidly and my wounds are slowing me down.

The rebel's attention drifts to the High Lord, who just leveled the playing field and is leaving torn bodies in his wake. Finding an opening, I don't hesitate and launch a final attack. When Nahtar tears through his chest, the loyalist is still frozen in shock, contemplating the Red Fury and his general at work.

My opponent drops to the ground and I stumble back, my boots squishing on the ground. It's a massacre. Azran seems to be in a trance, his eyes completely red, and his smile feral as gore splashes all around. My eyes widen when his face distorts in a sick smile showing off his red-splattered teeth. The ends of his blond hair are now crimson, and he is drenched in blood. I see where he gets the nickname from.

Cal doesn't notice the state Azran is in, or at least doesn't appear remotely shocked by it. I should be scared, but weirdly, I'm not. I'm merely hypnotized by the massacre unfolding in front of my eyes. He's in his element, and the slaughter is a part of his nature, a beast feeding off blood and death.

I let Nahtar drop on the red grass now covered in bodies. Unable to stand anymore, I slide to the ground, and my head turns until the rebel captain's stare meets my gaze. Only, he is not smiling anymore, and his head has been separated from his shoulders.

My fingers are absently rubbing the wet soil, and when Azran comes back into my line of sight, I realize the Lord of Bloodshed and I have more in common than I thought. Maybe I'm not the only monster roaming this earth after all. A glimmer of hope lights up in my heart as he rushes toward me, looking as ferocious as ever. He looks pissed, but I'm not afraid. It's the only state I've ever seen him in.

My vision blurs. My cuts are burning, and a familiar slumber is calling me. Exhausted, I close my eyes for a second.

⚬

Azran

The attackers poisoned some of their blades, but she's fine now. Mor made sure of it. Logic is telling me to attend to my responsibilities, yet, even with the healer's expert care, I can't leave her room. Savage is recovering by the fireplace, so I watch over them both, replaying the last hours in my head.

She finally flutters her eyes open and notices me on the edge of her bed. She tries sitting up, clearly in pain, and blows a breath in relief at the sight of her wolf.

"You are not to ever leave the palace grounds without an escort again," I say, unable to ease the tension in my voice. "And don't you ever give up on me again, you hear me?"

She meets my gaze but doesn't respond. She lifts the covers to examine the damage to her body. "No new terrifying scars to match the monster inside me, then?" Her weak voice barely reaches my ears, and I growl back.

A sudden urge to worship her body and show her how magnificent she is courses through me. I take a deep breath and focus back on the recent events. "You saw what I am." I didn't think twice before revealing myself to her in the forest, and there's no point in pretending I didn't see the shock in her eyes. "What I can do." She slowly nods. "We both carry a monster inside us, little one. The only difference is that you still have some light left."

She answers with a small smile, and a pit in my stomach opens, lighting me ablaze. It's the first time she's ever smiled at me.

"What happened to you?" She asks, her beautiful hazel eyes betraying her curiosity. I take a moment to study her face before launching into this tale I know all too well, enjoying the reprieve from the constant hostility.

"Back during the wars, I went to the Blue Mountains in search of a way to save my people. I didn't know it then, but I was about to find the prophecy. When I first touched the scroll, I felt nothing. The next second, my whole body was on fire, energy blasting through me, light burning my eyes. I was blinded, but I couldn't let the scroll go. It had become a part of me."

Her eyes widen. "After what felt like hours, when I couldn't take it anymore and thought I was going to die, it stopped. I came out of that mountain... different. A monster." I give her a small smile. "That's when my eyes turned red. Later, I discovered I'd been granted strength, speed, and a blood lust greater than any enemy seeking to harm me. When my power is unleashed, I become obsessed with killing anyone in my path." My shoulders sag as the weight of the secret I have been keeping for ages disappears. "Only Cal knows."

"I'm not the only one." A single tear rolls down her face, and I shake my head.

"And you don't have to do this alone. I'll help you. If we're to defeat the rebels, I'll teach you everything I know about control." She winces at the mention of the rebels. I forget she doesn't see and feel the same things I do.

"How do you do it? How do you deal with what you are?"

"You embrace it. You learn how to control it while making peace with who you are. I know you see me as a monster, but nothing is that black and white."

I lean forward, wanting to comfort her, show her I'm not the uncontrollable beast she thinks I am, and she lets me.

"Your eyes, they look different."

I pull back when I realize she's studying me, and her eyebrows imperceptibly twitch. She can't figure out what I've barely become aware of. "Get some rest. I'll come to check on you again."

⸻ ◆ ⸻

Elanor

Rina strolls in carrying the biggest breakfast I've ever seen as I'm getting dressed. Today, my sides and legs are not in as much pain. Soreness flares in the muscles of my thighs as I put on the second leg of the leather pants, but it's manageable. My Fae body has its perks and heals surprisingly fast.

"You need to eat something. It will help you recover your strength." Rina puts the tray down and sets the plates on the table, reminding me how nice it feels to be taken care of sometimes.

"Only if you eat with me," I say as I walk to the table, disregarding the disapproving look in her eyes. She finally yields and takes a seat next to me. With her usual reserve, she barely touches the food, and as soon as I'm finished, she stands up to clear the plates.

While her back is turned, I throw a piece of dried meat to Savage. She's still not entirely comfortable around him, but I'd say it's getting better. Overall, everyone seems to have adjusted to him being around as he spends most days wandering the palace grounds.

As soon as she's gone, a commotion sounds in the corridor. A smile springs to my face when Vesta storms into my room.

"How could you be so careless? Don't ever run off like that again without letting anyone know!" My smile freezes when her facial expression registers. She's pissed, all right. Genuine concern underlies her words, though, so I don't argue.

"I'm fine, really. And I learned my lesson, V." Adding her new-found nickname makes her flinch just like I had hoped.

"Hilarious, L. I can play this game, too, if you want." Both her hands are now resting on her hips.

I burst out laughing, unable to contain myself any longer. Shortly after, she joins me and pulls me into a tight hug.

"So tell me, what was *that* about the other night?" I say.

"What are we talking about? Do you mean you and our High Lord dancing and then him pulling you in for a discreet embrace away from prying eyes?"

My mouth gapes open. "That is *not* what happened. I- I was beginning to spiral, my power was slipping away. He actually helped me regain control. And don't turn this around! I'm talking about a certain general, dark and handsome, captivated by your beauty, and you looking the most uncomfortable, well, ever." She gives me a side-eye. "Is that usually frowned upon in Fae society?"

"No, you'll find Fae society to be rather... liberal. Basically, as long as it's consensual no one cares. And to answer your other question, I have no idea where that came from." I raise a skeptical eyebrow in response.

"Fine. Yes, I think he's good-looking, and I may have had a small crush on him before."

"Before? Did something happen?"

"No, that's the thing. I had just made the High Guard at the time, and he was my direct commander. The crush was pretty obvious on my end, and I didn't go the extra mile to hide it." I chuckle, but she continues solemnly. "Except, he never returned it. Forever the polite and charming general like he is with everybody else. So, I moved on."

"Oh, yeah. You've clearly moved on."

She gives me a sardonic smile. "I really don't want to get sucked into something like this with the war looming. I've found a good balance, and I won't jeopardize it for a Fae who suddenly realizes I exist. Especially if it's just him being his usual flirty self because he's bored or something."

"I understand. Well, I hope that whatever this is, he's not toying with you, or I'll give him another taste of my power."

She laughs. "Works for me! All right, I have to get to my rounds, or I'm going to be late. See you later."

Savage and I walk Vesta out and spend some time in the gardens, soaking up the fresh air and sunshine, before returning to my room.

A folded note is lying on my pillow.

*"Meet me at the training center at sundown. Bring your gear.
Az."*

Azran

Eyes closed, I'm executing a series of warm-ups and stretches. As ordered, the training center has been cleared out so I strike the air with full force, not bothering hiding my strength. In my element, tension leaves my body almost instantly.

My eyes snap open when she enters the room, her scent betraying her. She's watching me, whether in fear or admiration, I can't tell. Without a word, I point to an empty square.

I patiently wait while she positions herself, then jump on her without warning, testing her reflexes. She ducks just in time to avoid a blow to her lower abdomen. She's quick on her feet. Once the surprise of my attack has passed, I see determination settle in her eyes, so I keep on, attack after attack. She manages to evade most of my hits, but a few make it through.

"Aagh! What the fuck is wrong with you!" She says after my fist connects with her shoulder, sending her twirling to the side.

I pause and turn toward her. "I needed to assess your training to see where to go from there."

She snorts loudly. "I got stabbed several times yesterday, and I don't even get a warning?"

"Your enemies won't warn you. Now, I called you here to help you prepare and control your power. No whining."

She pinches her lips, clearly unamused. Let's see how she handles what I have in mind next.

I unsheathe my two-bladed sword and lunge at her. She has the common sense to grip Nahtar and counter my blow. I deal a series of strikes, each deadlier than the previous one. She's barely containing the assault but I'm smiling widely, showing I'm toying with her.

She is panting and fury radiates from her body every time our swords cross. Baring her teeth, she's determined to endure whatever I have in store for her. Cute. But I won't stop until she's on the floor, begging for a break. My smile turns feral, and I push on.

Her legs are visibly shaking but she's not giving up. She's properly exhausted, though. Color has left her face and she's struggling to keep her sword up.

I don't hold back, and she fails to block the next blow, losing her grip. I hit her with the flat of my blade and send her crashing to the floor with a kick of the leg. A cry escapes her lips when she hits the mat. She turns to face me and squints her rage-filled eyes at me. But the tip of my blade suddenly inches away from her cheek silences her.

We lock eyes for a second before I lower my blade. No comment is necessary. She knows her body failed her, and I just proved how important our lessons are going to be. She's been getting too comfortable in her routines.

When I step away, she tries to get back on her feet. I don't know how she still has the energy to stand. Pure hatred is probably fueling her.

"See you tomorrow, same time." As I'm about to turn the corner, I glance back at her. She's sprawled on the floor again, her chest heaving, and this time I don't repress the victorious smile blooming on my face.

Elanor

"What an insufferable, entitled *bastard*, bossing me around just to display my weaknesses and rub them in my face!"

Vesta bursts into laughter at my remark.

"What's so funny? He's set on riding my ass every day now. And all I can do is shut up and take it."

"Right, sorry. Not funny," she says, still smiling. "Look, it's going to help with your power and strength, right?" I nod. "Then endure it, it will be worth it. He's our High Lord, so it's not like he's going to train you forever. And maybe one day you'll be the one kicking his ass, who knows?"

That thought brings me comfort.

Several soldiers in the dining hall are looking in our direction, but it appears they're getting used to my presence here. The staring has turned into furtive glances, which I take as an improvement. I guess I'm also more accustomed to them and everyone around here, too.

My human life seems further and further away as each day passes, and it just leaves me wondering about the prophecy. I don't know how I could ever be what they all want me to be. Thankfully, Vesta offers welcome distractions, and so does my training, I guess. It gives me an outlet for my angst and fears.

Despite protests from every aching muscle in my body, I go back to the training center for more practice. I'll show the High Lord what I'm made of.

<hr>

Azran

As I'm pushing her to her limits, I glimpse the dark energy flickering a few times. Every time I push for more, and every time she surprises me by swallowing it back down. She's showing more control than I ever had when I first discovered my power.

She's also incredibly stubborn, refusing to show any weakness, which inevitably leads to her being completed exhausted by the end of our training.

After an insane sequence she handled well, I give her a break. "Drink and stretch, then I want ten laps around the courtyard."

Without flinching, she disregards the former and goes straight outside. Smart ass.

I lean against an arch by the entrance to watch her from a distance, counting her laps. And as expected, when she comes back she looks like she's about to collapse, but still no complaints.

"Drink. And stretch. You're going to hurt yourself." I leave no room for disobedience this time. She finally complies. Too tired to argue, I'm sure.

I try not to stare as she's stretching her legs, her thin shirt sticking to her sweaty body. "You're doing well, Ela. Keep it up, and you'll be in fighting shape in no time."

She lifts her head, stunned by my encouragement. And before she can hide it, the biggest smile escapes her lips. My heart instantly swells as I try to carve this image into my memory. Goddess of war and death, whose smile can light up a room.

In the following days, I'm called away several times to attend to urgent matters, so I leave her with an extensive list of exercises to practice on her own.

After the fourth missed session, I wrap up a meeting earlier than expected and decide to check the training center. As the garrison comes in sight, I slow down. It's almost midnight. She's probably gone by now, and I'm sure she's been doing just fine without me. I quickly go over the objections in my head but proceed anyway. I want to make sure she's not overexerting herself.

When I walk into the room, she pivots in an instant, with Nahtar pointed at me.

"What are you doing here?" She asks, panting.

"Checking on you."

"No need, I'm fine."

"Clearly." I consider leaving her alone but decide against it. "We've been making some headway with the rebels." She stills instantly, waiting for my next words. "Braern has organized pockets of resistance all across the territory, and it's been difficult to identify and crush them all." I cross my arms against my chest. "He's one of the sharpest minds I've ever known. He and Cal actually trained together long ago. But we're working on a strategy to draw them out. It will all end on a battlefield. The question remaining is where and when."

She nods. "Thank you for letting me know."

I nod back. "Good night, Ela. Go get some rest. I'll see you tomorrow."

As promised, I'm there the next day, ready to continue her training. We've been at it for weeks now. She's made significant progress with sword practice, and her physical condition has dramatically improved. So today, I'm going to be testing her mental resistance.

Realizing she's gotten a bit too complacent, I bring the difficulty up a notch. I launch relentless assault after assault on her, and I can see the frustration boiling anytime I hit her. With my next move, I elude her parry and hit her with my elbow on the back of her head, too fast for her to dodge.

She bares her teeth at me as frustration turns into rage. I don't give her a moment's rest to recover. I lunge at her again and hit her a few more times, even pushing her and sending her crashing against the wall. A savage growl tears from her throat. Oh, we're getting there. I can see the power flickering behind her eyes, slowly turning them black. I push on, not holding back my next blow and her poor riposte earns her a shallow cut on the shoulder.

"What's up, little one? Mad that you can't deflect a simple blow or touch me even once?" I'm about to send her over the edge. She's gripping her sword so hard her knuckles turn white, and her eyes darken. She's losing control. "Go on. Come on, show me what you've got! I'm not afraid of your little tantrum." I walk up to her and corner her against the wall.

"Asshole," she says, her jaw clenched hard. Dark waves ooze out of her body, trying to grip me. I step closer, baring my teeth in response. I can feel the dark energy pulsing against my body.

"Try me." I put my arm on the wall right next to her head and bring my face within an inch of hers. Our bodies are so close together I can feel the heat emanating from hers, her chest rising with each ragged breath she takes.

The atmosphere darkens, her fury almost palpable. I could cut through the tension with a knife.

She meets my gaze, and I momentarily get lost in her stormy, hypnotizing eyes. There, rage subsides in favor of something else. Something equally aggressive yet different. Something I never allowed myself to even consider or hope for. There, I recognize adrenaline mixing with anger and turning into desire.

The purpose of this exercise evades me, and, unable to resist, I close the distance between us until my lips crash down on hers. When her lips part slightly, encouraging me to explore her lovely mouth further, I don't make her beg. Pain courses through me as she bites my lip between her teeth. I respond by probing with my tongue, meeting hers eagerly, losing myself in her animosity.

I pull back, resting my forehead against hers, offering her a chance to catch her breath or slap me.

"I've been waiting for you for so long..." I can't control my thoughts anymore.

"To mold me into your perfect warrior and to fulfill your damned prophecy? To use me for more bloodshed because I, too, am a savage?" Her rage returns instantly, revealing the depth of her distrust in me.

"No..." I growl deeply as I grab her by the neck and push her back against the wall. Her breath catches in her throat, and she swallows hard, her chest heaving. The scent of her arousal overwhelms me. "I've been waiting for you, and you only."

I try to instill as much conviction as I can in these words while staring into her hazel eyes, all traces of darkness long gone. Then my lips are on hers again, and this time there is no stopping me. When a moan escapes her throat, I understand she doesn't want me to stop, and bliss courses through me.

My hands wander her body until I grasp her thighs and lift her up against the wall. Her legs close in around my waist, and she starts grinding against me, each of her movements rubbing against my hard length. Barely able to restrain myself, I devour her neck and rip her shirt open with one hand, uncovering a thin leather bandeau. Her sweet smell intoxicates me as I caress her scars with my lips and taste her skin. My other hand is roaming her waist, her back, and lowering to grab her round ass.

I pull down the last piece of fabric left on her chest and bare her before my eyes. I gently knead her breast and roll her nipple between my fingers. Her moans are my unraveling, so I grab her other nipple with my teeth, gently tugging, then biting. Her head rolls back, and as she's still grinding against me, I can feel the wet heat pooling between her legs. I need to feel her around me. I need to hear the sounds she makes when she comes around me buried deep inside her.

Footsteps echo down the hall, and Cal walks into the training center the next second, his gaze fixed on the letter he's holding. "Az, you need to see this!"

In an instant, I turn around to put myself in between him and Ela, shielding her naked body from his sight. She unwraps her legs and stands still as a statue against me, although I can feel her heart beating wildly in her chest.

"Out." My voice reverberates against the walls, loud as thunder. Cal looks up, then away, and walks right back out to wait in the corridor.

I turn to look at Ela, completely flushed in my arms. I reach to stroke her cheek, but she turns away before I can open my mouth. "I can dress on my own. Go see what this is about."

I move to face her, trying to meet her gaze, seeking confirmation, but she returns a cold stare. "Ela, it's not-"

"I said it's fine. Go."

I'll leave her be if this is what she wants. Without a glance back, I head out of the room and find my general around the next corner.

"Sorry, Az. I didn't realize I was interrupting-"

"What is it that you needed me to see so urgently?" I cut him off, pissed, more at myself than him.

He clears his throat. "Our network of spies caught rebel movements down south. They identified several hideouts with two to three dozen Fae in each. I say we strike fast and move on them tonight. We can't waste time and risk them being on the move again."

I consider his words as we walk toward the garrison. Ambushes in the night. They'll get slaughtered. My own people. I swallow hard as I nod my approval for another bloodbath.

Cal gives the order for the squadrons to move out and dispatches the soldiers orderly. They all look up to him. He's a natural. Me? They just fear the High Lord.

When it's just us again, he asks the question that's been on my mind for a while. "What is Braern doing, Az? You know him as well as I do. He must know a battle is inevitable."

"I think he's stalling, trying to gain more time. I don't know what for. More men or more weapons. Either way, this will end in bloodshed." I say, the weight of my responsibilities suddenly much heavier.

He nods.

As Cal is about to leave to join his soldiers and lead the mission, he puts his hand on my shoulder. "You deserve to be happy, Az. It's about time."

I shove him away, but I can't repress the smile tugging on my lips. "Come back in one piece, asshole."

"Always do." He winks.

***

Elanor

I'm holding my torn shirt closed with one hand and Nahtar in the other as I rush back to my chambers, a breeze in the wide corridor lifting the sides of my top.

My steps echo in the empty marble halls until I cross the threshold of my bedroom. Leaning heavily against my closed door, I let out a breath, my heart still pounding in my ears.

What the fuck just happened? I was so mad I didn't realize what the rage and tension were fueling in me. Not until it drove me to the point where the intensity just needed to be unleashed, let loose freely and aggressively in whatever form. The memory of his lips pressed on mine, his teeth around my nipple, and his hardness against me comes back to me in an instant, overwhelming me.

I close my eyes to push back these thoughts, but his intense gaze haunts me and wetness still soaks my underwear. God, I even moaned.

Out. Loud. Heat instantly returns to my cheeks as I realize I made a complete fool out of myself.

Somehow, deep down, I know he would disagree. I can almost hear him growling in my ear in disapproval, and the thought raises the hair on my arms.

I decide on a cold bath in the hopes that it will make me forget the last hour. Yet, even under the freezing water, I can still feel his hands all over me, his breath against my neck. And his confusing words still resonate in my head.

He said he wasn't referring to the prophecy, but this could be a part of the same elaborate scheme to make sure I stick by his side.

Savage is waiting for me on the covers, staring like he knows what happened. I narrow my eyes at him for a second before realizing I'm being ridiculous. This was just a much-needed form of release. All that tension built up from hours of training, of him getting under my skin, testing me. There is nothing more to it.

I know I can't trust him. There is a very real possibility that he's trying to manipulate me into doing his bidding. And if that's not it, there's still nothing for me to pursue there. It's too dangerous, and I have certainly nothing to gain by making myself vulnerable like that.

Sleep evades me, and my thoughts go back to him. When I close my eyes, my mind plays tricks on me. He's lying in bed naked. His right hand is stroking his length, his breath quickens, and his eyes snap open when he... I jerk up in bed. Savage nuzzles against me and I absently brush my fingers through his soft fur.

After what feels like hours, I fall asleep from exhaustion.

The next day, relieved I didn't see him after spending the better part of the day in the gardens with Savage and a few books I borrowed from the library, I head straight back to my chambers after dinner.

I climb the marble stairs leading to my floor as fast as I can, seeking the comfort of my room. I can feel the tension leaving my body gradually when it's in sight. My boots resonate on the floor, each step getting me closer to safety. Only a few more doors to go.

"There you are. Too tired to train tonight or just avoiding me?" The voice comes from behind me, sounding awfully close.

"I actually have other priorities than a Fae with an over-inflated sense of importance." Set on not letting him see a flicker of emotion, I turn around, putting up a neutral front.

"Is that what you think of me?" He chuckles darkly and moves to cage me with his body. I don't answer, unable to say another word while he's got me pinned against the wall. His body is way too close to mine. "Good girl," a devilish smile appears on his face.

My eyes snap up to his as a fire ignites inside me, and heat pools between my legs.

"Take the night off. Use that time wisely. You're awfully tense tonight. May I suggest an ice bath?" His red and amber eyes glimmer with mischief when mine widen in shock at the suggestion. The next second, he's gone, and I rush off to close my door behind me, only now releasing the breath I've been holding.

CHAPTER TEN

Elanor

The following morning, the garrison is in an uproar. Orders are shouted all around, horses are trotting on cobblestones, and the air is filled with tension. Squadrons are returning after being dispatched to deal with rebels.

Tensions are escalating, but the prospect of a full-out war reminds me of the damn prophecy and the role I'm supposed to play in it. How can I save anyone when I can barely control my power and almost got killed a few weeks ago?

Guilt looming in the back of my head, I'm also reminded of the reason why I initially went into the Dark Forest. There is one more mystery I need to uncover before deciding if I want to commit to the role I'm meant to play in the war. My parents. Their death is the last piece of the puzzle, I just know it. I need to find out how and why they died.

I sign to Savage and we head into the courtyard. We approach the palace walls and find two soldiers standing guard by the arch, their identical blond heads recognizable from a distance.

Wyn smiles widely at me when I'm within hearing range. "Good morning, Ela, great to see you in one piece."

"Hi, boys." Remembering the way Azran greeted them at the Solstice celebration has the intended effect and they both cringe. Savage welcomes them with a low growl.

I reveal a smile and extend my hand. "I'm kidding. What do you say we call a truce?"

Wyn looks at Varan for a second, then at Savage, and finally shakes my hand. "Thank God!"

"Sorry! We can't help behaving like pricks sometimes," Varan laughs.

"I've noticed," I say, smiling. "I'm heading into Averion. I'll stay within the city limits and be back before sundown. No need for an escort."

"Hmm, are you sure?" Stealing a trick out of Vesta's playbook, I rest my hands on my hips and don't look away. I'm ready to begin a staring contest when Wyn finally lifts both hands up in the air. "Ok, fine. Just don't leave the city."

I repress a cry of victory and motion for Savage to walk ahead. "See you later, boys!" I smirk as I walk past them.

Once in the heart of the city, I retrace my steps back to the streets I met Thalea in, with Savage quietly following me. She's my best bet at finding out what happened to my mother.

There is no stench here, no mud or puddles on the ground, and no trash lying around. Each building appears to have been crafted by expert hands, with arches decorating the windows and domed roofs reflecting the light.

As I'm walking the white capital, a cool wind at my back, energy buzzes around me. Radiant, hopeful, and profoundly welcoming. People walk the streets with their heads held high, not hiding in the shadows or trying to disappear under hoods.

The burnt-down building is not hard to find as it's the only part of the city that is not gleaming white. Workers have already cleared the rubble and are beginning to rebuild.

I quickly walk past it with rosied cheeks, and step into the paved street where I met Thalea. And that's where my luck ends. I have no idea how to find her, and I can't reasonably go knocking on each of those doors to figure out if she even lives around here.

I approach an older Fae and ask about her whereabouts. He steps back when he recognizes me and, without uttering a word, points at the door across the street before walking away. Great. I scare the shit out of Fae folk now, or maybe it's just Savage by my side. Before I can thank him, he's disappeared around a corner.

Facing the wooden door, I knock, hoping this is Thalea's home and not some stranger's. A few seconds later, the door opens and reveals the tall Fae I saw weeks ago.

"There you are! I've been expecting you. Come on in." She gives me a big smile, although it falters slightly when her gaze lands on Savage. I motion for him to stand guard by the door, and he obeys immediately.

I follow her inside and enter a small kitchen with pots and pans on the stove stewing with something that smells delicious. She points to an empty seat at the table and takes another one next to it. I quietly obey, and she takes my hand in hers.

"I'm so sorry for the way I handled things when we first met. I was so shocked by the resemblance to your mother, I didn't even realize how upsetting it must have been for you." Her voice trembles slightly as she gently strokes my hand.

"I'm the one who should be apologizing. I almost burned down the entire neighborhood."

"Nonsense. I would have done the same thing. And that just confirmed you are indeed Aerín and Tan's daughter." She chuckles, taking the whole situation rather lightly.

"What do you mean?"

"Oh, my dear. Your parents were the most fearless Fae I ever met. Aerín was the definition of intensity. Anything she did, she poured her heart into." A smile blooms on her face and she removes her hand. "She loved and fought hard. We were childhood friends, and as soon as she was of age to wield a sword, she did."

"Tell me more about her, please."

She nods with excitement. "I remember the day she barged into my house, the day after meeting your father. She was adamant she was going to marry him. She just knew she had found her mate."

"Her mate?"

"Another Fae destined for them, with whom they would share the most special bond. The mating bond is said to be unbreakable, even in death. When you're mated, you stop solely belonging to yourself. A part of you is always with them, and a part of them with you."

"And my father was hers?"

She presses my hand once more. "You're the fruit of the union of two Fae who loved each other very much."

"I guess that's why my father never recovered from her death," I say. "That's actually what I wanted to ask you about. Do you know how she died? I need to know what happened."

Her air saddens and she shakes her head. "I don't, I'm sorry. Her loss deeply affected me, and I never had the heart to try and find out. But there's someone who might be able to answer your questions." Renewed hope springs in my heart. "Her name is Ilyana. She took Aerín in when she was a baby and raised her. She lives on the other side of Averion, in the Arts quarter. I can draw you a map."

She pulls out a piece of paper and a pencil from one of the kitchen drawers when I nod. A mouthwatering aroma fills the air but I remain focused as she draws lines and arrows, my next stop already decided.

"Thank you for your help, Thalea. It means a lot."

"You're very welcome." After a pause, she says. "Aerín would be so proud of the strong Fae you've become."

My vision blurs with unshed tears as I nod, grateful for everything she shared with me today.

"Go on, now!"

I return her smile and head back, following the map she gave me, Savage strolling after me.

After several wrong turns, I make my way to the Arts quarters. The streets are filled with bright colors, stalls decorating the walls, and artists selling their crafts. The air is coated with the smell of paint, fresh leather, and clay. A beautiful tapestry catches my eye and relegates my angst to background noise. The thunder inside me is unusually distant, almost quieted by the hustle and bustle of the city around me.

I make it to Ilyana's home, command Savage to stand by the door a few steps away, and take a deep breath before knocking. After an interminable wait, an old Fae opens the door.

Wrinkles mark the corner of her eyes and forehead, but she has a kind face. Her white hair is neatly cut to her shoulders, and her brown eyes are studying me intensely.

"Good afternoon. I'm Elanor. Aerín's daughter. Thalea sent me-"

Before I can utter another word, she pulls me in for the tightest hug I've ever received. She's crushing me in her arms, her small frame able to hold incredible strength. Finally breaking the embrace, she guides me inside. "Come in, my child. Come in."

"You don't seem surprised by who I am," I say.

"You're her spitting image. And although Aerín kept you a secret from the rest of the world, I knew she was with child when she left Averion with Tannyll. I raised her myself. There was nothing she could have hidden from me," she says. A sad smile tugs on her lips. "I was hoping the child had survived all these years, and I would get to see them one day. My prayers have been answered." She closes her eyes briefly before pressing two fingers to her lips.

Once inside, I cut to the chase. "That's actually why I'm here. I have so many questions. I don't even know where to start..."

"Of course. Sit down. I'm going to make us some tea." She points to an armchair and shuffles towards what I'm guessing is the kitchen.

I take a minute to look around the room I'm standing in. Plush rugs and pillows decorate a corner, and books and artwork are everywhere on the floor and walls. This feels so homey.

I can't believe I'm standing where my mother once stood, crawled even. This is where she grew up. Nostalgia suddenly takes my heart, but this time I embrace it, feeling closer to her than I've ever felt before.

Moments later, Ilyana returns, holding a tray with a teapot and cups perched on it. I approach to help her, but she shakes her head, refusing assistance. Strong-headed despite her age, she settles the tray down on a low table in front of us, and I take a seat in the leather armchair she pointed at earlier.

"Can you tell me why she left Averion? I want to know what happened to her." I break the silence, unable to stop the words from leaving my lips.

I watch her pour the hot tea into the cups for what feels like an eternity, but I wait, inhaling the fruity scent filling the room. Finally, she hands me a cup and sits in the armchair opposite mine.

"Before I begin, you must know your mother always saw the best in people. And ultimately, that's what brought her doom." I patiently wait for her to continue, the steaming cup of tea warming my hands.

"She had joined the High Lord's army and met Tannyll around the same time. They were both working alongside Azran, trying to unite our people. After decades of fighting, although victory was near, Aerín was drawn into something bigger. And she made a mistake." I watch as she takes a sip from her cup, and I put my own down, untouched.

"I'm guessing by now you've learned about Braern, the loyalists' leader and former commander in our High Lord's army." Her eyebrow raises in question, so I nod, swallowing a lump in my throat.

"Braern wasn't always the lunatic he is now. I met him several times. He was friends with all of them, you know. Your mother, your father, the High Lord, the general. As he became more zealous, they all distanced themselves from him and his ideology. But not Aerín. She believed he was lost and needed help." She shakes her head slowly. "Even after he seceded and betrayed them by killing numerous Fae, she didn't forsake him. One day, he found a way to approach her without the others knowing, and that bastard tricked her." Her brows draw closer together. "He used her to gain intel on Azran's plans, which led to the slaughter of hundreds of Fae supporting Azran's vision. Her good heart led her to betray her High Lord, her mate, and everything she believed in. She didn't realize it until it was too late."

"What happened after that?" As much as I need to know how she died, I also don't want to hear it. She passed away so long ago that it's become easier to just remember the tight embraces and peach pies. I'm not sure I'm ready to tarnish those memories and be faced with the reality of her death.

"She came to me, told me everything, and asked for help. She was looking for a way to protect her family, to protect you, so I advised her to leave despite how painful it would be to see her go. That's when she and Tannyll disappeared, with you in her womb." She sighs heavily. "The next day, Calen stormed in here, asking about Aerín meeting with Braern. I never heard from her again, until years later when the general informed me she had been executed. I'm guessing it was in retaliation for the betrayal. That is all I know."

Tears are rolling down my face as I consider her words, my heart completely shattered. My mother was murdered because she betrayed them all, by mistake.

"I know your mother deeply regretted her actions, but what was done was done, so she did the only thing she could. She fled to have you and save you. Had I known you had survived, I would have found you earlier, dear child. You must believe that," she says, her voice suddenly shaking.

I knew this would not be pleasant, but I was thoroughly unprepared. My power simmers with the revelations but I hold it down tightly as I stand up. There is still one more question that needs answering before I can let my heart implode.

"Thank you for being so open with me, Ilyana, and for everything you've done for my mother," I say, trying to keep my emotions in check. "I need to go now."

"Wait, Ela. Please, stay a moment." I shake my head, already set on my next step. "Then please, visit me again. There's still so much I can tell you about your parents." Tears stream down her wrinkled face. If I look at her any longer, I'm going to fall apart, so I nod and head out.

⚬

Elanor

One more question, and then I'll be able to let it all out and collapse. But not yet. Not until I get this last question answered. A confirmation, really. Because who else could have given the order for her to be killed?

I'm running in the streets, heading back to the palace as fast as I can, my focus narrowed. My boots hit the paved streets loudly and Savage is running by my side, ever my guardian in this wretched place.

My power simmers, and instead of trying to extinguish it, I slowly fuel it with my anger and fury, readying myself. Darkness responds instantly.

I'm in the courtyard, crashing through the metal palace doors, sending them banging against the walls. I check the throne room, but it's empty. A deep growl escapes my throat, shaking the walls around me.

I pause just long enough to send Savage away before exiting the Great Hall. He's not needed where I'm going.

I make for the stairs, climbing them three at a time. Barely strained by the effort, I reach the top in less than a minute, cross the corridor in a breath, and lunge for the office doors, kicking them in.

Six pairs of eyes land on me, stunned by my violent arrival. But I only stare into his red irises.

"Out. Everyone. Now." Azran says, and I barely notice as the room empties. I'm still staring at him, standing behind his desk, cold as ever.

"Did you give the order to kill her?" Hate distorts the sound of my voice.

"Who are you-"

"My mother. Did you or did you not have her killed?" I ask, unable to contain my rage. He's still watching me silently, and right as I'm about to explode, he answers me.

"I didn't give the order."

"Who did?"

"No one. Because I killed her myself."

An eye twitch is the only warning sign he gets before I jump on him. Undoing any restraint I have left, I find purchase on his shirt, slam him against the fireplace with a snarl, and hit him with everything I've got. My fist connects with his jaw, bursting his lip open. Blood spatters on his face but he doesn't fight back.

I unleash my power, rage twisting my gut. Dark spirals explode out of me, burning and holding him against the wall. My wrath takes shape, sucking the light out of the room, and pouring black acid on his arms. His face grimaces with pain and his flesh sizzles, filling the air with an abominable scent. But it's not nearly enough to quench my thirst for revenge and death. So I hit him, scratch him, scar him, again and again.

Drawing blood with my hands, I want him to beg for his life, beg for me to spare him. But he remains silent, letting me hurt him as much as I can. As if that could earn him mercy.

With a snarl, I grip my knife and put it to his throat. Panting with furor, I press until a drop of blood appears on the blade.

My power is running wild inside me, lighting my body on fire, as he takes his last breath on this earth.

Something stills my hand before I can push further into his throat. His eyes have lost their red glimmer, now completely hazel. The tug inside me pulls me back from the dark precipice I nearly toppled over as I realize he's willing to let me kill him.

He deserves to die. For killing her. For taking her away from me. And for lying so damn much. But that's too easy and precisely what he wants. No. I won't give him that reprieve. He's going to have to live with himself, dealing with the monster he truly is, with the guilt and the self-hatred. That's a worse punishment.

I slowly put a lid on my power while I step back and let him go. He leans heavily on the fireplace wall, blood still dripping from his cut. My features settle in a cold mask, with only my eyes probably betraying the true emotions still raging inside me.

"I didn't know the whole truth at the time. No one did. I swear." Heaving, he doesn't look away. "When she ran away and went into hiding, it looked like an admission of guilt." My knuckles whiten as I hold back a punch. "I learned Braern tricked her when we intercepted a message confirming they had killed Tan four years ago." My gaze trails to the crimson streak decorating his corded neck. "After all those years, they found and murdered him, because he was willing to live among humans. They didn't know of your existence, or they would have killed you, too." He winces as he takes a shallow breath. "For the record, Cal pleaded for her. This was my decision only. If I could go back in time and change what I did, I would, Ela. I'm sorry." My shadows are still gripping his arms, burning through the fabric of his shirt as pain distorts his features.

"Fuck your apology. Don't you ever look in my direction or touch me again. You disgust me." I slap him hard and his face reddens under my palm.

I turn around and stalk out of the room. Still blinded by rage, I can't stay here. I run. Savage catches up with me in the courtyard. I can feel the dark shadows of power following me, like a cape around my shoulders and legs.

I don't stop until I'm out of the city and into the Dark Forest, hours later.

I collapse on my knees, digging through the earth, breaking my nails, tears streaming down my face. Unable to breathe and choking on my own sobs, I'm reliving that dreadful night on the cold forest ground. My throat and lungs are on fire, and all I can think about are my parents.

My shadows are now entirely cloaking me, and when my sobs calm down enough for me to breathe in, I let go of the guttural scream I've been holding inside for hours. My heart is being pulled out of my rib cage and burned in front of my eyes.

Azran

Her words were knives to my chest, and the slap was the final blow.

The first tears start rolling down my face seconds after she's gone, and I slide down to the floor, my heart in pieces.

I can't stop my body from shaking or control the pain flaring in my chest. Putting my head in between my hands, I let it all go. The hurt. The shame. And the guilt. I wish she had cut my throat. Anything would have been easier than seeing the hate and furor in her eyes. Anything.

Cal walks into my office at that exact moment. "Az! Soldiers have just reported seeing Ela leave the city."

"She knows. All of it." The words light my dried-out throat on fire. I don't lift my head to look at him, but he's by my side in seconds, holding me tight. I barely feel the burns and cuts on my body as more tears flood my hands and shirt.

"I'm sorry, Az. I'm so sorry."

"There is no way she's helping us now. I'm sorry, Cal. I've failed you all."

"Shut up. We'll be fine. We'll figure something out."

He stays with me for hours, his support unfaltering as I'm slowly dying inside. If only she had killed me, instead of leaving me to this torment, though I deserve it all. I've destroyed her, and now I've lost her.

When I think I can't hurt more than I currently do, her scream resonates inside me, tearing through what's left.

⚬

Elanor

I stay on the forest ground for an eternity with Savage's warm presence against my back as the truth about my parents' death crushes my soul.

When I have no tears left to shed, I realize it's nightfall. I can barely discern my surroundings. What now? I consider leaving, going far away from here, leaving Azran to an eternity of despair and self-inflicted punishment. He can rot away in hell for all I care.

But that would also mean leaving Vesta and everyone else to their fates. Where would I even go? The life I left, if that was even life, is long gone, buried away in a web of lies.

I sit back, my legs aching from kneeling too long. The cold and wet earth welcomes me as a gust of wind hits my face.

And what of the prophecy? That goddamn prophecy. Deep down, I know I can't just disappear. With the importance of my newfound responsibility weighing over me, I don't think I could live with myself if I fled.

I don't think I can ever face him again, and the thought brings fresh tears to my eyes. Unsure how to go on, but unable to leave.

I stand up, sore and exhausted, and Savage lets me lean on him. I start walking in the dark, inhaling the deep forest scent, still needing to clear my head. Somehow, even after all this, this place brings me comfort. Its familiar shades of green and brown, the rustle of the leaves, the cold and humid feel, everything about it grounds me.

Finding myself here at night, I realize I'm not afraid anymore. It's been so long since I last saw our shack, and I've changed so much. I wonder if I'll ever see it again. It's probably starting to decay now.

Another thought comes to mind. Leaving would also mean abandoning everything my parents once fought for, even my mother. And I can't dishonor them like that, especially my father. Somehow I'm certain he spent all those years training me to prepare me for this day, knowing it would come.

I take a deep breath as my mind is made up. I will fight in this war, fulfill the prophecy, defend the humans I lived alongside for twenty-two years, and slaughter the rebels responsible for my parents' death.

Or I will die trying. I have nothing left to lose. Savage's furry head tilts towards me, confirming I already have the only ally I'll ever need for this.

"It's just the two of us from now on." My hoarse voice disturbs the deafening silence around us.

I slip back into my room hours later, right before dawn, and glimpse my reflection in the mirror. My long brown hair is disheveled, and deep purple decorates the skin under my crazed eyes.

Instead of going to my bed, I lie down on the floor on Savage's spot by the fire and fall asleep against him.

The following weeks go by in a blur. I spend them training alone, my shadows surrounding me. Even Vesta is keeping her distance after I pushed her back harshly several times. She didn't do anything to me, but her allegiance lies with him. It always has. And I just can't stomach it.

Savage doesn't leave my side, though, and I go to sleep on the floor next to him each night. I'm woken up by violent nightmares, and only his warm presence calms me down enough to fall back asleep.

Rina tried convincing me to sleep on the bed, but I won't budge. I know she's trying to support me the best way she can, but I can't help the sharp words that come out of my mouth these days. She's backing off now, too, leaving me alone.

I've gotten much better at controlling my abilities, calling upon the shadows, feeling the power run wild inside me, and flirting with the fire that I know lies within the blade when no one is around. I can feel the darkness responding in a pulse when I summon it, and it's becoming like second nature.

But after a while, even the darkness is not enough to keep fueling my rage, and grief subsides. With it comes a trickle of guilt for pushing everyone who's been kind to me away. I just can't let anyone in ever again, not with what I'm preparing myself to do. Chances are I won't make it out alive, and I won't leave anyone behind grieving for me.

I'm just so tired of pretending, of constantly raging and attacking everyone around me. No one realizes I'm trying to protect them from the monster inside me and protect myself from another devastating loss.

After another day on my own, I enter my bedroom and find Rina tidying it up. Her eyes are filled with worry, so when she offers to run me a bath, I accept. I can at least give her that.

"Thank you, Rina. For everything. For your patience and service. You've been nothing but good to me. I'm sorry if I've been-" She pauses what she's doing and looks at me while I'm standing half-naked in front of her. She's not going to make this easier for me. "Sorry, I've been behaving like a jackass." She nods, clearly agreeing with my assessment. "I really appreciate everything you've been doing for me since I arrived, letting me wander around without reporting to the guards, feeding and caring for Savage. Everything."

"All is forgiven, but I'm too afraid to come near your wolf. The High Lord is the one who's been leaving food and water for him. I've even seen him pet him several times and-"

"And what, Rina?" She's clearly unaware that even bringing up his name could set me off.

"I once overheard him telling Savage to protect you," she says. "He's also the one who left you the black diamond necklace you were wearing for the solstice."

Feeling my blood boiling, I sharply nod to her, and she leaves the room. I finish undressing and sink into the warm bath, trying to calm myself down. That fucking bastard. All because of the damned prophecy, trying to lure me in, convince me to join the cause.

I'll play my part all right, but not for him. For my father and to prove to myself something good can come out of all that darkness.

Even though it means butchering a whole army alongside him. And butcher, I will. Braern is responsible for my parents' deaths. His days on this earth are numbered.

I now see the irony of it all. He tricked my mother, used her, and Azran tried using me, too. I'm just a weapon to them. Especially to him. Her murderer.

The bath overflows when I stand up abruptly, and water drips on the floor as I stomp through my room. I dig up the diamond necklace and hurl it through the open window into the void.

CHAPTER ELEVEN

Azran

Her presence haunts the palace but I make sure to stay out of her way, grateful she is still here. I'm not sure what motivated her decision to stay. She's probably plotting my murder for a day when I least expect it.

Somehow, I can't find it in me to even attempt to protect myself. The realm depends on me, and yet, I know for a fact that if she came after me I wouldn't fight back. I couldn't. Not after revealing the part I've played in destroying her family and her life.

The days turn into weeks, and I leave my door unlocked at night as I wait for her to come rip my heart out and end this suffering. But she never does.

The rare hours of sleep I get are shaken by dark and bloody nightmares. Yet, even that poor reprieve is better than the scorching pain flaring when I open my eyes at dawn. I'm being skinned alive day after day, doomed to live in agony for eternity. I thought the horrors of my childhood would have prepared me for everything in this life, but nothing prepared me for this.

I've started healing, but my body still bears the marks of her rage. And this barely scratches the surface of my suffering.

Anytime I catch a glimpse of her, she's nothing like herself, wearing her anger like a cape and her hate in a cold mask. Her shadows and Savage follow her everywhere.

I throw myself into the preparations for the war, taking council with captains to discuss strategies, sending envoys to the different Lords, and securing armies.

One afternoon, Cal marches into the office and drops something on my desk.

"I found it in the courtyard. I thought you should have it back." It's the black diamond necklace. "I know it means a lot to you. She can't hate you forever, Az. Maybe she'll come around."

"I murdered Aerín." My brows draw closer together. "This is not something you get over. It would take centuries, and that's if she ever does."

"Good thing we're immortal, then," he says, smiling. I know he's trying to cheer me up, but I can't even manage a fake smile. "I hear it can be repaired."

I shake my head. "You don't get it. I felt it snap."

When I finally lift my head from the stack of papers I'm reviewing, he's standing in the corner of the office, waiting. I raise an eyebrow.

"We've identified a rebel hideout. It's big. The biggest we've ever stumbled upon. By the chain of the Eidune, within a labyrinth of tunnels and caves inside the mountains."

"Why didn't you say something sooner?!" Shaken from my torpor, I immediately stand up.

"Look, no offense, but you don't seem like you're at your best right now. I think I should lead the raid."

"Bullshit. I've been waging wars since before you could wield a sword."

"Now you're exaggerating. I was already pretty decent with the wooden ones."

He manages to get a chuckle out of me with his stupid remark and is now beaming with pride.

"All right, smartass. Pick out your best warriors. It's at least a three days' ride. We leave at dawn."

***

Elanor

Vesta walks out of the barracks, and even at a distance, I can tell from the look on her face that she's fuming.

Seeing she's not going to stop for me, I catch her by the wrist, but she turns violently and snatches her arm away with a snarl.

"What's going on, V?"

"What is it to you?" She glares at me.

"I'm sorry. I haven't been the best of friends lately, but I'm still here for you." I say as I back away slowly. It's probably best I leave her alone. I know the feeling well.

But her shoulders sag, and her features relax. "No, I'm sorry. I know you've been going through a lot." She gets closer to me. "This whole day has been shit. There's a raid in preparation, and Cal has ordered me to stay behind. I'm not joining the squadron."

"Wait, what raid? And why wouldn't you join?"

"We've stumbled upon a massive rebel hideout in the Eidune range, and Cal won't let me go. No idea why. I've tried everything. I'm one of his best soldiers, damn it!"

"I'm sorry, V." She and I both know that with the general, there's nothing I could say or do to get her in. Defeated, she gives me a sad look before heading toward the arch leading into the city.

I'm still watching her walk away when Cal comes into view.

He spots me at the same time and comes toward me, a frown wrinkling his forehead. I know what he's going to say before the word leaves his mouth.

"*No.*"

I return a dark smile. "Try me."

"The wolf stays."

"Why?"

"Because the enemy knows you don't go anywhere without him. He's a beacon signaling your presence."

"Fine. When do we leave?"

"At dawn. Don't be late."

I nod before turning back. Retracing my steps, I enter the palace and go straight to my chambers to pack fresh clothes for the journey.

As I'm getting ready, Savage is watching me quietly. When I'm done, I walk up to him and kneel on the ground by his side.

"Hey. I'm sorry, but you have to stay behind on this one. I'll be back before you notice I'm gone."

He whimpers at me, tilting his head to the side like he understands my words. I stare into his white eyes, the same eyes that used to scare me and now belong to the one being I can count on to protect me.

"Not sure how I'll get a minute's sleep without you around, but I'll have to manage." I extend my arms and hug him tightly, burying my face in his warm fur.

Several hours later, we've left Averion and are riding across Fae territory.

I'm relieved to find Wyn and Varan among the soldiers on the raid. They offer a welcome distraction with Azran around. The twins are constantly bickering, which is fun to watch. I wonder if they do it on purpose to ease the burden on everyone's mind.

Ever since I attacked the High Lord and unleashed my power on him, he's avoided me. He hasn't tried talking to me, and I don't want him anywhere near me. But I swear I can feel him watching when he thinks I'm not looking.

I stay quiet for the better part of the first day out in the plains, taking in the land around us, almost soothed by the sound of the high-spirited horses. The muscles in my back and legs are barely strained from the ride, a silent confirmation of my improved physical condition.

From what Wyn told me, we're in Sun Fae territory, but we won't be stopping in any city or villages, even though I spot a few from a distance.

By the time we set up camp for the night, my mood has slightly improved with the twins around. Several Fae are patrolling the area while others are preparing dinner or resting. As I watch them all naturally take on tasks and organically organize themselves, my thoughts drift to Talín, and my heart sinks a little.

Not long after, Wyn and Varan walk into my line of sight, carrying several plates of food. After thanking them, I join them by the fire and start eating dinner.

"So, how does it feel going on your first raid with stunning Fae warriors?" Varan shoots me a wink.

"Stunning is not the word I would use. But so far, it's relatively entertaining, with you two bickering like children," I say, my hands pinching the air to mimic their constant chatter. They both burst into laughter.

"It's not my fault I have this nutcase as a twin. Imagine having to live with him day and night!" Varan says.

"So you even share a bed? Interesting." From what I understand of Fae society, two males sharing a bed is nothing shocking, but, just like in the human realm, two brothers is a tad more problematic.

The outraged looks on their faces do me in, and I laugh out loud for the first time in weeks.

"Very funny, Ela. We'll see who's laughing when I win the bet." Wyn says.

"What bet?" My interest is immediately piqued.

"Who kills more rebels by the end of the week." Varan reveals a devilish smile.

However sordid, this might be exactly what I need. "Oh, you're not winning that bet, trust me." I say as my gaze follows the High Lord walking around the camp. The twins exchange a concerned look, probably reading the tension in my body.

"So, what is that about, Ela?" Wyn cocks his head toward Azran. "Want to talk about it?"

I shrug off his inquiry, focusing on the fire burning in front of us. I extend a hand, playing with the warmth of the flames.

"We can tell something's not right. What happened?" Varan says.

After a moment, I give them the answer that will surely put an end to the questions. "He killed my mother." That shuts them up, and I go back to staring into the crackling fire in silence.

Varan clears his throat. "Hm. Well, I'll kick his ass if you want me to?"

Thinking back on the hurt I've already inflicted, I'm almost tempted to tell them there is no need.

"I'd like to see you try. Try touching me or her and you won't live to see another sunrise."

Azran is upon us, towering over Varan, who appears to be shrinking in on himself by the second. The High Lord looks like he hasn't slept in days, but his penetrating red gaze tells me he's lost none of his edge. He just looks more unstable, if that's even possible.

Feeling my rage already bubbling, I jump up with a snarl and leave without another glance at him. Entitled asshole. He's out of his mind if he thinks he still has the slightest claim on me. There's not a chance in hell I'll become his docile little warrior.

Elanor

I wake up tired from a night spent tossing and turning, followed by a day spent riding and listening to Wyn and Varan's usual banter. I kept glancing behind me, hoping to find Savage's comforting presence, in vain, and my heart dropped every time.

Cal gathers all units around the fire when we stop after sundown.

"We'll reach the Eidune range tomorrow at nightfall."

The whole camp falls silent, everyone carefully listening to him. Admiration fills the soldiers' eyes. The general is a natural leader who clearly cares about each and every one of his soldiers and will do anything in his power to bring them all back in one piece.

"Rebels are hiding in a network of tunnels and caves, making for the perfect trap. Each unit has been assigned a tunnel entrance and will storm it simultaneously. We'll have until dawn to do as much damage as possible." He paces around, meeting everyone's gaze. "Your captains will give you the location of the rendezvous point before going in." A horse whinnies at the back, but not one single Fae turns their head. "Remember why we're fighting. Remember your training. Protect each other." Cal is now looking straight at me. "Do not underestimate our enemy. They know these tunnels and caves better than you. Do not follow a rebel into a tunnel alone. You'll be dead before you know it." Thanks, message received.

"Now, get some rest, tomorrow will be a long day and an even longer night," he says.

As everyone disperses, Cal heads toward me and pulls me aside.

"You're with Az tomorrow. Do not go wandering off alone, you hear me?" Before I can argue, he shuts me up with a gesture of his hand.

"This is not up for debate. You either stay with Az, or you don't come." There is no mistaking the tone of the general of the Fae armies.

I swallow my anger and nod sharply. I try to sleep after that but barely manage to close my eyes for a couple of hours. Memories of dead rebels and of my parents keep swirling in my head.

Come dawn, I join the rest of the soldiers already mounted on their horses.

Around midday, we leave the plains for desertic lands, and several units split up from the group to take the eastern or western route toward the mountain range we can now see on the horizon. Wyn and Varan are part of the unit heading west, while Cal leads the eastern unit. I'm left alone with a small group of Fae I don't know, and Azran. Brilliant.

As the Eidune range gets closer, silence settles in. Still a reasonable distance away, we leave the horses hidden from sight by a barren hill and head towards the mountains on foot.

We're still climbing through the narrow paths of the Eidune with the last light of the day when I'm starting to think we're lost. Suddenly, Azran lifts his hand up, and our small group freezes behind him. He slowly turns back to us and points to a thin opening on the side of the mountain we're crouching against.

Then we're silently making our way into the tunnels. This is a labyrinth, all right, and I have a bad feeling about this. Crawling beneath the earth feels wrong.

We come across a junction of several tunnels, and Azran dispatches soldiers in pairs, sending them down the different arms. He motions for me to follow him down the last arm to the right. I silently obey, focusing on the danger ahead of us and not him.

Our tunnel widens to the point where a dim light is visible at the end of it. Azran sees it, too, and unsheathes his sword quietly. As we get closer to the light, another embranchment is revealed, our tunnel crossing another one.

Suddenly, footsteps echo in the tunnel ahead of us. Azran pulls me tight against his body and squeezes us both into the crevasse of a wall. One of his arms is around my chest, and the other is holding his two-bladed sword in front of me. Surrounded by shadows, his breath is warm on the back of my head. Tension radiates from his body like the embers of a fire.

With his contracted torso behind me and his strong hand holding me in place, I'm reminded of his remarkable strength and of the fact that if he had wanted to fight back when I attacked him, he could have. He once told me no one had ever been allowed to live after threatening his life, yet he pulled me aside without a second thought to protect me. I guess I am the exception.

I should hate this proximity, but I don't think I have it in me to keep fueling this venom. As the footsteps get closer, his grip tightens, and we wait, motionless, for the rebels to either find us or walk past us.

Thankfully, they do the latter, their shadows stretching out on the wall across from us. We finally release the breaths we've both been holding, and Azran steps in front of me to follow the rebels.

We've been walking these tunnels forever, and I'm grateful not to be alone.

I almost bump into Azran when he stops abruptly in front of me. What the hell? Several voices resound from the turn right ahead of us, too many to count. Azran turns to me slightly and gives me a nod. I return it, readying Nahtar.

The rebels receive no warning and barely have time to grab their weapons before we descend on them. Nahtar finds its first target within seconds. And the next one is already lined up by the time I withdraw my bloodied sword.

With at least a dozen rebels here, I unleash all my pent-up rage and start slicing left and right. Releasing my power, I send two crashing against a wall, knocked out or dead. Next, I lunge at the Fae baring his teeth in front of me. I dodge his blow and gut him as I move on to the next attacker. It's a bloodbath, and we're quickly gaining the upper hand. Azran is killing rebels behind me when I spot a Fae fleeing down a tunnel across from me. Without thinking, I break into a run after him. I can't let him warn the others.

As I'm racing towards the tunnel, Azran's dark voice is the last thing I make out above the sound of swords clashing. "Come back here! Ela!"

Knowing he's too far to reach me and surrounded by rebels, I keep running. I'm still chasing the fugitive, taking turn after turn, when I realize how reckless I'm being. Cal's warning comes back to me right when I come to a stop in another cave lit up by torches. The rebel is looking right at me. A wicked smile appears on his sharp face, revealing his pierced tooth, and six Fae step into the light, ready to face me. Before I can unleash my power, a presence looms behind me, a shadow in the corner of my eye. Then the world goes black.

Calen

With no stars or sky above us, it's hard to tell exactly how long we've been down here, and it's starting to feel like an eternity.

Rebels are now few and far between, but I can't tell if it's because they've been dealt with or because they managed to escape and hide deeper in the tunnels.

This network of narrow passageways runs so deep into the mountains that somehow I have a feeling we've barely scraped the surface with the attack. Braern is the most devious and cunning Fae I know and I suspect that the loyalists will have found a way to warn him by now. I don't intend on staying long enough to find out and most likely end up trapped underground with my soldiers.

We finish clearing another cave, and I pull everyone back not long after. Relief floods my body when we finally emerge from the tunnels. I didn't realize how suffocated I felt being down there until I breathed in the fresh air of the night.

I pause close to the entrance to wait for everyone to come out. When all twenty are accounted for, I'm relieved to find we've only suffered minor casualties. All are able to walk, with only a few needing wounds bandaged right away. I instruct the soldiers to take care of it as best they can before we leave this wretched place.

I quickly lead the way down the range, regularly checking everyone is keeping up with the pace. Shortly after, we find our mounts and are back on the plains by dawn, riding through the desert to get to the rendezvous point.

As the sun rises, I spot a cloud of dust rising in the distance to the west. The other unit is riding out to meet us.

Once we get to the meeting point, we set up camp, and the wait begins. A few hours later, the last unit returns. The weight I've been carrying on my shoulders finally lifts as horses appear in the distance wearing red and gold colors.

But not long after, my heart sinks. There are two riderless horses in the unit, and Az and Ela are nowhere in sight. The minute the soldiers get to us, I walk out to meet them.

"Where is your High Lord? And Ela?"

I recognize Milan's shaved head as he dismounts and bows before me. "They took a separate path through the tunnels, general. We waited for them outside the mountains, but dawn was near, and we were easy prey out there. So we went to the horses and brought them all back to avoid them being discovered."

I nod. He's a good soldier, and I would have done the same thing. Reinforcements should have arrived and the Range must be swarming with loyalists by now. Dispatching a few riders is the best I can do, as I can't risk marching on the Eidune. The position of the range puts us at a strategic disadvantage, and finding two Fae set on evading unwanted attention will prove nearly impossible.

Azran and Ela probably got out of the tunnels late because they couldn't stop screaming at each other. They're on foot, but they'll make their way back. Azran has survived way worse. They'll be here.

━━━━ ◆ ━━━━

Elanor

When I wake up, my ears are ringing, and my head is about to explode. I'm tied up in a dimly-lit cave with no furniture except a table across from me overflowing with papers. Shit.

I'm lying on the floor, my hands tied behind my back, and a collar on my neck is connected to the wall by a rope. Like a fucking dog. When the buzzing in my ears finally stops, sounds come back to me, and voices I don't recognize echo right outside.

I start tugging hard on the rope, but before I can make any progress, three rebels walk into the small cave I'm being held in. The one with long black hair steps forward, wearing leather armor and carrying a massive sword at his side. Looks like I've found the leader of the assholes, and he is studying me avidly, undressing me with his dark eyes.

"The whore is awake. I'm Onas. You don't know what that means yet, but don't worry. We'll get to know each other very well, very soon." He licks his lips, and his face distorts in an evil smile.

I swallow the lump in my throat, trying not to show fear, and look around for my weapons or anything that's going to help get me out of this mess.

"Oh, don't bother, it's just us. The blond bastard was long gone when we went back to the cave. Fucking coward."

My eyes widen and a pit opens in my stomach. Azran couldn't have left me. The only promise he's ever made to me was to keep me safe.

"Listen up, bitch. We have some time before the commander arrives, so my friends here are going to wait for their turns outside until I'm done with you." I'm almost tempted to let go of the nervous laugh I'm holding, but the two henchmen leave the cave, and I'm left alone with this repulsive motherfucker.

My blood freezes as I realize he intends to see me bend to his will. All trace of nervousness leaves my body, and survival kicks in.

"Go fuck yourself, pig!" I crawl against the wall to put as much distance as possible between us. My fingers are scraping the rock behind me, trying to find a sharp edge, anything that will help free my arms.

"Oh, fight me. That will make it more entertaining." He laughs darkly as he advances on me and grabs my right leg. His gross hand on my chin almost sends me gagging, and I kick him a few times with my left boot, but he doesn't let go. Instead, he secures both legs and starts pressing down on me with his body to keep me still, crushing my hands behind my back.

Pain flares in my fingers as the skin is torn against the hard rock. But that's the least of my worries. I start screaming and kicking, struggling, trying to get him off and away from me.

His disgusting hands are traveling along my thighs, groping my ass, and trying to tear my pants open.

What this monster is about to do to me will scar my body and soul if I make it out alive. Panic is starting to overwhelm me, so I try reaching for my power, but it's not responding. The blow to my head must have knocked me out hard, and I was already weakened by the sleepless nights and the fight.

Something hard pokes me in the thigh and his putrid breath is all over my face as he laughs loudly. Resorting to my last and only weapon, I try biting him, but he's fast and keeps his head and arms out of reach. Still screaming and kicking, I don't hear the sound of swords clashing until Onas suddenly lifts up to look around.

"What the fuck is going on back there?"

His weight is completely lifted off my body as his scream reverberates in the cave. Azran is pulling Onas by the hair, dragging him away from me, and pinning him to the wall.

He came. Az came. He didn't leave me. His blond hair is all bloodied, and his eyes are entirely red. Relief floods my entire body when he snarls loudly in the face of the rebel. He snaps Onas' neck with both hands, and his limp body falls to the ground.

The next second, Azran is by my side, cradling my face with one hand and untying my arms with the other. Then he's pulling me to him, hugging me so tightly I could cry.

"Thank you, thank you, thank you," I whisper against his strong chest. Not letting go, his tense body is shaking. "I thought you had left. They told me you had left."

He pulls back just enough to look me in the eyes, his forehead touching mine. "Never, little one. I'm never leaving you."

I nod and tears roll down my cheeks. He wipes them with his thumb and lowers his hand to my neck. He snaps the collar open, hurls it across the room, and puts his fingers back on my neck to gently rub my reddened skin.

"My hand makes a much prettier necklace." He stares at my lips before lifting me up. "Let's go. It's already dawn. Can you walk?"

My brows draw closer together. "We're not done yet. We came here for a reason."

"Are you out of your mind?"

"I heard them talking about something stashed in the lower tunnels." He raises an eyebrow, so I push on. "Let's check it out, and then we'll leave."

"Fine. But promise me to listen to everything I say. And at the slightest hint of danger, we're leaving."

I nod.

We find Nahtar and my knives before heading back into the tunnels, completely emptied out except for the trail of corpses. Taking several turns, we find a tunnel leading downward and head into it.

After an interminable descent, we land in a small cave where two Fae are standing guard. Their eyes widen at the sight of us, but Azran jumps on them in a second and decapitates one while gutting the other with his double-bladed sword. It's all over before I can even blink.

We step over the bodies and find a vast cavern filled with barrels. Azran opens the closest one, revealing a glittering dark powder.

"What is it?" My own voice sounds distorted in my ears, the voice of a stranger.

"No idea." He grabs a handful of it and drops it in a small satchel he pulls out of his belt. "Now, let's go."

CHAPTER TWELVE

Azran

Ela and I hurry out of the tunnels and emerge from the mountain. Without pause, I lead the way down the rocky path. We need to get out of here as fast as possible. Braern will have heard about the raids, and reinforcements must be on the way.

The sun is rising rapidly in the sky, indicating we have now run out of time. Adrenaline still rushing through my blood, I sprint ahead to look for the horses. Only, they're nowhere to be found.

Tracks hurrying away from the range mark the grounds. The rest of the unit must have taken our mounts with them, not wanting them to be found by rebels.

"Fuck." Ela has come to the same conclusion.

I repress a smile. Swearing is like second nature to her. Right after arguing with everyone around her.

Without a second of hesitation, she heads north and breaks into a run. She's the most strong-headed and determined Fae I've ever met.

I gladly let her take the lead, her smaller stature making it an easier pace for me to follow, given my state. What would have been a day's ride just turned into two full days, and I need to conserve my strength.

We're disadvantaged on foot, and we both know it, so taking a break is out of the question. Hours are beginning to blur together, and I lose all track of time as I focus on the back of her head. Her luscious brown hair is now crusted with blood and dust, reminding me of that piece of filth. I'm panting heavily, but rage keeps me going.

Ela looks back at me several times to confirm I'm following. I don't need her distracted, so I regulate my breathing and dig my nails into my palms to keep the pain at bay.

I check the southeast every now and then to make sure we're not being followed or chased. I squint my eyes at the horizon once more, and this time, dust is swirling in the distance. I catch up with Ela, pick her up before she can argue, and duck behind a small dune. I immediately crush her body with mine, trying to make us invisible and impossible to spot from a distance.

"Get off me!" She tries pushing me off, but I put my hand on her mouth and drop my gaze to hers, which silences her immediately.

I almost pull back when panic flashes in her eyes. I hate to be the one putting her in that state right after what she barely escaped. "Riders. Stay down." She stills and does as I say.

My attention now entirely focused on the horizon, I try to discern where the riders are headed. Once I'm confident they're not coming toward us, I relax and catch a glimpse of worry in her hazel eyes.

With my body against hers, there's no hiding my slowing heartbeat and shortness of breath. Or maybe she's worried about rebels finding us or about what I might be capable of doing to her in that position. A rush of disgust courses through me, and I quickly move away from her and get up. "Let's go."

"Wait-"

"We're too close to the range. Let's go." I break into a run, glad I'm already covered in blood, and there's no way she can notice my open wound.

⋘✦⋙

Elanor

We manage to put some distance between the mountains and us by the end of the day and stop for the night behind a dune. We should be in Sun Fae territory by noon tomorrow.

The sun will be setting soon but we can't risk a fire out here. And we don't have any provisions, anyway. I sprawl on the ground, hungry and exhausted.

Seconds later, Azran comes to slump heavily next to me. I didn't expect him to be so out of breath earlier when we hid from the riders. He's never shown any weaknesses before and is probably the strongest fighter I know.

He's covered in the blood of the Fae he butchered, and his usual golden skin looks deadly pale. Properly looking at him for the first time in days, my gaze widens when I spot the fresh blood oozing from his side. "You're hurt."

"I'm fine. It's nothing."

But his ragged breath tells a different story. Alarmed, I straighten my back and move to get a closer look at him.

"Given the look on your face, you won't make it to the rendezvous point in that state. And if you can't run tomorrow, I'm leaving you behind. So shut up and show me. Now."

He finally complies, sits up, and starts unbuckling the straps on the side of his armor. Once he's done, I push his hand aside and glance at his black undershirt. Even with the last light of day, I can tell it's soaked in blood and sticking to his torn flesh. Shit.

I help him completely remove his chest piece and shirt and grab the last of my water to carefully rinse off the wound. It's not a large cut, but it runs deep. Otherwise, it would have stopped bleeding by now. And that's as far as I go. I have no medical training whatsoever, and, given our history, I'm the one who has needed stitching up more.

He gently takes my hand to move it away from his abdomen.

"You need to close it."

I make a snorting noise. "And how would I do that?"

He looks at Nahtar on the ground next to me, and it takes me a second to realize what he's suggesting.

"Are you out of your mind? I could set your entire body aflame!"

"That will be a quicker end than slowly bleeding to death."

"For you, maybe. But that will also alert all the rebels in the area and get me killed. Unlike you, I don't have a death wish."

"It's either that or leaving me out here to die." He pauses a moment. "Your call."

I know what he's implying. There I have it. My chance at revenge. But anger suddenly wakes up inside me. "If I decide I want you dead,

I'll come for you head on. I won't just finish you off when you're already halfway gone."

A sad smile appears on his face while I sit back to consider my options. For several minutes, I'm just mulling over his words, gazing at the crimson horizon, and then at him.

When I realize the bastard is right, I reach for Nahtar. Either I manage to wield and control my power, or he dies by dawn.

I know I should loathe him and want him dead, but I can't simply leave him to die. I need him if I want a shot at avenging my parents and getting to Braern. After that, if I make it out alive, I'll have all eternity to craft the most devious plan to take him out.

But right now, at least with him on this earth, I'm not the only monster roaming the world. Even though that same monster killed my mother. Then again, in the last month, I've killed my fair share of Fae. I stop myself before I spiral down that dark path and get back to Azran.

I bring Nahtar close to him and focus on the blade as I take a deep breath to try and calm my racing heart. How can I light up Nahtar enough and not set his whole body on fire? The only time I saw the dark fire, it consumed everything in its wake.

Struggling to ground myself, I close my eyes and retreat inward. But my power seems to be evading me, just like in the caves. I don't notice the tears rolling down my face and my shaky hands until his calm voice stops me. "Ela. You don't have to do this. I have no right to ask for your help. I understand if you leave me. It's okay."

My eyes snap open as his contradictory nature hits me, forever puzzling me. Both the monster slaying enemies and the Fae seeking absolution. The fierce warrior and the one embracing death. The cold, violent High Lord, and the calm, almost tender, Fae in front of me.

"It's not that. I, I just don't know how to do it." I say before looking away.

Both his hands are covering mine now. "What did you feel when you first set Nahtar ablaze?"

"Anger. Betrayal. Confusion. I felt like I wanted to watch the world burn." It's the first time I admit that out loud. He's the only one I could ever say this to without fearing judgment or shame.

He nods. "Then focus on the opposite of that. Darkness cannot exist without light, nor death without life."

I've never looked at my power this way. Having only seen the darker side, I'm not even sure there's something else to it.

Still gripping my sword, I close my eyes and dive back into my own consciousness. I'm trying to recall memories of happiness and warmth when I'm brought back to our cabin in the Dark Forest and my father telling me stories. Although the stories were terrifying, his tender and proud gaze always eased my fears.

My mind drifts to another comforting thought. He would give the tightest hugs, a safe haven I miss so damn much. As I lose myself in memories of him, I can feel my power pulsing slowly and regularly through me, like a small stream coming down the mountains.

When I open my eyes again, Nahtar is softly glowing, and no dark flames are circling around its blade. Azran is studying me, but I stay focused on Nahtar and the memories as I bring the tip of the blade closer to his body. I quickly glance at him, and, seeing the determination in his eyes, press the flaming sword to his side.

His torn flesh sizzles under the blade, and the smell of his burnt skin fills the air. Nahtar's glow illuminates his grimacing facial features, clenched jaw, and pale skin, and I quickly remove it once the wound has been cauterized.

I release my power as Azran blows air sharply out of his nose, looking like he's about to faint. Frankly, I have no idea how he managed not to scream. My gaze wanders to his scar-decorated torso where I find the beginning of an explanation for his resilience. I wonder what he's seen, what he's gone through and survived.

With the moonlight above us, I can barely discern his face anymore. Needing to make sure he's okay, I instinctively extend a hand, reaching for him until my fingers come in contact with his bare chest.

"I'm okay, Ela. You did well, thank you." His hand is now on top of mine, his fingers brushing my skin, his breathing slowing down.

An unexpected wave of relief washes over me, and I remove my hand quickly. His Fae nature and power should help him heal well enough by tomorrow.

I listen to his breathing until it's regular again, and he's fallen asleep lying on his side. Then I bring my knees up, resting my chin on them with Azran at my back. Although I'm exhausted, I know that if I doze off, only nightmares await. So I postpone the inevitable, trying to focus on some point on the horizon.

⸺◆⸺

Azran

I don't remember falling asleep. I only remember the scorching pain of Nahtar on my side. When I wake up, it's still completely dark out, and my heart jumps out of my chest when I don't see Ela right away. After giving myself a few seconds to allow my eyes to adapt, I let out a slow breath. She's lying down a few feet away.

I watch her for a moment and realize she's shaking slightly. Her labored breathing confirms she's having nightmares. Without a second thought, I drag myself over to her, wrap my left arm around her, and bring her closer to me, hoping it will keep the nightmares at bay. I know all too well the price to pay for wielding powers. I relax against her when her breathing calms down moments later.

She adjusts in her sleep, arching her back to better fit against me. The rush of heat that courses through me is violently interrupted when her elbow settles in my wounded side. Air catches in my throat, and it takes me several minutes to recover regular breathing.

Despite the stabbing pain in my side, I don't move, not wanting to break the embrace I can only steal when she's asleep. Dawn is still several hours away, but I just lie there, carefully watching over her.

When she wakes up with the first light of day, it takes her a moment to realize the position we're in. She moves away abruptly, pushing me away with her elbow and sending another zap of pain through my body.

Her eyes widen as she realizes where her elbow has been this whole time.

"What... why didn't you-"

"I didn't want to wake you."

She stands up, looking at the horizon before facing me again. "How's your side?"

"Better." I turn to show her the wound neatly closed up and the burn that is healing.

The prospect of running for hours doesn't seem as dreadful. Strength has returned to my body and the pain is manageable, which is more than I hoped for. "We need to catch up with the rest of the units. Let's go."

I put my bloodied shirt back on, loosely buckle my armor over it, and then we're off, jogging across the rocky terrain. I cannot wait to leave this barren land behind us. I'm done eating dust and seeing nothing but sand and rocks.

A couple of hours later, the sun is high in the sky when we finally step into the Fae plains, sweat dripping down both of our foreheads. The first grass patches are a sight for sore eyes as nature reclaims its rights over this land. We slow down to a quick walk. We should be at the rendezvous point in a few hours, and the suspended truce she seems to have granted me will end.

"Ela, I know what I did is unforgivable and that nothing I could say would-"

Her menacing look stops me.

"Don't mistake me talking to you for something it's not." She stops dead in her tracks, pointing her finger at me. "Just because you couldn't deal with the added guilt of letting me get defiled by those bastards doesn't mean I forgot you murdered my mother. There's no coming back from that."

"You think it's guilt that made me come for you?" I jerk my head back as my eyebrows draw closer together, but she doesn't answer. "So, you're going to go back to pretending I don't exist, even though your staying means you're here to fight alongside us, alongside me?"

"I've realized now that nothing will shut you up. And I am here to murder the rebels responsible for my father's death and get my revenge on Braern. You're just a means to an end, even though every second in your presence disgusts me." There it is again, the sharp pain that had dimmed the past few days in her presence. "I know what I'm here to do. I clearly can't stop you from talking to me, but I can promise you're not going to like what I have to say."

I suppose that could be considered an improvement, so I don't argue.

We finally reach the rendezvous point and spot the camp further ahead of us. As we're getting closer, Cal rushes out to meet us, and even from a distance, I can see the tension on his face.

"Thank God you're both alive. What the hell happened to you? I was about to dispatch units, thinking you might have been captured or worse."

I give him a strong pat on the shoulder. "We're fine. How's everybody else?"

"Every soldier is accounted for, and we only suffered light casualties. By the latest report, we managed to put a severe dent in their numbers."

Relief instantly washes over me. Sending my people to war has always been and will always remain the heaviest burden to bear.

"Az. What happened to you? Did she do something reckless and stupid?" Cal is looking straight at Ela.

As fire sparks in her eyes, I cut in. "No, I did." Cal's eyes narrow but he doesn't persist. "She found this." I pull out the satchel still tied to my belt. "I've never seen anything like it."

Cal grabs the small bag and opens it up carefully.

"Me either. We should ask Mor to look into it." I nod.

Ela looks over to the camp and two blond-haired soldiers wave at her from a distance. Without a word, she leaves to meet with Wyn and Varan. They're so comfortable around her, grabbing her by the shoulders, and making her laugh. I loathe it. Exhausted, I don't repress the low growl that escapes my throat.

⸺ ◆ ⸺

Elanor

I'm relieved to find Varan and Wyn in one piece. They don't inquire about what happened, and I give them a grateful glance when they resume their usual banter. They tell me about their raids while I drink my fill of water and eat some food. Apparently, Varan won the bet, seeing the defeated look on Wyn's face.

My thoughts drift back to earlier today when I snapped at Azran. There's no questioning whether he deserves my wrath, but deep down, I know who my emotions are hurting most, and it's not him. Anger is the only voice my grief has ever had.

I've been to hell and back these past few weeks, trying to process what he's done and how to go from there, how to fight alongside him. With the revelation, the dam on my emotions started crumbling down. I've spent so much time trying to outrun them, and the years of unprocessed grief are crashing down on me. I can't carry on like this forever, being the instrument of my emotions. I need a way to deal with this head on. I'm still deep in my thoughts when Cal calls for us to move out.

The ride back to Averion is uneventful. I even nod off a few times on my horse, lulled to sleep by the regular movements. We ride through the night as everyone is eager to return to the capital.

When we stroll back into the gleaming city and the palace courtyard, a weird feeling comes over me as the white dome appears, towering over us. This place has harbored some of my worst moments, yet it's somehow become the closest thing I have to a home.

Savage is waiting by two familiar faces near the palace doors. I jump off my horse, and Savage meets me in a couple of swift leaps. Ignoring the looks I'm getting, I crouch down to meet him and pull him against me. His wet and raspy tongue finds my ear and licks it affectionately.

Vesta and Rina greet us shortly after, clearly relieved we're back. Vesta wraps me in a tight hug while Rina waits silently by us with a big smile on her kind face. Disregarding her usual reserve, I pull her in for a hug, too.

"Welcome back! You look like hell." Vesta shoots me a wink.

"Probably not my best look, but the rebels had it worse, I can tell you that."

They both accompany me toward the palace, and as we step inside, Vesta sends a glare in Cal's direction.

CHAPTER THIRTEEN

Azran

Mor meets Cal and me in my office a few days after the raid. His hair braided as always, the healer marches into the room carrying the small leather bag we gave him when we returned to Averion.

He bows slightly before handing the pouch back to me. "High Lord."

"Come on, Morthil. We've been fighting alongside each other for centuries, and you still hold on to the formalities." Cal cuts in, using Mor's full name and the healer twitches at the mention. A smile appears on Cal's face, satisfied with himself.

"Tell us what you've found, Mor." I interrupt before this degenerates into another bickering between these two.

"A whole bunch of nothing. After conducting all the magical and medical tests known to me, I have no idea what the powder is or does."

I let out a heavy sigh. "They had entire barrels of it, hidden away. Anything else you can tell us, Mor?"

"I can tell you it's not from this continent. And it's definitely not something that grows naturally."

I shake my head silently. Knowing Braern, I can't say I'm surprised. He's always had more than one trick up his sleeve. But this cannot be good.

"Thank you," I say before he leaves the office.

The minute Mor is out, Cal starts pacing around the room. "Whatever this is, it won't make a difference, Az. The entire legion is armed and ready. We have more than six thousand Fae to call upon when the time comes, and Mor is also gathering the healers." He nods to himself. "The only question remaining is where and when. Then we'll crush Braern's soldiers and finish him off."

Cal rarely reveals his true emotions, but whenever Braern is concerned, he can't hide the look of pure hatred on his face.

"I know. Keep me updated on all reports from our spies and scouts." He's still pacing in front of my desk. "Cal. We'll get him and put the centuries of battle and death behind us."

"Yeah, you're right. I will." He gives me a small smile and exits the room as well, leaving me to the pile of paperwork waiting for me. On days like this, I wish the affairs of the realm could wait.

After approving different budget requests for the army and signing new commerce licenses for the city, I head out. There's one more thing on my list of things to do today.

Since we've returned from the Eidune range, I haven't stopped thinking about Ela. When she closed up my wound, I could swear she was worried, and I can't get the thought out of my head. She hides her emotions behind a wall of rage, but I think it's a facade, and I have the feeling that she's been running away from it all for too long.

Hope is fueling me, a fool's hope I'm sure, but hope nonetheless. I can't let it go. It's all I have. I have to try, put the monster aside, and wait for her to see me, to see us.

Elanor

I'm back to my training routine with Vesta, and each day ends in troubled nights with Savage by my side. The only noticeable difference is I'm back in my own bed. Sleeping on the hard desert ground at least taught me to appreciate my mattress. I've also been practicing with Nahtar in my room, and I can now light it up without setting the whole place on fire.

Done with the day, I turn on the water faucet and undo my leather armor and pants. I'm standing in nothing but my white undershirt waiting for the tub to fill when Savage growls. I freeze, but the room falls silent again.

I quietly tiptoe towards my bedroom, readying myself for whatever awaits beyond the arched opening. Part of the room comes into view, and Savage is casually sprawled on the floor, his head tilted in welcome. My shoulders relax as I step into the bedroom.

Azran is standing a few steps from Savage, his long blond hair flowing on his shoulders, and I barely repress a huff.

"Sorry, I thought you-" He doesn't finish his sentence, and his eyes widen as he looks me up and down.

Unfazed by my own lack of apparel, I stand there, watching him fumble for his words, until he turns his back to me.

"What do you want?" I ask.

"I wanted to talk to you."

"Then talk." I walk past him to get to my wardrobe and grab some fresh towels.

"You seem busy. I can come back later."

"I can bathe and listen at the same time, you know. It's amazing what women can do these days." His jaw clenches tightly.

While I've decided not to seek revenge on him, at least not yet, I'm going to take a mean pleasure in doing what I do best. Talk back and push his buttons.

When I walk back into the bathing room, the tub is filled. I put the towel down, remove my undershirt and sink into the hot water. My skin tingles as my body adjusts to the temperature, the steam flushing my cheeks. This is by far the luxury I appreciate above all else.

I glance at the huge mirror occupying the entire wall to my left and spot him by the arch, his back still turned to me.

I start rubbing myself clean, adding ointments to my body still healing from the raid. I wash off the sweat from my hair, carefully detangling it with my fingers as I lather scented product in it.

He finally breaks the silence. "Back at the caves, what happened with your power?"

I finish rinsing my body while I consider his question. "What do you mean what happened? I used it to fight off the rebels."

I sink under water to rinse off my hair and stay there for a few minutes. I'm enjoying the quiet cocoon of warmth, well aware of his presence. When I can't hold my breath any longer, I stand up in the tub and wrap myself in the towel. I catch a glimpse of the High Lord, half turned toward me, the knuckles of his fisted hand turning white.

I finally get out and walk to the vanity as water drips on the floor. Now facing the mirror, the red scars contrasting with my pale skin inevitably attract my eye. My bruised legs also carry painful reminders of what happened in the small cave.

"Why didn't you use it on that bastard when he had you tied up?" Azran's penetrating gaze falls on me, his rage suddenly palpable. We lock eyes, and I take a moment before answering.

"I tried, but I got hit pretty hard on the head when they captured me. That, the lack of sleep and power already spent, I think I found one of my limits."

I can still feel Onas' fingers roaming my body sometimes. Even the thought makes the hair on my arms raise instantly. I repress the shiver of disgust and extend my hand to grab the hairbrush by the sink. As I'm running it through my wet hair, my eyes snap up to his when I realize he's still watching me.

"I'm sorry I didn't get to you sooner. I would have killed them all slowly and made them suffer endlessly if I had had the chance. No one will ever touch you again unless you ask."

I watch as his red eyes strangely glimmer in the light, and I look away again, unable to hold his gaze.

"Cal and I want you to join our strategy briefs with the captains of the legion starting tomorrow. My office at sundown."

By the time I look back up, he's gone.

Elanor

Over the next few days, I attend the daily meeting with the captains, and I'm surprised to find Mor alongside us. I didn't realize he was part of that close circle. The rest of the group is made up of half a dozen captains, mostly males, except one blond female. Each captain leads five squadrons, each squadron consisting of a hundred soldiers including a lieutenant.

I witness several heated arguments between Cal and Azran, Cal being the only person confident enough to challenge decisions and strategies. I admire how the general never backs down, even in the face of his angry High Lord. It speaks to their life-long friendship.

Everyone is growing tense as the days go by, and more reports of disturbances across the Fae cities keep coming in. Loyalist supporters are stirring up trouble, distracting our patrols, and we are nowhere closer to bringing Braern out in the open for a fight.

As inexperienced as I feel among those seasoned warriors, at least I'm learning about warfare. And if I'm being honest, I enjoy spending time here, as the room has a comforting warmth and scent, with its leather couches and fireplace.

One afternoon, I take a long stroll in the gardens with Savage. Ever my guardian angel at night, he is more than deserving of a nice walk, a reminder that I can be more than the disheveled and scared girl shaken by uncontrollable tremors and cold sweats after dark.

We quickly get there, as he knows the way by heart, and start wandering the grounds. Following a path through the small forest, Savage is trotting almost cheerfully, sniffing left and right and turning back towards me every so often to check I'm still following.

Anytime I come here, I'm always amazed by something new I hadn't noticed before. A small pond hidden behind bushes, a blossoming tree, or a new type of exotic vine reclaiming its natural right.

We turn a corner, and I stop dead in my tracks. Just a few feet away, Azran's back is turned to us, and he's looking in the distance, his hair flowing freely in the wind. Instead of his usual armor, he's wearing a simple dark tunic, and his massive sword is nowhere in sight.

I've stumbled upon a stolen moment, something secret and almost sacred. I'm about to turn back, but my attention is caught by the sight in front of him.

A gigantic willow tree overlooks a bed of ivory and onyx flowers, and nature's striking beauty hits me. With each gust of wind, the petals are dancing under the sunlight. And the smell is just heavenly, almost luring me in, daring me to make a bouquet and stick my face in it.

"Beautiful, isn't it?" His back still turned to me, his voice startles me. I was so hypnotized by the view I forgot for a moment who was here before me.

"I'm sorry, I didn't mean to disturb you. I'll go."

He immediately turns around. "Stay, please. This is as much yours to wander as it is mine." My gaze briefly drifts back to the willow as I try to come up with something to say in response.

"If you'd like, I could show you around?"

Guilt unfurls inside me as I remember the first time he offered to give me a tour, and before I even realize what I'm doing, I accept with an enthusiastic nod. Shit. I know I said I wanted to start facing my demons, but I might have skipped a few steps here.

He steps aside, inviting me to join him with a gesture of his hand. And, although tempting, I can't reasonably run away without looking like a scared little girl, so I comply.

As we start walking along the path, he breaks the silence. "It's peaceful, isn't it? Each living thing harmoniously grows among its peers. Some come from the most secluded parts of this world, others you could find just outside Averion. It took me decades to acquire it all and find a way to make them blossom here."

I've never seen him that open and vulnerable around anyone, especially not me. Unsure what to reply to that, I blurt out the first thing that comes to mind. "I didn't realize you knew so much about botany."

"There were very few things I had access to as a child that didn't entail endless torture. Books and plants were among them." His face turns to me, and he gives me a kind smile. "So when I was able to travel, I spent as much time as I could learning from each Fae race." I realize my eyes must betray my curiosity and sparkle with interest as he chuckles lightly.

"Tell me more," I ask, not seeing the point in trying to deny how eager I am to hear about his past.

"I learned the most with the Wood Fae, of course. They're masters of their craft, having the utmost respect for nature and life. The Water Fae taught me about trees and plants growing near water, like black ash or hyssop. And the Sun Fae have a more practical approach to their knowledge of things that grow, focusing mainly on crops and harvests."

"What about the Moon Fae?"

His gaze suddenly darkens. "I had already learned everything there was, and I left that place as soon as I could. Wars broke out everywhere not long after, and there was no time for all that anymore."

I ponder his words as we head deeper into the woods, surrounded by the rarest varieties of flowers, each shaped differently, but all of them white. The sweet perfume in the air is making me forget where I am and with whom I'm walking.

Suddenly a question forms in my mind, one I've had since I learned about his unique abilities.

"Would you do it again?" A frown appears on his forehead. "If you could go back in time, would you pick up the scroll again?"

"Yes." He answers without even taking a second to consider it. I tilt my head to the side, hoping he'll explain. "If I had to do it all again, I would. Bearing the burden of my power is a small price to pay to be put on your path. And living in a world where you exist will always be worth it, even if one moment with you is all I ever get."

I nod, unable to speak another word. Thankfully, he breaks the silence again. "I have to head back, Ela. Meetings." He motions towards the palace.

"Hmm. Yes, of course." And there it is. Reality rushing back to burst the imaginary truce bubble.

Right before he leaves, his face lights up. "Thank you."

I watch as he turns back and disappears behind some trees, mesmerized by this eerie moment we just shared.

I gaze in Savage's direction, who looks just as surprised as I am, before releasing an awkward chuckle. Still distraught by the interaction, we wander the grounds a while longer before heading back as well. I want to make it to the training center before dinner.

Elanor

The following strategy council is spent assessing which location could give us an advantage in the battle and discussing the latest updates on the rebels. They ambushed a commercial caravan en route to Morilanthe for the second time this month and attacked a Water Fae village. I would have thought the Eidune raid would have put a dent in their forces, but it's like they're everywhere and nowhere at the same time, and we can't seem to find them.

Even though I'm pretty much useless at those meetings, I find myself looking forward to attending. It's the only time I really get to study Azran without it being suspicious or too obvious. And I'm able to learn about the other Fae rulers and their territories.

There wasn't much information to get my hands on back at the library, so any insights are valuable. Especially on Amrynn, the Lady of the Moon Fae. I've noticed how one of the captains mentions her name with reverence in his tone and admiration in his eyes. With no drawing or portrait as a reference, I can only imagine how breathtaking she must be to elicit such a reaction.

Right when I think we're about to wrap this one up, Azran dismisses everyone but me. They all leave the room and I am left to face him.

"How are you doing with your training? How can we better prepare you?"

I hate how condescending he sounds. "I know you were basically born with a sword in your hand and have been killing since before you could read, but that doesn't mean you can talk to me like I'm a child." Right when I think I'm making progress in letting go of the anger and bitterness, the insufferable High Lord is back, and I just can't help myself.

"You're right. That's not what I meant to imply. I'm just curious about your abilities. Is there anything new you can do since we came back from the raid?" He's referring to what we discovered together while out in the desert. I shake my head, and he continues. "It took me years to master my power, so I thought maybe you would discover if there is something else to it."

"There's nothing but death to find. And it looks to me like you've just mastered how to slaughter the most enemies in a record time. Or is there something else you can do?" I can't repress the irritation already blooming in my heart.

He gives me a cold smile, though it doesn't reach his eyes.

"Strength and speed, I discovered later. I can focus my power in certain parts of my body to increase the impact of my blows, the velocity of my legs, etc."

"Cool. So that's how you became High Lord? By cheating when arm wrestling everyone who wanted your place?"

He closes the distance between us in a few steps, stopping right in front of me, a vein pumping on his forehead. "You think this is a game? It's our people's lives on the line."

"*Your* people's lives."

"When it comes down to the final battle, if you want to make it out alive, you'd better start taking this more seriously."

"What makes you think I intend on living after that?" A sardonic smile tugs on my lips.

A low growl tears from his throat. "I won't let you die."

I chuckle. "I will rip Braern's heart out of his chest or die trying. And there's nothing you can do about it. I carry death with me everywhere I go, remember."

"And I am the Lord of Bloodshed. I promise that out of the two of us, if only one makes it out alive, it will be you. I swear it on my life." As he pronounces these last words, a zap of energy goes through me, and my eyes widen.

"What did you do?" I push him away from me. "What the fuck was that?"

I freeze as I wait for him to explain himself, but he simply walks away. I follow him out of the office and into the corridor. When I realize he's not going to answer me, I sprint to catch up with him and throw myself hard at him to push him against the wall. "What the fuck was that?" I snarl, my face inches away from his.

He doesn't try pushing me back and just stares at me with his blood eyes. "If it comes down to it, it will be me and not you looking into Death's eyes. I just made sure of it."

Before I realize what I'm doing, I slap him hard in the face. I'm about to hit him again when his hand appears out of nowhere and tightly grabs my wrist.

"That's the second time you've slapped me. No one who's ever hit me has lived to do it again. Careful, now." His voice is so low I can barely hear him, but there is no mistaking the rage radiating from him.

"So hit me back. Unleash the monster I know looms beneath the surface." His gaze turns to surprise. "What? Like you wouldn't hit me?"

Still holding my wrist, he suddenly grabs my jaw with his other hand. My hand flies to his as I grip his forearm, trying to undo his deadly hold.

"Never. I have other things in mind for your pretty face, none of them respectable." All traces of anger have left his chiseled face and heat is coming from his body.

I try freeing myself from his grasp but instead, he twirls me around, still holding my face and wrist, and pins me against the wall.

"What? Is that not the monster you wanted to awaken?" He says, before letting me go with a dark laugh. I push him away and storm out.

Back in my room, I begin pacing around. Right when I think I have the upper hand, that insufferable jerk always finds a way to turn things around.

But once the rage recedes, guilt takes over. Or more like the absence of it when he's around me. I haven't forgotten what he's done, and yet, the hate is not as vibrant as it used to be.

It's the last thing I expected, and it feels like I'm betraying my mother. That's what haunts me at night. That, the memory of Onas in the tunnels, and the dead rebels in the forest. Everything is so twisted. I don't know who I am anymore. My only certainty is my propensity to bring death wherever I go.

⋯⋯◆⋯⋯

Elanor

After another troubled night, I visit Ilyana. There's something I need to get off my chest, and she's the only one who can help me with this matter.

When I knock on her door, she answers immediately, and her face lights up when she sees me. "Come on in, Ela. I'm so glad you decided to come back. And your wolf can come in, I don't mind."

Clearly, not much scares the old Fae, so I comply and lead Savage in. He goes to a corner of the room to lie down and attentively watch me as I sink into one of the leather armchairs.

Ilyana joins me shortly after with some hot tea, just like during my first visit. But this time she just stares at me, waiting for me to speak. Unsure how to start, I go with a relatively innocent request. "I want to hear more about my mother."

"I'll tell you anything you want to hear, my dear. But I can tell something else is troubling you. Talk to me." Damn. I didn't realize I was that easy to read.

"We both know who killed her, I think." She motions for me to keep going. "I'm around him all the time. He's saved my life on countless occasions, and he's also the most unnerving Fae I've ever met. I know I should hate him, and most of the time, I do."

"But other times?" Ilyana encourages me with a kind smile.

"I don't know! I'm just so confused because sometimes I don't even know if it's hate I'm feeling anymore. I should have killed him weeks ago when I learned the truth. I even had an opportunity to just let him die, without having to carry the burden of the responsibility. And yet, I didn't take it."

My vision suddenly blurs, and tears start rolling down my face. The old Fae gives me a strange look and grabs my hand gently.

"Do you know how your father and mother fell in love?" She says, changing the topic. I shake my head, trying to stop the tears from falling. "She tried to kill him." My eyes widen at the revelation. "He had cost her a promotion she had been working toward for years. In a fit of rage, she headed to his barracks, her knife in hand, ready to make him regret his actions. She was a fiery woman, I'll tell you that." I chuckle through the tears at the thought of her marching into the garrison, full of rage and thirsting for revenge. That sounds familiar.

"The line between hate and love is fine, my dear."

Unsure what to make of that, I ask her the question that's been burning through me for days.

"Did you forgive him? Did you forgive your High Lord for killing her?"

She doesn't hesitate. "A long time ago. I couldn't live with that hate and resentment. It eats at you if you let it. I know he did what he thought was best at the time, and I also know how much he regrets it."

"What do you mean?"

"Every year on her birthday he visits me. He comes to talk about Aerín and drops off the most beautiful flowers. There's more to him than the monster he's so carefully crafted to appear as his true nature. Throughout the years, I've seen him rise to be our High Lord and build Averion, making it into the city it is now, a safe haven for Fae and humans alike, filled with life."

"I don't know if I have it in me to do the same, Ilyana."

"No one is asking you to, my child. We don't forgive for others' sake, we forgive for ours. Don't let the guilt eat you alive when your mother would be so proud of you and who you're becoming." She reaches over the table to cup my cheek. "Her death broke my heart, and yet look at how much beauty she also brought into the world. Remember her for that, not for some revenge you think she would want you to hold on to. That was not her."

I take my leave shortly after. Needing to clear my head, I take a walk through Averion. I've barely explored the city since I arrived, so I stroll around in the Arts quarter, going from shop to shop, surrounded by vibrant colors. With the city buzz creating a semblance of ordinary, I'm just another Fae walking the capital

Now out of Ilyana's quarter, I get to the heart of the city and step into a huge plaza filled with merchants and citizens rushing from one stall to the other. Vendors are heckling passersby and I spot several humans among the crowd, living in harmony with the Fae. This view is still so strange and new to me. But it also brings me a renewed sense of comfort and pride. I never thought this to be possible, and I'm starting to understand why so many have rallied behind the High Lord and his vision. I realize a Fae-Human alliance is still far off, but it doesn't seem quite as impossible as it did before I came to Averion.

Savage is staying close to me, his presence alone creating a comfortable space around us that no one dares disturb.

I stop by a stall displaying stunning jewelry, rings, necklaces, and earpieces. Hypnotized by the shiny beads and gemstones, I extend a hand to hover over the beautifully crafted pieces.

I turn around when Savage's low growl sounds, a hand on the hilt of my knife, to find a wide-shouldered Fae standing in front of me.

"Your pet is in my way."

"My *pet* will rip out your throat if I tell him to. Move along, there's plenty of space to go around." I turn back around to take another look at an earpiece I spotted earlier.

Savage growls behind me again, only louder this time. In a second, I unsheathe my knife and put it on the large Fae's throat while sending a quick signal for my wolf to stand down with my other hand.

"Maybe you didn't hear me the first time, asshole. Get lost."

A crowd has gathered around us now, attentively watching the scene.

"I'm not scared of your toothpick, darling. Who the fuck are you, anyway? Walking around like you own the place. That doesn't sit right with me." He leans forward, letting my knife dig into his skin.

A familiar voice says. "Relax, Rick. You're talking to my friend, Ela, who happens to be under our High Lord's protection. Also, her wolf doesn't really care who you are and would probably have sunk his teeth into you already had she not given him the order to stand down."

Vesta emerges from the crowd, wearing a dark blue long-sleeved dress, her red hair loose around her shoulders, stunning as ever.

"V. I didn't realize she was with you," Rick says as he steps back. I lower my hand and sheathe the knife.

"Sorry, Ela. Rick tends to be a little territorial around here. He usually knows everything and everyone that comes through the plaza and takes his role to heart."

I carefully assess the guy before giving him a quick nod.

"Right. Sorry. I just saw you there with your wolf. I thought you were intimidating people and could be a threat or something."

"I'll admit Savage doesn't give off the friendliest vibes at first. I was simply admiring the jewelry on display."

He extends his massive hand toward me in a peace offering, and I shake it briefly while Savage observes the whole scene attentively.

"Good. Now that introductions have been made, we'll let you get back to your day, Rick. Thanks!" She waves him off and takes my arm under hers. The poor guy looks disappointed by the sudden dismissal, but Vesta turns to me. "Look at you making new friends. You're a natural!"

"Very funny. V?" I raise an eyebrow.

"We had a thing a while back. Nothing serious. Just fun."

"Right. So all your lovers call you V?"

"Most of them do. Others just call me goddess," she says with a laugh.

"Right."

"I'm glad I ran into you. I'm heading over to do some shopping, and I could use a second opinion."

I give another longing glance at the earpiece on the stall and follow her across the plaza, with Savage right behind us.

CHAPTER FOURTEEN

Elanor

Vesta walks into a shop down the main street and I send Savage away before following her in. He knows his way back to the garrison and clearly won't be needed in there.

Once inside, I'm overwhelmed by the amount of clothing surrounding us, but Vesta dives right in as the shopkeeper greets us.

"What are you looking for, V?"

"Dresses, shoes, anything stunning, really," she says from the other side of the shop. Well, that doesn't help narrow it down. "And we're finding something for you, too. You can't keep walking around looking like a soldier every hour of the day."

She meets me by a rack of clothes, dresses already piling up on her arms. The shopkeeper steps in to help her out and puts everything by the changing rooms at the back.

Before I can dissuade her, V pushes me into one of the stalls and hands me a mountain of clothes. "Try these on. I'll try on my selection, and then we can show each other."

I'm about to argue, but a squeal of joy sounds on the other side of the panel, and I stop myself. One carefree afternoon won't hurt me.

Knowing Vesta, I'm expecting to find nothing but revealing dresses showing three-quarters of my body, but to my surprise, she's also picked some day dresses that could accommodate Nahtar on my back. I try one of those on first and step out of the room.

Looking at myself in the mirror, it fits perfectly. The long-sleeved black velvet dress hugs my waist nicely and flows around my legs. The delicate fabric is soft under my touch and comfortable enough for me to wear all day.

"That looks great on you." Vesta's head pops out of her changing room. "You're getting it."

Heat rises to my cheeks. "I can't. I don't have any money."

She explodes in laughter. "Ela, you're the High Lord's guest. We'll just have the bill sent to the palace."

"Wait. I can do that?" My brows draw closer together.

"Of course. Now, how do I look?" She fully opens the curtains.

"Gorgeous," I say, smiling. The emerald dress complements her eyes and hair beautifully.

After trying on half of the dresses in the shop for the better part of the afternoon, I order the simple velvet dress in black, grey, and navy. I also couldn't resist a black satin flowy dress with padded shoulders encrusted in gems and flared long sleeves. I can easily wear a thin armored vest underneath it, and to be honest, it suits me.

Finally, Vesta convinced me to add a ball gown to that pile. It's ethereal, light blue, with beaded emerald gems along its V-neck cut, long asymmetrical sleeves, and a flowy skirt. The fabric is cut open on the front below the waist in triangles, revealing the skin underneath. And Vesta orders twice as much. The shopkeeper confirms we'll receive everything by the next day, and we head back into the street.

"Let's go get some food and drinks," she says.

I'm having so much fun I simply follow her, embracing this joyful moment. I'm starting to feel like... well, like I belong in this city and with these people.

We end up on the terrace of a small tavern on the east side of the city, right by the Aiduin River. A warm wind brushes my face, and I close my eyes, breathing in the scent of the air. I release a blissful sigh after taking in the buzz of activity around us.

When I open my eyes, a handsome white-haired Fae is dropping off our drinks and an assortment of appetizers in front of us. The tight shirt he's wearing shows off his defined muscles, and that's all I can look at. When I finally look up, his hypnotizing blue eyes and sharp jawline do me in.

Once he's gone to another table, V elbows me gently in the ribs. "Well, look at that! His name is Ayas, by the way. Excellent choice, might I add. He knows what he's doing in bed."

I turn to her in shock. "Have you slept with the whole city?"

Her laugh fills the air. "What can I say? I don't like sleeping alone. I'm happy to share recommendations if you need some." She shoots me a wink.

"I mean, I wouldn't say no if he was interested, that's for sure! Maybe I'll get myself a birthday present," I say as a smile appears on my face.

"Did you say birthday?!"

Shit. I should have known better. She's not going to let that go. "Please don't make this into a big deal. It's in a few days."

"Iiiih! I can't believe you didn't tell me before!"

"I don't want to do anything. I'm not huge on birthdays. I don't think I've celebrated mine in years."

"Nonsense. I'm getting you something. Or someone, maybe?" She smirks.

"I can figure that out on my own, thanks." I dismiss her suggestion with a wave of my hand.

"When's the last time you invited someone into your bed? Wait! Have you even tried it out as a Fae?"

"Of course not! When would I have had time for that?" I suddenly blush at the memory of Azran and me in the training center. "Plus, I think it's overrated."

"Overrated? Oh no, L. I think you've been picking the wrong partners. Wait. So you've never..." My brows draw closer together. "Well, you know. Orgasmed?"

"Shhh. Could you be any louder?"

"Damn, L. We gotta find you someone to explore that with," she says, before taking a sip of her drink. Her eyes are now wandering the terrace, on the hunt for a potential candidate.

"Stop that! You're killing me. I'm fine." I shove her shoulder gently.

"All right." She puts one hand up in surrender. "You just let me know if you need any pointers, then!"

"Will do." To avoid further inquiries, I try the drink in front of me, dipping my lips in the purple liquid. The alcohol burns down my throat nicely as I take my first sip. It's lovely.

Already emboldened by the liquor, I move on to another topic. "So, what's going on with you and Cal?" She narrows her eyes at me and doesn't answer. "Oh, oh. What's up, V? Are you still mad at him?"

"You could say that." I nod, waiting for her to continue. "After the raid, I confronted him. I've known him for ages, and he's never punished me like that. He said it wasn't a sanction and that he just trusted me more with keeping things in check back at the garrison if you guys happened to be delayed or something."

"All right. That doesn't sound too bad, does it?"

"Yeah, except it turns out it's complete bullshit!" She spits out. "The bastard later told me that he didn't want to put me at risk unnecessarily and that he cared about me."

"What an asshole, really," I say as I roll my eyes.

"You don't get it, L. He says he wants me, he wants us. After all this time, he finally has the courage to admit his attraction to me and then tells me he wants me to live in a golden cage while he goes off to war. What a prick!"

"Is that really what he said he wants for you?" I raise my eyebrows.

"No," she says. "It doesn't matter anyway. I told him to go to hell."

"What? I thought you liked him?"

"I only told you that I had a crush on him once. And that was a very long time ago." She pauses for a moment to take another sip of her drink. I do the same, giving her time to open up. "I met someone else after that. A soldier in another unit. I was so young, completely and utterly in love. Elis was the most handsome Fae I had ever seen. He had long black curly hair, and his entire body was tattooed. He swept me off my feet in a matter of days." A sad smile tugs on her lips.

"What happened?" Her use of the past tense didn't go unnoticed.

Tears are beginning to fill her emerald eyes and I put my hand on hers, pressing gently.

"Turns out he was my mate. We thought we had eternity ahead of us, but he was killed in the unifying wars. It took me a hundred years to recover." She swallows a lump in her throat.

"I'm so sorry, V."

"Thank you." She looks away. "You know, most Fae don't even meet their true mate, and finding another one is almost unheard of. But as much as that connection is the strongest thing you'll ever experience in this life, you also become a prisoner of the mating bond. You don't just share a bond, part of your soul merges with theirs." She turns her head toward me again, letting me see the ocean of hurt concealed in her gaze. "So you can imagine the price to pay if one of you dies. After it happened, I thought about killing myself every single day for years. I don't ever want to go through that again."

"How did you pull through?"

"Revenge. I completely lost it during the wars and butchered so many people, Ela."

I squeeze her hand a little tighter. "I know what it feels like to want to watch the world burn. When you have nothing else to lose, you're invincible. The mating bond sounds like the opposite of that. I don't ever want that. I don't ever want to be weakened like that."

Vesta tilts her head to the side and gently presses my hand back before letting go.

"Look at us trying to give each other advice about men when we're both set on running away from them all," she says, before bursting out laughing. I'm about to argue, but the ridicule of our conversation hits me, and I join her, giggling uncontrollably.

After receiving several disapproving glances from other tables, we manage to calm down enough to order another cocktail.

"Oh, and I've been meaning to ask you, V. What's the story with Cal and Azran?" One of her eyebrows shoots up, and a big smile tugs on her lips. Oh no. She's getting the wrong idea. "Come on, it's for research purposes! I'm trying to understand who I'm allying myself with."

"Right," she chuckles. "Azran met Cal during the clan wars. They started off on opposite sides until Cal saved his life. Azran had gotten separated from his unit, and a group of Sun Fae found him. They recognized the son of the Moon Fae Lord and wanted to kill him, but Cal stepped in front of them. He was the best fighter in his unit, so they didn't dare challenge him and cast him away instead, labeling him a traitor." She takes a sip of her drink. "That's when it all started. I think he was the only one who didn't judge Az's lineage, his mixed blood. And that's also when our High Lord realized uniting the Fae was possible. On top of saving his life, Cal gave him hope, you know?" I nod back, waiting to hear the rest. "Azran became Lord of the Moon Fae not long after that, and Cal never left his side. They became brothers by choice along the way, with Cal probably being the only person in this world who gets to see Azran's true feelings, and vice versa."

"That's a hell of a story."

"It sure is. Now, enough about them!" She shoots me a wink.

Several rounds of drinks later, we call it a night and head back to the palace. As we walk together, we continue joking, chatting, and laughing hysterically in the night. My legs are a little wobbly, and at this point, I'm not sure who's holding who. We part ways once we reach the garrison, and I finish on my own.

I get to the stairs leading to the upper levels my rooms are on, and my vision blurs a bit, but I hold on to the cold railing and make it to my floor.

With my door in sight, I walk along the corridor with one hand on the wall to help me stay upright. Damn. Maybe I should have slowed down a bit on the drinks. But I can't repress the dumb smile from blooming on my face.

"Where were you?"

Startled, I turn around and almost fall on my face, Azran's arm steadying me at the last minute.

"You missed the war council. Where were you?" He asks me again, his chest rising rapidly. He looks so... alarmed.

"None of your busy, uh, business." I free my arm and regain a semblance of self-control.

"Are you drunk?" He squints his eyes at me, and worry subsides for a more usual air of frustration.

The fact that he gets annoyed so easily when it comes to me makes me smile widely. "I was out, living a little. You should try it sometime."

He releases a low growl as he gets dangerously close to me, and his gaze catches on fire. His scent hits me, and a rush of heat courses through me.

"Don't you worry about me having fun, little one." Right, I'm sure the High Lord can have his fair share of fun whenever and wherever he wants. I manage to put a disgusted look on my face, slightly scrunching my nose.

His mouth gets dangerously close to my ear in response. "You can't fool me, you know. When I'm near you, I can smell it all over you. Your arousal."

My breathing instantly accelerates as his words register. Unable to control myself much longer, I step away and head to my room.

"See you tomorrow, little one."

His voice follows me, like a murmur in my ears, until I close my bedroom door.

Once inside, Savage greets me with a whimper as I run my fingers through his warm fur. Moments later, I undress, slip into my nightgown and fall asleep when my head touches the pillow.

Images of dead bodies, dark flames, and death start flooding my dreams, turning them into nightmares. I wake up in the midst of a particularly dreadful one. In the dream, I'm alone in the middle of a battlefield, surrounded by corpses, stepping on torn body parts, my boots making a squishy sound as I walk the bloodied grounds. Everyone I know is among the cadavers, covered in ashes, some bodies still ablaze and burning. I swear I can even smell the burnt flesh. There's nothing but death, and I'm all alone.

When I open my eyes, still shaken up, I find Savage on the bed next to me, attempting to soothe me. Drenched in sweat, I get up and remove my nightgown to get changed. As I'm standing there naked, I feel a deep tug on my power.

Following my instinct, I close my eyes and focus inward. I start calling on my power, and it comes effortlessly. Darkness surrounds me, its obscurity almost hugging me, a familiar and comforting presence, welcoming me in its warmth. When I open my eyes again, I'm wrapped in dark shadows twirling around me. I can tell my irises have darkened as my vision is lightly veiled.

I walk up to the mirror and realize I'm nothing but shadows. I can barely see myself through the black haze. I move my arms around, and the dark ribbons follow each of my movements, perfectly adjusting. I guess I can add cloaking myself in shadows to the list of things I can do. That could come in handy.

Savage suddenly growls at me, wary of this new trick. "It's okay, it's just me," I say as I call back the shadows, revealing my naked body. He calms down and walks toward me to lean his furry head on my legs. I get changed and try going back to sleep, unsuccessfully.

At dawn, I get up to start another day of training and endless meetings. And later that day, at the war council I attend, I keep my latest discovery to myself.

Azran

I'm pacing in my room, trying to remain in control of my emotions and not walk into her bedroom. It's been like this for days. Ever since we came back from the Eidune Range, her terror explodes through the bond. Just like in the desert, she's having nightmares.

But here, there's nothing I can do about it. She barely tolerates me as it is, even though I know she feels at least part of what I feel when I'm with her.

There's the terror, the helplessness, and then the part that scares me the most. It's the deepest silence, strangely comforting, almost welcoming. Until it turns into nothingness and an endless void echoes on the other side of the bond.

The first time I felt it, I thought she had died. My heart stopped, and I was in the corridor, about to burst through her door, when I sensed her again. It took me hours to calm down and fall back to sleep. And then it happened again on other nights. I felt her disappear and come back, each incident scarier than the last, as I was left wondering if this would be the final one.

I don't know how much longer I can endure this. Sensing her presence everywhere I go feels like agony. Yet, the further away she is, the harder it is. It's like I'm being crushed by an invisible weight. And when I'm around her, it's sometimes worse, with her rejections and jabs like nails to my heart. But if that's the best I can get, so be it.

❧

Elanor

Vesta's head pops in through the door of my bedroom. "L!"

"Hey, V! Were we not supposed to meet at the training center for evening practice?" I say, as I'm still gathering my equipment. She doesn't answer me right away, so I turn to her. She is wearing the emerald gown we got together, and she's standing by the entrance with both hands behind her back. "Oh no. What did you do?"

"I may or may not have thrown a little something in your honor." She shines her brightest smile but freezes as I don't return it and my brows draw closer together. "Kidding. I did no such thing!"

"Really?" A wave of relief washes over me, instantly calming my rising panic.

"No. I totally did," she blurts out with a laugh. "Come on, don't make that face. It's going to be fun! You can wear the beautiful dress we chose together, and I got you a little something to go with it. Happy birthday, Ela!"

She pulls a package from behind her back and hands it to me. I give her a disapproving glance, but open up the present. My jaw drops when the wrapped box reveals a stunning pair of silver cuffs encrusted with light blue gems. "Holy shit. That is absolutely gorgeous and completely outrageous. This must have cost a fortune!"

"Nonsense. They'll suit you like a glove. And I had to redeem myself for throwing you a surprise party, anyway," she says with a chuckle. "Now, get ready. We have a party to attend!"

I hesitate a moment longer before pulling her in for a hug. "V, thank you so much." She returns it happily and helps me put on the dress and matching cuffs. The light blue fabric complements my brown hair nicely, and the whole look is pretty... angelic. Ironic.

When we get to the throne room, everybody is there and came bearing gifts. I try not to cringe at the thought of all the attention, and thankfully, Wyn and Varan don't hesitate a second before greeting us. They hand me the most beautiful set of knives I've ever seen, offering a welcome distraction from the anxious thoughts already blooming in my mind.

"You shouldn't have, guys. This is too much."

"Come on, Ela. Anything for you," Wyn says.

"They're actually twin daggers," Varan adds with a wink that sends me laughing.

"Of course. I should have known better with you two. Thank you!"

Cal saunters in next to wish me a happy birthday and gift me a book on warfare. A typical gift from our general. I thank him and let him get back to the party. Before he joins the other guests, he glances at Vesta, who won't even look at him.

A few minutes later, she is called away by a group of Fae waving at her. She gives me a worried look that I dismiss with a gesture of the hand. "Go! I'll see you later." I can manage a Fae party on my own, right? Right.

After putting the gifts down on a table not far from the entrance, I turn back to face the room and momentarily forget how to breathe.

Thousands of candles of all sizes are hanging from the ceiling, lighting up the center of the ballroom and contrasting beautifully with the dark ribbons circling the pillars and the black velvet curtains covering the tapestries. A sky of lights in an ocean of darkness.

A scent, sweet and hypnotizing, strangely familiar, catches my attention next. Ivory and onyx flowers are diffusing their heavenly perfume all around the room. The more I focus on them, the more they seem to pop up everywhere, on the columns, the high tables, and in guests' hair. They look exactly the same as the ones I saw in the gardens days ago. Wait. Did Azran help arrange this?

Tucking that piece of information somewhere in my brain, I bring my focus back to the party in front of me. Faes are circulating around the room, carrying trays full of cocktails, and I get myself a drink that I start sipping slowly, set on being more careful tonight than back at the solstice or the tavern. Speaking of the bar, I spot Ayas walking toward me. He's even more handsome than I remember.

"Hello, birthday girl. Happy birthday!" He flashes a smile which somehow makes him even more attractive.

"Thank you. I'm Ela, by the way."

"Ayas. You and Vesta were at the bar a few days ago, right?"

"Right. Sorry if we got a little loud that night," I say, remembering the conversation revolved primarily around the specimens of the other sex.

His unrestrained laugh fills the air. "Don't worry. I know how Vesta gets when she drinks."

"She's definitely something!" His contagious laughter brings a smile to my face.

"To be honest, I couldn't help but overhear you might be looking for a partner. So, I'd like to volunteer for the job if you're interested." He winks at me before offering me another stunning smile.

Heat flushes my cheeks as I consider what he's offering. I didn't realize Fae could be this blunt when it comes to... well, that.

"Good to know, Ayas," I say with an awkward smile.

A commotion echoes behind me, and I turn around in an attempt to pinpoint the cause of it.

"You know where to find me, Ela," Ayas adds, still flashing his cheeky smile.

I'm watching him graciously walk away when Mor comes into view. Wearing his usual braid, he's ditched the armor for a more casual shirt and pants ensemble. He gives me a small smile that I return before resuming his conversation with a handsome red-haired Fae male I don't recognize from a distance.

"Ela!" I twirl around as my name is called out and find Thalea and Ilyana coming toward me. They pull me into a tight hug. "Happy birthday, beautiful," Thalea says.

"Thank you. I'm so glad you're here," I say, genuinely happy to see them both. This party is taking a turn for the better.

***

Azran

I'm still watching her walking around the room, looking celestial in that blue gown, when Cal comes to stand by my side after giving her his gift. I can tell something is bothering him, and I bet it has something to do with that flamboyant Fae. Cal is not used to rejection, so Vesta must be giving him a hard time.

I'm about to push some buttons when another scene catches my attention. A white-haired Fae is talking to Ela. I get closer to try and make out what they're saying.

"...looking for a partner. So, I'd like to volunteer for the job if you're interested."

"What the fuck did he just say to her?"

Cal pulls me back right when I'm about to lunge at this nobody. "Get a grip, Az! She can make her own decisions. And need I remind you, she doesn't owe you anything." I throw a dirty look in his direction even though I know he's speaking the truth. "Come on, let's grab a drink. If you want things to change, you should tell her."

"She'd laugh in my face. Or put her knife to my throat."

He shakes his head. "You won't know until you try. She could surprise you."

Cal gives me a worried glance as I down my drink, but I don't acknowledge it and order another one. He is called away by a group of soldiers wanting to share a toast with their general moments later.

My mood is darkening by the minute until she strolls towards me with a drink in hand. I watch as her hips roll, and the blue dress shows off her voluptuous cleavage.

"You could have given me a warning," Ela says when she's within hearing distance.

"Where's the fun in that? And I wouldn't have robbed myself of the opportunity to see you in that captivating dress," I say, emboldened by the drinks in me. "I'm glad my money is being put to good use."

She blushes at that mention. "Vesta told me-"

"Take all the money you want. If I had known the mention of money would make you blush, I would have brought it up earlier." I raise my hand to stroke her cheek but stop myself halfway. "So many more ways I could bring color to those cheeks."

God. I love seeing her mouth drop slightly and her eyes widen for just a second before she regains her composure.

Pretending she didn't hear me over the music, she switches topics. "Sorry about the other night. I may have drunk one too many cocktails. I'm not sure what I said to you, but I'm sure it was nothing nice."

"Don't apologize. It's lovely to see you having fun. I was worried about you is all." She swallows. "How are you sleeping these days?" I ask softly, even though I already know the answer to that question.

"Do they ever go away?" Her voice is almost a whisper as she gazes into my eyes. I'm not sure what she's hoping to see in them, but I nod, knowing damn well that mine have never left me. Except for that one night, out in the desert. "I'm just one door away if you ever need me."

Her face drains of all color. "Your room is next to mine?"

I burst out laughing. "You didn't know?"

"How would I have known?"

"I did offer to give you a tour when you first arrived. It's not my fault you turned it down." I say with a shrug, a smile still tugging on my lips.

"Right."

My thoughts drift to the small box inside my vest pocket.

"Well, I'll leave you to enjoy the party," Ela says, just as I gather the courage to grab it. She walks away before I can ask her to stay.

CHAPTER FIFTEEN

Azran

It's well after midnight when I'm standing in front of her door. I lift my arm to knock but freeze mid-air, my heart racing wildly.

I retrace everything that's happened since I met her, everything I've said and done to her for the millionth time tonight. Finally, I take a deep breath in and knock twice.

She opens the door seconds later, still wearing her blue gown, her hair falling down loosely on her shoulders. She's the most precious thing I've ever laid eyes on.

"May I come in?"

She steps back to let me in before closing the door. Savage is not around tonight, and it's just the two of us.

I don't give myself more time to overthink and simply turn to face her before taking the small velvet box out of my pocket and handing it to her. "Happy birthday, Ela."

Her eyes widen as she extends a hand and takes the box. Her gaze jumps between the gift and me, and I stop breathing, bracing myself.

She opens it up and her lips part. "How did you know?" I take the golden earpiece from its case as I raise an eyebrow at her. "V. Of course." She answers her own question.

"May I?" I lift the sparkling ear jewel to her face.

Her chest rising rapidly, she lifts up her hair, pulling it away to give me access to her delicate ear. I step closer to her and position the gold jewel on the tip of her ear, securing it by pressing lightly on it. It's like it was made for her. It fits perfectly.

Our bodies inches away from each other, her sweet perfume is almost intoxicating. I restrain myself from brushing my fingers down her hair and step away to let her admire herself in the mirror.

She lifts a hand to her ear, gently touching the jewel. "It's stunning. Thank you." I watch as her fingers gently explore the stones decorating the gold, in awe that she is letting me see this other side of her.

Her eyes lift to mine, and I can't help myself. I come right behind her, stopping a fingerbreadth away, feeling her heat radiating against me, and she tenses.

"Ela. Please." Cal's words come back to me. "Tell me you don't feel the same way I do when we're around each other. Tell me you don't want to feel my touch on you." My gaze is still fixed on her. "Tell me to go, tell me you don't want me."

⋯◆⋯

Elanor

I can't focus on anything other than his reflection in the mirror. His handsome face. His red eyes turning hazel when he's looking at me. His hair falling down on his strong shoulders. His sharp jaw and his inviting lips.

"Put me out of my misery, Ela. I want all of you. I accept all of you. The darkness and the light."

I slowly turn around to face him, and at this moment, I realize any remnants of guilt I was carrying are gone.

"What light? I've killed and I've burned. My life is nothing but death."

"It doesn't have to be. I've seen it." The question is frozen on my lips. "Your light. Your longing for life. You radiate the brightest fire when you take down the walls." Suddenly my eyes are watering, exhausted from trying to keep my defenses up, his words the key to melting them all. My last resistance is holding on by a thread. "Little one, you hide your smile because you're afraid to light up the entire world with it. But you don't have to be strong all the time, not with me. And I don't want to pretend around you anymore."

He lifts his hand to my face, stopping inches away, letting me decide, and I lean almost imperceptibly into his touch. I close my eyes as he strokes my cheek gently and takes away the fear.

He cups my face with both hands, lifting it slightly, and I open my eyes to stare into his. Ever so gently, he leans forward, brushing his lips over mine, removing the last barrier holding me back. He pulls back to give me another opportunity to back out, but I don't want to.

I crash into him, needing to feel his lips on mine. He responds immediately, pulling me closer to him and wrapping an arm around my waist. My mouth parts, and his tongue slides in, gently exploring. I meet each stroke eagerly, sparks lighting up in my core. A moan escapes from my throat, and my hands are on his chest, unable to refrain. Feeling his strong body under my fingers, I grip his shirt aggressively.

The next second, he's lifting me up in the air, and I wrap my legs around him, my heart pounding in my chest. His hand drifts towards the opening of my gown, going up my legs, sending electric sparks down my spine. He's now gripping my thighs and devouring my mouth. Arousal building inside me, I start grinding on him, needing to feel his hardness against me. A low growl escapes his throat.

He carries me to the bed in the middle of the room and gently lays me down in the center of it with my legs hanging off the edge. He pulls away briefly to reveal the ravenous look in his eyes.

"Are you sure you want this, Ela?"

Fuck the consequences. I've spent weeks in a constant state of fear, afraid to live, afraid to feel, afraid to do anything, and I'm so tired of it. So yes, I'm sure. I grab his shirt and pull him back to me, our lips crashing together.

He's kissing my neck eagerly, and my skin is on fire under his touch. His hands, still roaming my legs, find the edge of my dress and lift it up until I'm completely exposed. He pulls off my underwear with expert hands and starts caressing my inner thighs as his kisses move from my neck to my cleavage.

He makes quick work of tearing off the blue fabric and grabs my nipple in between his teeth. Gently tugging and sucking, zaps of pain mixed with pleasure send me grinding hard against his hand, needing to feel him closer. Wetness is pooling between my legs, his fingers teasing me but not coming close to where I need them.

"Touch me," I snarl as I lift my head to look at him. A feral smile appears on his face and he kneels between my legs. My eyes widen as he grips my thighs, pulls me closer to the edge of the bed in a tug, and parts my legs wide open.

I let out a loud moan when his warm mouth lands on me, his tongue gently circling the bud of nerves in between my legs. Tension builds up with each stroke. He reaches for my breast with one of his hands and tugs lightly on my nipple, sending pure bliss through me.

Right when I think I can't take the intensity anymore, he slides a finger between my wet folds and inside me. I'm panting hard, reaching for something to grab ahold of, when I find purchase on his blond hair. My hips are now fully grinding into his mouth, and my eyes roll to the back of my head when he slides a second finger inside.

"Az." I let out a gasp, still tightly gripping his hair. Overwhelmed by the intensity, my emotions are spiraling. Panic suddenly strikes me, and I push him away. "Stop!"

He pulls away immediately and takes several steps back. "What's wrong? Did I hurt you?"

"I, I don't know. I've never felt this much…" I'm heaving and struggling to find my words.

He's standing in the corner of the room, waiting for me to explain, when he finally realizes what I'm trying to say. "Pleasure?"

Heat rises to my cheeks and I close my legs and sit up. I drop my gaze when his eyes widen, unable to meet his stare.

"I can't lose control. Ever. With my power-"

"You don't scare me, Ela." He's in front of me in a few steps, cupping my cheek and lifting my head to face him. "I want you to lose control with me. I want to feel you unravel under my tongue. I want to hear you scream my name as I feel you come around me." A devilish smile appears on his face.

⁂

Azran

I scan her features, giving her time to decide. She's so beautiful. The only thing I want right now is for her to come on my face, to feel her warmth drip all over my jaw and in my mouth.

"Do you trust me?" My heart tightens as the words leave my lips.

After a pause, she nods, and relief flows through me.

I lift up my shirt to remove it and start undoing my pants. She's watching me, hunger still dancing in her eyes. God, I love that sight.

Once I'm completely bare before her, I walk around the bed and join her on it. I help her sit on her knees, remove her torn dress, and toss it aside.

Kneeling behind her, I slowly caress her body, starting on her back, shoulders, and arms. I kiss her everywhere I touch her, now focusing on her neck, and goosebumps bloom all over her warm skin. My chest against her back, she presses into me, feeling me hard against her ass.

Still kissing her neck, I pull her close while my hands roam her stomach, chest, and scars. She lets out a soft moan and my body reacts instantly, heat rushing through me. With one hand, I start massaging her full breasts, and the other explores between her legs.

Slowly circling with my fingers, her breathing accelerates under my touch. Dragging my fingers further down, her wetness drips all over my hand as I slide it back up. I keep teasing her tense bud of nerves and she turns her head slightly towards me. Accepting the invitation, I move away from her neck to kiss her face, jaw, and full lips.

She grinds into my touch, each touch of her ass against my hard length taunting me. My fingers slide down to enter her. She gasps and presses into my hand, demanding more. Pumping my fingers repeatedly in and out of her, I pinch her nipple with my other hand, still kissing her. When I know she can't take it anymore, I remove my fingers and go back to circling her clit slowly, teasing. I position myself by her entrance, lifting her up slightly so we're better angled.

"Yes. Please."

"What, Ela? I want to hear you say it." I whisper in her ear, rubbing against her wetness. I'm tempted to make her beg, for I know I could, but my own resolve is holding on by a thread.

"Fuck me, Az. Fuck me. Please."

"Good girl," I whisper back as I enter her. She lets out a long moan, arching her back to take me in fully. Slowly thrusting into her warm pussy, I keep massaging her and kissing her neck. My body pressed against hers in the most intimate embrace, her touch is intoxicating.

Unable to hold back anymore, I start ramming into her hard, sending her unraveling. I need her to scream my name, blinded by pleasure.

With my other hand, I grab hold of her beautiful hair and wait for her signal. She leans into my touch in seconds, so I pull hard as I move in and out of her. Her moans filling the air are like music to my ears.

"Damn." I'm barely containing myself from exploding inside her.

"Az…"

I don't know what's most hypnotizing. My name on her lips, her inability to finish a sentence, or how she feels as her pussy grips my length.

"Yes, little one. Tell me how you like it." Releasing her hair, I put my mouth on her neck, kissing, and biting, while she floods my fingers as I push into her again and again. I growl in her ear when she digs her nails into my forearm with each thrust and the sound of our bodies hitting together fills the air.

Kneading her breast with my free hand, I lick and suck on her ear with my teeth before groaning with pleasure as I sink inside her once more.

"Come for me, Ela." She does, as I pinch her clit between my fingers and hit that sweet spot inside her. She lets out a loud moan as she pulses around me.

"Deep breaths, little one. Let it flow through you." I say, gently massaging her.

When I can't take it anymore, I pull out of her and come on her lower back, seeing stars.

We're both panting hard as she sags in my arms, her head resting on my chest. I pull her into a tight embrace and gently kiss her head. Feeling her tremble in my arms, I carefully lift her up before turning her around to cradle her. She looks up to meet my gaze and dark embers dance in her eyes. I bend down and slowly kiss her reddened lips.

Even though the last thing I want to do is break away from the embrace, I stand and head to the bathroom.

She's sitting on the bed, her brown hair flowing wildly around her beautiful flushed face when I walk back in with a wet cloth in hand. I've got to have her again. But next time, I'll watch that stunning face of hers when she unravels under me.

As I step back on the bed and start wiping her body clean, I catch her studying my chest. Her fingers travel to my shoulder, down the thick scar that runs along my left arm.

"See. I've got them, too." I deposit a gentle kiss on her shoulder, and she gives me a small smile, striking me with that light, before lying down on the bed. Although I'm unsure whether I should stay or if I'm pushing my luck, I can't leave her yet. I join her and pull her close to me. She snuggles against my chest, gently stroking my abdomen.

"Talk to me, Ela. How are you feeling?" I give her another kiss on the head but she doesn't answer. Her regular breathing reaches my ears, and my heart tightens at the view of her peacefully sleeping in my arms.

I still haven't moved by the first light of dawn, too afraid to disturb her. But I know I must leave. Even though this was, without a doubt, the best night of my entire life, I don't think she returns my feelings beyond the physical attraction.

Not wanting to overwhelm her by still being here when she wakes up, I quietly sneak out of the room.

Elanor

I'm awakened by sunlight streaming through the windows, feeling surprisingly rested. I stretch out my legs, and my eyes fly open when the soreness in my muscles hits me. Flashes from last night come back to me, and I spring up in bed only to look around and find him gone.

A wave of panic washes over me. He left. Panic soon subsides to a whole other range of emotions. Anger. Confusion. Disappointment? What the fuck did I expect, anyway? I don't need that kind of attachment to tie me down, especially not to him.

The morning bliss completely evaporated, I get up and start getting ready after a scalding bath to wash his scent off me. Unable to completely shake off the fact that he left during the night, I try to make sense of the situation. He finally got what he wanted, I guess. And it's not like I didn't get anything out of it, either, remembering the shattering release I felt last night.

I catch a glimpse of my reflection and realize I'm still wearing the golden earpiece he gave me. I remove it and leave my room, set on going about my day as usual.

Savage spots me as I walk out into the palace garden and bounds towards me happily. I narrow my eyes at him in return. Of all the nights he decides to stay out, he picked last night. I'm starting to think maybe Vesta was right.

I decide to go for a morning walk with him inside Averion, needing to clear my head. When we return, Rina meets me back in my chambers with some food. She has the common sense not to comment on the rumpled bed sheets and torn dress as she makes my bed. I eat, thank her, and head back out with Savage to the training center.

As always, several Fae are training, and Cal is among them. He gives me a nod of acknowledgment before returning to his soldiers.

Vesta's cheerful voice fills the air moments later when I'm done stretching.

"Hey L, what's up? What did you think of the party?" She strolls in, joining me at the back of the room.

"It was great. Thank you again. I had fun." I say. I put a smile on my face, but a frown appears on hers.

"It's okay. You don't have to lie. Sorry, if it was too much." The corners of her mouth lift as she tilts her head, and I give her a genuine smile this time.

She positions herself in front of me, inviting me to join her and start my training. She knows me well. Grateful for the opportunity to get back into my routine, I unsheathe Nahtar, and we start sizing each other up. I launch an attack that she parries easily before countering with a riposte.

An hour later, I'm sweating and panting but feeling much better. We take a break, and I use that time to tie my hair in a low bun.

"Ela! What is that?!" Her fingers are pointing at something on my neck.

I turn around to check myself out in the mirrors alongside the room and see a giant bruise flowering on my neck. Shit. I quickly undo my hair, letting it fall down on my shoulder to cover the side of my neck again.

"What did you do, birthday girl?" Shock strikes Vesta's features. "Was it Ayas? Did I tell you he was good in bed or what?" She bursts into laughter.

Frozen in horror, no words are coming out of my mouth. Finally noticing my state, her mouth snaps shut and she pulls me away from prying eyes.

"Talk to me. What happened?" I remain silent. I don't think I can say this out loud.

"Oh. Wait. Was it-" She opens her mouth and her eyebrows lift as she mimes the first letter of the alphabet. "He left shortly after you did." I nod, surprised she made the connection so quickly. "Wow. How was it?" Her cheeky smile is back.

"Shut up, V. It's not funny."

"Come on. It can't have been that bad. Or was it?" Her hysterical laughter resounds in the room and I push her gently. But the sides of my mouth lift into a smile, unable to resist her contagious giggles.

"It was fine." She manages to raise an eyebrow in between a burst of laughter. "Ok, maybe it was more than fine. That's all I'll say. And that's all this will ever be."

Finally able to contain herself, she says. "Right. Well, good for you. You deserve some fun!" That's what it was, right? Just fun.

I stick my tongue out at her and sheathe Nahtar back in the scabbard on my back. "What about you? How was your night?" I tease her right back, glancing at Cal on the other side of the room.

She rolls her eyes at my question. "It was a rather unsuccessful one on my end, but not for lack of trying." She sends a murderous glance at the general, who happens to be watching her. "I think that asshole threatened every single Fae present at the party not to come near me."

"So, it's not your legendary charm faltering?"

"Nonsense! Come on, let's go. We've been here long enough," she says as she pulls me towards the exit. Someone's getting under her skin.

We stay together until dinner, after which I head to the war council. As I'm climbing the stairs leading to his office, I tense up at the thought of being in the same room as him.

CHAPTER SIXTEEN

Several captains are already there, including Lana, the only other female attending these meetings. She gives me a quick nod that I return before taking position against a bookshelf. Mor and one of the captains are talking in a corner. As I study them, I realize the red-haired captain was at the party last night. I didn't recognize him yesterday without his armor on. Naar, if I remember correctly.

Cal marches in, followed by the other captains of Averion. Eren's purple hair unmistakably stands out. Vesta told me he's from the Water Fae. Kharis, and Yhen, although both dark-haired, couldn't be more different. Kharis wears the Wood Fae colors. His sharp eyes are ever-watching and scanning the room he's in. Tall and thin, he always carries a bow with him. Yhen, the pale-skinned Moon Fae captain, is shorter than most, but what he lacks in height, he compensates for in width and strength. He wears a short beard and sports a mean collection of knives. Elion, Sun Fae, enters last. Thick golden blond hair and dazzling green eyes, with bronze-colored skin. Although I've only seen Cal fight, they're all deadly.

The general closes the door behind him and takes his place by Azran's desk.

"Good evening. Thank you for coming-"

"Is the High Lord not joining us today?" I ask, cutting him off. Several heads turn toward me, surprised by my interruption, but I keep my gaze fixed on Cal. I couldn't care less about their formalities.

"He's not." Seeing he's not going to give me any further explanation, I nod and let him go back to the regular agenda. Is Az avoiding me? I put that thought away, trying to dismiss the tug of disappointment I'm feeling and bring back my focus to the conversation at hand.

"We've spotted movements of rebels gathering by the mountain range, but no sight of Braern yet. And the Loyalists ransacked another village down south, so Tharrion is increasing his patrols. Let's keep all units ready to move out."

No change, then. I gaze into the fire burning behind Cal, momentarily hypnotized by the flames. I wonder what's taking so long. We've taken out several rebels' nests, but it sounds like it hasn't upset any of Braern's plans. I know I'm supposed to play a role in this war, but I wonder when and where that will happen.

Damned prophecy.

I lift my head when my name gets called, and all eyes are on me.

"Kharis. You're in charge of assembling and leading the unit Ela will be a part of. You're to ensure her safety and help fulfill her part. By any means necessary." Cal pauses to look around the room. "We don't know where and when Braern will show himself or if he will join the battle. So any sighting of him before or during the final battle should be reported to the Unifier and High Lord immediately. She could be the turning point in the war."

With his last words, the pressure settles in. I gaze around the room and stop on Kharis, who is proudly smiling at me. He gives me a quick nod, acknowledging his commander's instructions. I swallow the lump in my throat and return his nod. I guess I have my answer now.

"General. What of the unrest of the population? Reports are still coming in-" Yhen's voice breaks the silence.

Cal's head immediately turns in his direction, silencing him in a glance before changing the topic and asking about the squadrons. That was awkward. It's the first time I've seen Cal cut off one of his captains this way. But I soon forget about it as each of them gives a detailed report on the state of their units.

⸻ ◆ ⸻

Azran

With the Aiduin river behind us, the grey city extends for miles, its rooftops and skylights reflecting the sunset. It took us a full day's ride to get to Morilanthe, and, as expected, it is still buzzing with activity, its thousand lights sparkling in the night. It's beautiful. With that simple observation, my thoughts return to Ela.

I glance at the six soldiers accompanying me as we approach the city wall. This little display is unnecessary, but I need to keep up appearances.

It's close to midnight when we finally ride into the city, and I'm assaulted by its familiar busyness. Streets are crawling with merchants and art resellers. Nightfall brings renewed energy and life to this place. It's been like that for as long as I can remember. And I would know. I grew up here.

With my soldiers behind me, we finally arrive at the Moon Palace. Amrynn's residence. It's rather late, and she couldn't have expected me this early, yet we're greeted by a group of aides and… Sias. There is no mistaking Amrynn's right hand, even from a distance. Short blue hair, clean-shaven, svelte unlike most Moon Fae, with calculating aquamarine eyes.

Sias bows slightly as I dismount. "High Lord. Welcome to Morilanthe. We are honored to be receiving you. May I offer you some-"

"Take me to Amrynn."

He has the intelligence not to question me and simply motions for me to follow him. I glance back at my soldiers and dismiss them with a signal, although I know Cal wouldn't like that.

Sias leads me through the corridors, even if I could perfectly find my way alone. As we arrive at the upper levels, we cross several terraces opening up on the entire city and night sky. The wind brushes in my hair, bringing in the familiar scent of this place. I close my eyes for a second and let the memories from another time rush back. Everything was so different back then.

Sias pauses in front of the throne room, waiting for guards to open the heavy doors. Of course. Amrynn would never receive me in a place that wouldn't allow her to display her position. Although we are technically family, and she certainly attempts to use that to her advantage every now and then, there is nothing binding us.

We step inside the room and find Amrynn waiting for us on the dais. Everything about her is carefully crafted. Her hair lavishly falling on her naked shoulders, the long dark dress hugging her curves, the makeup on her face, every single piece of jewelry on her body, her stance... everything is a calculated move.

"Lady Amrynn." The depth of Sias' bow doesn't go unnoticed and clearly speaks to his loyalty.

She dismisses him with a gesture of her hand before turning towards me and bowing ever so slightly. "High Lord."

I watch Sias leave the room and wait for the doors to close until it's just us two. "I don't know how you trust him."

"Who says I do? Keep your friends close..."

I raise an eyebrow, not bothering to respond.

She reveals a devilish smile before stepping down from the dais and waving toward a table full of refreshments. I shake my head and remain silent, waiting for her to open the dance. I've learned to let her take the lead at times. It usually gives me an opportunity to better study her.

"So, is it true? You have found the Unifier?" Her crystal voice sings in the air.

I'm surprised that's what she's leading with. Amrynn is usually less direct about what she really cares about, always careful to layer it between other topics. I nod, cautious not to reveal anything of importance, and I join the dance.

"Your network of spies has probably already reported everything they could get their hands on about the Unifier. What do you really wish to discuss?"

"Right." She begins strolling around the room, taking her time before choosing her next words. "Attacks on our commercial routes have increased in the past months and merchants are growing restless. We want to end this more than ever, but there is so little information about Braern and his plans." She lowers her voice and gives me a worried look. "I'm not sure that our people will feel... confident in our leadership when the time comes."

"Amrynn, cut to the chase. What is it that you want?" I can see right through the fake distress. I've known her for centuries. Playing games is the only thing that brings her joy in this world. That, and power.

Her eye twitches before she recovers from my interruption. "If our High Lord were to lower taxes on commodities and maybe release a statement to the people, I think it would ease concerns."

"A statement that you would write and that wouldn't fail to highlight your achievements, am I correct?"

She gives me a small, calculated smile. "Azran, I am simply trying to ease some of the burdens you carry and ensure our people will follow us."

"I'll think about it."

After all these years, she hasn't changed at all. She just got better at hiding who she truly is. The girl who is scared to lose, scared of never being enough, who needs to control and overpower others. Although she is a handful, she does a good job at leading the Moon Fae, and I know she cares at least a little bit about her people, even if she would never admit it.

"I will see you tomorrow," I say, before walking away.

I don't even need to ask and head straight to my old rooms. As much as it pains me to spend another night in here, I won't give her the satisfaction of asking for another room. She knows better than anyone how much pain and abuse we both endured behind these walls.

I'm walking the cold corridors, pondering the Moon Fae dilemma. As much as this is where I need Amrynn to be, it's not a long-term solution. Not much has changed since I left. They never truly accepted me, and I know the respect the Moon Fae show to our ruling has very little to do with me. Their allegiance lies with her and not me, as ever. Which makes this territory the most unstable and vulnerable to Braern's reach and poisonous ideas.

Once in my childhood room, I efficiently strip out of my clothes, take a quick bath to wash off the remnants of the ride, and head to bed. I'm exhausted, yet sleep evades me. My thoughts irrevocably drift back to last night with Ela, and my heart tightens at the memory.

I still can't believe it really happened. I should get some rest, but I know what awaits me when I close my eyes, so I linger on her remembrance, flashbacks of our embrace playing on my mind until I can't resist the slumber anymore.

The next day goes by slowly alongside Amrynn. She updates me on the state of the Moon Fae army and the city's recent developments. I've already made up my mind about her ask. But I'll let her parade around me and attempt to woo me into doing her bidding.

Right before dinner, I stop by my room to find one of the soldiers I had dispatched earlier today waiting for me. Staying silent, he hands me a piece of paper. Walls have ears around here, so I dismiss him with a motion of my head and open his written report. After carefully reading the missive, I tear it into pieces, cast it into the fire still burning in a corner of the room, and head to the dining hall.

I'm eager to return to Averion, so we move out of the city the next day at dawn. Overall, this visit proved interesting, to say the least. Cal will have a field day when he learns about it. He could never stand Amrynn and her plots.

Elanor

The next two councils are more of the same. Rebels are still conducting random attacks and even ambushed one of our units. Azran doesn't show up. I don't even see him throughout the day. If he's avoiding me, he's doing a damn good job at it.

Tired of this little game, I decide to stick around at the end of today's meeting and confront Cal. On top of being the general of the armies, they're best friends, so he must know where his insufferable High Lord is.

Cal is wearing the usual red and gold armor and his black locks are tied at the back of his head. As he's tidying the stack of papers in front of him, he notices me standing in the middle of the office.

"Yes, Ela? Can I help you with something?" He says with a smile.

"Where is he?"

"Where is who?" His smile widens. Now I see why Vesta finds him so annoying.

"Don't play dumb with me. Azran. Why is he not attending the councils?"

He finishes stacking up the documents on the desk and walks toward me.

"He's away on a diplomatic mission up north. Amrynn, the Lady of the Moon Fae, requested his presence to discuss the war against Braern." I try to keep my features neutral and repress an eye roll. "A crucial part of his role is maintaining harmony between each Lord and Lady of the Fae. He wouldn't have gone if her alliance wasn't absolutely necessary." I clench my jaw. "Why do you care?"

"I don't. I'm just wondering why the High Lord leaves when war is on his doorstep," I say as I cross my arms in front of my chest.

He stares at me for a second before continuing. "He wouldn't leave if it wasn't important, Ela. Believe it or not, he cares about his people and about you."

"Right, the prophecy. I'm the secret weapon."

"That's not what I meant, and you know it."

"Sure." I dismiss his words with a wave of my hand and leave the office.

Back in my room, I get ready for bed, Savage alongside me. I brush my hair and attempt to fall asleep, but I'm feeling restless.

I'm pacing around my room with Savage watching me from the corner, the soft patterned rugs under my bare feet. My head is a fucking mess, the whole spectrum of emotions known to exist storming inside.

Do I regret what happened with Az? I'm not sure. I just can't believe I let it happen.

He'd paused several times to make sure I'd wanted it as much as he did. I'd had all the occasions I would have needed to stop before going too far. But I didn't.

I wonder how long he's been looking at me this way, wanting me. Or if this is just another elaborate scheme to ensure his weapon doesn't run away.

A tingle of guilt wakes up inside me, and my thoughts drift to my mother and father. Ilyana's words come back to me but I try not to dwell on them, and I keep stomping around the room.

Finally, a ton of anger is hiding inside me because that bastard left without a word. I can't read him! One day he's the cold High Lord, the next, his eyes are sparking with desire. And then he disappears to go wander off with some Fae. I don't care how important she is. His years of reign didn't teach him any fucking manners.

Suddenly, my vision darkens, and shadows emanate from me. My rage is unraveling, and I can feel my power boiling inside me, begging to get out.

Savage barks at me, trying to get my attention, but I'm perfectly aware of what's happening. I'm just flirting with the idea of letting it all explode around me, letting it all go to hell without a care in the world. This madness is pure bliss and I feel like having a good time.

The corners of my mouth lift in the semblance of a smile, and I growl. Power explodes around me and shatters one of the mirrors in the room. The rage and dark blur leave me instantly. I've completely lost control, letting my emotions take over. The realization has the effect of a cold bucket of water thrown on me, and that's when I put my finger on what's really bothering me.

Fear. That's what I can't get over. I'm scared. Terrified, even. I keep mulling the same question over and over again, wondering what his intentions truly are, too afraid to get to the bottom of it. Being used as an instrument of war is not what truly haunts me. What if he's being truthful with me, and even worse, what if the way I feel about him changes?

Above all else, I'm scared I've just made a huge mistake. I've been trying to keep everyone at arm's length, but that night everything imploded. I've repressed my emotions for so long that I fear I won't be able to let them out slowly. Deep down, I know this emotional storm is going to swallow me whole and there will be no containing it.

And that's not something I can afford. I don't know what's going on, but I have revenge to fulfill and that's the only thing that matters. I can't get distracted, and I can't get attached to anyone, certainly not him. Not having anyone close is best, nothing to lose and no one who can leave me. A shiver runs down my spine. No one can have that kind of power over me. Never again.

━━◆O◆━━

Calen

I let out a grunt the minute the door closes on Ela. Everyone is driving me crazy. I don't know how Az handles the ongoing parade of visitors, constant interruptions, and the never-ending pile of documents to review.

My thoughts drift to Vesta, as they often do. I knew she liked me a long time ago, but I didn't have the guts to try at the time. Then she met Elis, confirming she was meant for him and not me. He was a good soldier and didn't deserve what happened to him. Just like so many others we lost.

My feelings never wavered, but there was so much to build and work towards. Now, I have no idea how to get her to take her walls down. Threatening all Fae present at the party was clearly not the right move, but I couldn't help myself. The thought of her with another drives me mad. I realize I'm being a complete asshole and that it is pointless. She's the strongest, most independent Fae I know. She's a free spirit, and I never want to tame that in her. Hell, I would push away anyone trying to do the same to me. That's just one of the many reasons I- My hands go to my face, stifling the thought.

Of course, I've been with other Fae, females and males. But no one compares to her. And every day, I beat myself up for not trying, for waiting this long, and for not acknowledging my feelings sooner.

And look at me now, acting like a complete moron, full of regret. I always pretend that everything washes over me, but this is the one thing that gets to me. I've watched hundreds of Fae get mated, and I wonder if I'll ever have that. Deep down, I don't think I will. I don't think I deserve to. I've led too many to their death and have too much blood on my hands.

Just as I'm about to head down that familiar dark path, the door opens on its hinges. My head snaps up from the desk I've been staring at when Az walks in. His hair is tied in a loose knot at the back of his head, and his strange red irises contrast with the dark circles under his eyes.

"Well, you look like shit. As usual." I greet him. "How did it go?"

He sprawls on the leather couch before answering. "Good to see you, too. It went fine. I've secured her allegiance. Amrynn just wanted to use the recent attacks as a bargaining chip for a more profitable deal on commercial routes and import."

"Of course she did. Your cousin is always out for a good opportunity to use her people's plight to her advantage."

"Don't I know it," he says, closing his eyes and pinching the bridge of his nose.

"But that's not it, is it? What else have you found out?"

Opening his eyes, he stares at me for a moment before finally telling me what's really going on. "I dispatched one of our soldiers to the city while I was stuck at the palace with Amrynn yesterday. The report he gave me was most interesting." I raise an eyebrow, waiting for him to continue. "Apparently, merchants are thriving. There is little to no talk of the attacks, and no one really seems agitated or worried. And she asked about Ela." His jaw clenches tightly as he rests both arms on the sofa. "I think she's trying to gauge our winning chances. You know Amrynn, never putting all her eggs in one basket."

"Az, we can't let her go on unchecked like this!"

He lifts both hands up in the air. "We've been here before. This is what she does and how she survives. And you know as well as I do that I can't forsake her on unproved suspicions and risk losing the north to Braern."

I close my open mouth and swallow the hateful words stuck in my throat.

"For now, we need to reinforce our network of informants and wait to see how this plays out. She's always played with fire, and so far, she has always leaned our way. As long as we can maintain our advantage, she'll play along."

I know he's right, so I nod. However frustrating it is to keep playing this game with her, this new development is useful to us. "I won't swap out our informants to avoid raising suspicions in Morilanthe, but I'll dispatch someone new."

"Sounds good."

"And what do we do about the rumors circulating around Ela? These fanatics use her name to spread falsehoods and put crazy hopes in people's heads to sell trinkets and benefit from the fear-mongering. They've even started calling her the Saviour of the Fae."

"They're just a bunch of zealots. And we can't waste resources and time trying to crack down on our own people. Just make sure Ela doesn't hear about it. She doesn't need to know about that."

"I figured as much," I say, remembering Yhen's question from a few days ago.

Azran leans back on the couch and sags a little against the cushions, clearly exhausted. I know he hates visiting Morilanthe, yet I suspect another motive for his trip being cut short.

"You came back earlier than expected." I tilt my head to the side. "Any particular reason?" He doesn't grace me with an answer, but I won't let him off the hook that easily. "Ela's been asking about you, and she seems pissed." Az's eyes widen almost imperceptibly. "What did you do?"

"None of your business, Cal. Anything urgent I should attend to tonight?"

I shake my head. "Everything's under control. No other significant news from Braern."

His gaze turns to a deeper red at the mention of Braern's name. "I have a bad feeling about this, Cal. By now, Braern has to have gathered all the soldiers he can. His attacks are accelerating but it almost feels like a distraction. There's something else going on right under our noses, and no one has a fucking clue."

"We're doing everything we can to counter his attacks and ready ourselves. We'll deal with it when we get to it. Just like we've always done, Az."

His head turns toward me as he nods. "Thank you. I know I don't say it enough."

"Nonsense. I know the red roses I receive every now and then are from you. No need to keep up the masquerade with the anonymous love notes. Don't worry, I know." I shoot him a wink.

"Shut up, Cal." But a smile slowly appears on his face.

That's all I can do. He carries the weight of the Fae kingdom, and I assist as best I can. He's like a brother to me, and I'll follow him to the ends of this earth.

"Go get some rest, Az. You really do look like shit."

Elanor

After profusely apologizing to Savage yesterday, I take him to the Dark Forest after breakfast, needing to get away from the palace. The guards are now used to my frequent outings and just briefly nod to me, acknowledging my presence. I let him wander around the woods while I find a quiet clearing to relax after our walk.

My power is growing restless, like it has a life of its own. But I can't afford another uncontrolled outburst at a critical time. So I work on my self-control, calling on my power and letting it go. Increasing its reach, calling it back to me. Again and again. Surrounding myself in shadows, I'm getting more comfortable in the darkness, now able to better discern my surroundings even through the dark haze.

I unsheathe Nahtar and focus on lighting it ablaze, first softly, then letting the dark flames run wild, keeping a safe distance from the trees and branches. I go through several fighting stances, lunging forward, parading, and initiating a series of attacks. I can feel my power steadily simmering through me, and it's exhilarating.

For a moment, I forget everything. The hurt, the heartbreak, the loss, the death. It's just me and the familiar darkness. Power takes over me completely, and I feel nothing. I am nothing. Just this flowing energy. The sounds of nature are gone and I can't even hear my own heartbeat. I wish I could stay like this forever, time suspended, emotions gone. Numb, I let my power run wild inside of me.

I finally open my eyes, putting a lid on the flow of energy, and the real world comes crashing down on me. The sound of birds chirping and wind brushing through branches comes back first, astounding. The smell of grass and moss overwhelms my nose next. And a profound sense of loss and loneliness blooms in my heart. I wish it didn't have to be this way.

I can feel my eyes watering when something tugs deep inside me, bringing me back from the edge. I try to identify the source of this sudden change, in vain, until Savage emerges into the clearing. My stomach growls as I realize we've been gone all day.

Once back at the palace, I stop by my chambers to change, deciding on the black velvet dress. I check out my reflection in the newly replaced mirror and head out.

I meet V at the dining hall. She's her usual cheerful self, entertaining the rest of the table with banter and gossip. She winks at me when she sees me walking in, so I wave and come sit beside her. Wyn and Varan are there, too, both smiling widely at me. My heart breaks a little as I watch them. Those three are the closest friends I have here. But there used to be one more...

I stay silent for the entire meal, with my wolf sitting behind me, silently guarding me. I let Savage lick my plate clean once my hunger is nothing but a distant memory. When I'm done, I head out of the dining hall to take the stairs leading to Az's office and the council that's about to start.

As I walk the white stoned corridors, my boots echo on the marble floor and my thoughts escape to that familiar place of loneliness. Even among my friends, I'm utterly alone, in a different world, isolated, unable to reach them. My nightmares also come back to me, reminding me of what I have to lose and how monstrous I can truly be. A shiver runs down my spine, but I push back the memory. It's just a nightmare, nothing more.

The flashes haunt me until I'm up the stairs and the office door is in sight. As I walk in, all the captains are here, and so is Cal. I take my usual position, leaning against the wall, the whole room in view, and Savage sits by my side, his warm body weighing on my leg.

Right when I expect Cal to start the meeting, Azran saunters into the room, and my breath catches in my throat. He's wearing a dark tunic, his long blond hair is dangling over his strong shoulders, and his double-bladed sword is at his side. His red gaze goes around the room, barely stopping on me.

A dark-skinned Fae I've never seen walks in after him, closing the door. His head is completely shaved and tattooed with intricate symbols I can't really make out. He quietly stands in a corner.

"Reports." Azran's low voice gives me chills, and I can't help but stare at him. He's sitting on the edge of his wooden desk, his arms crossed against his massive chest.

Without hesitation, Naar speaks up to share the latest developments on his squadrons. Kharis goes next, and the rest of the captains follow.

The Fae with the shaved head is taking notes of everything, nodding every now and then.

"Let Barus know if inventory needs to be adjusted for your units," the High Lord says, pointing to the Fae with the shaved head. "That's it for today."

Before he's even done dismissing us, he walks around his desk and starts going through the papers on the table. Everyone but Barus seems to be heading out. Still shocked by his presence and his complete lack of acknowledgment of mine, I leave with the rest of them without a glance in his direction.

CHAPTER SEVENTEEN

Azran

It took all I had not to stare at her the entire meeting, torn between the memory of her body lingering in my mind and the distress she felt throughout the day, unable to read her features, talk to her, or reach out while surrounded by prying eyes. A few feet away from me and yet so far away. Separated by our past and divided over the future, with an ocean of guilt between us.

I couldn't help myself earlier. I tried calling her down the bond, risking her discovering it all. Thankfully, I don't think she noticed. The alliance we have achieved is too fragile for me to endanger it carelessly like this.

Back in my room, I sit on the bed and undo the laces of my boots. After removing them, I take a deep breath and put my head in my hands. Between the sleepless nights, decades of fighting, political headaches, and now the excruciating longing inside me, it's taking everything I have left to keep this menacing storm hidden. I have a pretty good idea of how destructive the aftermath of revealing the bond could be.

I spring to my feet when the door of my bedroom opens and crashes against the wall. Ela is standing before me, deadly beautiful in her black dress and clearly pissed off.

"I didn't take you for a coward." Her irises are already darkening.

I slowly walk around her and close the door. "I had obligations with the Moon Fae."

"Obligations you had to attend to in the middle of the night?" She narrows her rage-filled eyes at me, following my movements.

So that's what's really bothering her. "I thought you would prefer me gone by morning. Was I wrong?" I say, hope suddenly filling my heart.

"No." Her eye slightly twitches as she shuts me down with a word, leaving me with a sliver of doubt. "I don't like being dismissed without an explanation. I'm not a little toy you can play with or string along."

"Right. Trust me, I know." Tension is still oozing from her body, and her mouth is closed shut, her lips tightly pinched. "Is that all you came to tell me?"

The darkness in her eyes is retreating, and I walk up to her, expecting her to step back. She stays still until I'm inches away from her.

"So, what now?" I say. She tilts her head imperceptibly closer to me, her lips barely opening. I can see her weighing the pros and cons.

"Is this what you want?" I ask, leaning towards her slowly and giving her time to decide. I can barely contain myself at the thought of what might happen, but thankfully centuries in politics have taught me enough to keep a straight face. This will only happen if and when she wants it to.

"Don't read too much into this." Her words echo in my ears, but her eyes tell a whole other story.

"Then I'm all yours." A devilish smile appears on my face and her breath catches in her throat as I close the gap between us.

I grab her by the waist and pull her to me. She doesn't need to be told twice, and her lips come crashing down on mine the next second. I kiss her back ravenously, tasting the desire in her mouth.

Not wasting time, she undresses while I devour her lips. Following suit, I pull my shirt open, tearing the fabric off my chest before pulling away. She is standing naked in front of me, panting with need, her black dress pooled at her feet, and all I want is to worship her.

My gaze drops to her full breasts and gorgeous thighs before I put my hands on her neck to slowly caress her skin. I move down to her red scars, taking my time to savor each touch, and I finally cup her breasts.

My hardness is poking through my pants as her fingers travel down my chest. Her delicate hands land on the waistband of my pants, and she pulls them down, leaving me completely exposed. Her arousal fills the air and I close my eyes, inhaling the divine scent. My eyes snap open when she starts caressing me, and I find her kneeling before me.

Holding my gaze, she starts stroking me firmly, each movement sending electricity tingling in my body. I can't take my eyes off her, fire and eagerness dancing in my heart, the memory of her wetness dripping all over my mouth dancing not far behind. I haven't forgotten what she told me on her birthday, and I intend on showing her new realms of pleasure for as long as she'll allow it.

I release a deep moan when her tongue touches me, teasing and circling the tip of my cock. I put my hand on her shoulder, gently pressing and encouraging her. "You're killing me."

She takes me in her mouth fully, and I groan loudly as her warmth welcomes me. "The things I want to do to your face."

She starts sucking hard, pulling me deeper in her throat while massaging the base of my shaft. My hand is on her head, and I can barely resist ramming down her throat. She lets out a soft moan when my fingers grab ahold of her hair.

"I'm going to fuck your face, little one," I say. She immediately sucks more vigorously, swirling her tongue around, giving me consent.

I grab her hair with both hands and thrust into her mouth. At first, slowly, to give her time to adjust or pull back. Then I undo all restraints and she takes me deeply.

Engulfed in her wet heat, her saliva soaks my erection as her tongue glides around. She gently grabs my balls, her hollowing cheeks taking my full length. I pull out when I get too close to unraveling and exploding on her face.

She looks up at me, her lips red and swollen, her eyes questioning as she catches her breath. A small smile tugs on my face, and I release her beautiful hair before gently wiping the corners of her mouth with my thumb.

"I'm not done with you." She is still panting with need.

"I know, little one. I'm not done with you, either." I get on my knees beside her and pull her in for a heated kiss. My hands go to her body, caressing her back, and grabbing her ass.

She parts her legs for me, letting my fingers wander in between her thighs, and I find her dripping with wetness. My hand is drenched in her arousal as I explore her tensed clit, and slide a finger inside her. She moans, arching her back into my hand, and I start pumping into her. Using my thumb to rub against her engorged bud of nerves, I kiss down her neck.

Suddenly, she's pushing me on my back, taking control. As I lie down on the floor, she positions herself on top of me, pinning me with her body. Before I can stop her, she impales herself on me. The cold marble does nothing to extinguish the intense pleasure that radiates through my entire body and my eyes roll when I sink into her heat.

She starts riding me, not giving me a moment's rest, and I grab hold of her ass. She's the most beautiful Fae I've ever seen, her long brown hair running wild across her chest, her scarred breasts heavily bouncing with her movements. She meets my gaze, and that look alone almost sends me over the edge.

Moving one of my hands to her front, I go back to circling her swollen clit, sending her writhing with pleasure. Her head falls back, and long moans escape her lips as she keeps rolling her hips. I let her set the pace and fuck me. Buried deep inside her, I can feel my release nearing as I meet each of her movements.

My hand still rubbing in between her thighs, I grab her breast with the other. She rides me faster, almost begging for her release, so I pinch her nipple between my fingers. Her lips part open as she screams my name. I come at the sound of it and she unravels seconds later.

Sensing her pulsing around me, I watch as euphoria washes over her. Shadows start oozing out of her rhythmically, and I grab her tighter, securing her in place to let her explode freely. The room goes completely dark, her shadows hiding us from the rest of the world for an instant before they're gone.

Heaving, she opens her eyes and puts her hands on my abdomen. Needing to feel her closer, I pull her to my chest, letting her rest on top of me and caressing her hair.

"Did I hurt you? The shadows just escaped me." She asks in between breaths.

"No." I keep brushing her hair and she sighs in relief. "Even if you did, I wouldn't have stopped you, little one." She abruptly sits up, pushing back on my chest, her eyes widened at my response. "Don't you get it? You can do whatever you want with me."

My voice is barely more than a whisper but she pulls away and stands up. I shouldn't have said that. Propping myself on my elbow, I watch her go around the room to grab her dress and put it on.

She makes for the door five seconds later, and I barely have time to gather my spirits and lift myself up. "Wait. Ela."

She hesitates, her hand on the handle, and without turning back, swings it open. "Good night."

❖

Elanor

I didn't realize my power was let loose until it was too late, but it was pure ecstasy.

When my head touches the pillow, my entire body is invaded by the most intense calm. It's like my release reset my nervous system. I get why Vesta was so insistent I find opportunities to...test things out.

Even Az's confusing words won't shake off my inner peace. I won't let this get to me, whether it's another pretty see-through attempt to manipulate me or something else on his part. This doesn't mean anything.

I just didn't like the way he wandered off to go see some other Fae the other day, so I went to say my piece. I may have gotten a little sidetracked but it doesn't matter. Everything is under control.

I know what I have to do. Braern is my only concern, and I won't be distracted by anything or anyone.

When I wake the next day, I take a walk with Savage and train with Vesta in the afternoon. As I'm about to leave, Kharis pulls me aside by the garrison.

"I've assembled the Unifier's unit. I'd like them to train with you in the coming days if that's all right with you."

Although it feels weird to have a team whose sole purpose is to support me and ensure my safety, I think it will be good, so I nod. The Wood Fae disappears moments later, already off to other obligations.

After dinner, I attend yet another pointless council where there is nothing outstanding to report and everyone is on standby. At night I drift off to sleep with Savage by my side, but my nights are filled once again with nightmares.

They feel so real it's almost like I've already lived them, or maybe I will. It's hard to tell whether they're premonitions or just ghosts haunting my dreams. There's the one with everyone I know dead on the battlefield, and then another one that loops in my head.

Still on a battlefield, this time I'm wielding two swords I don't recognize. My vision is blurred, and a warm liquid rolls down my neck and temples. Surrounded by enemies, although I can't make out their faces, I'm slicing through the mass of bodies around me. Too fast for them to even stand a chance. Blood is splattering all over me.

I can't feel pain, just the fury burning inside me as I slay soldiers like a demon unleashed on its prey. Once there's no one left standing, rage subsides to a crushing wave of guilt. My bare arms are entirely red, and blood is dripping from my blades onto the soaked ground. I turn around and contemplate the hundreds that have died at my hands.

A faint male voice echoes behind me. I recognize its familiarity, but I can't clearly make it out. And every night, before I can turn around and identify who's calling, I wake up drenched in sweat with guilt lingering in my heart. The battlegrounds keep changing, but it's just more of the same. Slaughtering enemies, bathing in fury and blood until it's over, and I can't turn around fast enough to see who's talking.

Although never fully resting at night, I've gotten used to the nightmares and short nights. I can count the nights I've slept peacefully on the fingers of my hand. Once in the desert. And the other two times. Well, here.

In Azran's office for another council, I'm leaning against the bookshelves. Expecting nothing new, I lose myself in thought as the wooden spine digs into my back. Before I realize what's happening, memories from the nights with Az come back to me, and I find myself staring at him.

Today his long blond hair is half-up, tied in a knot at the back of his head, the rest falling on his shoulders, revealing his striking features. With the fire crackling at his back, giving warmth to the room, the flames nicely match the color of his irises. And even from where I'm standing, his forest scent hits me, mixing with the leather smell of the office.

As usual, he barely acknowledges my presence, but an idea forms in my mind. A theory I'd like to test.

After everyone is dismissed, I stay behind. As soon as the last captain exits the room, Az's head tilts up from behind his desk to meet my gaze.

Without a word, I slowly make my way to the wooden counter. Not breaking eye contact, and not giving myself time to hesitate or for my courage to falter, I put both hands on the desk and send everything crashing to the floor. One of his eyebrows raises in question.

"So, now I have your attention."

"You always do." He rises from his chair and puts both hands on the table. His fingers are almost brushing over mine and embers are dancing in his eyes. "What can I do for you today?"

I gather what's left of my determination before I lose myself in his gaze. "You can take me right now." His eyes flicker at my words. I've surprised him. Good.

He swallows, hard. "Right here?"

I nod. There's an interminable pause, and I'm seconds away from fleeing the room when he leans forward across the desk. He grabs my jaw tightly between his fingers, bringing me closer to his face, and growls in my face.

"I hope you don't talk to anyone else this way."

"I can do whatever the fuck I want. And right now, I want you to fuck me on this desk."

I close the distance between us, my lips finding his. His mouth welcomes mine instantly, and all traces of fear leave me.

I bite his lips slightly as he pulls me closer. I lift a leg up to climb on the table, and he drags me over to his side while still devouring my lips, each stroke of his tongue sending electricity down my spine.

I sit on the edge of the wooden desk, my legs spread around his waist, and he doesn't waste a minute. He lifts up the skirts of my dress and grabs a handful of my bare ass. Bliss courses through me as his hands travel my body.

An unfamiliar tug reverberates in my heart, almost calling me to him, but I shut it down. I'm not going to fall for this illusion of safety. I just need a release. One last time to keep the anxiety at bay. Sex and nothing else.

He's now disposed of my underwear and is undoing his belt with one hand, still caressing me with the other. Lost under his touch, I let him do whatever he wants. I just need to forget everything.

His pants are halfway down his muscular legs when he pulls my hips forward and pushes on my chest gently. I lean back on the desk, silently obeying his command. The next second, his hand is between my legs, gently circling, wetness already pooling in my slit.

I lift my head as I let out a soft moan, encouraging him further. And he returns a wolfish smile, clearly enjoying the view. He's stroking himself as he caresses me, and the sight of his erection sends a rush of arousal through me. His thumb is still brushing over my clit when he pushes two fingers inside me, making me gasp.

I can't take my eyes off him. I wish life could be easier. I wish the past and future didn't have to be. I'm truly seeing him for the first time, with his strong jaw and handsome face. Needing to forget about my responsibilities, I want to get lost in his gaze, but I think his smile is what really- I abruptly sit up with his fingers still buried inside me, needing to interrupt my train of thought.

"What do you think you're doing?" His hand grabs me by the throat. He's pumping his fingers inside me as he holds me up, slowly pressing on my neck, and I can feel the tension building between my legs.

"Take me," I say hoarsely, staring at his lips so I won't gaze into his hypnotizing eyes.

So he does. Taking my lips and my pussy at the same time, he enters me in a slow thrust, still choking me. My eyes roll as I arch my back to take him in fully. A deep moan escapes us both when his tongue meets mine. His other hand is behind my back, supporting me as he starts pushing in and out of me.

"Harder," I say against his mouth, needing all of him. He complies instantly, pounding me strongly against his wooden desk. His grunts fill the room, mixing with my whimpers.

He pushes down on my neck to have me lie down and gain better access to my whole body. Still thrusting into me, his thumb is on my clit, circling the engorged bundle of nerves. His body smashes against mine, sending waves of electricity every time he fills me entirely.

We're both panting, and it's like my body catches on fire when my climax nears. Letting go of my neck, Az pinches my nipple hard through the fabric of my dress. The zap of pain focuses all my attention back on my body and sends me unraveling.

As the orgasm shatters through me, I don't hold back, screaming my release. He comes inside me moments later and collapses on top of me. I barely notice when my shadows dance all over us and retreat back within me.

An intense sense of calm settles over me. My whole body is tingling with pleasure, and his scent is overwhelming my senses. I close my eyes, his heavy chest on top of mine.

He's panting, his heartbeat pounding against my body, and his soft hair brushing my shoulder. I turn my face slightly but stop myself an inch away from resting my head on his, reason making a comeback.

He lifts his head, and his hair falls on either side of my face, leaving me no choice but to meet his gaze. He deposits the most gentle kiss on my lips and rests his forehead on mine before I can utter a word.

I freeze, unable to return his kiss, bewildered by the sudden mark of affection and tenderness after his repetitive avoidance in front of everyone else.

Az suddenly pulls away, leaving me bare and empty. I lift my head just in time to see him turn around to put his pants back on. My brows draw closer together as I sit up and pull down my dress as best I can. I guess that's my cue. I stand up and walk around the desk towards the door.

"Thanks." My voice fills the air, sounding darker than intended. Az turns around and returns a cold stare. Right. Job done, I guess.

The next day, I walk into my room after a morning run with Savage and start discarding my sweaty clothes. I strip naked, barely glancing at my scars, and dive into a warm bath. The deep red marks are just a part of me, a representation of what's hidden beneath the surface, of the damage I carry and can cause.

The hot water enveloping my tight muscles, memories of last night come back to me in waves. I was right. Anytime I experience a physical release, I get to enjoy a peaceful night, free of the bloody nightmares. Of course, that doesn't explain the one night out in the desert, but I'll conveniently disregard that one as an anomaly.

Once I'm done bathing, I walk back into my bedroom with a towel wrapped around me, and my gaze lands on the black diamond necklace I threw out the window weeks ago. It's back on my bed.

I stop dead in my tracks. When did he drop it off? And what's up with that necklace, anyway? I imagined it would have shattered into pieces when I threw it out. It's more resistant than I thought. Looking back on the past several months of my life, I guess we have that in common.

Maybe Azran realized his weird dismissal was not very in line with his long-term strategy for the Unifier, and he thought a shiny jewel would do the trick. I snort out loud before putting it away in my wardrobe. Nice try.

I put on my gear and head to the training center. Azran is standing among the other soldiers when I walk in. He's everywhere today. Just when I, for one, could use some distance to figure things out. Conveniently, he ignores me anyway, clearly back to his usual self.

Everyone else greets me, though, and I realize I'm staring at the Unifier's guard when I spot Kharis standing proudly in the middle of his fighters. I only recognize a few other familiar faces among the twenty soldiers standing before me. The captain of Averion doesn't waste time introducing everyone and motions for his unit to begin training and for me to take my place at its center.

The group organically shifts around me as I position myself and begin going through the different fighting stances and repetitions that are like second nature to me now. To my surprise, the soldiers start adjusting their fighting styles, moving as I move, filling in the gaps around me.

We train like this for hours while Kharis goes around the room correcting his warriors and adjusting techniques. His unmistakable voice sounds in the air at intervals, but there is no trace of anger in it. He's simply doing what he has to in order to ensure that as many of them make it back home as possible once it's all over.

When we finally wrap up, he pulls me aside.

"You have excellent technique. I'll work with them to ensure we're at our best when the time comes."

I give him a small smile in thanks and finally ask the question that's been on my mind since I arrived. "Shouldn't I go introduce myself to each of them?" I lower my voice, unsure what's the best course of action here.

He returns a kind smile before gently shaking his head. My heart sinks at the realization of what this means and what they're all prepared to do. Each of these soldiers would die for me. Knowing their names, relating to them, and caring for them would hinder me. These people are warriors. They've all seen Death before, and they're prepared to face it again with me.

Although this could seem heartless, I appreciate his candor. He doesn't lie or evade the truth, which means I can rely on him, and I guess that's the most important thing.

Once I leave the training center, I remember that Vesta is out on a recon mission, so I can't spend time with her. Instead, I take a walk through the city and drop by to see Ilyana and Thalea.

At night, I'm woken up by another violent nightmare, and my thoughts drift back to the necklace in my wardrobe. I search for Savage but he's not in the room, which means he's probably out in the gardens.

A night stroll sounds like exactly what I need right now, so I grab a long robe before leaving my room. Just as I do, Azran is exiting his room at the other end of the corridor, and his head turns in my direction.

⸻ ◆ ⸻

Azran

I wake up from yet another horrendous dream. They've become a part of me, a part of what sleeping is like. As the nightmares have been my faithful companions since the day I touched the scroll, I know I won't be able to go back to sleep. I get dressed and decide to head to my office to go over the latest missives received from our scouts. I'm not expecting anything unusual, but I need to keep busy.

I can't stay here aimlessly when I know she's next door. I thought I could give her what she needs and pull away, but every minute I spend trying to ignore her is hell. Being in the same room with her is torture. Unable to claim her as mine, unable to look at her because I'm too afraid my eyes will betray my true feelings.

I head out, but just as I do, she's there, at the other end of the corridor. Her hair is a mess around her pretty face, and even the distance can't hide the purple beneath her eyes. Those don't take away any of her beauty. They're just a reminder that she's unable to rest in my home.

My breath catches in my throat as I realize I cannot do this right now. I'm on edge and so close to telling her everything. I head into the corridor and walk by her without a word.

"Why did you leave the necklace?" I'm about to step into the stairway when her voice stops me. There is no mistaking the note of frustration in her tone.

"It's yours. Wear it or don't."

"I don't want it," she says. My back still turned to her, I close my eyes, trying to refrain from revealing too much. "Why give it to me in the first place when all you do is ignore me? If you want it back, just say so."

I spin around in an instant to face her, pain tearing through me as the words leave her mouth. "It was meant for you, and you only. Do with it what you will." I turn away. I've already said more than I should have.

"Meant for me? What do you mean?"

I pause to take a deep breath.

"It's a family heirloom. Now enough with the questions. I have things to do." Forcing myself to put one foot in front of the other, I head out. As I do, her anger radiates through the bond. I already knew she didn't want me the way I want her, but the confirmation doesn't hurt any less.

Message received. I need to keep my distance. Yet I can't refuse her when she seeks me out the way she did yesterday. This will be the death of me, but if it's all I can get, then so be it.

CHAPTER EIGHTEEN

I storm out of the corridor, in the opposite direction as him, and start stomping around the palace corridors. The cold marble beneath my bare feet helps keep my power in check after his unnecessary display of irritation and self-importance. Prick.

I'm wandering the castle aimlessly, going up and down stairways and walking past dozens of closed doors, just trying to clear my head.

When I finally stop, I'm in the empty Throne Room, its giant terrace waiting beyond the glass panels. I step outside in the cold air of the night and go towards the edge. With the metal railing reflecting the moonlight, I narrow my eyes to discern its patterns more clearly. Shapes of each element of the Fae, suns, leaves, water drops, and moons, are intertwined together, symbolizing his dream.

With the peaceful city below, I hold on to the handrail, absorbed in contemplation. I wonder if this is all it will ever be, a fantasy, and the hope that I could somehow bring them what they've been seeking for hundreds of years.

I lift my head to gaze into the darkness beyond which I know lies the woods. I close my eyes for a second, picturing myself there, back in our cabin, with both my parents. I wonder what my mother would look like today and how different my father would have been had she not left us. And for the first time, I consider what their deaths also mean.

They've been reunited at last. Able to live out eternity in death together, with nothing left to separate them. Strangely, the idea brings me a deep sense of calm and comfort. And when the wind brushes through my hair and the fabric of my robe, it feels like a soft caress.

I still can't believe everything that's happened since I first saw Azran in the Dark Forest. How far I've come, how much hurt and loss I've suffered, and how much I've changed. Letting out a slow breath, I stay here a while longer, staring into the dark, before heading back to my room.

Once there, I realize I don't want to sleep. What I really need is to blow off some steam, so I change and grab Nahtar. I'm a caged animal here, waiting for Braern to show his hand. I have this feeling we're being taken for fools, and waiting around is becoming harder each day.

As I walk out, I dive back into my thoughts, and those irrevocably go to the High Lord.

A family heirloom. I'm not sure what's more disturbing about this latest revelation, his behaving like an asshole or the fact that the concept of family is no stranger to him. Does he have siblings, parents, or cousins that are still alive? And why give me the necklace in the first place? When he's not buried inside me, he ignores me or acts like it's painful to even look at me.

I get to the training center a little before dawn and finally give up on trying to make sense of it all. Thankfully, the room is completely empty, so after stretching, I begin a series of strikes with Nahtar. Balancing my weight on my legs, I'm flying across the room.

Ever since I got to Averion, and after having my previous life torn apart in front of my eyes, the one thing I've gained is a lethal skillset with a sword and knives. And an even deadlier power that I can constantly feel gently pulsing beneath my skin, waiting for my call.

Sweat is forming on my forehead and trickling down my warm back. My breathing the only sound in the air, I keep dancing with my blade, keeping my core tight with each move.

I've somehow come to terms with my new life in the past weeks. I'm not celebrating it, but at least I have a purpose now, revenge to fulfill. Before I stumbled upon Azran, I was barely surviving, so in a way, I'm grateful for this new life. At least I'm not living a lie anymore, and if I'm being completely honest, I finally feel like myself in my Fae body. I had just never realized how out of place I felt before.

And when I'm fighting, when I unleash my power, a sense of quiet and peace like I've never felt before washes over me. It's a welcome reprieve after more than two decades spent in fear. It's good to be the one inflicting it on others for once. I know how twisted that sounds, but I can't help feeling this way.

Still swinging Nahtar around, I turn around violently and stop my blade an inch away from Wyn's angelic face.

"Wow! Good morning to you, too." He slowly steps away, his hands in the air.

"Sorry! What were you doing sneaking up on me like that?" I ask, still panting from the exertion.

"What he usually does. Wreaking havoc and leaving me to fix the mess afterward." Varan's voice comes from the arched entrance as he gives me a big smile.

"It's good to see you, guys. What are you doing here so early?"

The blond twins exchange a knowing look.

"Look, Ela. Even if we tell you, you can't come. We've all received explicit orders not to let you come with us on recon missions."

"Orders? Then why didn't you avoid me when you spotted me here, hmm?" My eyebrow raises in question. They're up to something.

"Told you she'd figure it out!" Wyn elbows his brother in the ribs. "We know you've been cooped up here for weeks. We've been sent on a recon mission to patrol the Wood and Sun Fae border, not far from the Eidune range." As Wyn blurts out every single detail of their secret mission, I make a mental note never to tell him a secret.

"But what I said still stands, we can't take you with us. Orders and all," Varan says, smiling widely.

"Right. So you can't take me with you. But nothing prevents me from, let's say, leaving Averion and coincidently stumbling onto you both on your way to the border..."

They don't answer, but a smile tugs on my lips. I'm like a child who's just come up with a brilliant plan to outsmart her guardians. Varan winks at me and glances by the entrance. I follow his gaze and spot their small packs. They're leaving now. Good.

I nod back at them both and sprint back to my room to pack a small pouch with a change of clothes and my waterskin. I find Savage in the palace gardens as usual, and he comes by my side instantly. We head to the stables, where I saddle and mount the black horse I rode before.

A brief thought for Kharis crosses my mind. I hope he doesn't get in trouble for this. And then I'm out of the palace, riding through the city. I barely nod to the guards at the wall and break into a gallop as soon as I'm on the vast plains. With wind brushing in my hair, Nahtar on my back, and Savage running by my side, I'm alive again.

After a few miles, once I'm past several hills, Averion is not in sight anymore. I spot Wyn and Varan waiting for me ahead, and I catch up with them.

"Fancy seeing you here," I say. They're both smiling. "So, tell me more about this recon. Anything I should know about?"

Wyn shrugs my questions off. "It's the usual. Patrol the border and report anything out of the ordinary. If we spot rebels, don't engage, follow to obtain information, and report back."

"Don't engage?" I narrow my eyes at them both.

"Ela. Don't engage. We're here to observe and report, that's all." Varan says.

"This makes no sense. We're on the brink of war, and we do nothing? Sit back and wait while Braern gathers more resources or God knows what." I mumble to myself as anger slowly wakes up inside me. The twins' raised brows stop me. "Sorry. I've just been restless, is all. I'll do as you say."

Varan gives me a kind smile. "Us, too. But Azran and Cal are the best commanders we've ever had, and they know what they're doing." Somehow, I doubt they know more than I do about Braern's plans, but the twins don't need to worry about that.

"All right, let's get moving before Varan goes back to babbling about his favorite exotic bird," Wyn says, a cheeky smile striking his features as Varan's turns red.

Laughing, I lead my horse down the path after them.

We spend most of the day traveling toward Sun Fae territory, following the Dark Forest on our right. As we get closer to the southern regions, we tone down the banter to stay on the lookout for movement or anything out of place. Beasts still roam these grounds, and I definitely don't want to face a darkclaws or anything of the sort ever again. Thankfully, the only tracks of monsters we spot all lead to the Dark Forest. And as usual, Savage is quietly strolling alongside us, glancing my way every now and then.

We're taking turns, with one of us scouting ahead while the other two stay behind to make a loop. We're making good progress as we're traveling light. So far, we've ridden past several small Fae villages and found them undisturbed. By the end of the first day, we're a little more than a day away from the Eidune Range where rebels were last spotted.

We stop for a few hours at sundown to eat and rest by a barren hill. I take the first watch while the twins sleep. With no fire to light up our surroundings or signal us to others, I let my eyes adjust to the moonlight.

After an hour, I walk the perimeter with Savage. We're not far from the forest, so I make rounds in that direction, quietly listening for any disturbance. We're camped far enough from villages for any crops to be near. And all I can discern is patchy grass until the edge of the wood. I'm about to head back when something stops me.

I crouch and freeze, and so does Savage. In complete silence, I scan the area as best I can in the dark, but nothing moves. There is something out there, though. I can feel it. Ever so slowly, I unsheathe Nahtar, careful not to let the moonlight reflect on its blade.

Letting out a slow breath, I call on my shadows and wrap them around Savage and me, knowing it will at least hide the humanoid form of my body. With my power set free, my vision improves, and I start walking quietly, trying to identify the source of the threat I know roams around.

I'm about to turn back when a group moving alongside the Dark Forest comes into sight. Their shadows are barely perceptible among the trees, but there must be at least a dozen Fae, maybe a few hundred feet away from me. They're heading south, and I could be on them in minutes with my shadows cloaking me.

Before I can second guess myself, I run towards them with Savage by my side. I won't engage, but I need to figure out what they are up to and where they are headed. I let my shadows entirely cloak the both of us and slow down to a fast walk when I'm within hearing range, matching their pace. Rebels. There's no mistaking the mismatched group of mercenaries in front of me.

When they abruptly stop, I think they're on to me. But as I watch them gather in a circle by the edge of the forest, I realize they are taking a break. Some lie down on the ground while others crouch over their packs, panting. Are they fleeing? Or in a hurry to get somewhere? Most likely the latter.

Using their exhaustion to my advantage, I get closer. I can now make out the heavy armor they're all carrying. This is no random group of rebels. They're armed for war.

But they're weakened right now, and that's the realization that I can't shake off.

I can take them out. I know I can. My power is already pulsing strongly when it occurs to me that my father's murderer could be among them. The thought almost sends me over the edge, and it's too late when I realize that my anger distracted me enough to undo my cloak of shadows.

I freeze when the first Fae to spot me jumps on his feet and unsheathes his short sabre. Just like the rebels from the forest, this one is wearing black marks on his face.

There's no hiding now, so I don't waste another second and sprint toward him. Savage, already ahead of me, jumps on a Fae lying on the ground. His fate is short-lived as he dies under my wolf's sharp canines.

His screams wake the whole squadron, though, and when I gut the first assailant, three others are facing me. I unleash my power and send them crashing while parrying a deadly blow on my left side.

I don't have time to think or look at their horrible faces. My sole purpose is to kill. I block another assault, pivot, and run my attacker through with Nahtar. Savage growls and attacks another soldier. Eight left, including the three I sent crashing moments ago.

I can't risk being hit by a poisoned blade, so I call on my power once more, sending my shadows around us, hiding me from their view, confusing them. And I butcher them all. Dancing in the dark, Nahtar is flying around me, cutting and slicing through bodies and armor alike. Seven to go. Pivot and slice. Six. Duck, parry, gut. Five. My power is now running wild inside me, pure bliss in my veins. Four. Each death is fueling me. Three. Warm blood splatters on my face. Two. Numb, there's only the void inside me. One. I call my shadows back to me, and my gaze falls on the terrified Fae in front of me.

"Please. Please, don't!" His words are meaningless to me, he's already dead. He's been dead since I laid eyes on the group. It was inevitable. This is what I was put on this earth to do. Kill and destroy.

The rebel tries to bolt, but I extend my hand, and my shadows sink into him, bringing him back. He's lying at my feet, begging. Tears are running down his face, but I can't hear a word or feel a thing. I grip Nahtar and swing it above his shoulders, separating his head from his body.

Savage's warm fur brushing against my leg brings me back to the living world moments later. I'm covered in blood, left to contemplate the horror and the torn bodies around me.

Sounds are coming back to me with Savage's labored breath. Wind brushes in the trees nearby, and blood drips from my blade. A copper taste on my tongue, guilt comes next. Just like in my dreams.

"Ela! Thank God you're alive!" Wyn's voice comes from behind me. I turn around, startled. "You were gone when we woke up. We thought you had gone scouting, but when you didn't come back, we came looking and heard the sounds of a battle."

Still trying to catch my breath, I can't utter a word.

"Wow." Varan's gaze jumps between the bodies and me. "Are you hurt?"

"No," I say in a weak voice, trying to fight off the tears and the overwhelming sense of shame crushing me. Seeing my distress, Varan proceeds to take me back to our encampment while Wyn gathers the bodies to bury them.

Spent, I wipe the blood on my face with a wet cloth and wait for Wyn to get back.

Once reunited, the twins are giving me concerned looks. "I was scouting the area when I spotted the group. At first, I followed from a distance, but when they caught me, I had to defend myself."

I leave out the parts about my shadows and powers. They already know about the prophecy and certainly don't need any more details to believe I'm a monster. They've seen what I can do.

Thankfully, they leave it at that and don't question me further. Instead, they pack up our small belongings and ready the horses so we can head back to Averion. I get changed into the fresh set of clothes I brought and mount my horse.

Elanor

It's nightfall when we get back to Averion the following evening. After dropping off our horses by the stables, we make for Cal's quarters to give him our report. I have a feeling I'm in for a memorable scolding.

We cross the threshold of the palace and the general greets us, the frown on his forehead revealing the depth of the trouble we're in. I attempt a small apologetic smile, but it earns me another cold glance. If looks could kill...

He leads us to the throne room without a word. Fuck. I know who's waiting beyond those doors.

As we step into the Great Hall, Wyn and Varan lower their heads to bow. I've never bowed to anyone, and I'm not going to start now, so I look straight ahead into Azran's deadly gaze. His blood eyes are the cruelest I've ever seen them. He's wearing red armor, and his double-bladed sword is hanging on the back of his white throne.

"Anybody want to tell us what the hell happened?" Cal bursts out the minute the doors close on their hinges.

I step forward before the twins have the chance to try and take part of the blame. "I stumbled upon Wyn and Varan while I was out with Savage on a ride to clear my head. They protested, but I couldn't be dissuaded, so I went on the mission with them." I pause to catch my breath and notice Cal glancing severely at his soldiers.

"I was told not to engage if we were to encounter rebels. So when I spotted a group of them heading South along the Dark Forest, trying to sneak past our patrols, I followed at a distance. I saw they were heavily armored when they paused to rest." Cal raises an eyebrow and motions for me to continue. Right, on to the tricky part. "I got closer to have a better look, but they spotted me and attacked. I had no choice, so I defended myself. Savage was with me, and we managed to neutralize the threat." I try to keep a neutral face, just like I had seen the captains do during war councils.

Cal slowly turns toward the twins, waiting for their confirmation. They both nod, and I let out a slow breath, relieved that that part seems to be going decently well. But then I glance back in Az's direction.

Big mistake. His eyes are like daggers, his jaw is tightly clenched, and his hand closed in a fist is whitening by the minute.

"How many?"

Az's voice startles me, and the hair raises on my arm. Red embers are dancing in his eyes, revealing his fury.

I can't bring myself to answer and dig my nails in my palms instead. I just can't. I know what's coming if I do.

The twins flinch when the High Lord stands up with rage carved on his features, but I stay still, readying myself for what's to come.

"A dozen, High Lord." Varan cuts in before sending me an apologetic look.

The temperature drops and I take a deep breath, bracing myself for his violence, knowing damn well that nothing could ever prepare me well enough.

"What the *fuck* were you thinking?" His voice resounds in the Hall so loudly my ears could explode. He seems taller and wider than ever, towering over me like I'm a mindless insignificance. Even Cal looks small next to him and the twins are shaking.

I can't help but lower my gaze. Not out of fear but because I can feel my own wrath waking up, a silent threat and a promise. I can't look at him right now because if I do, I know I'll see the same monster that exists inside me. And the world might explode if we both collide.

His steps echo on the marble floor as he walks towards me, his fury radiating from his body, directly fueling mine. How dare he talk to me like I'm beneath him and some reckless brat!

"Do you have a death wish? You were told never to leave without me knowing about it!"

His voice trembles with emotion, but I've had enough. I look up, revealing my darkened eyes. "I am *not* your loyal little pet! You wanted me to be the Unifier, then here I am. I did what I had to do!" I say behind clenched teeth, my power pulsing beneath my skin, so close to jumping out of me.

My blood turns to ice when he reveals a wicked smile that doesn't meet his eyes. Cal takes one glance at his High Lord before sending the twins away and leaving us alone.

The tension increases tenfold with their absence. Az is standing right in front of me, shaking with fury. Right when I think he's going to lose control, his mouth opens slightly. "Do you have any idea what the past two days have been like for me?" He steps closer to me, grabbing me by the arms. "*Any* idea?"

Savage barks at him as his grip tightens on my arms, but I'm just staring into his red eyes. Unable to move or speak, I'm trying to keep a lid on the power thrashing inside me and not get us both killed.

Fury subsides to horror in his gaze. Without letting me go, he growls through clenched teeth. "You were gone. You disappeared. I felt it!"

I finally manage to shake off the shock. "What the fuck are you talking about? You weren't there. I took care of a threat." I can tell he's about to argue, but his mouth opens and shuts abruptly.

The cold mask of rage is back, his red eyes glaring at me, but he lets go of me.

"Don't you get it? They cannot get their hands on you or figure out what you can do. We can't lose this element of surprise."

I take a step back, almost physically hurt by his words. This is all about the prophecy, it always is. That's the only value I have in his eyes.

"I was careful. There was no living soul around, and no one left to tell the tale. Since that's all you care about." I say as disgust and guilt come back to me.

He tries reaching back out to me, but I dodge his hand, simply giving him a cold stare.

"Ela, that is not all I care about."

"Really? What are we doing then? What is it that you want from me? Apart from my fulfilling of your damned prophecy. You hate me. I hate you."

He takes a step closer but doesn't try touching me this time. He's just looking into my eyes, trying to decipher what's going on. "Does it look like I hate you?"

Rage seems to have left him, but rage hasn't left me. "One day, you fuck me, you tell me all sorts of things, you give me a family heirloom. And the next, you ignore me, dismiss me, and call me out in front of everyone, treating me like a child." Shock paints his features. "Or maybe you're just treating me like the weapon that I am. Carefully crafting it, trying to manipulate it. And then kissing it when you feel like having a little fun with it!"

Time suspends as he freezes, his eye widened.

"What else do you want from me? You've made it very clear you only wanted my body. You've shut down any attempt I made to turn this into something more!"

"All I wanted was to not be treated like a toy! You just want me because of your damn prophecy, to keep me close, imprison me, and make sure I don't leave when you need me the most!"

"Fuck the damn prophecy!" His scream reverberates in the hall, his lips shaking as he scans my face.

Silenced by his outburst, I'm trying to wrap my head around what he's suggesting.

"Don't pretend this is news to you, Ela. I've wanted you since I first laid eyes on you," he says, with yellow lights dancing in his eyes. "Do you think I let anyone walk into my room in the middle of the night? Insult me? Reject me like I'm some random Fae? I'll take anything you'll give me, even if it's just scraps!"

He steps toward me, and I step back. Suddenly he calms down, and I realize I'm trembling.

"Don't you know? Deep down, have you not realized yet?" His voice is almost a caress in my ears.

"Realized what?" I don't want to hear what comes next, but I can't help the words from leaving my tongue.

He closes the distance between us to gently cup my face, and I let him.

"I love you, Ela. More than I could ever put into words. I adore you. All of you." My mouth drops open, and my eyes start watering. Unable to refrain, exhausted from the constant fight, rage, and games, the tears start rolling down my face.

"What? When..."

"I realized it the first time you went into the Dark Forest and the assassins came after you. Then in the caves, when those-" His jaw clenches hard and he swallows a lump in his throat. "I love you unconditionally. I love all of you, both the darkness and the light." His hazel eyes sparkling with emotion render me speechless. "I didn't want to push you. Not after everything I had done. But I couldn't resist when I was around you. I thought you knew and weren't interested. I thought this was one-sided."

I hold my breath as a familiar tug pulls inside me. Somehow, I think he feels it, too.

"No. No..."

He gently nods his head. "It snapped into place when I rushed to get to you during the assassination attempt. I could hear your thoughts. I could hear you giving up and getting ready to die. It tore through my chest."

"No..."

"I felt it snap when I broke your heart and told you about your parents. I thought that was the end of it when my heart shattered into a million pieces." He pauses a moment to stare into my eyes and my vision blurs with fresh tears. "But somehow, in the caves, when you were captured, I could feel you again. I could feel your panic guiding me through the tunnels. I could hear what that bastard was telling you, what he was going to do to you. And I knew."

My heart is beating out of my chest as I wait for his next words. "You are my mate, little one. There will never be anyone else." He's looking at me with pure adoration in his eyes. "I promise to show you how much I love you until you can trust me. I'd walk through the gates of Hell and relive the horrors of a thousand lives to find you because you are mine, as I am yours, and I will never give up on you. It's *never* been about the prophecy."

The walls built up inside me crumble down, revealing the bond pulsing between us. A thin thread tying us together, radiating with light. I step away, freeing myself from his hands. "*No.*" No. No. I can't do this. Alone in an ocean of emotions, a threatening storm is rolling in and a wave is about to drown me. I can't.

I do the only thing I can think of. I call on my power and my vision darkens instantly. For the first time, I let the lethal energy course through me freely, completely unchecked. I cloak myself in shadows, welcoming the void accompanying the darkness, pushing everything back. The panic, the shock, the bond. Everything is put under wrap while my power runs free.

With all senses muted, everything quietens and his scent disappears. I can't feel the cold tears on my warm cheeks anymore.

I close my eyes, visualizing the darkness swallowing me whole, obliterating any remnants of feelings, securing it all away in an unbreakable safe, and I lose track of time.

I'm in a trance when Savage's wet muzzle on my arm brings me back to the Great Hall. The High Lord is gone, and I'm alone in the gigantic marble room. I turn around, not feeling a thing with my power on a simmer, shielding and protecting me. I never want to turn it off

That's it. I can block away all of this to focus on the only thing that matters, my revenge. I can see clearly now that emotions are no longer clouding my judgment.

My thoughts drift to the war as I absently pet Savage's soft fur, and I realize I'm done waiting. The night sky beyond the glass panels reminds me of the council that's about to start. I need to go to the meeting, but this time, I won't be sitting through another useless series of reports.

A plan forms in my mind as I head out of the room, walk through the corridors, and up the white marble stairs with Savage in my wake.

I'm almost the last one there. Cal, Mor, Lana, and Naar are already seated. Kharis and the other three captains are there, too. I quietly observe the group as we wait for the High Lord. Cal lifts his head to meet my gaze and gives me a quick nod, to which I don't respond.

Azran walks in moments later and stands in front of his imposing desk, his eyes scanning the room and pausing on me for a brief moment. I don't look away. With a gesture of his hand, he invites us to start the usual reports. But before I can cut in, the door swings open.

CHAPTER NINETEEN

Azran

I stare into her eyes and see nothing. I still don't understand how she does it. She feels dead to me through the bond, although she's standing before me, alive and breathing. And my heart has been ripped out of my chest once more.

I didn't expect this revelation to go well, but I certainly didn't expect it to go that badly. She's become an emotionless version of herself. A deadly instrument with nothing to shackle her wrath.

Bringing my attention back to the meeting, I motion for my captains to begin.

My head snaps towards the door when it crashes against the opposite wall, revealing one of our scouts.

A tall Fae stomps in, her armor full of mud splatters and deep purple beneath her crazed eyes.

"What is it?" I say, eager to learn the cause of this interruption. Cal is already standing next to me, waiting.

"Braern. He's marching on the human kingdom." She lowers her gaze. "He's been spotted by the Eidune range with at least three thousand warriors. They've crossed onto Brimora, and we think they're headed for Adria." The silence the room falls into couldn't be any louder.

I freeze for a second before rage takes over. I turn around, grab hold of the wooden desk, and send it flying against the fireplace with a growl. Paperweights, books, and ink bottles crash on the floor. We won't get there in time. The humans will be slaughtered.

I squeeze my eyes shut as power thrashes inside me. One moment is all I'll allow myself. One moment for rage to explode. One moment to let this sink in.

When I turn back to face the council, resolve has replaced shock in my captains' eyes. We've all come to the same conclusion.

"That sick bastard!" Cal's voice fills the air. "That's what he was after all this time. Stalling to advance on the human realm."

"But why Adria? He knows he can't win against us and the Brimora army." Kharis asks.

"It's not about winning. It's about permanently damaging any Human-Fae alliance, making it impossible for us to ally ourselves with them no matter the outcome against him. Because we'll be too late." Cal says before looking at me, waiting for me to make the call.

There is no way for us to prevent the massacre, and in that, Braern has already won. The only thing we can do is stop him before his madness destroys the whole continent.

"What are we waiting for? Let's go after him and end him." Ela joins the conversation, only it's not her I'm looking at. I stare into her eyes and see Death dancing in her darkened irises.

An army is about to raid and destroy the human territories, and it doesn't seem to be affecting her in the slightest. She just wants Braern dead. Well, that will have to do.

"They're forcing our hand, making sure we're chasing them and playing catch-up," I say as I look around the room. However horrifying that sounds, I know we're out of options. "We move out by first light. Send word to all squadrons to gather south along the Dark Forest by dawn the next day. Then, we're marching on Brimora."

The whole room is in an uproar. Mor leaves first to gather Averion's healers and organize the supply wagons with Barus. The captains and Ela head out right after, and only Cal stays behind.

When it's just us, he turns to me, his jaw clenched tight. We've gone to war more times than I can recall, and I know he's feeling as heavyhearted as I am.

"Damn it, Az. This is worse than I thought. As much as we tried anticipating his moves, he just landed a huge victory, and he knows it. We'll have no choice but to adjust and improvise based on the terrain when we get there." He closes his eyes and pinches the bridge of his nose. "At this time of the year, Adria could already be marshy." I nod in agreement. Everything is out of our control now, and there's nothing I can say that will change these circumstances or make him feel better.

"I should have killed him when I had the chance. This is all my fault," Cal says.

"Shut up. None of this is your fault. Braern lost his mind and morals long ago. We're not going to spend energy worrying about what could have been when this piece of shit is still alive and out there. We're going to ride out and end him, and we'll help as many humans as possible."

I instill as much strength and conviction as I can in my words. "We outnumber them by far, and odds are in our favor, two to one. You know I hate this as much as you do, but this could be the last of it for a very long time." I step forward and grab him by the shoulders.

"I know. You're right." He lets out a long sigh before straightening his stance and looking back at me.

"Plus, we have Ela and my abilities," I add.

"No, Az. We've talked about this. You can't reveal your powers. Not unless it's absolutely necessary."

"I know. All I'm saying is we're not defenseless here. We've been dealt a shitty hand, but this won't be the end of it. This will all be over in a few days, and Braern's head will be rotting on a battlefield."

Cal finally gives me a small smile, and I let him go before taking a few steps back. My thoughts automatically drift back to Ela as I realize this couldn't come at a worse time. A sad smile tugs on my lips as Cal is studying me. He knows me too well.

"I told her." I glance around the office, unable to look him in the eyes. "She lost it and blocked out all her emotions with her powers."

"Shit. Well, that explains her reaction."

"She feels dead to me, Cal. I've never felt anything like that. It's... insane." My eyes widen as I say it out loud and my heart breaks once more, pain tearing through me.

"I'm sorry, Az." Cal steps forward but I stop him with a wave of my hand.

I lift my head up to face him. He needs me at my strongest and not completely unstable with a wounded heart. "It could never have been anything more. I killed her mother and wrecked her life. Now, enough about this." He's about to argue but I extend my arm in his direction. "We're off to war, and I've got an entire battlefield on which to unleash my rage."

Silenced, Cal walks up to me and grabs my forearm tightly.

We don't need to say anything else. He knows. I know. Until whatever end.

Elanor

Savage and I head to the garrison to get my horse. Knives are strapped to my thighs, Nahtar on my back, and I'm carrying a small pack of fresh undershirts and leather pants.

It's still dark out when I meet Wyn and Varan in the courtyard, both ready to move out.

"Hey, Ela. Are you okay? You've heard?" Wyn asks.

"I'm fine." My own voice sounds unfamiliar to me, almost foreign. Distant.

"Sorry about earlier in the Throne room," Varan says, giving me an apologetic look. I dismiss his words with a shrug, unaffected.

The gallop of a horse resounds on the cobblestones. Vesta hurries through the arch, covered in dust, her red hair a complete mess as she returns from her mission. She still manages to gracefully hop off her mount as Cal steps out of the garrison to meet her. He tries grabbing her by the arm to pull her aside, but she frees herself.

I hurry towards them and join the two as Cal shares the latest development. Her head snaps to mine when she notices me. "Are you okay, Ela? I'm so sorry."

"I'm fine. Why is everyone apologizing to me?" I roll my eyes at her words.

Vesta's brows draw closer together, but I head back toward the twins where my horse has been brought out. I secure my pack on its back before checking its saddle and mounting it.

Cal and Vesta are still talking and glancing over toward me.

The general heads in my direction when Vesta rushes to the garrison.

"Ela. Ride with whoever you want, but when we get there, you're staying with your unit, Az, and me, until we assess the situation."

I nod. Sounds fair to me. I want to be there when reports of Braern's movement arrive. I promised myself I'd end him, and I intend on keeping that promise.

Vesta emerges from the barracks shortly after, changed and heavily armored. Dawn is still a few hours away, but the first readied squadrons are moving out of the palace grounds.

I join the twins with the High Guard, and Vesta catches up with us right when we're crossing the arch leading into the city. Kharis is riding not far behind me.

As soon as we're out of the city, we break into a gallop. And from here on out, it's a race against time.

For the first time since I've met them, the brothers are silent, and so is everyone else. Hundreds of hooves beat the ground as we trot through the plains and we're joined by several other units heading to the rendezvous point alongside the Dark Forrest.

Every now and then, I glance at Savage running by my side. We haven't stopped for hours but he doesn't seem affected.

As I'm staring in the distance, I make out the Eidune range. I don't know what lies beyond it, I've never been there, but I know it's not going to be pretty.

Eventually, the horses tire by the end of the afternoon, and we finally come to a halt. I dismount and lead my horse to follow the rest of the High Guard into the biggest Fae encampment I've ever seen.

Hundreds of small triangular tents are installed by the edge of the forest, with fires lit up all around as daylight fades. There are warriors everywhere, going from one side to the other. Most of them are wearing green and brown colors. Wood Fae.

I'm walking behind Wyn, Varan, and Vesta, galloping hooves still echoing in my head, until a different clamor sounds around us. Fresh squadrons are joining the army, settling in, and soldiers are breaking into conversations everywhere.

Several heads turn in our direction, following us as we head deeper into the ocean of tents. When we get to the center of the camp, we stop by a pavilion, and a Fae comes to grab our reins and lead the horses away.

"Come on, L. This is where the High Guard stays. There's room for you here." Vesta points to a small tent next to what I imagine is hers before nodding toward the big tent behind us. "This is the High Lord's pavilion." I follow her gaze and see that one of its sides is rolled up, and its entrance is guarded by two Fae warriors wearing Azran's red and gold colors. "The Wood Fae are already here. The rest of the army will get here by dawn."

Feeling sore from the long and hard ride, I find an empty container to give water to Savage before taking some time to stretch and hydrate myself. The twins drop off some food for us both moments later and I eat the stew silently by my tent.

The extent of my exhaustion hits me once I put the empty bowl down next to me. I need my full strength when we get to Brimora, and I haven't had a minute to rest since before the recon mission. I don't want to let go of its reassuring presence, but my power is sapping a chunk of energy I can't afford to waste if I want to make it to the battle with enough reserves.

I have to take the risk to dim it. I just need to isolate the one thing I can't process right now and let the rest be.

Closing my eyes and retreating into myself, I follow the thin thread of energy flowing within me until I find its source. I call almost all my power back, focusing only a tiny amount on what I barely sensed late last night. As I'm working on spinning this intricate web, I can feel darkness retreating.

I take a deep breath and keep going. This has to work. Staying focused on the task at hand, I slowly let some feelings and life back in.

Reality sets in with the crushing weight of where we're headed and what we're about to do. The familiar wave of fear is next, and with it comes the dread that always accompanies my nightmares and never really leaves me. Utter loneliness and isolation follow and hit me the hardest.

I'm about to be overwhelmed by the emotions and spiral down, but I tighten everything in place, holding my breath. After several long minutes, I realize my world has not shattered yet, and the web of energy inside me is holding.

I open my eyes and find Vesta, Wyn, and Varan looking at me. I exhale and finally recognize the worried glances coming my way. As blissful as it is to lose myself in the darkness, coming down from it is the worst wake-up call. It's like I'm switching planes of existence and the mortal one is no fun. Never has been for me. My eyes dampen as I realize how comforting the idea of death has become to me. It would be so... freeing.

My face must betray my new state as the twins give me a small smile, welcoming me back.

"The High Lord requests your presence, Unifier."

I turn around to identify the person calling me by the stupid title. A human soldier wearing the Wood Fae colors is standing there, waiting for me to follow him.

It's now completely dark out, but the campfire still reveals his innocent and beardless face. I didn't realize some humans had joined Azran's army, given their short lifespan and frailty.

I'm about to scold him but refrain from it at the last second, noticing the hope and pride in his gaze. Although I'm far from being the savior he seems to think I am, I don't have it in me to break his spirit before the fight that's to come. His chances of making it out alive are low enough as it is. Yet, he doesn't seem scared. Just in awe.

I stand up and nod solemnly, waiting for him to lead the way. With a movement of my hand, Savage stays put.

"What's your name?" I surprise myself when the words leave my mouth.

"Alan." He glances back at me, startled by my question.

"How old are you, Alan?"

"I'm 22." My heart sinks instantly at his response.

Moments later, Alan stops by the guarded central pavilion and steps aside to let me in. He's looking at me expectantly, and so are the two Fae standing guard. So I say the only thing that comes to mind.

"I'm glad to know you'll be fighting alongside me, Alan."

The boy is beaming with pride. "I will be honored to do so, Unifier."

Not letting my smile falter at the mention of the prophecy, I give him a nod and step inside.

The High Lord's tent is spacious, well-lit by lanterns, yet basic. Several seats have been arranged around the room, the ground is covered in rugs, and a simple bed has been installed in a corner.

Averion's captains, Mor, and two other Fae I haven't met are already inside. The svelte female is wearing green armor, and a delicate braided crown is resting on her forehead. Irann, Lady of the Wood Fae, if I had to guess. And the robust male conversing with her must be Tharrion, Lord of the Sun Fae. His golden crown contrasts beautifully with his dark skin and hair. I read about them back at the library.

Finally, Azran and Cal are standing silently at the back of the room. A pit opens in my stomach when I lay eyes on the High Lord, afraid my power won't be able to contain the bond I know lies deep inside me. But nothing. I know the facts. I remember every single word he said to me. And it doesn't overwhelm me. It just doesn't mean anything to me right now. Satisfied, I take a few extra steps in the tent.

"Irann, Tharrion, meet Elanor." Azran begins, introducing us.

I shift to face them and stay still, repressing the need for my fingers to toy with the hem of my shirt.

"So you're the Unifier." Tharrion's deep voice resonates in my ears but I don't respond. His eyes go from my face to Nahtar before the Sun Fae turns towards the High Lord with a scoff. "You're asking us to believe that this formerly human stranger will be the turning point during the battle and to put all our trust in her abilities. I hope you know what you're doing, High Lord."

Cal is about to interject, but Azran stops him with a motion of his hand. With his red eyes glimmering, the High Lord steps forward. "You know better than to question me, Tharrion. Or have you forgotten what happened last time you tried?" His gaze digs into the eyes of the Sun Fae before his striking features reveal a dangerous smile. "I haven't."

"That's not what I meant, High Lord, I just-"

"I know what you meant. There's still time for you to switch sides since you seem to be harboring doubts about humans. I'm sure Braern would welcome any ally he can get his hands on."

Everyone stops breathing as there is no mistaking Azran's glacial tone. Tharrion is now staring at the ground, smart enough not to object.

"This is your last warning," Azran says.

"What Tharrion might have been suggesting, Az, is that we have no idea what she's capable of. Maybe a demonstration would ease concerns and give us the extra confidence to walk in the fight." A high-pitched voice fills the air as a new shape appears in the corner of my eyes, circling around me to come forward.

The most stunning Fae I've ever laid eyes on is standing in front of me, with blond hair falling down to her rounded hips, striking silver eyes, pale skin, and full lips. Her tight grey armor hugs her every curve. She slowly turns around to meet everyone's gaze, knowing precisely the kind of effect she has on people, and Tharrion sends her a grateful glance.

"Overconfidence is the downfall of an army, Amrynn. All those centuries roaming the earth, yet your strategy lessons still haven't paid off." A menacing smile appears on Cal's face, and Amrynn's cold eyes turn to flames as she snarls back at him.

"Enough." Azran silences them both.

Her name sinks in as she meets my gaze, not hiding her animosity. I tilt my head to the side, not breaking eye contact, slowly wiggling my fingers. Oh, try me.

She returns a superior smile and my vision darkens. A brisk gust of wind lifts a side panel and warmth leaves the room. I will erase that stupid smirk off her face. She wants to see what I'm capable of? I'll make her choke on her pride and beg for mercy.

Seconds later, her smile loses its edge when condensation leaves her lips and her breath catches in her throat. Lanterns flicker and it takes me another minute before realizing I'm sucking the life out of the space.

"Ela." His voice breaks the silence, and I release my power. "I owe you all no explanation, and this is no freak show. Now the next one with a death wish can speak up and will see it granted." He pauses a moment, but everyone remains silent. "Reports."

Acting as if nothing happened, Amrynn opens. "The Moon Fae have joined. I bring a thousand fighters with me."

"So do I. We're ready to fight alongside you, High Lord." Tharrion adds, having recovered from his mishap.

"All Averion's units are here, High Lord," Kharis says.

"We've received word from Ker. He's at least a half day behind." Cal checks his sword as he explains.

"We cannot wait for him. He will cover the south of the range and any possible retreat of Braern's force with his archers. No prisoners." Azran doesn't flinch as the orders leave his mouth.

Irann speaks up for the first time since I arrived. "Our healers have joined Mor's, and our soldiers are ready to fight. Scouts are keeping watch on Braern's forces and reporting burnt-down villages across north Brimora. He doesn't seem to be in a rush to get to Adria."

"Braern won't try to march on Adria. It's pointless. It would take him days, maybe weeks, to take the fortified city. He knows the fight is with us. He just wants to set the region ablaze, kill and destroy as much as possible until we get there." Cal interjects.

It's getting harder to keep my power under control with the news from Brimora, but I remain silent.

"He will meet us out in the open. Cal and our captains will lead the main offensive on Braern's force. Irann and Tharrion, I need you on his west flank. Amrynn, you're taking the other one. We'll adjust based on the terrain as we get there." Azran looks around the room, pausing on each Fae present.

Although he's not wearing a crown, there is no mistaking the High Lord standing in front of us. "You've trusted me this far. This is what we've been working towards, and our shared dream is within reach. We move out before dawn. Do not disappoint me."

Every single Fae present nods solemnly and bows to their High Lord. Beneath the egos and arrogant facades lie true loyalty and respect for him. After all, he built this realm. They have been chasing Braern for so long that they got lost in political games, but it's time for the final move.

I'm the only one still standing, so we stare into each other's eyes and his gaze softens. Mate. The word echoes in my mind, devoid of meaning. I'm staring at this giant blond Fae with crimson eyes. The very same warrior I first met in the Dark Forest. The one who killed my mother and saved my life countless times. The commander of the Fae armies. I know I can't hide from this forever, but I'm glad I'm able to right now.

And just as I'm studying his face, a strain flares within me, like a door being rattled. I realize what he's trying to do as everyone finally straightens their backs. Without hesitation, I send my power crashing against the barrier I erected.

I take one last look and see him flinch before I turn around and leave the pavilion.

CHAPTER TWENTY

Elanor

Stepping into the night, I head back to the High Guard and find Savage waiting for me. The twins and Vesta are nowhere to be seen, probably resting or, knowing V, spending some more energy in good company.

I enter my tent and find a simple cot on the ground. Exhausted from the past few days, I lie down and close my eyes. I barely feel Savage nuzzle against me before falling into a deep sleep.

I spring awake a few hours later, my heart racing after the usual night terrors. The nightmares are even more terrifying out here, like a promise of what's to come. Sitting up on the cot, I grab my waterskin and rinse off my face. I splash the cold water on my forehead and heated cheeks several times until the bad dreams are relegated to distant memories.

I lean forward to lift the sides of the tent, only to find it's still dark out. It won't be long before dawn, so I get up and ready my weapons. Exiting into the night with Savage, I sit by the dying fire. My stomach in a knot, there's no way I can eat anything right now.

Moments later, the whole camp gets ready to move out. The boy from yesterday is bringing back our mounts, and I spot Wyn and

Varan leaving their tent. I can't imagine what today must be like for them. Going to war with an unbreakable bond such as theirs must be terrifying. Depending on Braern's position, we could be fighting as early as tonight.

"Hey, Ela, short night, huh?" Wyn greets me.

I give him a small smile, seeing the concern in his eyes. "So you two really do share a tent, if not a bed!"

"Call it a tradition!" Varan winks. We're all doing our best to make the most out of the situation, but the tension is palpable. I've killed and fought more than I'd care to admit, yet I know nothing could prepare me for this next fight.

"What is it like? A battlefield of this magnitude?" Even with the captains' reports on our numbers, I just can't picture it. That many warriors fighting. Dying.

The twins exchange a look that tells me more than a thousand words could. Fuck.

"What I can never get out of my head are the screams. Fury, terror, and agony. The crash of bodies and swords." Wyn squeezes his eyes shut.

"The smell. Blood, bowels, piss." Varan is looking at the soldiers hurrying around us, probably wondering which of them will make it back.

We fall into a heavy silence.

"Perk up, ladies! We've got a long day ahead of us!" Vesta jumps on the brothers, pushing them apart to settle in between them.

"And where were you all night?" I ask, raising an eyebrow at her.

"Oh, you know! Checking on the troops, making sure everything is functional." She says with the biggest smile on her face.

"Another tradition, am I right?" Wyn elbows Vesta. Varan bursts into laughter, and I join him seconds later, letting go of some of the stress that's been building up inside me. God, it feels good to laugh again.

Less than an hour later, we're riding through the Dark Forest to bypass the Range and get to Brimora as fast as possible. Although the familiar smell of moss and trees brings me back to where it all started, I find no comfort in being in this part of the forest. Usually incredibly silent, the sound of thousands of hooves beating the ground is astounding. Yet it's not loud enough to silence the terrifying thoughts storming in my head.

Surrounded by known faces, Vesta, Wyn, Varan, and so many others I've trained with, yet still utterly alone. My heart tightens as I watch these seasoned warriors, unable to hide the fear in their eyes and the tension in their shoulders. Even Vesta's aura seems to have darkened since we stepped into the forest.

Numbers are in our favor, but I know some of us won't make it back to Averion. Maybe it will be me. Maybe it will be one or all of them.

When I can't take it anymore, I ride ahead to join Kharis, Cal, and Azran at the front of our column. I press my thighs to the sides of my horse and don't look back. I'm not good at goodbyes.

I pass several scouts racing up and down the long line of Fae warriors heading south to exchange reports. Curious to hear the latest word on Braern, I speed up while checking that Savage is following.

I finally spot long white-blond hair flowing and a two-bladed sword rising above the sea of soldiers. Azran's head snaps in my direction once I catch up and fall back at their pace. His red eyes are studying me, and I brace myself for another invisible assault, but it never comes. Good.

As we're riding through the woods, I'm feeling a little calmer now. Contemplating the absurdity of my situation, I even crack a smile.

It's so weird being around him, knowing what I do, and yet not feeling a thing. We've come so far, and I can't deny how much he's helped to shape my life, control my power, and discover who I am. Knowing the truth about how he feels about me, I can't help but wonder where that puts me.

I've barely grazed the surface of the bond, only getting a glimpse of its crushing weight and left to wonder what lies beyond. Is it all but darkness for me? Simply a prison, a cage I can't be free of, or could there be something else?

I wish it had been under other circumstances. I wish I hadn't been born in Death. Death. My oldest friend. The only constant presence I've known. The only thing I've ever been sure of. It comes for us all, and it will come for me, too. Maybe tomorrow.

Deep down, I know there's nothing for me to live for beyond ending the life of the Fae responsible for all of it. This is what my life has been leading up to. Or... there it is again. The underlying fear twisting my stomach. What if there is something else? I turn to look at him once again, trying to objectively consider the impossible.

The gallop of a horse interrupts my train of thought as a scout rushes toward us. Cal immediately rides out to meet him, and, as much as I'm dying to do the same, I remain in position, aware of the dozen pairs of eyes on my back. Maintaining my composure, I keep my gaze fixed straight ahead until we've caught up with them.

"Braern's army is half a day's ride outside the Dark Forest to the southeast," Cal says.

"We'll stop by the edge of the forest for a few hours tonight. The horses need to rest and so do the soldiers." Azran's tense voice surprises me. You would think he'd be used to all this by now.

We don't set up camp when we stop later that night. All too aware of how close we are to the enemy, everyone uses the next hours to rest and deal with the nerve-wracking chase we've been forced to join.

I find a trunk to sit on and share some water and dried meat with Savage. Too tense to feel my body's exhaustion, I stay there, absently caressing Savage's soft fur and observing the movements around me.

Cal and Azran are talking among their soldiers, and I watch them for a time.

Momentarily distracted, I don't see Mor approach until he's sitting on the other end of the dead tree. He's wearing his usual braided hair, and he seems so... calm. I wonder how many of these nights he's lived through. He finally shifts to meet my gaze.

"A lot seems to be resting on your shoulders, Unifier."

His words hit home as I've been trying to focus on anything but that. That and the bond.

"I see them looking at me with hope in their eyes like I have the power to even prevent this massacre and bring them all home."

"No one has that kind of power. Your role will be revealed soon enough."

"I'm not even sure what that is." I exhale slowly. "I've seen them give you the same look. How do you do it? How do you deal with the weight of responsibility and the aftermath?"

Mor sighs heavily before answering. "You're looking at it like you have a choice. What will be, will be. All you can do is your best, given the circumstances." He looks around, his gaze pausing on several warriors sitting down, sleeping, chatting, living, until he stops on the red-haired captain. "I know I can't save them all. Although I wish I could, I've learned to let Death do its work and take back those whose time has come."

"You talk about Death like it can take form and has its own will."

"My beliefs are my own, and I believe in many things most would consider impossible. I've been on this earth for countless centuries. I remember things most have forgotten."

"What if I fail?" I let out in a whisper.

"We're not all powerless in the face of Death. Remember that." His gaze burns into mine, and I squint my eyes at him, but he doesn't grace me with an explanation.

We sit in silence for a moment, his words lingering in the night.

Naar is still standing by a wide tree, checking his mount. The words leave my lips before I can think twice. "Is he your mate?"

Mor doesn't answer at first, but a small smile appears on his face. "For your information, it's considered rude to ask. But yes, he is." Letting Savage be, I rest a hand on the hard trunk, feeling its ridges with the tip of my fingers. "I met him centuries ago. I come from a long line of healers, and our magic is shared with our children when we're granted the honor to bear them. As such, for us, it is frowned upon to pick a partner with whom that's not possible."

I stay quiet as I wait for him to decide whether he wants to tell me more or not.

"I forsook that responsibility when I met Naar. Easiest decision I've ever made, although it wasn't a decision, really. This is what was intended for me. I'm grateful for the years we've been given, I know it's more than what most get. But that's the one thing I'm truly afraid of in this world. Not being able to save him and Death taking him back."

I can see love mixing with dread in Mor's eyes, but my heart remains cold as ice. I imagine that is how I would feel, too. I gaze at the High Lord again. Why? Why him? I repress the thoughts before I venture too far down that path and bring my focus back to the healer.

"I will do everything in my power to fulfill my part. Braern has a date with Death, and I will make sure he gets there on time."

━━━ ◆◇◆ ━━━

Azran

We step into Brimora with the first light of day. Ela is riding by my side, Kharis and the High Guard not far behind.

I know Braern is waiting for us after ransacking the region. Smoke rises in the sky as we ride past burnt-down villages. And before long, the smell of putrid and burnt flesh is in the air.

When we're still a few hours away from Braern's latest reported position, we come across a massacre and lead the army through it.

Bodies are piled up on the bloodied ground, with children among the dead corpses. Braern picked his location to make sure we'd ride through this slaughter.

As I contemplate the destruction once more, I can't help retracing the events that led to Braern's betrayal. Trying to find when and where I could have foreseen all of this. I come up empty and am just left with the confirmation that nothing could have prevented this madness. All I know is that Braern needs to be stopped. He's long past saving, and my faith in our path toward unity has never been stronger.

Clenching my jaw as we ride through the human plains, I glance in Ela's direction. Her eyes have darkened, and tears of rage are rolling down her face. She meets my gaze but it's an empty stare. I wish I could reach her, support her, and help her survive the sea of fury she must be drowning in.

I know she hasn't been conserving her powers but I can only hope the state she's in will suffice for the fight to come. I can't let her out of my sight, though. Braern knows the Unifier is riding with us, and I can't predict what he'll do.

In my mind, there is no way he comes out victorious, but Braern is not stupid. He wouldn't bring us out for a fight in the open unless he knows something we don't, and that's what scares me.

I don't know how things will play out with Ela, but if there's one thing I know, it's that there is no telling her to stay back.

I spot several Wood Fae scouts in the distance, riding back. My heart sinks before they're even here. We've arrived, and Braern is waiting for us beyond that hill.

Cal and I exchange a knowing look before bringing the whole army to a halt.

The scouts confirm our guess, and Cal immediately goes off to ensure all captains are readying their units while the camp aides organize and protect our backs. I spot Mor dispatching healers with the units. The tension around me is palpable.

I turn to look at Ela. Her face is a cold mask, but I can see her chest rising and falling rapidly and her breath catching in her throat. Without thinking, I reach for her, cupping her chin to lift her head up. "Be careful out there. I won't be far."

I let go of her when she nods. I know things are bad when she doesn't even have a smart comment to retort. "If we get separated, you know what to do to call on me." She sensed me through the bond, and she knows I will unleash hell on earth to get to her if she needs me.

When Cal returns, I know there's one more thing left to do. Calling on my power to increase the reach of my voice, I ride out along the front line of our riders, looking each warrior in the eye.

Our army extends as far as the eye can see and I spot Irann and Tharrion ready to march. Amrynn is nowhere to be found, but that's no surprise given her orders. She needs to get ahead of us to encircle Braern's forces from the east.

I unsheathe my two-bladed sword and wield it high in the burning sun with a roar. Thousands answer me. Again. Roars fill the air, making the ground tremble, shaking off the fear and paralyzing terror.

"Brothers and sisters. Today, we fight for unity. Today, we bathe in blood, return victorious, or meet our fate." My voice resonates across the plains, so even the last line of infantry can hear these words. "To Death."

"Death!" Their answer shakes the ground. And I scream with them before turning my horse around and launching into a gallop across the plain.

The ground trembles as the cavalry follows me, with Cal right by my side leading the High Guard. I have never let my soldiers go to battle without me, no matter what lies beyond, and I won't start today. I don't turn back to make sure Ela is there. I know she is.

Climbing up that last hill, I emerge on the other side to face the mass of soldiers waiting for us down a small slope, and I don't stop. I press my knees against the sides of my mount and give voice to a deadly roar. I want Braern to know I'm coming for him. At last.

In a glimpse, I know we outnumber them. Some rebels are riders, but most of them are infantry. With the thunder of our riders in my ears, I barely hear the rebels launching toward us and dying as our first arrows rain on them.

⚬

Elanor

On first contact, we hammer through the front lines of rebels. There's no time to think, I just let Nahtar do what it does best. Slaying left and right, we push through their infantry, furor fueling us. Making us give chase was a big mistake. It only gave us more rage to unleash upon them all, and that pent-up tension is about to be released savagely.

Keeping my power in check and reserving it for when I truly need it, I swing my blade toward a rebel, slicing his face in half. Blood splatters over me and the warm liquid rolls down my cheeks.

A spear comes straight at me, so I jump off my horse, meeting Savage on the ground. My feet dig slightly into the wet ground, and I realize Braern made sure to pick a location where our riders couldn't push their advantages. Most of us are already on the ground, abandoning our mounts, volleys of arrows flying above our heads, striking down at random on both sides. The next second, I strike a loyalist down.

Screams are already filling the air all around me, but I block it all off, focusing on one kill at a time. More of our soldiers are on the ground next to me now, advancing on the rebels. Nahtar buries down the side of a Fae, and I pivot to throw one of my knives at another attacker. Savage chops through what's left of a rebel, the torn flesh making an unmistakable sound.

Freeing my blade, I swing it before it connects with a sword, sending a shock through my arm. The Fae in front of me is covered in dark runes and baring his teeth at me. I snarl back before ducking his next blow and returning a strike to his chest.

All tension and fear have left me as I'm dancing with Death. With the smell of blood in my nose, I lunge at the next rune-covered face. Glimpses of red and gold armor twirl around me, which means Cal's High Guard and Kharis' unit are not far. The Wood Fae is shouting orders and insults, his colorful words fueling me more.

I got separated from the twins and Vesta a while back, but I can't afford to lose focus. I size up a huge Fae coming into my line of sight and lunging at me with a roar. Leaving an opening in his defense, he hammers down his strike toward my head with brutal force. I duck at the last minute and respond with a stab to his open side. I pivot just in time to see him come at me again, madness dancing in his eyes. He is not trying to avoid my blows, he just wants to see me bleed, attempting attack after attack. I finish him when I tear through his jugular.

Realizing I've created an opening in their line of defense, I don't think twice and let my rage take over. Killing my way through the mass of enemies, I'm seeing fewer and fewer red armors around, but I don't care. Each blow is getting me closer to the revenge I've been seeking.

"Ela!" I turn around just long enough to see Kharis coming after me into the opening I've created. He's a hell of a fighter!

I come back to the scene before me when the tip of a blade rips against my thigh. Seconds later, a rebel collides with me, sending me flying. My body hits the ground hard, knocking the air out of my chest and I bite the inside of my cheeks, drawing blood.

By some miracle, I'm still gripping Nahtar, but when I turn around to get up, two Fae are on me. Before I can strike, Savage jumps at the throat of the rebel on my right. The other Fae is momentarily distracted, and I kick him down and away from me, buying myself just enough time to get up and run him through with my blade.

Tasting copper in my mouth, I turn to Savage, still standing over the first attacker. "No!" The Fae pulls out a knife and my cry is drowned in the fracas around us. The blade digs into the fur as my wolf rips the rebel's neck out.

I lock eyes with Savage before he jumps on another attacker. Relieved, I bring my focus back to the fight around me. My gaze lands on a black leather pouch attached to the belt of a dead rebel. But another Fae covered in runes comes at me. I dodge the blow and strike back, gutting him. He falls to the ground, wearing one too.

After striking down another enemy, I crouch to grab the small sack hanging from his side. Opening it reveals an all too familiar black powder. My stomach drops instantly. Something's wrong. Something is terribly wrong.

I'm about to turn around to alert Kharis, fighting not far behind, but a sword is swinging at me. Off instinct, I unlock my power and light Nahtar ablaze to block the strike. I fend off the attack and run my blade through the rebel's abdomen. It cuts through his armor like butter.

I'm readying myself again when several rebels run by me, retreating to the back of their lines.

My brows draw closer together when some of us break into a run to follow the rebels and cut off their retreat. Moments later, Savage and I join them. With my power set free, there is no stopping or escaping me.

We've got the upper hand, and they've now realized it. We close the distance with some rebels and re-engage them immediately while the rest of my unit runs past us to catch up with the other loyalists trying to run away.

Finding my next target, I chop off an arm and pierce the rebels' armor through the back. My gaze falls on another leather pouch as the body crashes to the ground. Remembering the powder, I stop dead in my tracks to call for Kharis. Before the words can leave my mouth, a crushing weight pulls me down, and the world explodes.

CHAPTER TWENTY-ONE

Calen

Withdrawing my blade from the guts of a rebel, I turn to face the next fighter, my movements precise and controlled. As I block his assault, I look to the east, hoping to spot Amrynn. She should have already joined the fight.

We need to push our advantage and break through their defenses. We quickly recovered from the marshy grounds and Ela dove into an opening in the front lines, with Kharis not far behind. We've strengthened our position and can't falter now.

As the thought crosses my mind, several rebels retreat in front of us. And I'm not the only one noticing. A rush of energy pushes in my back, and the entire army gains momentum to go after the rebels. Several soldiers start running after them.

Vesta is fighting off two loyalists not far from me. One of them lunges at her from behind and I throw a knife at his throat right before an attacker collides with me. My sword is knocked out of my grip, so I grab his head with my bare hands and push my thumbs down his eyeballs, popping them with a disgusting sound. Horrified screams tear from his throat, but I push him away to grab my sword and finish him off. Thousands of cries already haunt me. What's one more?

Soldiers around me are now fully breaking into a run to go after the retreating rebels, and their victorious screams resound ahead of me.

Turning back to where Vesta was standing a second ago, my knife missed its mark and stuck to her attacker's thigh, piercing through a leather pouch. A dark powder is spilling from it. I narrow my eyes, but it's out of my sight when Vesta's sword connects with the rebel's chest, sending him to the ground.

My blood freezes as everything falls into place in my mind. Without a second thought, I lunge at her and pull her back by the waist.

"Retreat! Retreat!"

Vesta's head snaps in my direction but she immediately obeys. She starts running back, grabbing as many of our soldiers as possible.

I'm shouting orders as loud as I can, hoping to attract the attention of my units.

"Pull back!"

I'm running too now, hoping I'm wrong, and this is not what I think it is. My eyes land on a dying rebel on the ground, smiling widely at me. And the battlefield explodes.

Azran

Cal's voice rises above the dying screams and I instantly know something's wrong. We were separated when our cavalry hit the marshes, and I got stuck on the western flank. I have no idea what he saw out there, but I freeze when I spot him running right at me, his soldiers with him.

"Fall back!" I grab hold of one of our own, put him on his feet, and send him running with the other soldiers around me. I call for our retreat immediately, trusting Cal's judgment without a second thought.

Cal is almost upon me, gesturing widely at me, when a huge explosion resounds in the air, sending us all crashing to the ground.

My ears are ringing as I lie in the cold mud. I'm not sure how much time passes. When I finally open my eyes, I'm still blinded by the blast. Braern found a way to set fire to the battlefield.

The white dots disappear from my eyes as smoke swirls above me, and for a moment, I lie there, hypnotized by the ashes dancing in the air. But when the smell of fire and burnt flesh reaches me, urgency jolts me.

I'm the first to get up, with dozens of motionless soldiers at my feet. I stumble toward one of them and look around to contemplate the aftermath of Braern's atrocious weapon. Not a single soul still stands.

Studying the bodies around me, most appear intact from the blast or not too badly burnt, and some are starting to move. Relief mixes with horror as I realize we were not at the heart of it.

Cal. I need to find Cal. My vision blurs and a headache explodes behind my eyes but I drag myself forward, calling his name with a raspy voice.

Fighters are beginning to get up and help others. Astounded by the blast and unable to process what just happened, I'm just relieved to find most of our soldiers alive. Or at least relatively unharmed physically, though their crazed eyes tell another story.

Several of them stumble over corpses, still trying to get away from this hell, shock painted all over their features. Others turn their distressed faces towards me, hoping for an explanation, for something to make sense of this madness. But I have none of the answers they seek.

A pit in my gut opens when Cal's face is not among the Fae standing up and the thought of losing my brother crosses my mind. A cry tears through my dried throat and I keep searching. My heart is pounding in my chest, my sanity dancing before my eyes, but his body remains hidden in the ocean of corpses.

I look up in the distance towards Braern's forces and finally spot the origin of the explosion. Doom sets in and my hope is instantly crushed. A sea of charred cadavers is waiting within the radius of the blast, smoke and flames still dancing in the air.

I was simply far enough to escape the deadliest hit. Rage wakes up inside me as my hearing returns, and I watch my people calling for help, screaming in pain. Then my world shatters when the most excruciating agony reverberates through me.

Ela.

⊰•○•⊱

Elanor

Pain wracks my body as I regain consciousness. I roll over on the bloodied ground and try stumbling back up. My head is spinning hard, warm blood is running down my temples, and my ears are ringing loudly. I crash back down, unable to lift myself up, as fire surges in my skull and everywhere in my limbs.

The air is thick with smoke, stinging my eyes, and burning embers are flying everywhere. Sounds start coming back to me, broken cries and screams of dying soldiers, and with them, reality sets in. My gaze stops on Savage, lying a few feet away from me.

I try calling for him, but the words won't come out. So I crawl, dragging myself over to him until my hands reach him. I let out a ragged breath when my fingers come into contact with his warm fur, instantly relieved.

I'm brushing his coat gently, fighting the pain in my body. When Savage doesn't respond, I try lifting my head to take a better look at him. Stabbing pain flares in my neck and my forehead slams into mud and ashes.

Once the shock dulls, I withdraw my hand and bring it before my eyes. It's covered in blood.

My breath catches in my throat and I choke on the muck. I push as hard as I can on my forearms and lift myself up enough to see the gigantic hole punctured through my wolf's back.

"No. No. No. No. No." He was with me right before the explosion. I saw him. I, I felt him.

I collapse and tears start streaming down my face, tracing a path through my ash and blood-coated cheeks. It was his weight I felt pulling me down. He pushed me away and shielded me from the blast, forever my guardian angel. I extend my hand and grip his soaked fur.

My sobs are shaking my body, sending tendrils of pain down my legs as Braern's evil plan fully hits me. He crafted this destructive powder and sacrificed his own soldiers to turn the tide of the battle. Sick fuck.

My next thought goes to Kharis. Shock numbs me again, and I let go of Savage to get on my knees. I look around but I can't see Averion's captain.

The atrocious smell of burnt flesh fills my nose, and I'm surrounded by corpses. Broken and charred bodies are everywhere, with pieces of armor sticking out of them at weird angles. Rebels carrying pouches were obliterated in the explosion, only leaving bits and pieces behind as their fucked up legacy.

The plates of metal must have done even more damage than the blast, tearing through flesh and shredding body parts. My gaze falls on the cadaver lying by my feet, its skin still sizzling, and on the thin piece of metal lodged on the side of my thigh.

My head snaps up when roaring cries resound. A horde of rebels is coming straight at me, stomping bodies, hate and hysteria deforming their faces. They're chanting and celebrating.

Looking around for Nahtar, I spot it under a destroyed corpse. I drag myself over there, and the second I grip the blade, I unleash my powers.

Rage and madness rush through me, giving me a new life, and I get up to face the monsters responsible for this. My vision darkens in an instant, and I close my eyes, embracing the darkness, letting it run wild inside me, calling it to me. A sick smile blooms on my lips when I light Nahtar ablaze.

They unleashed fire on us, and it's time to return the favor. Today, I will be Death.

My eyes fly open when the first rebel reaches me. She's dead before she knows it, her head severed from her shoulders in a clean cut. Her body touches the ground, and others are on me.

Rebels are coming at me from all sides, stomping on the dead. I send my shadows at a group of them trying to encircle me. Darkness burns through them like acid, and their screams are music to my ears. But that's not enough.

In a deadly trance, I'm dancing with fire, letting it consume everything. Their bodies turn to ash, their flesh blistering and filling the air with that fetid smell. Their eyelashes catch on fire and their eyes melt under my dark flames. I keep dancing.

I'm the only one alive within the explosion's radius, and just like in my nightmares, I'm standing on a pile of bodies. Nobody could have survived this if they were within range. I only did so because of Savage.

Blood splashes my face once more, filling my mouth with the familiar metallic taste, and I stop counting the kills. I'm slaughtering left and right, annihilating anyone approaching me, but more are still coming.

The reality of it all is starting to dawn on me. Braern has found a way to invert the odds, rebels are fighting with revived furor, undisturbed at the sight of their fallen brothers and sisters crushed under their boots.

I'm beginning to feel pain again, and my blade's flame is not as bright as it was before. I have failed them all. My power falters at the realization and fear swells in my heart before I remember that I've been here before. Alone and on Death's doorstep.

A weird calm comes over me, replacing the panic. It will be okay. I did my best, and I will join my parents at last, leaving this wretched place behind me. Tears start rolling down my face, and I let the grief and guilt run free one last time. It's time to let it all go.

I'm striking down another fighter when a wild roar flares behind me, shaking me to my core, and I spot a glimpse of him. Alive and fighting his way to me. His bloodied blond hair is dangling in front of his face, but I can see the frenzy in his eyes. He's coming for me, even now, keeping his promise to never leave me.

My power responds immediately, recognizing the monster joining the fight. Death will have to wait a little longer. I have someone to kill and revenge to fulfill. With renewed strength, I shove the rebel next to me and unleash darkness on them all.

Moments later, Azran pierces through the dark shadows and takes up a position against my back. Energy flows through my body at his contact, and a feral snarl escapes my throat.

I can see clearly again with him by my side. There's nothing that could stop us now. I'm the only one who could truly hurt him, just like he's the only one who could be my demise. But right now, it's me and him against the hordes of barbarians. We will end them all and raise hell on earth together.

⚬

Azran

I let fury take over and unleash the rest of my power in a roar. I slay two rebels with one strike and crush the skull of another one with my elbow. Each blow fueled by magic, I slaughter blindly, Ela fighting right by my side. There's no hiding my powers now.

Time stops as we're fighting like demons. I won't let them get to her. I won't let them take her away from me. Not now, not ever. She's all I have left in this world.

There's no need to talk. I can feel her presence and every single one of her moves. I join her in harmony, swinging my two-bladed sword, enthralled in a deadly trance.

In this instant, amidst violence such as I've never witnessed before, I'm at peace. She's my shelter, welcoming me, keeping me warm, keeping me alive. I'm fighting for her and her alone. And I know she's doing the same.

After what feels like an eternity, her dark ribbons retreat when several units join us. I release a shattering roar to try and shake off the shock and fear from my soldiers' hearts, rallying them to me.

But when the sun sets, we're still fighting the never-ending mass of soldiers. Both armies are now back at it, eye for an eye, and we're losing ground. Our soldiers remain unsettled by the blast, wide-eyed, in a stupor, and fighting for survival, not for victory. Braern's warriors know they managed to turn the tide, and they're killing ferociously, pushing their advantage.

I'm starting to question how much longer we can do this when a reprieve finally comes.

"Ker's coming! He's joining the fight!" Soldiers are screaming around me.

Moments later, I can feel Ela's relief and the whole army pushing forward as fresh troops join the ranks. A series of arrows fly over our heads and land in the mass of rebels in front of us, so I lunge forward, wielding my blade.

"Forward! To your High Lord!" My blood freezes as I recognize the voice sounding above the battle. I turn around and my gaze lands on Cal, fighting a few feet away from me. Covered in ash and blood, but still alive.

He lifts his head and we share a glance that a thousand words couldn't describe. He nods and we both head back into the butchery.

Moments later, what's left of the High Guard joins me, giving me enough respite to go to him.

"Sorry I'm late. Got held up back there for a minute." He greets me with a wink, but I can read the same relief in his eyes.

I reach for him with my free hand and pull him into a strong embrace. I'm so fucking happy to see him that I could crush him. But there's no time for this, so I release my hold on him and bring my focus back to the battle still raging loudly around us.

"Our flanks are gaining on them, we can encircle them!" Cal shouts next to me.

Finally, some good news! The blast was contained to the center of the battlefield, where it would hit us the hardest. Thankfully Amrynn and the others must have managed to escape it.

Suddenly, a horn resounds, and I stop dead in my tracks, preparing for another of Braern's tricks. But to my surprise, his soldiers are pulling back. The rebels we were fighting off moments ago are now trying to free themselves and get out of our reach.

"Should we go after them?" Cal is looking at me expectantly, his brows drawing closer together.

My head is spinning as I'm trying to figure out Braern's plan. "No. We don't know what awaits us if we do, and I've had enough of his deceit."

He complies, already sending orders for our soldiers to retreat to the camp and gather and bury the dead. Everything is set in motion quickly, but Ela doesn't react. She's standing still, surrounded by bodies, covered in blood with Nahtar still in hand.

I'm with her in an instant. "Ela." She doesn't move, so I step in front of her. Finally, she lifts her head and her gaze breaks me into a million pieces.

There's nothing I can say to erase the crushing guilt in her heart, so I pull her to me, and she sags against my chest weakly. I tighten my hold as her pain blasts through the bond and burns everything in its wake.

The most destructive tempest of fire and ice is raging inside her, but it's her soul being pulled apart. My chin dips to the top of her head as I caress her hair gently, trying to contain my tears and stay strong for her. How she withstands such violence is beyond me. I'm racking my brain for a way to comfort her, stop the pain, or for anything that could help. But I come up empty.

Clenching my jaw until it hurts, I'm keeping an eye on our surroundings, waiting for the storm to break. "Let's go." My voice is merely a whisper but she abruptly tries pulling away.

"Savage. I need to find him. I need to bring him back." Her widened eyes are scanning her surroundings as she sobs uncontrollably. "I, I need to."

Catching her face between my palms, I press my forehead to hers. "I'll find him. I promise. I will bring him back to you."

Not giving her time to react, I gather her tightly in my arms and carry her away, her blade secured on my back.

When we get back, the camp is in a complete uproar. I lock eyes with a healer and head to the main pavilion to deposit her on the bed. She's trembling and I stay by her side until exhaustion takes her moments later. Once asleep, I check her body briefly and notice the piece of metal sticking out of her thigh.

Thankfully that's when Mor walks into the tent. I step away to leave him room to care for her. He scans her body and pulls out the metal piece before applying pressure to the wound. Closing his eyes, he calls on his power to stop the bleeding. It's all over in a matter of seconds.

He gets back up but doesn't manage to hide his trembling legs as he motions for me to sit down. "I'm fine, Mor. Go. Thank you." I dismiss him without a second thought.

He gives me a severe look, but we both know he could save one of our own instead of taking care of my superficial cuts. He hands me a bandage and leaves without a word, just like he's done so many times before.

I don't wait until he's gone to kneel before Ela, clean cloth and water in hand, to rinse off her wound that's already healing and wrap it in a tight bandage. I don't know how she survived the blast, but the damage she sustained is not merely physical. Once I'm confident she's out of danger, I let out a sigh of relief and head back out there.

On the deserted battlefield, dozens of our soldiers search the corpses for survivors and abbreviate the suffering of the ones slowly dying. It's still completely dark out, and I stumble on several bodies as I make my way through the graveyard.

Once at the heart of the explosion, I search the grounds extensively before finally spotting Savage. I don't notice his torn body until I'm back at camp. I find untouched ground to deposit him on, give orders not to move him, and hurry back to my pavilion.

***

Elanor

Azran walks in right as I'm standing up and trying to buckle my sword in place. "I found him."

"Thank you." My voice barely reaches my own ears and my eyes water instantly as I secure my harness. I try to take a few steps forward but barely make it before crumpling down.

I brace myself for the shock, but it doesn't come. I'm in his arms, his strong body holding me up. Even after everything I've put him through, he's still here, carrying me, being whoever I need him to be. The commander, the monster, and more.

I wrap my arms around his back and pull tightly. He returns my embrace immediately, pressing his warm body against mine, and I close my eyes.

Letting the tears flow freely, I'm sobbing against his bloodied chest, unable to control the words coming out of my mouth. "I saw this. In my dreams, I was standing on a pile of bodies. A butcher. I couldn't stop it. I couldn't save them."

He rests his chin on top of my head. "I know, Ela. I've had the same dreams. There is nothing you could have done." His words bring new tears to my eyes.

"Az." Cal's voice breaks the silence and I pull away. He's standing by the entrance, in bad shape like the rest of us. "The captains are waiting outside."

Az questions me silently. I wipe the tears off my face and nod.

Cal lets them all in. Amrynn, Irann, Keryth, Tharrion, Yhen, Lana, Eren, Elion, and Naar. Everyone but Kharis. Although I didn't see his body, I know he didn't make it.

As they walk in, they're all staring at Azran and me, unable to decide who is more terrifying now that his power has been revealed, too.

Naar comes in last, looking terribly pale. The only face not coated in ash belongs to Ker. Even Amrynn looks completely disheveled. We all take a seat, and only one remains empty.

Azran's cold gaze goes around the room, pausing on each of his captains before turning to Cal. "Casualties?"

"At least a thousand in the blast. Reports are still coming in. By the latest count, almost two thousand have died or were heavily wounded and are unable to fight." The general's jaw clenches hard, and Azran closes his eyes before letting out a long breath. "We estimate Braern's force at a little over a thousand able-bodied fighters now."

"A thousand of my soldiers are still stationed by the Range," Ker says.

"They let us get through. Braern sacrificed hundreds of soldiers to let us break through the first lines and run into his trap. To draw in the most of our army and do the most damage." A vein is pumping on the High Lord's forehead as he tries to contain his rage.

"We saw the explosion from afar and came as fast as we could, High Lord." Ker briefly bows.

Tharrion's gaze has been fixed on me since he entered the pavilion. "How did you make it out? Your units were in the middle of it. And what the hell was it?" He's breathing heavily, and his arm is tied to his chest, a bloodied bandage keeping it in place.

"Kharis didn't make it," I say as all eyes land on me. "He was with me when it happened. We were further inside enemy lines when I noticed rebels wearing small leather pouches on their belts. I got my hands on one and found a dark powder in it. I tried warning the others, but I was too late. I only survived because my wolf shielded me from the blow." I manage to spit this out without falling apart, digging my nails into my palms until I draw blood.

"I noticed the pouches too, barely in time to pull back some of us," Cal says.

"I had never seen anything like it." Yhen's voice is shaky and he can't seem to take his eyes off Kharis' empty seat.

Naar winces in his seat as he repositions himself. "What if they have more?"

"We know what to look for now. And a blast this huge will have required a huge quantity of that powder which matches what we found in the Eidune caves." Azran pauses to look around the room, gauging everyone's reaction to the revelation. "We couldn't identify the sample we brought back with us."

Amrynn's high-pitched voice fills the air as she stands up, sending her chair flying. "More secrets! Were you going to tell us had your hand not been forced?"

"Watch your tone, Amrynn," Az growls at her. "I don't answer to you." Fire flickers in his eyes, reminding everyone who they're talking to. "Will another demonstration of my wrath be the only thing to keep you in check? Do you only respond to threats?" His face is now tight with rage, his gaze crimson.

The Moon Fae doesn't seem to want to back down, and her fingers flinch in the direction of the knife at her side. Unable to refrain, I snarl at her loudly. Her head snaps towards me, but she stands still.

"Still interested in playing political games after today's massacre. Which one of us is the monster, huh?" I stand up. "I've heard enough."

If I stay one more minute in there, I'm going to lose it. I lift the entrance panel, and step into the night. A cold breeze hits my face and I pick a direction. My whole body is in pain, so I simply focus on moving my legs. Before I can stop and rest, I need answers. One thing at a time.

I spot Mor running around with other healers wearing white silk in their hair. They're trying to attend to as many wounded as possible. Screams and laments reach my ears in between the gusts of wind.

Death and destruction are everywhere. Bloodied Fae are staring at me with wide eyes. Others send me hateful glances, not bothering to hide their true feelings.

Heading towards the screams, I get to the infirmary. A mass of bodies is lying beyond the wide tents, waiting to be put in the ground.

I let out a gasp when Vesta walks out of the infirmary. "V!"

Her head snaps up, and I break into a run. We crash into each other as she pulls me in. I hug her back tightly with trembling hands.

"Thank God you're alive," she says. "I saw you go through the enemy line right before the blast."

She pulls back, still holding onto my hands. Her eyes have lost their usual gleam, and several shallow cuts decorate her beautiful face, but she appears to be relatively unharmed. I offer her a small smile as she studies me, too.

"Savage. Savage saved me." My eyes water again, but this time I push back the tears.

"I'm so sorry, L."

I nod, accepting her words of comfort before looking around us. "Where are the twins?"

She doesn't answer and lines appear on her forehead as she gives me a pained look. Panic takes me in an instant. "It's Wyn, he's badly wounded. Varan is by his side. I was just with them."

I step away from her to head inside, but she catches me by the arm. "Ela, it's not looking good." I nod, barely listening. I need to see for myself.

I stalk toward the entrance of the infirmary, Vesta following behind me. As I step inside, the smell of blood and bowels assaults me. Dozens of wounded soldiers are lying on cots. Some are screaming, calling for loved ones, and others are crying. A young Fae is holding his own entrails in with his hands. His empty stare follows my steps, but when his gaze meets mine it turns feral.

Vesta places her hand on my shoulder and pushes me forward. We stop when I spot Varan crouching over a cot. His brother is lying down, a bandage soaked in blood around the head. I get closer and see his entire left side is badly burnt. Blood and pus are oozing from the charred flesh.

"Varan-"

His blond head lifts up when he hears his name coming out of my mouth. Before I can kneel down next to him, he turns back to face me, his brows drawn close together. "What are you doing here?"

Taken aback by his anger, I blurt out. "I heard Wyn had been wounded. I came to check on you both. I'm so sorry."

"We don't want you here. You were supposed to stop this!" His words are like daggers to my heart as he gets up to snarl in my face.

Unable to process his words, I step back and bump into Vesta, still behind me. "I, I-"

I recover before falling down and start running. I don't stop until I'm out of the infirmary. But the bodies piled up around me do me in. An ocean of torn and bloodied faces greets me, sinking into my brain, and Alan's empty stare is among them. His jaw is crushed, and the rest of his body is entirely burned.

Varan's words finally set in. Why didn't I stop this? I could have prevented this horror back in the caves, burned it all down. I should have noticed the pouches earlier, alerted the others, and found a way to save my people. My head feels like it's going to explode as I realize their deaths are on me. When I can't take it anymore, instinct takes over, and I walk away.

When I stop, I'm in the middle of the camp. I catch my reflection in a mirror by a soldier's tent and barely register the crazed eyes staring back at me. I'm covered in ash, and my hair is crusted with blood. I fall to my knees, too exhausted to stand.

CHAPTER TWENTY-TWO

Elanor

It's like I'm back in the Dark Forest. I'm lying on the ground by my father's cold body, digging my hands into the earth, and a giant sinkhole has opened before me. Unable to resist, I fall into it and let it swallow me whole.

Stuck in the darkness, I can't find a way out. And maybe I don't want to. Horror is eating at me and each second is an eternity. I'm drowning in the sea of the dead, assaulted by images of a battlefield where nightmares now mix with memories. My punishment for failing.

When I finally look up I find a water basin next to me, probably dropped off by a soldier who didn't recognize me and took pity on a wrecked Fae.

I take another look at myself in the mirror propped against a tent, and rage replaces everything. Braern must be celebrating his devious scheme, congratulating himself on the death of thousands.

But it's not over. I'm still breathing.

Plunging my hands in the water, I rinse my face and hair as best I can. As my fingers trace the outline of my face and absently brush through my knotted hair, a plan forms in my mind.

I scan my body quickly. The cuts to my thigh are superficial, and the bandage around it is holding. Granted, my entire body hurts and is covered in bruises, but there is no severe damage. I'm guessing I have Azran and Mor to thank for that.

My power responds when I call upon it. Although depleted after I used a massive chunk on the battlefield, the fury bubbling inside me confirms I'm not done yet. I check Nahtar on my back and the straps on my daggers before standing up. This will have to do. I can't waste any more time feeling sorry for myself and the ones we lost. If I come back, there will be plenty of time for that once Braern is dead.

I stand up and use the High Lord's pavilion as a compass to guide my steps. Once I get closer to the side of the camp, now guarded by soldiers, I call on my shadows. My vision darkens instantly and adjusts to the night. I bypass the guards and step into the destroyed plain.

Rebel bodies are still covering the land. Their commander sacrifices them and defiles them even in death. I repress a shiver of disgust and push on, carefully stepping in between the bodies.

When I come in view of Braern's encampment, dawn is near. Thankfully, my shadows keep me hidden from the rebels guarding the perimeter, and I sneak past them with ease.

At first glance, there is no differentiating between both sides. Wounded and bloodied Fae are everywhere. I stop on the side of a small tent to catch my breath and reevaluate my next steps. I need to locate Braern.

I'm looking around, trying to find a clue that will lead me to him, when my gaze falls on a dark pavilion installed on the hill at the far end of the camp, towering over the rest of the army. That sick bastard must have had a front-row seat to today's massacre from the comfort of his tent.

It takes me longer than expected to get closer. Soldiers are swarming the grounds, and there are only a few places for me to take cover, even with my shadows. When I am several feet away from the pavilion, I realize it's not even guarded. Egotistical maniac.

I don't even know if he's in there. I can't make out any sounds coming from the tent. On my guard, I unsheathe Nahtar before stepping in.

It's almost entirely in the dark, except for a small firepit in the center. With the cold metal of my sword in my palms, I release my shadows and it takes a second for my eyes to adapt to the room. It's covered in plush rugs, pillows, and luxurious seats. There's a table at the back, overflowing with food and drinks.

"I was beginning to wonder whether you would have the guts to come, Unifier." A dark voice sounds to my right, and I freeze instantly.

Remembering Cal's words, I silently scold myself for dismissing the absence of guards outside without even considering the implication. Shit. I played perfectly into his plan.

Braern steps out of the shadows. With grey hair falling over calculating green eyes and a neatly shaved square jaw, he looks... ordinarily good-looking and nothing like the evil captain I had pictured.

I tighten my hold on Nahtar when he steps closer to the fire, letting me see the long scar that runs on the side of his face and the hole in place of his ear.

"Come in, make yourself comfortable," he says, waving towards the seats and refreshments. His cold smile reveals blackened teeth and the image engraves itself in my brain.

"I came here to wipe that sick smile from your face, not sit down and chat." I lift Nahtar a little higher.

Braern stalks towards the table at the back with a cruel laugh. "Before you get to that, there's something I'd like to discuss with you first. Elanor, right?" He's pouring liquid into a cup. "I saw you fight out there. Impressive. You could accomplish great things with that much power."

"I'm not interested in your lies and manipulation," I say, baring my teeth at him. I step into the light cast by the brazier to show I'm not buying into his little games.

He turns around to study me and surprise flashes on his face before his brows draw closer together. "You look awfully familiar. You remind me of someone I knew."

My vision darkens immediately and I let out a vicious snarl.

"Could it be? Aerín's daughter?" His eyes widen before he bursts into laughter. "The irony!"

"Get her name out of your mouth." I grip Nahtar hard, letting the metal dig into my palms to keep me clear-headed.

"You do realize you're fighting for her murderer?" My silence sends him chuckling darkly. "I've got to hand it to you. That is pretty ruthless. I tried helping her before he got his hands on her, you know."

"Helping her? You're the reason she's dead."

"The entitled asshole calling himself High Lord of the Fae killed her, not me. Is that what you call him, too? Or do you have another nickname for Aerín's executioner?"

"Shut up," I utter behind clenched teeth, trying not to let my emotions take over.

"Tsk. Tsk. So sad to see how deeply his lies have influenced you and to watch you desecrate her memory like that." He shakes his head before taking a sip of his drink, and a red drop runs down his chin. "I wish I could have saved her. My only regret in this life. Maybe there is still time to change your fate, though."

"You tricked her, you bastard. And you want me to believe you're not the lunatic I know you are? My father's murderer?"

He sends his full cup crashing into the fire and the radiating heat hits me.

"Tannyll deserved to die! Arrogant little shit!" As he stares at me, wide-eyed, I get a glimpse of the madness dancing in his irises and the gold medallion dangling from his neck after the sudden movement undid the top of his collar. "I remember killing Tannyll as if it was yesterday. Then, he was but a shadow of himself. If only I had known of your existence back then, we could have changed the world, you and I. You have your mother's beauty and spirit." He regains his composure and gives me a small twisted smile.

"Wrong thing to say, motherfucker."

Closing the distance between us to lunge at him, I don't see him take out his sword, and he counters my first assault easily.

"Come on, Elanor. I don't want to hurt you." He parries my attacks, holding back his blows, and making me dance around him.

"You should have thought about that before sealing my mother's fate and slaying my father. I'm not walking away until one of us is dead, asshole."

"You can't blame me for trying, but it looks like you've got more of your despicable father in you than I thought." His face transforms into a terrifying rictus as he launches his first attack.

I jump out of his reach, and my training with Az comes back to me instinctively when Braern ripostes with more speed and furor than I would have imagined. His long sword connects with Nahtar with strength, almost knocking it out of my hands.

I quickly realize I'm going to need my power to defeat him. My training is barely keeping me alive as Braern deals strike after strike. I pivot after a parry and light Nahtar ablaze as I swing it toward him. He doesn't even flinch and blocks my assault easily.

My eyes widen as the shock of our blades reverberates along my arms and sparks burst into the air. What the f... My blade should have cut through his easily! Maybe I'm more weakened than I thought.

Not giving up, I keep pushing, but Braern blocks my attacks, a victorious gleam in his eyes. He's dodging almost effortlessly, while my breath is quickening, and my muscles are tiring with each strike.

Changing strategy, I send my shadows at him, but the dark ribbons go through him like ghosts. I step back as my stomach twists in a knot. It can't be. Braern has found a way to protect himself from my powers. They're useless against him and he's a better fighter than I am.

His face lights up in a satisfied smile. He's been toying with me, waiting for me to come to this realization. In a last attempt, I search my power for an anomaly to try and figure out what's wrong. But it's right there. I can feel it, and nothing seems different.

Panic threatens to take over, and I keep scanning my power for an answer. As I sense the strings of energy flowing through me, I realize the lock on the bond is gone. It probably imploded after the blast or when I unleashed my power on the rebels.

There is no mistaking it, I can feel the bond pulsing inside me, fueling me. The overwhelming grief and heartbreak must have over-powered it earlier, clouding everything else after the battle.

But the shock of this discovery is short-lived as Braern strikes straight at my head. I duck at the last second and manage to untangle myself from this deadly dance.

"What's wrong, Unifier?" His distorted voice brings me back to the fight right before his sword swings at me again, aiming at my side this time. I jump out of reach, and Braern deals another blow I barely escape.

I can't do this alone. I need help. I need him. My heart is racing, and I'm panting heavily now. I won't hold out much longer, but I don't know how this godforsaken bond works!

I block another assault and picture my mate with his raging eyes and wild hair. I have no idea if I'm successful, and I'm still calling out to Az in my mind when Braern's sword finally finds its target.

I snarl loudly as I pivot, and pain explodes in my back.

Azran

After dismissing everyone but Cal, I consider our plan once again. I know the risks. Although unlikely, more explosive powder could be out there. But we don't have another option.

We'll begin the attack at dawn, avenge our dead, and it will be the last sunrise Braern gets to witness.

"Go get some rest, Cal. You look terrible."

"Right back at you. You look like-" He freezes when I hold up my hand. My heart almost gives out when her voice flares in my head, and a storm of emotions follows.

"Ela." I look around frantically. "She went to Braern. Launch the attack, now!" I'm wreaking havoc in the pavilion to find my weapons but Cal is standing still. "Cal!"

Snapping out of it, he rushes out and I follow him. He dispatches several soldiers and I break into a run.

How could she be this reckless? I almost lost her earlier, and I can't go through that again. I'm storming out of the camp as fast as I can while it's still dark out. My head is spinning, trying to come up with a plan as I realize I can't just walk into the enemy camp.

When I step onto the blood-soaked lands, an idea forms. I scan the lifeless bodies around me until I find what I'm looking for. Kneeling on the ground, I strip the dead rebel before me to don his armor, and I smear some of his blood on my face. I search for a helmet but can't find any, so I cover my hair in as much mud, ash, and blood as I can. Finally, I tuck my blade under a torn cape. I can't risk anyone recognizing it.

I've already stopped for too long. I need to move. Using the last hour of darkness to provide cover, I sprint across the battlefield until I'm in view of Braern's camp. Once within range, I slow down and limp toward the fires circling the encampment. When I'm in view of the guards, they begin shouting as they notice me.

"Help me. Please." I croak in a broken voice, extending a hand. One of the guards comes up to me and catches me as I crumple to the ground. He drags me inside the camp where he drops me heavily. My eyes are half-open and he's squinting his at me. His hand is hovering by the hilt of his sword. I don't have time for this. I need to get to Ela.

A ruckus breaks out on the other side of their camp and the rebel's head snaps in that direction. Soldiers are springing up on their feet, gathering their weapons, and shouting orders. Cal.

"They're coming! Move out! Move out!"

I sneak away while the guard is distracted and escape in the commotion of soldiers running around. I don't need to search, I know where she is. I can feel her presence up the hill right when my eyes land on the dark pavilion leaning on the side of the slope.

A horn resounds in the whole camp, calling all fighters to arms. Able-bodied soldiers are sprinting, bumping into each other, trying to get to where they need to go. The confusion plays in my favor as I make my way through the camp, my target in mind.

With the pavilion in sight, two figures leave the tent, fighting. A pit opens in my gut when I recognize Ela's small figure, and the rest of the world disappears. She's holding her sword up but, even from a distance, I can tell something is wrong.

In a roar, I sprint towards them and unsheathe my sword.

"Braern!" As his name is called out, the leader of the loyalists steps back to look around.

I close the distance between us in seconds, gathering the last of my power to me.

Braern hasn't changed since I last saw him and his torn face transforms into a grin when he recognizes me. The same hysteria and hate still dance in his eyes.

Ela freezes in place several feet away from him, blood covering her back and legs. As the scent registers, rage takes me and I jump on Braern. Our swords cross but he twists his blade free.

Ela circles him to attack from behind but Braern is faster and anticipates her move, lunging at her. She dodges the blow at the last minute, avoiding his strike but not the shove that follows and sends her flying across the hill.

"Finally reunited, brother!" Braern's scream fills the air when he turns back toward me.

I bare my teeth at him, before engaging him again. "Not for long." The battle is raging down below. "Look around, Braern. It's over!"

"Oh, but to the contrary, Az. It's just the beginning!"

I glance at Ela as she tries to get up, needing to make sure she's okay. *Your powers*, I send down the bond, but she shakes her head, defeated.

"What is this I'm seeing, Az?" Evil laughter tears from Braern's throat. "After centuries butchering your own people, you have finally found someone crazy enough to care for you! It's too bad she has to die, really."

The threat undoes my last restraints, and I snap. Unleashing the rest of my power, I aim my sword directly at his hateful face and hit him with my full strength.

I almost lose balance when he deflects the blow with a swift move. How? My gaze jumps between Ela and my weapon. She won't or can't use her powers, which can only mean that Braern found a way to neutralize our advantage. He knew the Unifier was coming and made sure to be prepared. A light tug pulls on the bond. A confirmation.

I have no idea how he managed to pull this off, but however unexpected, this won't change today's outcome. I won't let it. He's one of the best fighters I know, but he can be beaten. I've seen it once before when Cal disfigured him. And there are two of us now. We can get to him.

When Ela rejoins the fight, we both move on Braern at the same time. She aims low so I go high. Braern twists around, blocking her assault, but mine meets its target. My blade plunges right above his shoulder and Braern lets out a guttural scream.

The cut doesn't slow him down though, and he jumps on me. As he gets nearer, the wound I inflicted moments ago closes up. Stunned, I lift up my sword too late and his cuts high on my thigh. Pain ignites in my head as I fall on my back.

"Az!" Ela's scream echoes and with it, a picture appears in my mind. A medallion dangling from Braern's chest.

My injury sends searing pain down my leg but I manage to get back up. I know what I need to do. Using some of my power to push away the hurt and strengthen my stance, I get back into the fight.

I release a growl of frustration after several unsuccessful bouts. I'm trying to find an opening in his defense but I can't get close enough.

I'm about to start another assault when Braern unexpectedly strains from the effort. Breathing more rapidly, he's slowing down as Ela readies herself for another offensive.

This feels like deja-vu. I'm still trying to place it when the feint Braern is about to execute hits me. Before I can warn Ela, she leaps toward him.

With no other choice, I do the only thing I can to keep my eternal oath. Mustering the remainder of my power, I jump in front of her.

Braern's sword connects with my abdomen in the next second. The cold metal pierces through me and I find purchase on his shirt, pulling him closer as the blade further cuts my flesh.

Knowing this will be the only chance we get, I don't hesitate. Releasing his vest, I rip the medallion off his neck and see a glimpse of fear in his eyes before he shoves me away.

"Ela, now!" I shout as I fall heavily to the ground, the medallion still in my hand.

⸺◆⸺

Elanor

I freeze when Az leaps in front of me. It all happens so fast I barely register when he snatches Braern's medallion away.

Az's voice rings in my ears and my power responds instantly, flowing unrestrained and exploding around. Stronger than ever, it numbs me instantly, clearing up the panic and fear.

Braern's scarred face turns towards me right when I set Nahtar ablaze and swing it across his neck. His head detaches in a swift movement, his features forever sculpted in a mask of shock.

I watch it roll on the ground as darkness flows through me, victorious over the mysterious enchantment. For a moment, all I can hear and focus on is the pulse pounding in my ears, overwhelming all my other senses.

My eyes snap back to Braern's dead body, and a wave of relief hits me as my power retreats. It's over. He's dead.

Distant screams confirm the battle unfolding before us is still raging, and rebels are getting massacred by our army.

My head turns to Azran lying a few feet away, covered in blood as usual.

He lifts his head to look at me. The crimson in his eyes is fading, revealing the most tender gaze. He smiles at me affectionately and his love overwhelms me through the bond, exploding freely for the first time. Pure contentment swells in my heart as I finally let him in.

The utter loneliness retreats, leaving room for his undying support. The certainty of his unconditional and unwavering devotion and acceptance is piercing through me like the sun through dark clouds after a storm. All my walls crumble down as a smile comes to my face.

Completely mesmerized by his beauty and strength, my soul is on the verge of exploding.

Even when the world has turned to ashes, I will love you, little one. I vowed to protect you and fight for you. And my vow is fulfilled. To whatever end.

My smile fades away at his words. Why does this feel like a goodbye? Letting go of my blade, I run up to him and kneel on the ground by his side.

A warm liquid is soaking my knees as blood pools around him, oozing from a wound to his abdomen.

A cry escapes my throat and I press my hands to the gash, trying to stop the flow. Blood is leaking through my fingers and a red river runs on the green grass around us.

A frenzy takes over me. I try to gather the liquid in my hand and put it back inside his body. My gaze snaps to his when the bond tears through me as life leaves him.

"No. No, you can't abandon me! I won't let you!"

Not after everything we've been through.

"Help! Help!" I'm screaming as loud as I can, for someone, anyone to come save him. "Please, stay with me, Az. Please."

I glance around to see if someone heard. Someone must have heard.

Down the hill, soldiers are fighting, but no one is looking over here. How can the world go on when this is happening? I'm shaken by violent sobs as my gaze returns to his body. Warm blood is still flowing through my hands.

I focus to find the faintest heartbeat still going, but slowing down. "I've got you. I've got you. Just stay with me." My voice cracks as I cradle his lifeless body.

My heart is getting ripped out of my chest. He never knew, I never told him. He never knew that I had been waiting for him, too. He never heard the words. He only ever heard me call him a monster but he never knew he was my monster.

"Please." I look to the horizon and the rising sun bringing its first light, painting the sky in shades of red and orange. "I don't know how to save him. I know Death, not life. Please. No. No. No."

I cup his face with my crimson hands, lifting his head, expecting him to open his eyes, to wake up. I squeeze my eyes shut as tears roll down my face, praying for someone to come help me.

His heart stops.

A searing pain burns through me, and time stops. There's nothing but this shattering agony. My whole body is on fire, and I'm being skinned alive. Acid is crawling everywhere in my body, tearing through me. My eyes widen in terror and my head falls back.

Somehow, the only thing that comes to mind is my father's face. I can't imagine surviving this, life without Azran, without my mate. Death is calling me. It has to come, anything but this. Paralyzed, I can't take it anymore.

I release a deafening scream as my heart fractures. Fury mixes with agony and my power blasts out of me. Thick ribbons of darkness tear through my chest, and the world goes dark.

CHAPTER TWENTY-THREE

Elanor

The agonizing pain is gone. An emotionless void welcomes me, and Death's comforting presence pulls me into an embrace. I have come home, at last.

I'm kneeling on the ground with a lifeless shape lying next to me, the world around me blurred. Instinctively, I reach out to touch him, but my hands go right through, like clouds made of shadows.

My body is weightless and free of pain when I stand up. Numb, my absent gaze watches as the universe shifts in tones of black and grey.

I focus in the distance where hundreds of lights twinkle softly before going out. Souls, dying. The realization rings so clearly in my mind there is no room for doubt. Soldiers are being taken away.

A familiar shape comes into focus beyond the battlefield. A wolf's spirit is running free on the plains. Liquid pools in my eyes and rolls down my face, though I'm not sure why. The wolf stops and warmth comes over me when our souls greet each other.

Savage. The name echoes in my ears, a confirmation and a reminder, as his shape flickers away. My chest tightens as I let him go, grateful for our time together and his protection.

I understand now. When my heart shattered, so did my soul. And with it, the world.

A presence looms behind me, and I recognize her before turning around. Death is staring at me, her shapeless black figure flickering with lights. Darkness is twirling with its antagonist. They're part of the same entity, intertwined, and inseparable.

Death extends a hand, hovering over the lifeless form at my feet. A Fae is lying down, his features peaceful although his cheeks bear bloodied imprints on them. His muddy blond hair is splayed around his face like a crown, highlighting his sharp jawline and pointy ears. His eyes are closed like he's resting, and my gaze stops on his lips. I've seen him before. I could never forget a face as striking as his.

Absorbed in the contemplation, at first I don't notice the thin thread of light floating away from his body and into Death's arms. His time has come. Death is taking away his soul.

An even smaller filament shines between our two forms, catching my eye.

No. This feels wrong. I step forward. "You can't take him, he's a part of me." A distorted voice says, and it takes me a moment to realize it belongs to me.

Death freezes. *That is beyond your reach, my child. Not even you can do that.* The words resonate in my soul like thunder, and something changes in the air, upsetting the balance of this world.

The tug inside me gets louder, alarming, screaming for me to do something. With it, pain comes back to my body. At first, only a throb. It flares until brutally blasting through my entire back and mind.

It's all coming back to me, searing through the numbness and apathy. The battle, Braern, Azran's dead body under my hands, and the reason I'm here. I have to save him.

Shaking uncontrollably, I'm trying to move, to cut the cord, and free his soul. But my body won't obey me. I try calling out again, in vain. My throat is closed up and the words won't come out.

Fire is burning down my back as I glance around for a way to help and come up empty. Helpless, panic is soaring through the pain, blinding me. A horrible tug tears through me, leaving me praying I wasn't powerless. If only I could move and-

We're not all powerless in the face of Death. Mor's words come back to me. But how? My head is spinning as a flicker of truth attempts to pierce through the pain. Something else is fighting its way back to my consciousness. Something I'm trying to put my finger on and remember. A way to stop Death.

I'm going over everything I know and every single mention of Death I've ever witnessed when the prophecy echoes in my mind. *Death will separate the worlds.* I'm so close to figuring it out, but the answer still evades me.

Separating the worlds. Deep down, I know this is where I am, in between realms. Not quite in the living world, not quite on the other side. And something brought me here. No. Not something. Someone. My scream shattered the universe. I opened a portal. I tore through the veil of Death.

An invisible veil on my mind lifts and I recognize Death. My kin. We're one and the same, or at least part of me is. I am Death, too, and I belong in this place.

After my parents' enchantment ended, I thought I had uncovered the full extent of my nature, but I'm only now seeing its true essence. Everything finally makes sense.

The utter loneliness I've always felt and the isolation no one could understand. No one except for him. It took me so long to realize this, but for the first time, I wasn't alone anymore. I knew that he didn't entirely belong to the mortal realm either.

I have no idea how this is possible, but I have never been more sure. We are not Faes. This is simply the form in which we present ourselves to the world.

Azran.

The thin thread of light is flickering, ready to snap and go extinct. Piercing anguish rings through me, and a crazy thought forms in my mind. A last resort.

The weight on my belt confirms the twin daggers are still secured in their sheathes, although I can't get to them. Still paralyzed, I picture reaching toward a blade, gripping it tightly, and pointing it against my heart. It's the only thing I have left for this gamble, the only thing I can think of. A threat for what's to come, for there's one thing I'm willing to bet my life on.

Although it's still unknown to me, there is a reason I came to this earth in this form and alongside him. And that gives me leverage. My own fate is the last thing I have to try and save him.

I close my eyes and focus all my energy on visualizing the blade. I imagine the cold metal in my palm and the steel under my fingers, its weight perfectly balanced in my hand. I imagine the sharp sting of the tip ripping through my flesh. I imagine the first drop of blood rolling on the weapon.

And when I open my eyes, I'm staring into Death's abyss, the knife pressed against my skin. She freezes, preventing the thread of light from going extinct, but that's not enough. A wailing call reverberates in my core but I don't stop. I push the blade into my chest.

Calen

In the end, confidence was Braern's downfall. We stormed into the rebel's camp at dawn and took them by surprise while Az snuck in. They didn't see us coming until it was too late.

I swing my sword at another fighter, slicing his hand off. His terrified gaze crosses mine before I finish him, but I'm already moving on to the next loyalist standing in my path. The tide turned and a massacre is unfolding before my eyes. Ferocious roars sound around me as revenge runs its course, confirming the loyalists are defeated.

I manage to extract myself from the fight to evaluate our situation. I lock eyes with Vesta, still fighting a few feet away, and motion for her to join me. She fends off a rebel before another one of our soldiers takes her place.

"Have you seen Az or Ela? Has Braern been spotted?" I pull her behind me to make sure she's out of reach of the attackers. Still keeping an eye on the fight a few feet away from us, I turn to her. Her face is covered in splashes of blood, and her eyes glimmer with vengeance and brutality. Even now, her untamed beauty strikes me. She returns my gaze for just a second before answering.

"No, and I haven't seen Ela since last night."

A shrieking sound fills the air, and my head snaps in the direction of the scream. My blood turns to ice when I recognize Ela on the hill. She's kneeling beside a body on the ground.

I look around, hoping to spot a white braid, but in vain. Damn it! I clench my fists hard, my knuckles whitening as I freeze in place. I can't leave the army. Not now. Not when we're this close.

Tears of rage are pooling in my eyes when Vesta grabs me by the shoulders. "Go. Go! I can handle this."

I nod, shaking off the paralysis. She's the only one I would trust with this responsibility.

I look toward the hill one last time, and Ela's body goes limp over Azran's.

I break into a run, racing through the camp and screaming my head off for a healer. I'm calling out for Morthil when I come across a small group of rune-covered rebels fighting for their lives. With no time to think as they jump on me, I parry the first assault and run my blade through one of the attackers. Baring my teeth at the other two, I dodge the first hit and deal a series of deadly strikes before finishing them off.

Urgency is shaking me and a pit forms in my stomach as I rush through the battlefield. Deep down, I know I'll be too late.

"Mor! Mor!"

Elanor

The sun is hitting the side of my face, caressing me with its warmth. My skin tingles under its comforting glow until a soft breeze brushes my cheek, relieving it from the heat.

My eyelids are glued shut, a welcome protection against the warm light. I never want to open them again. My only wish is to remain in this peaceful and carefree state, with the sun's rays as companions.

Stabbing pain blasts through my chest, sounds of a raging battle explode in my ears, and my eyes snap open. Blinded by the daylight, it takes a few seconds for my vision to adjust.

Recollections of a dark place come crashing down on me. I'm trying to tell reality apart from imagination as I remember fragments of this realm. Souls of fallen soldiers. Savage's spirit dancing on the plains. Memories are piercing through my suffering.

Death. Death was there. I'm reliving it all, the agony, the shattering of the worlds, and my bluff. I look down and the trail of blood running down my chest confirms it.

Finally, the stakes come back to me, and my gaze lands on my mate, still lying on the ground a few feet from me. The heartbreak instantly consumes me, tearing through what's left of me. I try crawling toward him, but a scorching pain explodes in my lower back and I collapse.

My eyes are closing again, unable to resist the call of the darkness. It's coming to collect its debt, promising to take all my pain away.

Thump.

Right before darkness takes me, it echoes again.

Thump.

A beating heart.

ACKNOWLEDGMENTS

I don't think I could fit the long list of people who helped make this crazy adventure possible on a few pages, but I'll give it a shot. An immense thank you to:

- You, dear reader, for getting this far and entrusting me with hours of your time. If you enjoyed this journey, don't hesitate to leave a review as I'd love to hear all about it.

- Enzo, for agreeing to read my very first (terrible) draft and challenging me. I'm so damn proud of you and couldn't have done this without your help. Sorry for the awkward bits, though, little brother.

- Capucine, for always being here when I need you. For reading the book in two days. For sharing killer feedback. And for giving me the boost I needed to keep going. I love you so freaking much. Ma femme.

- Ariel, for being such a driven and caring friend. I wouldn't have come this far without your unwavering support. I'm so incredibly proud and grateful for our friendship. To even crazier dreams. I love you.

- Carla, for your responsiveness and amazing insights. This past year has been crazy for us both and you never stopped rooting for me. I'm eternally thankful for you.

- Lauryn, Isabella, Rachel, Raeanne, and Sarah, for beta-reading and providing the most crucial feedback. You helped make this dream of mine come true.

- My ARC team, for taking the time to review Wielder of Shadows. I appreciate all your encouragements and constructive criticism.

- Cyndi, for helping me step up my writing game. Your tips are forever engraved in my brain and so are your jokes.

- To Christina and Steven, for showing interest in the book from the minute I started talking about it. It meant the world to me.

- H, for always being a supportive partner and remaining patient even when I spend all our evenings writing. Thank you for creating a safe space for me to explore my creativity. I love you more than you will ever know.

- A very special brotherly mention to Hammam. I can't wait to take you along for the sequel.

Thank you all.

www.ingramcontent.com/pod-product-compliance
Lightning Source LLC
Chambersburg PA
CBHW030627310726
48979CB00003B/910